RUSSELL JAMES

is a British crime-writer known for his hard-hitting, low-life thrillers, mainly set in south east London, though his latest novel, *Oh No, Not My Baby*, is set in and around the city of Bristol. He had an author's conventionally unhappy childhood: his father committed suicide and he was a bright child, physically abused by wicked relations, before being sent to military boarding schools. Subsequently, he has never been able to stick within an organisation: he is an observer, a lone wolf.

His previous novels include *Underground*, *Daylight*, *Payback*, *Slaughter Music* and *Count Me Out*.

A paperback original.

First Published in Great Britain in 1999 by
The Do-Not Press Ltd
16 The Woodlands
London SE13 6TY
www.thedonotpress.co.uk
email: thedonotpress@zoo.co.uk

ISBN 1 899344 53 5

British Library Cataloguing in Publication Data. A catalogue
record for this book is available from the British Library.

b   d   f   h   g   e   c   a

Printed and bound in Great Britain by
The Guernsey Press Co Ltd.

Oh No, Not My Baby

A *NOIR* MYSTERY BY
Russell James

MYSTERY
BLOODLINES

For Henry, Jennifer and Hannah, and all my other friends in
Bristol.

1. OH NO, NOT MY BABY

(OH NO, NOT MY SWEET BABY)

WHEN ZANE REPLIED, Shiel was peeling potatoes.

Zane said, 'I know. You think, "I'm a decent guy. I don't want to kill innocent people. It isn't right." You don't feel good about it. You think, "Every man's death diminishes me. No man is an island." Don't you?'

Shiel said, 'These are awful potatoes.'

Zane said, 'I can read you like a book.'

Shiel dunked his knife in the water.

Zane said, 'You're having second thoughts. People have to die, Shiel, to make them see the point. Otherwise we're just another lost voice in the wilderness. A dozen lives maybe, to save millions.'

Shiel frowned. 'Half these potatoes are black to the core and the others are pitted with deep eyes. How come they're so different?'

'Different types.'

'They're just rotten potatoes.'

'From different places. Potatoes nowadays come from all over the world. Jersey last week, Egypt this – and next week, who knows? It's no surprise they are different.'

'I remember when potatoes were just potatoes.'

He had been waiting half an hour. In the car parked outside the yard, Nick blew on his hands. It wasn't really cold but after half an hour in the dark a chill had set in, a cool damp breeze moving across from the Severn estuary. His fingertips were balls of ice. To warm his hands he slid them beneath his thighs. His cheeks were shadows, like craters

5

on the moon. Nick could look haunted at the best of times, and this was by no means the best of times.

Though approaching midnight the plant was still working. From ground floor windows, lights shone across the yard through wraiths of steam. The high wire netting fence made it look like a prison and from what Babette had said, the level of security on the front gate was prison tight. But she was inside. Through the quiet evening air Nick heard humming, occasional clanks, and once or twice the machinery groaned like a truck with a rickety gear. Escape pipes on the wall gave out jets of steam. Ten minutes earlier he had heard a muffled hooter, and two women had come from a side door and stood in the dark to smoke their cigarettes. They wore white overalls and tied-on hats. After they had finished and gone back, the yard was empty again. Nick wondered whether they had found time to grab a mug of coffee or milky tea before the hooter ended their short break. It sounded a grim way to earn a living.

The humming stopped.

From where he sat in the car it left a silence like dead of night. He could make out fainter sounds now: the squeak and rattle of a metal trolley on a concrete floor; some tinny music, even voices from inside. Somebody shouted something. Someone else called back. The tinny music would be a radio. He heard another shout. Then a bleeper started – not loud, but irritating – the kind of noise that pricks at your ear and makes you narrow your tired eyes.

Nick exhaled, casting a slight film of mist across the windscreen.

The bleeper changed pitch to become an oscillating howl. He saw someone run out of one side door into another. Two men trotted across the gloomy compound like hospital doctors in trailing white coats. Everyone had to wear overalls. Even Babette had worn one over her red blouson and matching jeans. Another door opened, and a dozen people emerged and stood milling about the yard as if on fire practice. If fire wardens were going to check everyone off, Babette would be in trouble – she wasn't supposed to be there. Perhaps she could hide inside and not come out. It might even help: with everyone out in the yard she could roam around taking photographs. Maybe *she* had set off the alarm – a neat trick.

But they didn't seem to be on fire practice. The staff had drifted out and were now milling around, unsure what to do, while a couple of supervisory types buzzed about as if *they* had some idea. Nick wiped the side window and squinted through. Though the yard was poorly lit and the small shifting crowd was anonymous he couldn't see Babette among them. She wouldn't be.

He began chewing at his lip. She hadn't explained what she meant

6

to do inside, though how much was there to say? She had the camera, and it wouldn't be hard to find where the carcasses waited to be processed. Starkly lit, no doubt, bodies sprawled across the floor – they'd make good photographs.

Babette hadn't worried about the risk. The worst that could happen was she'd be evicted from the premises. The company would not make a song and dance or complain to the police. They'd want the whole affair kept quiet. Their need for privacy would help Babette if she got caught – which she wouldn't, she'd assured him. She'd been in there before.

But it was worrying. The people in the yard seemed uncertain what to do – and although sitting in the car left him helpless, he could do nothing else. Babette had told him to come back at half past eleven and wait inside the car – ready, if necessary, for a quick getaway.

The bleeper stopped.

It left a slight ringing in his ears, and this time he could hear the voices from the yard. He wound the window down.

It was like a radio in another room. The rolling Bristol accents carried in the night air, but though he could make out some words he couldn't get the full gist of what they said. He'd have to get out. He could stroll across to the wire netting fence but... if they saw him outside the fence, nearly twelve o'clock at night, they'd be bound to ask why he was there. Perhaps he could pretend he lived in one of the nearby houses. No. He mustn't draw attention to himself or Babette's car.

He watched the people in the yard. Had something happened in the factory? Was Babette safe?

It was when the police arrived he began to worry. First the sickening heave of a distant siren – which he tried to tell himself was going somewhere else – then the noise grew louder, lights flashed, and a white panda car arrived. As it approached the gate the barrier rose, and the car glided through without breaking stride. Straight to the main door. Straight inside.

It looked bad. If Babette had been caught, there was nothing he could do. He could only stay in the car in case she needed him. He began to wonder if he should back further away. No, the police might be looking around for her confederates, and if they saw his car – *her* car – starting up...

Please don't let it be Babette. Let it be some kind of fire practice. In that case maybe the police would have to come, as if for a real emergency. But wouldn't there be a fire engine too? He looked at the workers. It wasn't a fire practice.

7

Another siren. Faster, more urgent. Coming closer.

An ambulance.

Again, the barrier was lifted to let the vehicle speed through. Two men jumped out and rushed inside the building. What had happened? Had Babette been caught? Had she been hurt? Nick knew that whatever was going on had to involve Babette. It was too much of a coincidence that on the very night she slipped in, another drama made them call the police. And an ambulance.

Another siren now.

People were appearing in the street, drawn from their houses by the sirens and flashing lights. Nothing like an accident on your doorstep to pep up the night. It *had* to be an accident, didn't it, if there was an ambulance?

Another police car arrived, and went straight in. Nick wondered what would happen if he drove across in Babette's car – would they let him through as slickly as they had the others? Don't even think about it.

Yet another police car. Three? This was serious. Nick got out of the car to join the onlookers from surrounding houses. Silence returned. Comparative silence. People chattered in the darkness as if at a theatre before lights dimmed. Inside the compound, small groups of white-coated staff drifted aimlessly – low-grade factory staff. Because of their work, he looked for blood stains on their coats, but he couldn't see any.

Beside the fence a woman called to those inside: 'What's happened, darlings? Been an accident?'

No one answered.

'Elsie!' the woman called. 'Someone been hurt?'

From the far side of the compound a thin sliver of a woman wandered over. Her voice was deep – a croaky West Country burr. 'Nothing to worry about, no. Well, I'm all right, anyway.'

'Oh, that's all right then,' the woman laughed. 'We can all go back to bed!'

Elsie shrugged. 'Just a practice, I expect.'

'With three police cars?'

Nick had joined them at the fence. He had the kind of face made older women want to mother him, but in the darkness they hardly noticed he was there. Some wore overcoats over pajamas. Elsie's friend outside the wire was fully clothed but slippered. She said, 'Better than working. We can have a fag.'

'Left mine inside, haven't I?'

'Just like you.'

The woman took out a packet and passed a cigarette to Elsie.

They both lit up. The night air began to flicker with tiny flares. Other workers came to the fence. No one knew why they had been sent outside.

'Some kind of emergency,' Elsie suggested.

'Someone ate one of your old pies.'

'Not one of us!'

People laughed. Nick glanced back along the front fence to Babette's car, but there was no sign of her. She must be inside.

A factory door opened and the two ambulance men appeared. One was carrying an empty stretcher. As he slid it into the back of the ambulance some of the women in the yard approached to ask a question. Whatever he told them caused a stir. One of the women broke away and scuttled to a colleague to spread the news. No one approached the fence. Nick said, 'Someone's heard something.'

'Can't be much,' a woman said. 'The ambulance is going home.'

The driver had shut the rear door but instead of getting in the cab he and his partner went back towards the factory. Someone called: 'Who was it then – anyone we know?'

If the driver replied, Nick didn't hear it. The men disappeared again indoors. Elsie called: 'What's up – a false alarm?'

'Bit more than that,' someone called back.

'Oo!' cried Elsie. 'I think I'll stay and finish me fag.'

No one at the fence seemed in a hurry to move away. As they stood chatting, Nick wondered if he looked as conspicuous as he felt. All the others lived in nearby houses. He'd be the only stranger.

The door opened again and a man in a crumpled suit came out with a policewoman. One of the workers groaned. 'Tea break's over.'

The manager ignored the watchers outside the fence. He said, 'Right, everybody, if you'd all come back inside. Please?'

Nick wondered if the manager always looked this grim. The policewoman addressed those outside the fence: 'There's nothing to see, so you might as well go back to bed.'

'I wasn't in bed, darling, I was watching a video,' said Elsie's friend.

'I'm sure that's a lot more interesting than what's happening here.'

'What *is* happening?'

'Nothing. You've all got homes to go to.'

She might as well have spoken to the fence.

Inside the compound, the staff wandered back indoors. The policewoman gave a last 'Don't hang around all night,' and turned away.

Someone called, 'Why not? We live here, don't we? We do as we please.'

But the policewoman didn't turn round. As she paced across the compound, she passed Elsie running back to the fence. 'Here,' called Elsie. 'You'll never guess.'

'What?'

Elsie had reached the wire. 'Someone's only fallen in the pulveriser.'

'No!'

Everyone crowded in to her. Everyone except Nick. He stood stock still.

It was several seconds before he made sense of their gabbling voices.

'They *think* it was an accident.'

'Of course.'

'You'd have to be bloody stupid to fall in that.'

Nick couldn't trust himself to speak. Elsie rushed back across the compound. As she reached the door the ambulance men came out, talking with the policewoman. Nick stared at them, as if by staring hard enough he might hear their words. He felt like a robot whose rusty mechanism had seized up.

Slowly, the small crowd began to drift away. The ambulance left, then one of the squad cars, leaving the compound empty of people. The factory doors were closed.

Nick returned to the car and sat inside. There was no reason why the accident should have been to Babette. There was no confirmation that an accident had happened at all. The ambulance had gone and the factory stood locked behind its fence and closed front door. He saw another car arrive, to be let straight through. Management, presumably. Two police cars were still on site, so it didn't seem likely *nothing* had happened. Perhaps Babette had been caught. Perhaps she had escaped. No: whatever *had* happened, Nick knew it had to involve Babette. He tried to forget Elsie's words. They were too terrible to contemplate. Babette could have been caught by Security – she could have struggled and been hurt... She could not have died as Elsie said.

Nick got out of the car. Although it had only been ten minutes the night air seemed colder now and damper. No one else was in the street. He walked beside the fence to the security hut at the gate.

'Excuse me for bothering you, but I wondered if there was any news... about what happened.'

'What would that be, sir?'

'You know, the accident.'

10

'Accident?'

'When someone was hurt.'

'Don't know anything about that, sir.'

Nick glanced across the half-lit compound to the unrevealing building. 'I don't want to be a nuisance but I live here. We heard about what happened and if someone's hurt, it could be someone we know.'

'The ambulance has gone now, sir.'

'Look, I'm worried.'

'And why would that be, sir?'

Nick sighed and walked away.

It was when the staff were sent home that he knew it was bad. He had been sitting in the cold car for twenty minutes, playing the radio low, when suddenly the factory doors opened and people flowed out across the yard. They no longer wore their white coats. They were dressed for home.

As he ran back to the gate he was joined by people from the houses. When the factory workers came out the gate, Nick feared they might stay shtum, but they didn't: they talked among themselves and to those waiting. What had happened was too out of the ordinary to be contained. They talked so freely that Nick wondered if they had been briefed on which story to release outside, but he told himself not to be paranoid.

Someone said it was not a member of staff. Someone else said they couldn't be sure. Either way, the factory was shutting down for the night.

'God knows about our wages.'

One of the women shouted back to the man in the security hut: 'I suppose you'll be staying all night?'

'Yeah, but if you don't want to go home I can make room for you in here. I've got it nice and warm.'

'I bet you have.'

They laughed. Nick wanted to hit them. But he asked, 'Is it true – did someone really fall into the pulveriser?'

'Seems like it,' someone replied.

'And she's dead? I mean, it was a woman who fell in, wasn't it?'

'Whoever it was, they're going to be dead.'

An older woman added, 'It wasn't staff, don't worry. We're all accounted for.'

The other sniffed. 'Perhaps a tramp came in to keep warm.'

'How's a tramp going to get in here?'

The woman nodded at the security man. 'He wouldn't notice anything in trousers. Thinks he's guarding a beach hut, him.'

11

He leant out of his window: 'You've got a surprise night off – your old man still thinks you're working.'

One of the women laughed. 'He'll get a surprise when I turn up.'

'You don't know what you'll find,' another added.

'When the cat's away…'

The security guard said, 'If you're looking for a tom cat—'

The woman reached up and prodded him. 'I'd make Kit-e-Kat out of you!'

The others laughed. Nick stood among them as if invisible. Every word was like a whiplash. He saw the policewoman coming across the yard and he tried to read her face.

She said, 'Hurry along now, please. Time we all went home.'

'What happened, Miss?'

Everyone was interested.

She said, 'There's been an accident.'

'We know that, dear. But is someone dead?'

'We're looking into it.'

'Well, either they *are* dead or they ain't, darling. It can't take much looking into.'

The policewoman paused. 'There does appear to have been a fatality.'

'It wasn't one of us, dear, was it? I mean, we're all right.'

'At this stage we can't say.'

'We're not bloody stupid. We wouldn't go up on that gantry.'

'Not when the machine's working,' another agreed.

One of the women asked, 'Have they got the body out?'

The policewoman shrugged.

The woman said, 'It wouldn't be easy. I mean, if it had slipped right down inside…'

'Ugh!' exclaimed a younger woman, laughing nervously.

'Because all the bone and meat is crunched up together. That's the point.'

'Oh, don't,' said someone.

Nick put a hand against the wall. 'Someone fell into the meat pulveriser and…'

'Seems that way.'

He shook his head. 'With all the meat?'

'Not just meat, love, is it? It's where they tip the carcasses in.'

He slumped against the wall.

The policewoman asked, 'Do you know someone in there – perhaps someone who went inside?'

He opened his mouth but couldn't say a word.

'You don't work here, do you, sir?'

He was feeling faint.

'He don't work here,' someone answered. 'He don't live round here neither, do you, son?'

A large woman asked, 'D'you know something about it, then?'

Nick raised a hand as if to fend off blows. 'No… I'm just… I'm just passing by.'

The policewoman came closer. 'Could you tell me, sir, what you are doing here?'

'I was just…'

He stopped.

'Passing by – at this time of night?'

He had to have a drink. Water. He needed water.

'What's your name, sir?'

'I've got to go. It doesn't matter.'

'I think it does, sir. What's your name?'

The group of women was drawing tighter now, and the police-woman was waiting. He said, 'Chance.'

'Chance of what?'

'Mr Chance.'

'Mr?'

'Nick, then. Nick Chance.'

'I see. Do you have some identity?'

'What… Why should I produce identity?'

'Do you have identity, Mr…?'

'Chance. No.'

'What's your address?'

'Brendon Road. 30, Brendon Road.'

She was writing it down. 'And where is that exactly – in Bristol?'

'Clifton.'

'Then you're some way from home, sir, aren't you?'

He no longer knew what he was saying. 'No, it's only… three or four miles away. I don't know. I mean, have you found a body in there?'

'Whose body might that be, sir?'

'I don't know. But have you got her out?'

'Her, sir? A young lady, do you mean?'

He stared helplessly.

'And what would be the name of this young lady, sir?'

Zane said, 'You shouldn't swear so much. It demeans you.'

'Ah, to fuck, you know that's a load of shit.'

When Shiel looked up, he saw Zane pointing a pistol at his heart. 'Jesus Christ, Zane.'

13

'I asked you not to swear.'

'But for fuck's sake—'

Zane cocked it.

'Put the gun away.'

Zane said, 'You're like all the other heathens: you won't listen, you won't do as you are told. Nowadays no one responds to a polite request. They think they can do anything they like. Regardless.'

He raised the gun till it was pointing at Shiel's face.

'To get what you want, you have to show you mean business.'

'Right. OK, Zane. Just put the gun away.'

Zane smiled. 'You and I mean business.'

2. RAINING IN MY HEART

THE ATMOSPHERE IN Bristol West police station at this late hour reminded Nick of the time he had been stuck on Leeds railway station overnight. Dumped up there at one in the morning, no useful train till after five, too late to find a small hotel, he had sat in a heated stuffy waiting room with three drunks who had missed their train, several more without a home and a couple of teenagers without a brain. They had sat on hard chairs at garish tables. Occasionally someone would get up and fetch a coffee from the battered vending machine. One man had tried to read a book, but for the most part they had sat slumped, head on hands at the shining tables, trying to snatch some fitful sleep.

But tonight they wouldn't let Nick sleep.

Instead they subjected him to half an hour of questions, left him alone for twenty minutes, then came in and started again. They did this three times. He wondered whether it was the way they softened up a suspect. The neatness of their technique was that towards the end of each twenty minute break his head would sag and he would sink into the shallows of a pool of sleep. Then they would come in and start again.

'Mr Chance, we can't find you on the voter's records.'

'I haven't been at the flat for long.'

'A transient, are you?'

'Rent the place.'

'And you have no proper job?'

'Musician. I told you before.'

'Oh yes, a rock musician, but not a proper job.'

'Is there any news yet – about Babette?'

'Miss Hendry? No, nothing yet. You were close, were you, Mr Chance, or did you just work together?'

'Friends.'

'A little more than that, I think. Getaway driver, shall we call it?'

'I was waiting for her.'

He was numb. His head felt dry, hollow, beyond sleep. He remembered Babette walking across the road to the security gate, turning to wave before going in. He had waited another minute in case she was refused entry. Then he had driven on.

'What time were you expecting her out?'

'I told you, eleven thirty.'

'And you had dropped her at…?'

Nick didn't answer. He would let the man glance back through his notes. But the man just repeated: 'You dropped her at?'

'Nine thirty,' Nick sighed.

'Well, at least you remember your story, Mr Chance.'

That wave at the gate had been the last that he had seen of her. She had smiled. She had looked so pretty in her tomato-red blouson, hair primly pinned up. He remembered it like a photograph in his mind: one arm raised, her legs astride, her bright daredevil smile.

'Nine thirty to eleven thirty – what did you do in all that time?'

'Went home. Tidied up.'

The man was checking through his notes. 'Into Bristol. Back out. Seems a bit unnecessary.'

Nick waited for him.

'By the time you'd got home, it would've been time to drive back out again.'

'Not at that time of night.'

'Even so.' The man stared.

'I had to kill a couple of hours.'

She had apologised. She had told him to go because she had arranged everything with some woman – she'd have two hours to sneak the photographs. Earlier, she and Nick had spent the evening in his flat, first in bed, then eating supper on the floor. They had smoked a joint together, just enough to enhance the luscious feeling of relaxation and contentment.

'Did you speak to anybody during that time?'

'No.'

'Telephone?'

Nick shook his head.

'I'd prefer you to answer in words. You know your answers are being recorded?'

'Yes.'

'Did you telephone anybody?'

'No.'

'You made contact with nobody at all?'

'That's right.'

'And who did your friend Miss Hendry contact during the day?'

'Just me. We spent the day together.'

'And the previous day – you spent that together, you said?'

'Yeah.'

'So for two whole days, Miss Hendry was – what, never out of your sight?'

'Practically.'

That wasn't quite right, although Nick wasn't feeling co-operative. This morning when they'd got up she had driven back to her flat to fetch some things. He had made some lunch. Preparing food for her had been almost as sweet as lying beside her in the dark.

'You went out to… where was it again?'

'The Arnolfini.'

'Very cultured, Mr Chance. Were you there for long?'

He and Babette had laughed at a typically far out exhibition in the upstairs gallery showing feminist use of once masculine materials: hemp netting and steel; railway timetables. There was a wall parodying pin-up centrefolds behind a ten foot plastic resin statue of a Barbie Doll with a two-foot staple through her midriff. There was even a rugby ball split in half to form a brassiere.

'We went for lunch,' he lied pointlessly.

'And who did you meet?'

'No one.'

'And after that?'

'Wandered around.'

It had been a breezy summer day, perfect for exploring the Bristol docks. They had strolled like tourists along the quayside to the SS Great Britain, and had taken a ferry back to the Watershed. Coffee at the harbourside tasted fine.

'Filling in time, were you?'

Nick grunted.

'Or getting to know each other – you say you'd only recently met?'

'Known her for years.'

'But you hadn't seen each other since…?'

'School.'

'And where exactly did you meet this time?'

The same questions, the same answers. His band had been booked for an animal rights gig at the Bath College of Art, less than an hour's drive away. The two towns were quite different – Bristol

17

was brash and metropolitan while Bath was darker and more grand – but in students' club those differences melted away. Students came from all over the country, but were an émigré population wherever they ended up. Bath students had more in common with students from Sheffield or York than with the mature residents of Bath.

The gig had been hot, dark and noisy. For a small band, Blue Delta made enough noise to fill a larger hall. There had been another, semipro band that evening – hired because it too had an animal rights connection – which put its emphasis on natural sounding acoustic guitars. Blue Delta blew them away. The other band was committed and skilled for amateurs, but to pit them against the raucous jazz-rock group had been a programming mistake – especially that night, when Blue Delta were without a vocalist. The band made some attempt to choose numbers with an animal rights theme ('Nothing from Meat Loaf,' Homer had said) but they didn't have that many sweet and caring numbers in their repertoire. ('We could do Hound Dog,' Homer continued. 'If you ain't never killed a rabbit, then you ain't no friend of mine.') They concentrated on rock classics refashioned for jazz, in which guitar and drums played rock while sax, brass and keyboard added jazz. Typically they would play a straight verse, chorus, verse again before letting either Nick or Tiger attack the melody. Nick played sax and Tiger trumpet. Once those two had started, Quinnie would hold the line on keyboard while Cleo shifted from a metronomic drum beat to her more fluid jazz sound, like Gene Krupa on speed (Cleo's own words). Homer Jefferson played guitar. The band had a repertoire of rehearsed riffs but on a good night like the Bath gig they broke free and played what came.

'That's where you met her?'

Babette had appeared in the second interval. For a moment he hadn't recognised her. Her hair was longer than he remembered and they hadn't met for several years.

'Hey, Nico,' she had murmured. 'Teacher always said you'd waste your life.'

She had the same grin that he remembered – and among all the heaving people Babette looked calm. Just like at school. Only now she was older the school beauty was in a class of her own.

'You studying here?' he asked.

'I'm through. Been out of Uni more than two years.'

'You got a First, I bet.'

She grinned modestly and shrugged. He said, 'What else would you have got?'

'So Nico, what d'you do for a day job?'

'This is it.'

'You make money at this? Wow. Only you.'

'We can play that – Only You.'

She smiled.

'Are you living round here?' he asked.

'For a bit.'

He leant forward. 'We can't talk in all this noise. Why don't we meet up tomorrow? We could talk about old times.'

'We don't need an excuse to talk, do we, Nico?'

When she smiled it was as if someone shone a torch into his face.

Babette said, 'I'll still be here when you finish.'

At around two o'clock the police offered a cup of tea.

'I'd prefer coffee.'

'All comes out of the same machine, sir.'

As he was drinking it he noticed that their attitude had shifted – not a lot, but for the better. Perhaps they could see that his uncommunicativeness was not because he was fighting them. It wasn't the main reason.

'This girl, then – you hadn't met her for several years, then she suddenly turned up out of the blue?'

'We went to school together.'

'Do you know where she lives now?'

'Bath, she said. I think her parents moved house.'

'But they used to live in Bristol?'

He had never been to their house. He had never been – properly – out with Babette. At school she had been a star – always top in the class, effortless at exams and good at sport. By rights she ought to have been Head Girl, but in their school that position was voted for by pupils, and Babette had not put her name forward. Sometimes the brightest pupils try to dim their light. Nick spent his own time at school quite differently. Like many teenage boys he found school irksome – he could do the work (reasonably, though not as effortlessly as she could) but he found the rules and day-to-day repetitiveness got him down. Fortunately he had his sax. Instead of dropping out and drifting, he practiced music and joined a band – several bands, until Blue Delta.

'You lost contact with Miss Hendry when she left school?'

'Yeah.'

'And didn't go to university?'

He had worked in a garage and played gigs at night. At around the time Babette would have been graduating, he decided to give up the day job and try to earn a living from the sax. No compromise. Half measures don't get results.

19

The policeman began again: 'How many years is it since—'

'Look, what happened to her? Are you going to tell me?'

'What *happened* to her? You don't know?'

'Come on, for Christ's sake – they said she'd fallen into some kind of meat processing machinery, and… Christ, you're quizzing me as if I pushed her in. Is that what you think?'

The policeman stretched and grimaced. 'No, we don't think you pushed her in, but we do think you were in league with her.'

'I don't care what you think. I want to know what happened to her – is she dead, for instance?' The words caught in his throat.

The policeman stared at him. Seeing he wasn't going to answer, Nick stood up. 'You wonder why people hate you.'

'I don't think that's called for, Mr Chance.'

Nick moved for the door, but the policeman blocked his path. 'You were waiting for her outside the plant tonight.'

'So?'

'Then you know what happened there.'

'I heard what they *said*—' Suddenly Nick lunged for a chair and sat down heavily. 'It is true, then?'

The policeman paused. 'You thought it mightn't be?'

'I—'

Nick began to gasp as if about to throw up. The man slid a plastic cup of water towards him. Nick glanced at it, then suddenly lashed out and knocked it across the room.

Neither of them spoke.

Eventually the policeman asked, 'What exactly did she intend to do in the factory?'

Babette had begun telling him yesterday on the beach at Clevedon – their first day together. The sun had shone, though a salty breeze whipped off the sea. Families sat on the sand while old people walked on the promenade. A few children paddled. 'Just a bit of a lark,' Babette had said.

Her auburn hair was down, and the wind had blown it into rattails. Her brown eyes sparkled. 'No one knows how disgusting the whole thing is. We use the word meat but we're talking about dead animals. Can you imagine a factory hall littered with dead bodies? I mean *real* bodies – heads and eyes, complete – lying in ungainly heaps. A room full of staring eyes – it'd be hard to believe they couldn't see you, wouldn't it? You'd wonder whether all those animals were really dead. People in waterproof boots wander among them, blood on their aprons. Do they go home at night, d'you think, and tuck up their kiddies in their beds?'

Nick said, 'I would think so.'

'You don't want to think about it at all, do you, Nico? Most people don't. They just turn and look the other way.'

'Nature isn't civilised. Animals eat other animals. They hunt and kill. In the wild they rip into the flesh of their victim before it's dead. It's a horrible thought, but that's reality.'

They were not arguing. They were too new together. But she stood a moment with the sea behind her and focused intently on Nick's face. 'That makes everything all right?'

'Civilisation… well, it hides unpleasant truths. It's only in recent years we've distanced ourselves from what we eat. Animals kill their own food, but *we* have always divided the tasks – sending some people to hunt, hiring some to farm, leaving others at home to cook.'

'Women.'

'Traditionally.'

Nick changed the subject. It wasn't something that he felt strongly about. The previous night's gig had been sponsored by a local animal rights group – which was presumably why Babette was there – and afterwards, she had hung around only long enough to take his address, then disappear. He had slept nervously, unsure if she'd reappear. And that morning when she drove round to his flat, Nick had not invited her in – he wanted neutral territory, somewhere bright, somewhere outdoors.

They spent the day in Clevedon, eating a surprisingly pleasant lunch in a small wholefood cafe overlooking the abandoned pier, and afterwards walking the length of the beach to the broken promontory of rocks pointing to the estuary. They plunged their hands into cool rock pools like children. She had kept some shells.

Later that evening – much later, when they were no longer nervous of each other – she told him more about the plan for the following day.

'Remember I was talking about that meat factory?'

'Mm. This topic is forbidden out of season.'

But she turned to him beneath the duvet. 'When exactly is the season?'

'When there's an R in the month.'

She thought for a second. 'Pig,' she said. 'That rules out the whole of summer.'

He stretched luxuriously. 'Then you'll have to wait.'

She ran her finger down his chest. 'I know someone who can get me inside.'

He frowned.

She said, 'I want to take some photographs.' She ran her fingers lower. 'You don't mind that, do you?'

She said she'd photograph as much of the ghastly process as she could, then release the pictures later with a detailed statement.

'So you're not on your own?' he queried.

'No.' She twirled her finger slowly. 'Like you, I'm with a group.'

Which he hadn't told the police.

When she told him, Babette had stressed it was a secret. But the policeman asked: 'You and Miss Hendry were in some kind of group?'

'No.'

'Just the two of you?'

'It was something she did on her own.'

'Oh, come on, Mr Chance – on her own! Which group are you working with?'

'I'm not.'

'Animal Liberation Front, is it?'

Nick shook his head and yawned.

'I know how late it is, Mr Chance, but if you want to get some sleep you're going to have to be a little more co-operative.'

Nick thumped the table. 'I've had enough of this!' He stood up. 'The girl I love is dead, and you're pumping me with questions.'

'Oh, you *love* her, do you?' The policeman stared up at him incredulously. 'Yet you only met two days ago. My, my.'

Nick lurched at him across the table, but the other man was faster and better trained. He grabbed Nick's wrist, twisted, and Nick was too tired to resist. The officer held him in a half Nelson: 'Things are livening up, son. Are you on for more?'

Nick crumpled. When the man let him go, Nick sat down and put his head in his hands. The policeman spoke clearly for the tape recorder: 'Mr Chance attempted to strike me but has calmed down. Do you wish to add to that, Mr Chance?'

There was a period of silence.

'Tell me, sir, what would be the point of this set of photographs?'

Nick didn't answer.

'We're having them developed, you see, at the moment. So you might as well tell us.'

'You've got her camera?'

'Oh, yes. Maybe there'll be a nice picture of *you*. Something revealing, shall we say? Or are they holiday snaps?'

'Bastard.'

'I've been called worse names before. What sort of pictures are there on the film?'

Nick shook his head.

'Not very helpful, are you? We'll soon find out. She left the camera beside the pulveriser, see? Put it down on the gantry.' The man was studying him as he spoke. 'What do you think happened? She put the camera down, looked into the vat, leant over... Is that what you think?'

'How do I know?'

'It might have been like that. Of course, you were outside all the time?'

Nick stared at him blankly.

'Weren't you?'

Nick continued to stare.

'OK. So let's say she put the camera down, then leant into the vat and fell. Do you think that's likely?'

'No.'

'You think she jumped?'

'What?'

'Did she say anything beforehand that might suggest she would?'

'Jump?'

'Was Miss Hendry the suicidal type?'

'For Christ's sake.' Nick shook his head. 'Haven't you been listening to anything I told you?'

'About what, sir?'

'About... about our time together.'

'Suicides are not always miserable, you know. How strongly did Miss Hendry feel about this group of yours? Was she fanatical?'

'That has nothing to do with it.'

'I think it has. Most certainly. Maybe she fancied herself as a martyr.'

'She did not commit suicide.'

'No? Well, it might have been an accident. Up there, you see, no one saw Miss Hendry fall. That was the point, wasn't it – no one should notice her? Even so, she must have chosen her moment. Wasn't that the plan?'

Nick muttered, 'I don't know.'

'She'd placed her camera carefully on the gantry.'

'Carefully?'

'It's a narrow gantry. If she'd dropped the camera, it would almost certainly have fallen through to the floor. No, she placed it, carefully. Then she fell into the machine.'

'Maybe she was... trying to find out...'

'Find what? No, it doesn't gel, Mr Chance. Of course, the whole thing could have been an accident – except that the machine has warning devices. One of those shut it down – a sensor, you know?

23

But, of course, the machine couldn't cut off quickly enough to save her life.'

'I don't believe it.'

'You're in denial, sir, I can understand that.'

The policeman paused, then changed his tone. 'Well, what's done is done. Look, Mr Chance, this has been pretty distressing for you, so I think you'd better go home and get some sleep. When you've had a good rest, I'd like you to think things through more carefully. We'll have another talk, and maybe you'll realise that it would be better if you told us everything. Incidentally, do you have the address of the young lady's next of kin?'

'No.'

'I'm serious, Mr Chance. We have to let her parents know.'

'I don't know it. I don't know where she lives.'

'Didn't you used to go to school together?'

'They moved.'

'I see. Well, you might as well go home.'

Nick began towards the door, then stopped. 'You haven't told her parents?'

'Not yet.'

'Has anyone… Do you want me to identify the body?'

'Um, no, there's no need for that.'

'I'd like to see her.'

The policeman looked away. 'Mr Chance, I'm afraid there's no question of that.'

Nick looked at him. '*Is* there a body?' he whispered.

'Yes, in a sense. But you wouldn't want to see it.' He saw Nick's face. 'No, you wouldn't,' he said. 'I'm sorry, son.'

When Nick left the station the rain was falling, soft and salty from the estuary. It was a cold bleak dawn.

3. I HEAR YOU KNOCKING

(BUT YOU CAN'T COME IN)

SOMEONE DOWNSTAIRS WAS cooking breakfast. As he passed their door it occurred to Nick it was unusual; nowadays, people don't cook bacon and sausages to start the day – too much cholesterol, too much fat. Too much trouble. Too many well-meaning articles in the press insisting that the diet which once sustained us will shorten our life. Instead of warming eggs and bacon we must eat muesli or plain toast. But we must eat *something*, the preachers say – to omit breakfast is to leave the body open to calorific temptation later in the day.

To modern families the smell of bacon is unfamiliar. It belongs to childhood, to the days when Nick's mother fussed in the kitchen before he went to school. But had she done that? Had his mother really waited in the kitchen, apron clad, or was it a piece of fake nostalgia installed in his mind by TV dramas and commercials? What had he really eaten for breakfast as a child? He couldn't remember. He had a distant memory of rushed mornings, of running down the garden path clutching a thick slice of bread and marmalade, his tie undone. Or was that image also fake nostalgia? Were all his child-hood memories supplanted by sharply etched pictures from adver-tisements?

Either way, he'd cook a proper breakfast when he got in.

Perhaps whoever lived downstairs also faced an undemanding day, no time pressure, no reason not to linger in the kitchen deliber-ately preparing a luxurious and forbidden meal. Other people rush off to work without time for a leisurely breakfast, and the days when

Mother prepared it are long past. Only the unemployed have time for breakfast. So maybe it's not so healthy after all.

His brain was swirling with stupid thoughts – anything to displace what he didn't want to think about. Nick climbed the stairs, took the front door key from his pocket, but when he touched the lock his door swung inwards into the hall. He felt a chill. Someone was in his flat. He could hear them moving. He moistened his lips and stepped inside.

In the living room two men were searching through his things – two men he had never seen before. One glanced up casually as he came in. 'Mr Chance?'

'Who the hell are you?'

'Good morning. Badly out of order last night, weren't you, sir?'

The other man sniffed and turned away from him, continuing to rifle through a pile of paper Nick kept on his desk. Nick snapped, 'Get away from that.'

The first man said, 'I'm sorry, Mr Chance, we have a job to do, and we're being as careful as we can.'

Nick said, 'You got a warrant, or what?'

'Don't excite yourself, sir… Don't do that!'

Nick was moving toward the man at his desk, but the taller, lean man stepped in his way. He had an accent Nick couldn't place: 'Don't do something you'll regret.'

Nick paused. The man continued: 'I'm afraid I must trouble you with a few more questions. It shouldn't take long.' His accent was Northern Irish, and it sounded out of place here – familiar yet menacing. Conditioned reaction, Nick thought.

The man said, 'I don't suppose you got much sleep down at the station? Well, if you're co-operative, you can be tucked up in bed in thirty minutes. What do you do for a living, Mr Chance?'

'I've been through this.'

'You know how we are, sir – we keep repeating the same old questions, just in case.'

'In case of what?'

The man smiled. 'Why don't we sit down? Leave my colleague to his duty.'

'I'm not standing here while he goes through my things.'

'Then you'd better sit.'

There was still a smile on the man's face, but he did not look friendly. He had the look of a pub fighter daring Nick to swing the first blow. Must have been his accent.

He repeated, 'What do you do for a living, Mr Chance?'

'I've told you.'

'No, sir, you've not told *me*.'

Nick sighed. 'I'm a musician. Have you got a warrant?'

'We can do this the easy way, sir, or the hard. I believe you claim to be an innocent party?'

Nick stared at him. The man looked tough. He had white blond hair. He said, 'Your words at Rendox were, 'I'm just passing by'. Except, of course, you knew the girl – so you were hardly passing by.'

'I've explained all that.'

The man nodded. 'It's been a long night, I know. But I think you'd feel better if you sat down.'

He was right, but Nick was obstinate.

'Why didn't you go into the factory *with* her, Mr Chance? Were you just the driver?'

'I was in the car.'

'You drove it. That was your job?'

Nick felt very tired. 'It just happened. And it wasn't a "job" as you call it. She was taking photographs, that's all.'

'No, sir.' The man smiled.

'What the fuck do *you* know about it?' Nick shouted.

The man paused. 'You're tired, sir. I understand. Please sit down.'

Nick might have, if at that moment a third man had not wandered in from the bedroom. 'Nothing in there,' he said, looking at Nick. He was a big man.

The man questioning Nick was clearly senior. He ignored the big man and frowned at Nick. 'Where did you meet her?'

Nick's throat was dry. 'I'm not going through this again.'

'Then we'll have to wait. We've got all morning. Though we might become less patient as time goes by. Where did you meet her?'

After a moment, Nick mumbled, 'We went to school together.'

'And then?'

'Nothing.'

'And what is "nothing" supposed to mean?'

Nick noticed that one of the men had moved to another small pile of paper and was lifting each sheet and examining it, holding each sheet to the dim light from the window as if trying to find a water-mark. Nick said, 'That's just sheet music. Leave it alone.'

'We'll be off as soon as you've answered our questions. When you and Miss Hendry left school, what did you do then?'

'Look, she's dead, for Christ's sake. I don't… I can't…'

'Sit down, Mr Chance.'

Nick did.

They asked more questions about *him* than about Babette – what were his politics, what contact did he have with extreme organisations? While the questions continued, the other two men gave up their search of his small flat. One sat in an armchair and gazed at Nick, and the other disappeared to stand outside the door. Nick felt hollowed out, a husk. His questioner remained quiet and unflappable, the Northern Irish accent colouring his words. Every now and again he would run a hand through his tight blond hair and stare at Nick as if he were a piece of clay he wanted to sculpt.

'You're a musician, you say?'

'I play sax.'

'That sounds nice, sir – very relaxing. But what do you do to earn a living?'

It seemed easier to drone out answers than to resist this placid man. Nick wanted them to leave. He felt bitter, sad, depressed. He wanted to lie on his bed and cry.

'What do you think of Rendox, Mr Chance?'

'*Think* about it?'

'Yes, you know – d'you disapprove of what the factory does?'

'I don't give a damn.'

'Your friend paid a hell of a price for someone who didn't give a damn.'

Nick moved his tongue around his mouth to help him salivate. '*She* gave a damn. I don't.'

'How wise.'

The man held the pause, but Nick had nothing useful left to say.

When the men had gone Nick closed the curtains in his bedroom. Instead of darkening the room they cut out only enough light to make the room more drab and miserable, so he reopened them. The sun had risen high and the sky was blue. Tile roofs of nearby houses soaked up morning light, and the soft grey Victorian brickwork looked warm to touch. People walked purposefully along the residential street. Someone tried to start his car.

Nick had one task before he could go to bed. He picked up his mobile and dialled a number.

'Steve? It's Nick.'

'This is early for you.'

'I've been up all night. I'm going to have to skip today's rehearsal.'

'We don't start till two o'clock.'

'I know, but… I've had a bad time. OK?'

'Well, it's the usual material. We're only doing it for Miranda.'

28

She was the new singer with the band. 'Run through the material, get her used to it. She seems pretty quick on the uptake.'

'Better than Selina.'

'I hope she lasts.'

Nick yawned. 'Lasts?'

'Didn't she seem kind of… fragile to you? I know we only saw her at the audition, but she did not look strong. She could have a history.'

'We've all got history, Steve.'

Nick put down the phone and looked at his bed. Though the sun cut a triangle across its foot, the bed looked chilly and unwelcoming. Back in the living room the tobacco odour lingered from his visitors, and he tugged at the wooden window to let in some air.

His saxophone stood in the corner. He picked it up and slumped his body into the supporting angle of the two walls, hunching over his instrument as if sheltering it from rain. Then he ran his fingers across the keys and began to play. It wasn't his normal material but a slow, monosyllabic extended blues in which the bass notes of the saxophone seemed to rasp and grunt with pain. Flexibility seeped into his fingers. This couldn't have happened. She couldn't be dead.

His sweet Babette could not be dead.

4. BYE BYE LOVE

(BYE BYE HAPPINESS)

I LIE HERE, staring at the ceiling, listening to the erratic trickle of everyday life as it passes my window. Cars glide by like gusts of wind. A starling chatters. Snatches of banal speech hang in the summer air like icebergs floating in the sea. Somebody laughs. I remember a day – I must have been thirteen – when our collie dog died. He had been as much a part of our lives as the carpets underfoot. The night before, he had slunk in late, ears drooping beside his face, gazing up at the family who could save him. We could see no outward sign of harm. He lay on the kitchen floor beside the boiler while my father gently felt round his body, searching for tender flesh that might suggest where the dog had been hit by a car. The only sensitive part was his soft belly. When my father touched him there, the collie growled.

I found his basket but when we tried to lift him into it he growled again. My mother took the blanket from the basket and placed it over him on the floor. But he shook it off. Then he stood up and crawled into the basket on his own and let my mother lay the blanket over him there. I don't know what time it was, but I had come downstairs in pajamas, having heard the fuss. I remember sitting on the kitchen floor stroking his head while my parents muttered about calling the vet. It was after surgery hours. They didn't think he'd come so late, and there was no all-night centre where we could take him. Eventually my father went to the phone, and when he came back he said the vet – a vet, some kind of vet – had said we might as well wait till morning. He would come out then. There was an animal hospital, apparently, but it was an hour's drive away, and since the dog hadn't been involved in an accident and wasn't bleeding, the problem could wait.

We *all* waited. My sister Helen was there, though I don't remember Alwyn, my older brother. He must have been away. At any moment throughout that night one of us would be sitting on the lino floor, stroking the dog. We wouldn't go to bed.

As the hours passed we realised that this was not a sickness, it was death. I think my father phoned again. My mother made hot milk for us – and she opened two tins of dog food, as if a different flavour might tempt the dog to eat. She turned off the harsh fluorescent light, lighting the kitchen from a little table lamp, one my parents sometimes used for supper when they wanted to make an occasion of it, the two alone.

Mother said, 'Helen, go to bed – and you too, Nicholas.'

Helen would have been eleven, if I was thirteen. But that night she stayed up long after midnight until her head sagged and my father had to carry her upstairs. I refused to go. When my father returned he agreed that I could stay up a little longer – even on that dreadful night he maintained the childhood difference in our bedtimes. As I remember, I never went to bed. Certainly I remember the cold dawn filtering into the kitchen – yet could it have been a *cold* dawn? We surely had the central heating on all night. I remember the changing light as daylight augmented amber from the table lamp, and I remember the collie shifting in his basket, tongue hanging from his mouth, and the way I gave him water from a kitchen spoon.

All through the night the dog lay in his basket like a broken toy, but in daylight he stirred restlessly, looking for a more comfortable position, and we asked each other whether this was a sign for the better or for the worse. I took a smear of dog food on my finger and placed it to his mouth. He lapped gratefully, and I began to hold out fingers of slippery meat, hoping that somehow I could nourish him back to health. But it didn't work. He quickly tired of the meat and lay in his basket staring at the floor.

The vet arrived around breakfast time, and while he knelt beside our dying dog we stood hollow-eyed like extras in the last scene of a tragedy. Remember that final scene in Hamlet where Fortinbras marches into the stricken hall? Hamlet and Laertes are dying, the king and queen dead, the whole palace awash with shock and mourning; and after three long hours of blood and tragedy the brisk young soldier – the heir apparent – makes his first appearance on the stage. He calls abruptly, 'Where is this sight?' When he sees they're all dead and he is too late to intervene he rubs his hands and says cheerfully, 'With sorrow I embrace my fortune... Take up the bodies. Go, bid the soldiers shoot.'

We stood watching the vet playing Fortinbras. 'Your dog's eaten

31

something,' he announced cheerfully. 'I expect it's rat poison. Did you lay bait?'

My father shook his head and my mother, voicing all our thoughts, said, 'It's the farm next door.'

The vet said, 'That'll be it,' and filled a syringe. 'Can't hold out much hope,' he continued airily. 'If he's swallowed Warfarin he'll have internal bleeding now. Not long to go. There's just a chance I can kick him back to life.'

My mother echoed, 'Kick him?'

'Figure of speech. This is adrenaline, to give his heart a shock. It'll either kick him back into life, or…'

'He'll kick the bucket,' my father said.

The vet looked up from the floor. 'I can leave you alone a few minutes if you want to think about it. I know how wretched this can be.'

'Don't go,' said mother. She glanced at my father but he looked away.

Helen asked, 'Are you putting him to sleep?'

The vet stayed on his knees and answered her: 'You'll have to be very brave.'

How many times, I wonder, had he used those words? At the time, I thought him cold and heartless. He had come to us from a good night's sleep, he had looked at an animal that must have seemed as spent and finished as an old tube of toothpaste, and he had thought: I'll give the tube one final squeeze. Which he did. But there was nothing left.

Later that day we buried the dog in the garden, and my mother tried to explain that there had been no alternative. We had waited all night, and the dog was in constant pain. Whatever was to happen would. For Helen and I, that day marked the end of a chapter in our life, and within six months my father changed his job and we moved to Bristol, leaving our beloved dog buried in the garden beneath the twisted maple tree that we'd never see again.

I lie here, staring at the ceiling, listening to my memory.

Babette asks, 'What ever happened to your frogs?'

In the first year at my new Bristol school the kids called me Frog King because I'd bring frogs in a plastic box and release them in the classroom.

'Still in the pond, I guess.'

'Won't the people who bought your house have got rid of them?'

'Not unless they filled the pond in.'

This was two days ago on the beach at Clevedon as we clambered over the rocky promontory looking into pools. The wind moistened her hair.

'You said your frogs had Devon accents.'

'I'd brought them with me when we moved.'

She sat beside me and her skirt dangled above a pool in which the sea water was spectacularly clear and where bright green seaweed waved in unseen currents. 'Perhaps you survive in their folk memory as the great frog god.' She smiled up at me. 'Imagine them croaking: many years ago, my children—'

'Generations ago.'

'There lived a huge and gangly boy—'

'I was never gangly!'

'You were so. When you first came to school you looked like a country scarecrow. Carrying frogs around in your pocket!'

'Not in my pocket. I kept them in a box on a bed of damp leaves and grass, and if they were lucky I'd put a snail in.'

'I always knew you were horrible.'

'Was that why you wouldn't talk to me?'

She smiled again. 'There were other reasons.'

I wanted at that moment, just as I do now, to grab her in my arms and stop our silly chatter with a kiss. But it was our first day. We were treading gingerly.

'One day, you little pest, you dropped a frog inside my dress.'

I have no memory of it. On the beach I denied it had happened, but Babette insisted it was true. We would have been about fourteen, maybe fifteen, and at that age a boy finds nothing innocent about a young girl's dress. I can imagine myself, a fourteen year old boy in sexual torment looking for an excuse to touch her – but I don't remember that I ever did. She was on that secure pedestal young boys erect for teenage girls. Perhaps in those days I *was* a country boy, but Babette seemed so sophisticated. Most of the boys in our class were in love with her: she was beautiful, she was bright. Yet she never seemed to have a special boyfriend – and believe me, I watched. I would have known. I protected her once when an oaf called Hywell Jones pestered and pawed her. He was a big boy, Hywell, but I knocked him down. Afterwards, when I turned to Babette she smiled and walked away. Now, of course, I would have followed her. But not then.

'You should have done,' she said. It was later that day, in her car, as we drove back to Bristol. 'I wanted you to.'

I turned, surprised.

'I walked away from the crowd,' she said. 'Because I couldn't kiss you in front of the others.'

In the front seat of her car I was as speechless as I'd have been at school. At that moment we had spent the whole day together and still hadn't kissed. We had never kissed. There had been a day, years later, in the summer – which summer? – yes, the year before we both left school. We'd have been seventeen. Our class, or some conglomeration of us, went in a coach to Tintern Abbey – a tall ruin, lost among trees on a hillside running down to a river. Woods enclosed the abbey. It was a gorgeous day. I expect most of us had gone on the trip simply for a break from the monotony of mugging up for exams. We weren't interested in abbeys, ruined or otherwise, but a day out in a coach, and two or three hours when we could get lost in the woods beside the River Wye, was too good to miss. After ten minutes at the abbey I doubt there was a single one of us still inside the formal grounds.

And that was the day – finally, after so long at school – when Babette and I found ourselves alone together in the woods. And two days ago, when we'd driven back from the beach; when she was standing in my flat for the first time, awkwardly because we'd just arrived; when she was looking at every piece of furniture as if it might have had significance – she remembered too. She noticed a vase of flowers on my windowsill, and laughed.

'Flowers! You're the only boy I know who would have flowers on his windowsill. Do you remember Tintern Abbey?'

I nodded. 'I'm the type who has flowers on his windowsill?'

She smiled. 'You're not any type at all. You're a country boy. Do you remember when we were in those woods?'

'Yes,' I whispered.

'You knelt down in a clearing and showed me a tiny plant. I wouldn't have noticed – it was just a weed. But it had this strange green flower – not a flower at all, really – a little square pellet with four flat faces.'

'Moschatel.'

'Town Hall Clock, you called it. I thought you'd made it up.'

'That's the common name. It's like a tower clock, one face each side.'

'Then you showed me lots of other flowers – weeds to a townie – but you knew all their names. I don't remember them now – just the Town Hall Clock. No, wait a minute, there was some kind of... Ladies Bedstraw. I remember now. You said it was fragrant, and in the old days they used to stuff a ladies mattress with it.'

'A pillow, more likely. You'd need a lot of bedstraw for a mattress.'

We smiled at each other, each remembering in our own way. It wasn't the flowers I remembered – it was the excitement of being

34

alone with her in the ancient woods. Sunlight filtered through the trees. In the clearings the warm sun dried the grass and Ladies Bedstraw. This was an adolescent dream come true: the girl I longed for, the afternoon stretching ahead of us; silence, birdsong, the leaves backlit and shimmering, Babette no longer talking, the two of us drawing together – and then that voice, that wretched Hywell Jones stumbling through the trees, saying, 'Hey, what's all this then? What have we here?'

And he wouldn't go away. When he arrived Babette and I hadn't even touched, and I was paralysed with teenage nervousness, not knowing whether she would let me kiss her. What could I say to Hywell Jones? We were so young. And the sneering Hywell hung around us while we trudged out of the trees back to the others. Among them we behaved as if nothing had happened – which it hadn't. But I spent the rest of the afternoon racked with doubt. She seemed cool, untroubled, and on the way home in the coach she sat with the girls.

Standing at the window of my flat two days ago, Babette spoke of it for the first time: 'You kept showing me different flowers and I waited for you to kiss me. I'd almost planned it. When we got off the coach at Tintern I had to find a way to drag you off from all the others. I'd been after you for ages.'

'You're joking.'

'I'm not. Then when I did you get you on your own I was convinced, you know, that this would be our moment. I suppose you were shy?'

'Yeah, kind of. And there was that bloody Hywell Jones.'

'Hywell?'

'He came barging in.'

'Hywell did?'

Incredible. The whole day ruined by him, and she had no memory of it. Or maybe she was no longer interested in the past, because now, standing sombrely by my window she asked, 'Well, Nico, are you still shy?'

Suddenly it was like the woods all over again. We were alone together, we had spent the day together, we were so close we could read each other's thoughts – and yet even then, trembling on the brink, when our thoughts were so loud we'd have to have been deaf not to hear them, I felt uncertain. She was such a prize that I didn't dare reach out and shatter what lay between us.

But she held my gaze and I kissed her where she stood. Anyone passing in the street could have looked up and seen us framed at my window.

Now I look through the window from the other side. From my bed I can see the roofline of terraced houses opposite. The sky is a non-colour between blue and grey. Above the roof a gull wheels aimlessly. I hear it cry. Out there it is midmorning and I have been lying on my bed for two hours staring into unchanging light. Memories drift by like the seagull in the sky. I keep them distant like the white soaring bird. Last night's memories are so painful that I cannot face them, and I rest on a cushion of inconsequential thoughts – shopping in the supermarket, cleaning the windows of my car. But every now and then I am jolted with a vivid flash of reality – the interrogation room, the men who searched my flat this morning – and I make myself remember years ago.

In our last term at school some of the seniors went on a school nature camp weekend. The field study was held each year on the south Wales coast, and was for younger pupils really. I had gone at fourteen but now I could go as one of the seniors helping control those unruly fourteen year olds. Babette had put her name down, which was why I went.

On each annual trip the party was accommodated in an old scouts' hall in a damp field on the edge of the village. Knowing that boys and girls would sleep in the same hut always built a tremendous head of anticipation among the pubescent tykes – though in fact the dormitory hut (in which the teachers and seniors also slept) was as antisexual and chaste as the waiting room at Temple Meads station. Nevertheless: three days of rambling in the fields, lonely strolls along the beach, the rough rolling shore. Yes!

But Babette didn't come. I don't know why. For some reason she dropped out at the last moment. However: among the band of supposedly responsible seniors was a girl called Rosemary Butterfield. Rosie was a pleasant natured, easy going girl with a plait of long blonde hair that hung down to her bottom, and she had an unjustified reputation as a slag. (Boys of seventeen sneer at any girl who 'does it", despite the fact that 'doing it' is the most desperate thing on their minds.) Rosie had been known to do it, and during our three days in Mumbles she did it with me. This was a matter of some consequence, since it was the first time I had done it with anyone. Losing your virginity should be a memorable experience, and I'm grateful that I lost mine behind a sandhill on a deserted beach, with the sun beating on my backside and little grains of sand in my toes and crotch. I remember Rosie fondly – despite the fact that when we got back to Bristol she was sufficiently proud of her conquest (I was not exactly a difficult conquest) to brag and show me off at school. My main fear at the time was that she would blurt out that I'd been a virgin – which she didn't – but the revelation wrecked any chance I might have had with Babette.

'I hated that girl,' she murmured. We were safely in my bed. It was that lazy black velvet hour straight after midnight. Street lamps glowed through my uncurtained window.

'You must have realised, Nico. I'd wanted you for years.'

'No way!'

'Months then,' she chuckled. 'Half the girls in the class fancied you, and you went off with that fat slag Butterfield.'

'She wasn't fat, and she wasn't a slag.'

'She was to me.'

'What d'you mean – half the class?'

'Looking for compliments? You were the one we looked up to, the one free spirit.'

'Oh yeah!'

'You didn't give a toss for anyone, did you? The system would never get you down. We slogged at revision, and you joined a rock band and played your sax. That made you God.'

It was unbelievable. 'I was a mess of mixed-up emotions.'

'Wasn't everybody?'

She moved onto her side and ran her fingers across my chest. 'We should have done this years ago.'

No dispute.

Later, I told her that in that final term I'd had a huge sense of hopelessness. I knew I'd fail my exams, and though I hardly tried to pass them I couldn't fool myself I didn't care.

'The worst time was watching the rest of you go off to university and leave me behind. You were stepping up to adulthood, and I was left in the same old Bristol.'

She paused. 'You were in a rock band.'

'A couple of gigs a month if we were lucky. And that wasn't a rock band. We were amateurs, making a lot of noise.'

'Untold Harm. I remember the name.'

'It lasted barely six months. Did you hear us play?'

'No. My parents kept a pretty tight hand. Things were easier at university.'

'That's where life began for you. Several of us stayed behind – including Hywell Jones, I'm glad to say – and we knew we were rejects. Life hadn't started for us. In the holidays I'd see you all back around town, but I wasn't part of your bright new lives. I was still in Bristol, and you had all moved on.'

'Yes, Bristol looked... tame and dull.'

'I'd have looked tame and dull as well.'

She lay against me and gave a little squeeze. 'Just as well I never saw you.'

'I saw you. Where was it? Broadgate – you were doing Christmas shopping. You looked ten years older.'

'God!'

'I felt like a child. I stood in the shadows and then slunk away.'

Now, lying in this cold bed, I taste sour vomit in my throat. We had two days and a night. And now she's dead.

The stark light outside gave no indication of time. Nick stared at the window, aware that the light had changed but unaware he had been asleep. He looked at the alarm clock – nearly three o'clock. Mid-afternoon. His throat felt dry. His mouth tasted as if he had a hang-over. For a minute he lay unblinking, but then the memories returned and he got up.

He had a wash, and when he saw his face in the mirror he remembered why he looked so haggard. When the kettle boiled he remembered the steam outside the Rendox factory. Her car might still be there outside the plant.

The police might have moved it – there was nothing *he* need do about it. He didn't even know where Babette lived. Somewhere in Bath. Or near Bath. Her parents had moved – to somewhere near Bath. Perhaps they were in the phone book. He put down his coffee cup and flicked through the directory: Hendry, there were twenty-two of them. But which one? Only a few were in the Bath area, but he couldn't be sure that Bath was where they lived. He could phone the numbers… No. They might not even know she was dead. He couldn't be the one to break it to them. He turned to another page of the directory.

'Yes – Mr Chance. How can we help you?'

'It's about last night.'

'You've remembered something?'

'I wondered if you'd picked up her car?'

'*Her* car? You were driving.'

'Someone should collect the thing, you know? Let her parents have it back.'

'We haven't located them yet, Mr Chance.'

'Oh. Anyway, you'll want the car. It's a Vauxhall. Hatch-back. I don't know the number, but it's a kind of greenish colour.'

'We'll find it. Are the keys in the dash?'

Nick winced. 'No. I've got them. I suppose I'll have to come out with you?'

'We'd better see you anyway, Mr Chance. We'll want your finger-prints to eliminate them from any in the car.'

But they didn't need his fingerprints, because when he arrived at the factory Babette's car had gone. Nick found the police car waiting outside, and a quick glance down the road showed that her car was no longer there. In the afternoon light the officer – lightly built, sandy haired – seemed more sympathetic than those the night before.

'Not the best place to leave a car,' he said. 'Round here...' He gazed glumly at the surrounding buildings. 'New car... They wouldn't need a key. D'you remember its number?'

'No.'

The man studied him. 'Well, never mind, we'll find it on the computer – provided she registered it, of course.' The man was think-ing. 'Of course, we don't have her address. Cast your mind back, sir. Try to think. Her address. Her family's address. Anything else about the car.'

'Her people moved to Bath, I think. That's where I met her.'

'Would she have been staying with her family?'

Nick paused. 'Probably not. She was living somewhere over that way, because I met her at Bath College at a gig.'

The policeman was watching him. Waiting.

Nick said, 'Yesterday she went back home to collect some things. Took about an hour or so. Hour and a half.'

'Some things?'

'Change of clothes. You haven't told her parents, then?'

'Not until we've found them, sir.'

Nick screwed his eyes half shut and stared at his feet. 'And have you... identified her? I mean... Do you want me to?'

The man touched his arm. 'I'm afraid that won't be easy, sir. That machine...'

'The pulveriser?'

'Exactly, sir. We found some scraps of clothing – a red material. I believe the young lady was wearing red?'

'Yes, and a white topcoat, a sort of overall.'

'They all wear that. Yes, the red was a denim material. Would that be right?'

'Yeah, a blouson and her jeans.'

'Red jeans, sir?'

'They matched. She had a black handbag. Did you find that?'

'Leather, sir? It's hard to find leather in a meat pulveriser.'

Nick closed his eyes.

'You feeling all right, sir?'

39

'No.'

'Although the car's gone missing, sir – been stolen – we still need your fingerprints. Perhaps you'd like to pop down to the station with me now? Best to get it over and done with, isn't it?'

Nick mouthed assent.

'You might take a glance at those scraps of red material, sir. See if they are the same as you remember. All right? And excuse me for suggesting this, sir, but would you like my colleague to drive you in your car? We wouldn't want another accident, would we?'

5. LITTLE RED ROOSTER

AFTER THE SHEEP had trotted, clambered and fallen from the back of his lorry Andy watched them mill around the yard – their last moments in cool daylight. If this had been a field they would have had sun on their backs but here in the abattoir yard the walls were high. There was deep shade. The red brick walls looked permanently damp and there was a smell of blood and animal feces. Every time he came, Andy wondered whether the sheep could tell, whether it was an intuitive fear that made them scramble in panic around the yard. Perhaps it was just that they had been released into daylight – they ran for relief and exercise, not from panic. You couldn't tell with sheep.

His own face gave little away. In his truck he spent hours alone, no one to talk or react to except radio and tapes. He'd listen to those and give nothing back. And at either end of his journeys he would dip briefly into other people's lives, nodding at so-called pleasantries, taking instructions. Most of his work came from West Country farmers, collecting animals from green fields where they had been reared, and hauling them to the rank and bleak termini where they met their death. Until the day he took them the animals would have been carefully fed and tended, kept in good health and, on smaller farms would have been known individually to the farmer and his hands. When the animals were being crammed into Andy's lorry those farmers' faces showed satisfaction mixed with grief. They had known their animals. This was the last they would see of them. Andy felt like Father Time – hooded, almost invisible – collecting doomed souls for their last ride.

He was the go-between, barely noticed, seen differently at either end of his grim journey: at the start he was the man who took the animals but at the abattoir he was the man who brought the next cargo, part of a world outside the walls. He felt for the farmers, who as far as he could tell genuinely cared for the animals in their charge – sheep, chickens, cows – and were beleaguered by falling prices, regulations, quotas, BSE, scrapie, prejudice, vegetarianism. Abattoir workers must feel even more isolated, he thought: the true butchers, a profession no one talks about. In each plant he went to Andy knew that the abattoir men bonded and supported each other against those outside. They had to, he thought. And, like him, they must be careful not to think too deeply about the animals. Those two men striding briskly round the yard couldn't let themselves view sheep as thinking creatures; they were simply items to be shifted. Animals were not living, breathing, fearing beings. They didn't know what was about to happen to them.

One of the men came across to speak. He had shouted something but his words were drowned beneath the bleating in the yard, and he came closer to chat to Andy by the gate.

Because of the clamour no one heard the motorbikes arrive outside.

One of the bikes waited near the gate while the other broke away and roared round to the far side of the enclosure, outside the wall. Each rider paused as if they were counting a given time. The first rider reached inside his pillion case for a grenade, lifted his visor and bit out the pin. As he spat away the strip of metal, Zane's thumb depressed the safety catch – the grenade comfortable in his hand as a large pebble from the beach. It felt pleasantly heavy, as if the explosive power locked inside increased its mass. Zane turned his bike around and paused, savouring the moment. He angled himself in the saddle to face the gate. With an underarm bowling action he lobbed the grenade towards it, swivelled forwards and urged his bike forward to get away. He had five seconds. Five seconds during which Shiel would remain beyond the rear wall. Five seconds before the bomb exploded, shattering the gate behind Zane as he shot into empty countryside.

Pandemonium inside the yard. Sheep leaping in the air, skidding, crashing against each other. Men fell to the ground. Behind the rear wall Shiel lit his first bundle of fire crackers and hurled it high across the wall. Crackers began firing before they hit the ground and the loose bundle tumbled cracking and spitting among sheep who, shocked by the first explosion, skittered in terror from the sizzling rat-a-tat ball of sound. As they careered wildly around the yard one of the sheep saw the gates blown open but it hesitated, unsure

42

whether the smell of cordite came from inside or out. Several sheep dithered behind it – until Shiel's second cartridge fell like a fusillade from the sky, and the animals scattered through the gate and rushed into the surrounding fields.

Shiel roared off on his bike, and from the corner of his eye he saw a group of sheep galloping loosely across a meadow. He smiled to himself. Liberation had been achieved.

Inside the yard, chaos continued. Many of the sheep were too stunned or stupid to find the gate and they barged around the walled enclosure, trampling on the three men as they began rising from the ground. Beside the shattered gate Andy sat, head reeling, heart pounding, half deafened by stampeding sheep and snapping fire crackers. He had been sitting for almost a minute, and the running sheep kept stumbling against him. He had to get up. But he felt so tired. Reluctant, almost. When he tried to stand he found he couldn't. Something had happened to his leg.

Hit it. Yes. Make the noise so damn loud it bends and buckles the walls. Smack this last chorus at 'em so strong the people fuse together into a block. Sail out now, in unison. Make 'em weep.

Nick could feel the vibrating reed shrieking back at him and the tube of the saxophone seemed to expand to become a fat conduit of gleaming metal. His elbows moved out from his body to accommodate its broadening size. He had to subdue the other instruments: Quinnie sailed on the keyboard like Jerry Lee Lewis and Tiger's trumpet was a rabid dog. Homer took his guitar into the stratosphere, and Cleo pummelled her set of drums.

They screeched into the last note like a Ferrari at the flag, but the applause came from a crowd weak as a baby in a rainstorm – only a few dozen of them in the hall. It was the smallest venue Blue Delta would play in their pre-Glastonbury tour – a hotchpot collection of dates they had lined up for these two weeks. But despite their small size the crowd were enthusiastic, and the band stood sweat-sodden before them to acknowledge half-time cheers. Nick watched their big guitarist ease the new singer to the front. Randi was so small that Homer could have picked her up and sat her on one hand. She was skinny, almost emaciated, her cropped blonde hair glinting in the overhead spots. She looked as if to blow the candles out on a birthday cake she'd need three attempts (what was she – a little older than Nick – twenty-five or six?) yet she sang as if made of steel.

House lights, such as they were, shuddered into life and the band became six ordinary people tidying their things. Homer unplugged his Gibson while Tiger Guffrey shook out his trumpet. Cleo bent to adjust the tension on a snare drum. Quinnie wiped his keyboard with a yellow rag.

Randi looked unsure what would happen next, so Nick went across and unscrewed his mouthpiece beside her. 'Good singing. Did you enjoy it?'

She nodded. 'I'm still fitting in.'

'You'll fit.'

He tilted the saxophone and shook drops of moisture to the floor.

She sniffed. 'Do we buy our own drinks, or does the newcomer get lumbered?'

He grinned. 'Never buy your own, not even in a dump this size. The least the owner can do is buy us a drink in the interval.'

'That'll be a step up from my last band. We sometimes had to pay to *appear*.'

'And pay again to be let out?' He grinned. 'Were you that bad?'

She shook her head as she walked away. 'The last band is always that bad.'

As Steve said, she looked like a girl with a history – and recent, from the look of her. Fragile. A bad time with drugs, or just a bad man? She began talking to Steve as the club manager arrived.

'Mr Quin?' he asked Nick, who shook his head and sent him on to Steve.

Tiger slouched across. 'Didn't get a chance to speak earlier,' he began awkwardly. Whenever he was uncomfortable, Tiger's Liverpool accent became more slurred. 'I mean, that was terrible, man.'

'I thought we were pretty good.'

'I mean the accident, the factory. And you were there, like?'

'Ah. Waiting outside.'

Tiger stared at him dumbly, then reached forward and touched his arm. 'You know, anything I can do.'

Nick grinned. 'I can rely on you for a pick-me-up.'

'The only cure for the summertime blues.'

Tiger was renowned for his pick-me-ups: he often popped a couple before the show, which was fine for the first hour but meant that by the end he was unpredictable. He grinned. 'Want something for the second half?' He slipped his hand into his pocket.

Nick shook his head. 'Last thing I need.'

Tiger seldom offered his drugs. When he had first joined the band he was using speed, but he'd forsaken it for coke. 'Cleaner,' he had said. 'Better for long term use.' He was a regular but light user, able to source stuff anywhere. As he said, 'You just recognise people, right? If you know where to look.'

44

Tiger was watching Cleo but she had quit the drums to talk to Homer. Nick saw the sadness in Tiger's face: that little triangle of tension had grown these last two weeks. He tried to break the mood: 'Randi was good. A nice surprise.'

'A right powerhouse. Who'd have thought it? And you know her real name? It's Miranda! Would you credit that.'

'Oops. Bet she turned out a disappointment for her parents.'

'Didn't we all?'

Tiger was trying not to look at Cleo. He patted his hair – dark, unruly, so wiry it would break a plastic comb. 'Anyway, I'm sorry about your woman, man. She was at the last gig, right?'

'Yeah.'

The manager passed by. He said, 'I told Stevie Quin – anything you want from the bar. Within reason.'

'Fine,' Tiger said. 'I'll take the barmaid.'

Two or three girls from the audience were waiting beside the stage, and although one of them laughed loudly for Tiger's benefit, he ignored them, saying, 'I'll get the drinks in. You want something?'

'A beer.'

'Right,' said Tiger, leaving. 'I see Quinnie's already scored.'

Steve Quin held a pint of lager in his hand and talked with two schoolgirls crossing their legs beside his keyboard. He was slightly built, almost delicate, and wore his blondish hair soft and long. The girls always gathered round Quinnie. Though they might think Homer sexier, young women were afraid to approach him first. Quinnie looked safer. Even black girls came to him first. There was something animal about Homer Jefferson, something so wild that strangers stood apart from him and watched. He was tall, fit and looked as if he had violence barely suppressed. On stage he showed off his well-exercised physique, his huge forearms glistening, his mass of dreadlocks swaying like snakes. The daunting effect was intensified by the outlandish sunglasses he always wore. He had a collection of large forbidding shades, each with opaque or mirror glass, and tonight's were electric blue. That collection, Nick scoffed, cost more than his cruddy guitar.

Homer was acting as if he hadn't noticed Cleo coming on to him more strongly than ever. He was Mr Cool. Or Mr Magoo: because when Cleo came on to a man he'd *have* to notice – even Homer, unless he was wearing his reflective shades back to front. She had been brunette originally, but had dyed her hair green blonde. In the band she wore it scraped back into a bun and, like Homer, played to the crowd – tight linen trousers and either a ragged cotton singlet or a bolero jacket: leather against bare skin. Cleo always looked about to expose something, though she never did. Even after fifteen months with Blue Delta – fifteen months and not a flash – the boys were convinced one day she'd slip.

'Great sax,' a slim girl said.

She was one of three waiting by the stage, but her two friends had left to join those round Steve.

'Thanks. Excuse me,' Nick said and left. He wasn't ready yet to talk to girls.

Tiger returned from the bar with four pints of beer. 'I got 'em for Cleo and Homer,' he said.

Nick extracted one carefully. Tiger said, 'See we even pulled the local MP?'

'Explains why the audience is so small.'

'Local election. Do anything for a vote.'

Nick shrugged. 'And there's an *A*genda stall over there. Didn't know this was an animal rights event.'

'That was the Bath gig. But nowadays there's always an *A*genda stall, and vegetarians, and Greenpeace and the anti fur trade gang.'

'We're the side-show, Tiger.'

'This is a trade fair.'

Tiger went to the stage, nodding to Randi threading through the throng. When she reached Nick she said, 'Four beers, eh – so I don't get a drink?'

'They're on the house. Ask at the bar.'

She looked tired, he noticed. He said, 'Tiger wasn't cutting you out, Randi – he thought you and Stevie were already on. Let me.'

He took her to the bar and she asked for orange juice.

'Don't drink?'

'Gave it up.'

He nodded.

'Mind, I could start again. The place is full of health freaks.' She glanced at his beer. 'You're not into alternative health, then?'

'This is my alternative.'

Now they were stationary, fans drifted close.

Randi said, 'Over here,' and leading him away she muttered, 'Don't we get a break?'

'Imagine what it'd be like to be really famous. I wish!' Nick laughed.

'I don't. I just want to sing.'

She seemed to shrink inside herself and become more compact, but she surprised him by adding, 'You did the right thing coming back tonight. You mustn't grieve.'

'I'll try not to.'

'No, I didn't mean you mustn't mourn her. Of course not. But the worst thing anyone can do is crawl into their shell.'

'I've just popped out.'

'Good.' She smiled up at him – still tight and compact. 'Let's keep moving.' He shouldered someone aside. Randi said, 'You went back a while, didn't you – you and Babette?'

'Yeah.'

'At the Bath gig – you know, when I watched the show? I was standing by her when she saw you on stage. She said, "That's my Nico." She seemed… pleased.'

She sipped some orange juice.

He licked his lips. 'She say… anything else?'

'Just that she'd known you way back. She didn't say where.'

'School.'

'Oh.' Randi chuckled. 'She made it sound quite mysterious. So you were only school friends? That's not so bad, is it?'

Nick's throat constricted.

'Drink up,' she said. 'Steve wants us back on stage.'

He couldn't swallow the beer. It tasted rancid. But he took it on stage for the second set and sipped it between riffs. They opened with three raucous welcome-back numbers and then slid into their own slow version of 'Little Red Rooster'. He tried to lose himself in the dragging rhythm of the tricksy blues, but tonight he couldn't express his sadness. He just sounded angry.

'Hey – aren't you Nick Chance?'

It was behind the club in the darkened car park. The band was stacking PA in Steve's van and the summer night was chilly with estuary dampness. Six men approached.

One said, 'It's all right for you, boy. Isn't it?'

'What?'

'Free publicity.'

Nick stared at him in the dark. Tiger hovered beside the van. Steve said, 'I'll get Homer.'

Nick said, 'Don't bother,' but Steve slipped inside the club.

One of the men said, 'Is that it, then – publicity? A fucking laugh?'

Nick shook his head.

'We're from Rendox,' one said. 'Mean something now?'

Nick sighed.

'Another night without our wages. All of us, the whole fucking place. I suppose you think that's really clever?'

'I don't need this,' Nick said.

One of them started toward him. 'Oh, *you* don't need it—' he began.

The back door opened but Nick didn't turn round. Homer said, 'You folks want trouble?' He had taken his sunglasses off.

A man laughed. 'Four of you now – think that's enough?'

'Five of us,' said Cleo.

Nick glanced round this time. She was a tall girl, Cleo, and these men wouldn't have seen her in a fight. Randi Page appeared. 'Six,' she said.

The man laughed louder. Another chuckled. 'Musicians,' he sneered. 'They think they're hot.'

'Want to try something?' Homer asked.

'You wait a minute.' One of the men stepped forward. 'If you're not part of this animal rights malarkey you can bugger off. But *he's* staying here.'

Nobody moved.

The man continued: 'You and your girlfriend, *Mr* Chance, you closed down our bloody plant. That's two nights now, and probably another night tomorrow.'

Steve said, 'The girl died, you know.'

'It's what she wanted, wasn't it? She jumped in the vat.'

Nick said, 'She didn't jump.'

'She didn't get up there by accident, boy. She went deliberate. Wasn't that the plan?'

'She was taking photographs,' Nick said.

The men shuffled nearer. One had a length of pipe in his hand which he tapped against the van. Tiger said, 'Stop that.'

Another man: 'Are you *all* in this, or only him? He was at the factory, but your whole band's up to its arse in this animal rights crap, right?'

The man banged his pipe against the van. 'So we better do the lot of you. Teach you all a lesson.'

'Let me tell you something,' said Homer, strolling casually to him – and the man raised his metal pipe in alarm. Too late though – too slow. Homer grabbed his wrist, punched him in the stomach, and kicked the pipe beneath the van. As the others closed in, Homer picked the man up and heaved him above his dreadlocked head.

Nick shouted, 'Let me talk to them.'

Homer glanced back across his shoulder. 'The time for talking's past.'

Nick spoke quickly to the Rendox men: 'The girl was just taking photographs. And she's dead, for Christ's sake. She went in the factory but she paid for it with her life. What else do you want – our lives too?'

Homer said, 'My arms are tired.'

'Put the poor guy down.'

Homer sat the man on top of the van and gripped his shirt.

The men were watching Homer. No one would try him on their own. Someone said: 'Were you lot mixed up in that bomb today?'

'Bomb?'

'Listen,' said Homer, and they did. 'What daydreams are you people having? Bomb? Are we the IRA?' He shook the man on the van. 'What the hell you talking about?'

'Someone threw a bomb at a Rendox abattoir. Was that coincidence?'

'Enough of this,' said Homer. 'I think it'd be quicker to have the fight.'

The man persisted: 'You don't know nothing about it?' He turned to Nick: 'How about you?'

Nick shook his head.

'There was a bomb today at our Somerset place – an hour away from here. A lot of damage. A man lost his leg. Animals all over the countryside. Now they're shut down too.'

Homer said, 'Why don't you go home and listen to some decent music?'

When he did get home, the trouble having fizzled out, Nick wondered how the Rendox workers had known where to find him. At the gate he had given personal details to the police – someone might have overheard. The gateman could have written it down. But surely he hadn't said anything about Blue Delta? His recall might be unreliable, but no – why would he have told them anything about the band? He hadn't even said he was a professional musician. To the police, yes, later – but not at the gate. What *had* he said there? He had given his name.

Oh yes: and his address as well.

6. I HEARD IT THROUGH THE GRAPEVINE

MAYBE IT WASN'T so early, but it seemed early to Nick. Daylight leeched through his curtains but it was midsummer: daylight came before the milkman opened his eyes. Any morning after a gig was a lost cause to Nick: nothing to get up for, nowhere to go, and he needed sleep. Someone was rapping at the door. The noise continued monotonously, two raps at a time. Rap, rap, pause. Rap, rap, pause.

He turned over. They'd go away. Couldn't be the postman – he didn't come to each separate flat. What was the time? Ten. Late for the postman, even on Saturday – this *was* Saturday, wasn't it? For what it mattered. Rap, rap, pause. Rap, rap.

He cursed as he got out of bed. A pair of trousers was draped across a chair, so he slipped them on, zipped up and wandered to the door. Just as he reached it the door opened and a man stepped into the room. There was someone behind him. They both came in. They *came inside!*

'Oh, you *are* in, Mr Chance. Not answering the door?'

The man behind him pushed it closed. Nick recognised them now: the Plain Clothes who'd been before. 'Have you got a warrant?' he spluttered. 'You come in here—'

'Don't get dramatic. We want a chat.'

'How'd you get in my door?'

'It's a simple lock, Mr Chance. Where were you yesterday lunchtime, around two o'clock?'

'Get out of my flat.'

The other man spoke. He had a local accent, warmer than the first man's flat Ulster twang – but his words weren't friendly: 'You'll be on a stretcher, boy, you don't watch out.'

Nick stepped forward, but they didn't budge. The Ulsterman repeated: 'Yesterday lunchtime?'

'Eating lunch.'

They waited.

'At a pub.'

They asked simultaneously: 'Which one?'

'You've got an alibi?'

Then the local man shut up.

'Who saw you in this pub?'

'The people in it.'

'That isn't helpful.'

Nick shrugged angrily. 'Well, the staff. Ask anyone.'

'They'll vouch for you?'

'Probably.'

The man raised an eyebrow.

Nick said, 'It was lunchtime. They may remember.'

'Were you on your own?'

'Yes.'

'Oh, dear.'

There was a pause.

The local man asked casually, 'Where d'you park your motor-bike?'

Nick stared at him. 'I don't have one.'

'But you can ride a bike?'

'I've got a car. What's this about?'

The white-haired Ulsterman took control: 'There have been two attacks now on the Rendox group. Is this to be a long campaign?'

Nick hesitated. 'I don't know anything about it.'

'You were at the first attack and for the second you don't have an alibi. I understand you support animal rights?'

'No.'

'Your rock band appears at events they organise.'

'We'll do anything for money.'

'Anything?'

The man looked at him. He was taller than Nick, lean and straight as a telegraph pole.

'This is waste of time,' Nick said.

'How long had you and Miss Hendry known each other?'

'I've been through this.'

'Where did you meet?'

51

'For Christ's sake, do you guys spend your entire lives repeating the same boring set of questions?'

'Where is your motorbike?'

'I don't *have* a motorbike!'

'Then how did you get there?'

'Read my lips: I didn't go near their bloody abattoir.'

The man smiled coldly. 'But you know it was an abattoir?'

Nick grunted in exasperation. 'Yeah. Some guys from Rendox came to our gig last night. They told me.'

'So you're in touch with Rendox staff?'

'They came to *me*.'

'And why would they do that?'

Nick sighed. 'They thought I might have had something to do with it.'

'That seems to be the majority view. You don't deny you took Miss Hendry to the processing plant – how did you get there?'

'In her car. I've told you this.'

'*Her* car? You still have it?'

Nick paused. His face hardened. 'You guys aren't from the police, are you?'

'Did we ever say we were?'

'Get out of my flat!'

'When you've told us what we want to know.'

'*You're* the ones should be answering questions. Jesus! What gives you the right to break in here?'

'I don't see any damage.'

'Not so far,' added the local man.

'Is that a threat?'

The Irishman leant towards him. 'If it was, Mr Chance, what exactly could you do about it?'

How does that Sam Hinton song go, Nick wondered? Yes: *What can you do in a case like that? What can you do but stamp on your hat? – On your nail file, your toothbrush… And everything else that's useless.*

If he'd had a cat he'd have kicked it. Animal rights!

They'd behaved as if they had every right to be there. Clearly they thought Nick knew more than he did, and the fact that he'd only met Babette that week was a story they did not believe. The Ulsterman kept asking what sort of campaign they had in mind – whether she had intended to kill herself: 'Like one of those Buddhists who sets light to herself in the street.'

'Or the IRA man who starves himself to death?'

Nick was angry and frustrated that he couldn't get rid of them. Their calm audacity made him wonder what had really happened inside the plant.

'Bloody strange accident,' he blurted out.

'It was indeed. Very strange,' they challenged back.

Only when they had gone could Nick surrender to his grief. They seemed to think Babette was linked to the abattoir bomb attack – but Nick had been with Babette those last two days. She had been almost flippant about her escapade. When she had gone to the Rendox plant she had worried she might be caught, but only like a schoolgirl on a prank. She had not intended to kill herself, and her jaunt had certainly not been part of a bombing campaign. Whatever had happened in Somerset must be coincidence. Her death had not been suicide – though it seemed an unlikely accident. True, she had climbed above the pulveriser to take her photographs – a gantry, someone said. So she might have slipped. Except that she had placed her camera down on the gangway. And was it really likely that, with all today's safety barriers and precautions, she could have tumbled inside? Wasn't it more likely someone pushed her?

Nick closed his eyes. It was too horrible to contemplate, but there seemed nothing he could do about it. These men, presumably from Rendox, had been to his flat twice but nothing they said established them as Babette's murderers. In any case, if they were part of the firm's security force, the police would only take their side. If he were to phone the police, what could he say?

These were morbid thoughts, and he had a life to lead. It was Saturday morning, nearly lunchtime, and he had to pack. There was a three hour drive ahead.

After the performance they felt washed out. Unlike the previous gig, de Montfort University had a proper auditorium and a crowd above a thousand. There were two other bands – a heavy metal outfit and a student group with a loyal following. All three were good, and Stevie Quin called it honours even. Rather than get drunk in the all-night rave after the show, he and Nick were in Steve's room. Visiting bands had accommodation in student halls.

'This is the life,' Steve said. 'All found. Even get their rooms cleaned.'

He had just finished running a long thin cable to the telephone box downstairs and was powering up his portable PC. Wherever they went he maintained Internet contact. He began keying their journal. 'Would you say we were top group tonight?' he asked.

'No question.'

'*We're* writing this story.'

Steve was updating the web diary with a piece he'd copy to rock music news groups. The Blue Delta site held music samples, photographs and the tour schedule, but Steve felt a daily journal encouraged fans to check in more frequently. While he typed, Nick sat on the bed and sipped a beer. Steve's untouched bottle stood by his laptop. He could nurse a beer for hours.

There was a knock at the door and Randi Page came in. 'There's been a cock-up with the rooms. We've only been given four.'

Steve said, 'Cleo's gone to Birmingham. Her brother's there.'

'That still leaves five of us.'

Steve shrugged apologetically. 'I'm sorry, Selena used to… share with Homer.'

'It's not part of the contract, is it?'

'Of course not,' Steve said. 'Someone will have to double up.'

'Oh yeah?' said Randi warily.

Steve blushed. 'I didn't mean that.'

'You and me, babe,' said Nick. Randi shot him a look. '*Steve* and me,' he clarified.

She remained on her guard. 'You sure?'

'Yeah, Steve's got the bigger bed. Not big enough for two, but… I'll come and fetch my things.'

'Thanks. Have you unpacked yet?'

'I don't till morning.'

Steve said, 'He's always ready for a moonlight flit.'

Randi relaxed. 'I'll bring your bag across. Which room is it?'

When she had gone, Steve gave Nick a cautious glance. 'You sure about this?'

'You're not going to eat me in the night, are you – darling?'

'I wish!' laughed Steve. He raised submissive hands. 'But seriously?'

Within the band it was an open secret that Steve was gay, but they kept it quiet from the fans.

'It's a fairly wide bed,' Nick said. 'We'll sleep top to toe.'

'I'll put a sheet between us if you want.'

Nick shook his head. 'I think I can trust you.'

They smiled at each other. Steve looked away. 'Right,' he said. 'Let's have a gander at our fan mail.'

Every night Steve dutifully skimmed the daily emails.

'You're not answering all those now?'

'It doesn't take long. I've half a dozen standard replies, so I just paste the right one and whoosh, there goes another email. Kerplop.'

'In the old days, big groups hired secretaries and sent postcards.'

'When we're big we'll have one. Ugh. No, thank you.'

'What was that?'

'Weren't you watching? A few nasties on here tonight. Delete. Splat. Hey look, here's a fan letter from Japan.'

'Really?'

'I bet he's never seen us. Jomo – is that male or female, do you think? I live in hope.'

'One of us should be satisfied.'

'Only if we ever see him or her in Tokyo. He says he likes reading our itinerary. Japanese: most British fans wouldn't know how to spell itinerary.'

'Do you talk to many people outside Britain?'

'A few. Let's face it, we're not really relevant out there. Oops, another nastie. Zap.'

'Bring it back.'

Steve pulled a face at him. 'There's always one or two, Nick. Ignore them.'

'What sort of one or two?'

'It's this tour. People think we've gone political. The animal rights gigs.'

'We have to. Glastonbury's coming up.'

'And we've had emails from that Rendox place.'

'Shit.'

'I *said* you wouldn't want to read them.'

'Let's see the one you deleted just now.'

'Deleted, baby. That means gone.'

'Never mind the buzzcocks, Steve. Bring it back.'

Steve sighed and clicked his mouse. 'A few more days and it'll stop.'

Nick read the email on the screen. It looked hastily written, as emails often are, and though it attacked animal rights groups in general, it attacked Blue Delta and Nick personally. 'How do you think it feels,' he read, 'to know you basterds want us to lose our livelyhood' ('Don't they have a spell check?' Steve asked.) 'and want to bomb us wihle we work?'

'They'll be bombing *us* next,' Nick muttered.

Steve said, 'There've been several of these.'

'Threats?'

'Not exactly threats.' Steve grinned reassuringly. 'Look, there's every freak in the world here, living out their fantasies. On the Internet everyone does what they damn well like. No laws, no bosses. It's therapy, man.'

'It's about time this Rendox business stopped.'

'Oh, it will,' Steve said, staring at his screen.

Then Randi arrived with Nick's bag and they changed the subject.

Two in the morning, Nick woke up. Steve was moaning in his sleep and had his arm across Nick's leg. When Nick moved it, Steve's elbow brushed his balls. Steve mumbled, 'Paul, please – Paul!'

He snuggled closer. Nick wasn't sure if he was awake, but he grabbed his hand and hissed, 'Steve! Steve, this is Nick.'

'Huh?' Steve was surfacing from deep sleep. 'Paul?'

'It's *Nick*.'

'What're you doin'… upside down?'

'It isn't Paul, Steve.'

Steve propped himself up in bed. 'Nick?'

'It's OK, man.'

'Jesus.'

'Just old Nick.'

Steve sounded as if he had come in from a run. 'I thought… A dream, I guess. I could have sworn… Did you touch me just now?'

'You touched *me*. You had your hand on my leg.'

'It was a dream. Oh, Jesus!' He began to cry. 'He'd come back, you know? And… I thought you were Paul, lying in my bed. He touched me. It felt so real.'

He controlled himself. 'I'm sorry, Nick, but… what's the opposite of a nightmare?'

'Try to get some sleep.'

Steve sniffed. 'Yeah, sorry. Did I wake you?'

'It's OK.'

Steve hesitated. 'You didn't think I was…' He exhaled. 'I still think about Paul. I miss him.'

'I know.'

'Christ, both of us in mourning. I'm sorry, Nick. It's only because you're in my bed.'

Steve shifted position and exhaled again. 'Just as well you were lying upside down. I could only kiss your feet.'

'And call me Jesus.'

Steve chuckled. 'Did you think I was coming on to you?'

'You haven't so far.'

'No.' There was a pause. 'Perhaps I should have done?'

'No way!'

'Well, a girl can ask. Sorry, Nick. God, I'm cold. Are you?'

'Not that cold. Go back to sleep.'

Steve grunted, but Nick knew he was lying on his back staring

56

into the darkness, remembering Paul. They had been a couple until Paul had been stabbed three months back outside a pub. No one knew exactly what had happened, whether it was random or provoked. Paul had simply not come home. The case aroused local publicity because, although knife fights weren't uncommon, knife murders were. Nick and Homer advised Steve not to go to the inquest, saying it was publicity he did not need.

'We've both had a lover killed,' Steve said. 'You want to talk about it?'

'No.'

'I felt like that. People kept... approaching me, as if they felt they *had* to talk about it – it'd be good for me, you know? I just wanted to hide away.'

'I know.'

Steve gripped Nick's thigh, but it was soothing, not sexual. Steve said, 'I never wanted to talk to anyone again. Crying helped – eventually.'

'Yeah.'

'But crying on your own is painful.'

'I'll get there.'

'Look.' Steve was moving in the bed. 'I'm going to help you despite yourself.'

'What the hell are you doing?'

Steve emerged from under the duvet by Nick, so that they were at the same end of the bed. 'Don't worry, I'm not going to seduce you.'

'Get off.'

'Don't be so macho, Nick. Listen. Haven't you ever held a girl just to comfort her – without putting your hand inside her dress?'

'For Christ's sake, Steve—'

'When you hold somebody it doesn't have to lead to sex.'

'I am *not* having sex with you.'

'I'm not offering it. This is about maturity, Nick – we're not teenagers now.'

'Get back to your own end.'

Steve laughed. 'Don't tempt me. Come on Nick, come to Auntie and have a cry.'

'You're the one who woke in the night.'

'Then why don't we cry together? I won't tell if you don't.'

'I'm not—'

'Grow up, Nick.'

'I can't do this, Steve. Understand?'

'OK, have it your own way. But one day, Nick, you're going to have to take the big step and let go.'

7. NOT FADE AWAY

STAN HOCKENDALE THREW down his newspaper. At the dining table Laura frowned over a clutch of forms, pen in one hand as she brushed aside her errant hair. Other strands sprang from the clasp to fall in wispy curls across her forehead, and Stan saw the bright creature that had captivated him years before. Without looking up she queried, 'Mm?'

'Story in the paper.'

'Funny ha ha?'

'Not funny either way. Politicians!'

'*Tell* me about them,' she sighed. 'You know what these are about?' She waved a form. 'Accountability of need. Thirty "questions we should ask to assess core requirements of the terminally ill" – to help us find "alternative provision", as the government so charmingly puts it. In other words, to find someone other than the State to foot the bill.'

Stan snorted sympathetically. 'There's no place for the terminally ill in today's society. No chance of their paying for their treatment. They're a drain on the sacred taxpayer. Isn't that the point?'

'I'm afraid so.' She dropped the photocopied form. 'At the hospice I try to help people enjoy rather than suffer their final weeks. Or at least to get something positive out of it. Now I'm supposed to take them through all this!'

She smacked the papers on the table. 'It's so irrelevant. I have to give them a score, you know? And when I hand in my forms they'll be collated to give *me* a score, to gauge my effectiveness at helping the State shirk its responsibility. We're not carers any more; we're tax inspectors… Oh, cheer me up – what was your story?'

Stan chuckled. 'Hardly cheerful. Just some prat from the government rambling on about their year-on-year increase in expenditure on health research when this year *we've* lost another two hundred thousand from our grant. If the government is spending more, I'd like to know what on.'

'Accountability. More money is spent, but only on officials and administration. I'm supposed to calculate the number of "support credits" each patient is entitled to – though of course, the questions are designed to reduce the credits. To earn credits on this scheme you'd have to be a homeless alcoholic hit by a bus.'

Becky looked up from her magazine. She was approaching twelve and very precise. 'Doesn't it occur to grown-ups it would be cheaper to pay people what they need in the first place, rather than spend twice as much and take twice as long trying not to pay anything?'

'All the time,' her father said.

Laura concurred. 'Politicians are not that clever.'

'They're stupid. I don't know why we bother with them.'

Her parents waited for any further pronouncements. Laura glanced at Stan. 'How serious is that two hundred thousand cut?'

He shrugged. 'It won't close us down. It just means we'll be a little less effective. Timothy says his prime objective now is to turn our balance sheet from deficit to profit.'

'But you're a research lab. You don't make a profit.'

'Oh, we can't *not*, it seems. We must be an income generator.'

Becky said, 'If you invented something sensible you'd make lots of income.'

'Ye-es,' Stan answered slowly. 'But we don't actually invent things.'

'You just kill animals.'

Stan took a breath. Laura answered hastily, 'They don't *kill* animals, darling.'

'They do experiments on them.'

Stan intervened: 'I know it upsets you, Becky, but a lot of medical research has to be done on animals. Let's face it, until recently, doctors had to experiment on humans. We can't go back to that.'

'It'd be more honest.'

He didn't want an argument. 'To make progress you sometimes have to make difficult choices. There's no easy answer.' He smiled encouragingly.

Becky sniffed. 'How many animals are killed every year just so companies can sell new types of make-up?'

'We're not testing cosmetics. You know that.'

'Three quarters of a million – in Britain alone.'

'I doubt that.'

'It's true! It's on the Internet. Gary printed me off this fact sheet—'

59

'Last night?'

'And the awful thing is there's no need for us to involve animals at all. Every year, two hundred thousand rats and rabbits—'

'Was this during last night's homework, when you were supposed to be finding out about Madame Curie?'

'Oh, I've got all that, but there's an organisation called The International Fund For Animal Welfare – which means they know what they're talking about – and they've got all these masses of statistics—'

'But did you get the material on Madame Curie?'

'Yeah, she was a right cow. Supposed to be such a saint, but she did it for money, really.'

'Come on!'

'It's true. She spent all the money on tons and tons of fertiliser or something—'

'Pitch-blende.'

'Industrial waste, tons of the stuff. Can you imagine? Blackish gunk, full of mud and pine needles from the forest where they'd dumped it. She processed all this horrible muck for years – years! – in her garden shed to extract a tiny gram or two of radium.'

'Decigram actually.'

'Exactly. Then what did she do? She sold it.'

'Sounds highly commendable to me – week in, week out, *month* in, month out, boiling up all that raw material. That's real science, Becky. Dedication.'

'She had a screw loose. Can you imagine filling *our* back garden with industrial waste, just to… it'd be like looking for a needle in a haystack.'

'And she found it.'

'Oh, you scientists are all alike. What was it for? Just to make nuclear weapons.'

'That wasn't what Madame Curie had in mind.'

'It's what happened, though, wasn't it? She was supposed to be looking for a cure for cancer, just like you.'

'She was a research scientist. She's not responsible for everything that's happened since.'

'That's so convenient! Huh.'

Laura coughed pointedly and rose from the table. Stan didn't respond. He picked up the paper, glanced at a page without reading it, then stood up to help Laura clear away. There was no point arguing with Becky. She argued about everything nowadays.

On Sunday evening when Nick arrived back at his flat it felt cold and lifeless, as if no one had lived in it for some time. No longer his own place. Less than a week ago, Babette had been here. Yet she had left nothing behind; he couldn't even smell her perfume. He wondered whether the security men might have come back and searched through his things again. It was possible. Both times when they called they had slipped the lock to let themselves in. He wondered why he hadn't called the police. He'd had two calls from the security men – two that he knew about. Rendox workers had come to a gig, and might try it again. There were messages on the Internet. Pressure from Rendox could go on for weeks if he didn't respond.

On Monday morning he drove to the plant and asked the gateman for the manager.

'Personnel?'

'The general manager. Whoever runs the place.'

'You have an appointment?'

'No.'

'Then he won't be in. What's your name?'

But to their surprise the manager agreed to see him. Telephone in hand, the gateman leant from the hut window and pointed Nick toward the main entrance.

'Mr Reeves,' he said. 'Someone will meet you.'

The gateman may not have remembered Nick's name, but presumably Reeves had. As Nick walked across the compound he scanned the windows to see if anyone was watching his approach. No one was. Workers didn't have time to look out the windows – though there were two women standing a few yards from the entrance smoking cigarettes in the yard: tea break at the food processor's. The women looked him up and down as he passed. He was used to that.

Inside the entrance was a cheap reception area where a girl wearing a telephone headset sat at a desk with a plywood front. She nudged a visitors' book across the desk and Nick signed in. Her call finished, the girl ripped off the top copy of the slip he'd signed and handed it back to him, together with a clear plastic holder to clip to his jacket.

'If you're not going in the factory you won't need a coat.'

He looked at the pale brown vinyl chair behind him and decided that he'd stand. The clip to attach the visitor's pass to his casual jacket didn't work whichever way round he tried to fix it. He was still fiddling when an older woman appeared.

'Mr Chance?'

She was in her forties, solidly built, and her grey hair was so heavily lacquered that it looked as if it had been pressed onto her head from a jelly mould. Any fly landing on it would slide straight off. She took his visitor's pass and in one deft movement clipped it to his lapel. Their chests brushed – not that she would have noticed. She straightened his jacket like a mother on her son's first day at school. 'That's better. Please follow me.'

Reeves had an office on the upstairs mezzanine. Like the rest of the office block it was clean but sparsely decorated. The walls had a temporary look as if they could easily be shunted away to create more working space for the plant. They bore framed certificates and an aerial photograph of the factory. There was also a sentimental picture of brown cows in a field.

'I assume you're from the animal rights group?'

'No.'

'But you were with Miss Hendry.'

'I'm... just a friend.'

Reeves nodded, watching him. He was slightly built, in his mid-thirties, and his tightly curled hair had begun to grey beside his ears. His gaze shifted beyond Nick's shoulder.

'All right, Sylvia. I'll buzz when we're done.'

Nick waited for the door to close. 'Thanks for seeing me,' he said.

Reeves smiled briefly. 'A friend, you say? Well, it's an unfortunate business.'

'Unexpected.'

'I assume so – though she might have intended... some kind of gesture?'

'She didn't kill herself.'

'The police don't seem convinced of that.'

'I was with her. I'm convinced.'

Reeves stared at him for a moment. 'Does that mean you were her boyfriend?'

Nick looked away. 'I only met her a couple of days before she died.'

'Really?'

'But we went to school together.'

'I see.' Reeves was chewing his lip. 'Mr Chance, perhaps you'd better say why you're here. Though I should point out there's no possibility of the factory being held to blame. If you or the family are thinking of litigation—'

'That's not why I came.'

Reeves seemed to relax. Nick said, 'I've come about your security people.'

'They shouldn't have let Miss Hendry in – but she tricked her way inside before.'

'I'm concerned at the way your security people are hounding me. It's got to stop.'

Reeves seemed to be thinking of something else. 'I'm sorry?'

'Your people have come to my flat twice already – and both times they picked the lock and let themselves in. For all I know, they could be there now.'

'I don't follow.'

'The first time they pretended to be police – or I assumed they were, I don't remember. Now they've admitted they're from security.'

Reeves shook his head. 'Whose security?'

'Yours – who else?'

'Is that what they told you?'

'Yes. Security.'

Reeves sighed. 'They didn't come from here. Look, Mr Chance, I realise that you and your animal liberation friends believe all sorts of sinister things about our business, but the only security Rendox has is the man on the front gate. Well, *almost* the only…'

'So there *is* other security.'

'No, no, our secure delivery service – that sort of thing. We certainly don't have the kind you're talking about – men going round to people's houses. Good God, no. Hee, hee.'

The giggle seemed out of place but Nick ignored it. 'I don't know who *else* these guys would have come from. And I've had trouble from your workforce. A gang came round after me. I get messages on the Internet.'

Reeves smiled, but it was the smile of a man in pain. 'The Internet? That doesn't sound too serious. And a gang?'

'They came round after a gig.'

'Gig? Oh, you're some kind of musician, aren't you? Hee, hee.'

Nick picked him up: 'Who told you that?'

Reeves seemed suddenly tired. He ran a hand through his curly hair. 'The police asked if I'd heard of you – whether you might be part of her animal rights group.'

'How much do you know about me?'

'Don't get paranoid, Mr Chance. I haven't had my "security" run a check on you.'

'Well, someone did.'

'This "gang" you mentioned – they don't seem to have done much harm. And even if they *were* from my workforce, you can hardly blame them for wanting to have a go at you. We had to close the plant down for forty-eight hours. They lost a lot of pay.'

'How long are your people going to keep this up?'

Reeves shrugged. 'Depends what else your friends get up to. You notice I pay you the compliment of assuming you are not personally involved.'

Nick exhaled. 'I'm not involved. I just drove her here. Christ, she only wanted to take photographs.'

Reeves snorted. 'So you say. And was your group "not involved" in the bomb attack on our abattoir?'

'What? Oh yeah, your security people mentioned something about that.'

'Not *my* security people, Mr Chance. Perhaps it *was* the police – they may be more interested in you than you think. I may be prepared to take your word that you're not an activist, but I dare say the police will be more suspicious. That's their job.'

Nick stared at him. 'They weren't police.'

'Well, I don't know.' Reeves glanced at his watch. 'Perhaps they were journalists.'

'Journalists?'

'Well, that's what... Miss Hendry said she was.'

Nick frowned. 'A journalist?'

'Mm. From the *Guardian*. Isn't that true?'

'The *Guardian?*'

Reeves gazed at Nick hollow-eyed, then smiled. 'I seem to have put you at a loss for words. Hee, hee. Didn't you know she worked for the *Guardian?*'

Nick shook his head.

'Oh yes, she was doing a piece on us, she said – well, not on us specifically, but on the food processing industry. Didn't you know that? It made what happened all the more of a surprise.'

'She wasn't a journalist.'

Reeves sniffed. 'Apparently not. Well, I prefer journalists to animal rights activists.' He paused. 'She was most convincing.'

She phoned me two months ago. I was a touch suspicious – we've had the occasional crank try that approach – but Miss Hendry quoted her credentials and said she'd bring them with her. Since we have to be careful how we deal with a national paper – a refusal often offends? – I said I'd see her.

Miss Hendry is of course – *was* a most personable young lady. She arrived neatly dressed, carrying some impressive files, an NUJ card *and* an introductory letter from Jenny Morris – you know, the *Guardian*'s environmental correspondent? I have the letter here. Nothing wrong with it. I know because I phoned Miss Morris *at* the

Guardian. She said it was kind of me to agree to see Miss Hendry and she hoped her paper would be able to give us a favourable write-up. I wasn't too optimistic about that. This was the *Guardian* – very liberal, no friend of ours. But when she arrived, Miss Hendry reiterated what Miss Morris had said. The paper hoped to show that meat processing was not necessarily the ugly business it's made out to be, and that our industry practices are now scrupulously hygienic. I was still suspicious. The *Guardian* is a trendy, vegetarian paper, and what she was saying sounded well laced with eyewash. I told her so.

She smiled. She had a lovely smile.

'There's one sure way to convince me,' she said. 'And since you've agreed to see me, all you have to do now is show me round.'

I thought I'd pretend reluctance – to draw any cards she had hidden in her hand – and it worked. She said it would help discredit the rumours.

'Rumours?'

'About what goes on here. There have been a number of complaints recently from nearby houses. They say your factory is making worse smells than it ever did before.'

'I'm afraid we've always made smells, Miss Hendry. It's inevitable – a bit like living beside the kitchen, you know?'

'But the smells *have* worsened?'

I shook my head. Though our business has boomed over the last couple of years, the smells aren't any worse. But clearly, the *Guardian* had got a *sniff* of something from our neighbours.

I said, 'You've surely not come about the smells, Miss Hendry?'

She gave another attractive smile. 'This can't be a nice place to live beside?'

'Ah, but we were here first. The nearby houses may look dowdy but when they were built, our plant had already been here twenty years. In a sense, that's why the houses were built at all: our plant and the other factories round here need a labour force on tap. It suits us to have casual workers within walking distance, and it suits the residents if they can walk to their job.'

She noted this down in her little notepad, though I suspect she was only writing it down for show. She hadn't got round to her real objective. But she was a pretty girl, and I was content to spar with her.

Crouched over her notepad she asked, 'Why *have* the smells got worse?'

I saw that her trick was to ask the sharpest questions while she wasn't looking at you, so they appeared more casual, like the one killer question you ask as you leave.

I said, 'Our neighbours like us, Miss Hendry. We pay their wages.'

Babette smiled again. 'This is awfully good of you. Could you spare someone to show me round?'

I could have let Sylvia give her the guided tour, but I thought that if I went I could help her understand what she saw. Let's not beat around the bush: for many *Guardian* readers – those delicate vegetarians – our process would have them throwing up their muesli. We have a lot of red and bloody flesh. We have bones. We have easily recognisable body parts – whole carcasses, for goodness sake. We deal in meat. Rendox turns dead bodies into food – and put like that it sounds disgusting. A *Guardian* journalist, seeing it for the first time, could easily faint. Or write a lurid account. When an outsider sees a heap of dead bodies lying on the floor, then sees them swept along and scooped into our processing equipment, they might have second thoughts about biting into a meat pie.

I have to say, Babette took it well. We were both kitted out in regulation whites – spotlessly white, of course – and her mass of lovely auburn hair was pinned inside a cap. She stood beside me with her notepad, and something about the way she stood – erect, the notepad poised, a sharpened pencil tapping against her teeth – reminded me of a fantasy nurse from a pin-up magazine or saucy movie. I know I shouldn't be talking like this – it's not PC – but I'm trying to place you in there with us. There was no hint of the militant vegetarian in Babette, you see, nothing to make me consider her a threat. Does this strike you as a curious picture? The blood-red flesh, the smell of meat, the pounding, crunching, metal machinery – and a lovely girl in crisp white tunic, sweet and innocent as she made her plan.

Nick glared across the room to hide his feelings and the plant manager edged towards him as if his story made a bond between them. 'Lovely girl,' Reeves muttered. 'Bloody awful shame.'

Nick's throat was dry. 'I don't want more aggravation.'

'Mm, mm.' Reeves touched his arm. 'Nor do we, of course. Listen... in case you *are* in contact with her organisation – forgive me, but we might as well be realistic – we've doubled up the guards at each of our sites. You shouldn't run a campaign against us.' He stared at Nick. 'That wouldn't be fair.'

'I don't want your people running a campaign against *me*.'

'Right. Point taken. Hee, hee. I'll see what we can do.' Reeves started moving him towards the door. 'If you get any trouble, give me a ring. Where can I get hold of you?'

'Your people know. They've already found me.'

They had reached the door. Reeves said, 'They weren't my men. Honest injun. You live locally?'

Nick hedged. 'I'm often on tour.'

'Got a mobile phone?'

'Why?'

'You never know, something might turn up. I mean, you were her friend, weren't you – you're not a member of her organisation?'

'What is this *organisation* you keep on about – I thought you said she was a journalist?'

'Oh, I don't know. That's what she told me. But the police said she was an activist.'

Reeves now seemed reluctant to let him go. Nick shook his head. 'She wasn't an activist – not seriously. She was just… unlucky.'

'A terrible accident.'

'Let's assume it was.'

'You don't think so?' Reeves watched him intently. 'But… If something happens, you'll keep in touch, right? If you find something out?'

'Yeah. You too.'

Reeves seemed frozen to the spot, so Nick opened the office door. He asked, 'Am I allowed to find my own way out?'

Reeves said, 'Of course. Sylvia will show you. But give me your mobile number. Just in case.'

8. IT HURTS ME TOO

THE GILMAN THOMPSON Research Centre was tucked away in a semi-rural setting in north Somerset. Its three pale cream low-lying buildings absorbed the summer sunlight and lazed in the tarmacked car-park like cheddar cheese on a slate slab. Green laurel hedging disguised the surrounding wire netting and concrete posts, and from the nearby hill the few cars glinted like toys. Fields around the site were fallow and, in one or two of them, brown cattle grazed. Beside each gate the green grass had been trampled into mud which now lay dry and flaky in the sun. From the gentle hill the quiet landscape appeared criss-crossed with winding lanes and tangled hedges. There were scattered farms, a few cottages, and a grey flat-towered church some miles away. In the late afternoon stillness, few birds sang.

Zane and Shiel were leaning against a wooden gate half way up the hill, four hundred yards from the research centre. They both wore motorcycle leathers and Zane had binoculars strung around his neck. Shiel barely glanced at the centre. Most of the time his face was lifted towards the sun, his eyes closed as he allowed warmth to seep into his skin. He kept his eyes closed when Zane stirred.

'Here's another one,' Zane said.

From one of the three buildings a man emerged and crossed to his car.

'Hockendale?' asked Shiel.

'Not sure.'

Zane followed the man through his binoculars. 'Someone else.'

Shiel yawned and opened his eyes. 'That's the third one. I'm getting bored.'

'I reckon Hockendale is in there, though.'

'No guarantee when he'll leave.' Shiel stretched. 'But it's *one* of the bastards, isn't it?'

'Mm.'

'They're all the same, so let's do *him*. It's getting late.'

'You in a hurry?'

'There's football tonight and I didn't set the video.'

'For Christ's sake.'

'It's important – second leg.' Shiel was already moving towards his bike. 'I'm stiff, I'm bored, and that Hockendale could work all night.' He cocked his leg across his saddle. 'Coming or what?'

'All right,' Zane muttered. 'Let's get on with it.'

He stood with one hand on the wooden gate, watching the car leave the centre below and turn right. 'Yeah, it's coming this way.'

He moved swiftly to his machine but Shiel had already kick-started his into life and was cruising down to where the narrow lane joined the slightly wider road coming up the hill. By the time Zane caught up with him, Shiel was at the junction, pulling a painted canvas sign from his bag. He shook it out and stood it on a flimsy frame.

'POLICE. ACCIDENT.'

The two men waited on their bikes, engines growling, visors down. The small car came groaning up the hill and while Zane flagged it down Shiel coasted past. Zane had his bike across the road as an additional barrier. The car slowed and stopped but the driver did not get out. He didn't even wind his window down, merely tilted his head and peered suspiciously at the obstruction. By now Shiel was at his side window. He leant from his bike and smashed the side window with a hammer, showering the man with pellets of glass. The man cowered away as the helmeted rider leant inside and switched off the car. Shiel took the key.

'Get out.'

His voice was muffled and the man could not quite hear. Shiel grabbed his collar. The man tried to squirm across his seat but there was nowhere to go. Shiel tugged at him. The man raised a hand, nodded, then opened the door. As he tumbled out he gasped, 'OK, OK, don't hurt me. What d'you want?'

'You,' Shiel said. From behind the visor it was just a grunt.

'D'you want my money?'

Zane had left his bike and was foraging in the bushes for the five-gallon canisters he had put there earlier. Shiel jumped from his. He was shouting orders at the man, but since the terrified driver either couldn't or wouldn't hear what he was saying, Shiel grabbed his jacket and pulled it roughly off him. Then Shiel began tugging at his

69

tie and the man fell back against his car and raised his arms to ward him off. The knot tightened, would not come loose, so Shiel yanked at it. The man clutched at his tie as if losing it would deprive him of protection. But by now Zane had joined them. He tilted his visor and the perspex shield jutted forward like a glass beak.

'Get him off the road. Round the corner.'

Shiel twisted the noose of tie and hauled the man away. For one desperate moment the man slipped, and as he scrambled for a footing he was half throttled. Zane busied himself removing the bikes and makeshift barrier. By the time he had carried the canisters round, Shiel had removed both the man's shirt and tie and was tugging at the waistband of his trousers. The man was blethering and Shiel was shouting through his visor. Shiel pulled at the loosened trousers and slid them down in a tangle round the man's ankles. When he pushed him, the man fell backwards, unable to stop himself, and struck the tarmac heavily. A stab of pain shot through his coccyx. Shiel was pulling his shoes off, then his trousers, but by now the man was too terrified to resist. He clutched his underpants. Shiel stood up. He didn't need to strip him naked. Instead, he stood over the man, his booted foot thrusting on his chest as if there were any chance the man might escape. Zane's shadow fell across his face and as the man squirmed to see him, Zane tipped the contents of a five gallon can across his chest. The man gasped. A thick, warm, treacly liquid slurped heavily from the can like congealed blood. A huge dollop hit him in the face, and he spluttered, floundering on the tarmac like a landed fish. Zane was shaking out the can. He threw it aside. Now he picked up a second canister and ripped off the top. A flurry of feathers floated in the air as Zane upended the container and shook them free. The feathers had been dampened and fell in wads. Some floated crazily in the air. The men were kicking the feathers at him, trampling them onto his body. Shiel was shouting again and Zane cried, 'Turn over! Roll in 'em.' For a moment the man lay still, but Shiel kicked him to make him slither over onto his belly. He kicked again. The man began to slide among the feathers. He wept in the dirt. 'Turn over,' he heard, and he scrambled over, half sat as Zane rammed a fist of feathers against his face into the dollop of stickiness around his mouth. Zane was shouting at him. He tried to listen, to make out the words. Whatever they told him, he would obey.

Zane yelled, 'Count yourself lucky this isn't tar. Because tar's hot. Right? You're lucky, aren't you?'

The man whimpered.

'This is oil,' Zane said. 'You've been oiled and feathered – like a duck.'

'Ain't that lucky?' Shiel reiterated as he pushed another wad of feathers against his face.

All three paused at the sound of a car trundling up the hill. It approached the junction and the engine noise surged as it went past the end. The three men stayed motionless. Each registered the driver, alone in his seat, eyes front, manoeuvring his car up past the other in the narrow lane. He didn't glance to either side. By the time he'd have turned he'd have been past the turning and whatever he saw wouldn't have mattered anyway.

Zane knelt closer to his victim's head: 'It isn't over yet.'

The man tried to speak but the words blurred. Zane said, 'You're a vivisectionist, right?'

'Nuh,' he gulped.

'You cut up helpless animals.'

The man could see his attackers waiting for him to speak – one kneeling at his side, the other looming over him like Darth Vader. He didn't know what to say. He heard, 'You think that's legitimate?'

The standing motorcyclist had unzipped a pocket and pulled out a knife. A wave of fear shot through the fallen man and in a sudden movement he tried to scramble to his feet – but the tall figure kicked him in the stomach and the other wrapped his leather arms around his sticky torso and wrestled him down. In one deft movement, Zane pinned him to the ground, his leathered shins pressing either side of the man's head and his knees pressing down hard on his shoulders. The man bucked and in his panic might have thrown Zane off, except that Shiel now stepped inside his threshing legs and kicked him in the balls. The man let out a long low groan. A flood of sickness engulfed him. He didn't notice that Shiel had taken one of his hands. He was aware of nothing until the sudden sharp horrific pain, the stabbing, searing flame in his left hand – a pain far greater than the nausea before. It didn't stop. He was screaming, hammering his feet upon the ground. He couldn't see through the black leather across his face and he felt as if his eyes were filled with blood. The wave of nausea came back and as he vomited he felt the leather jerk from his face. His head beat wildly from side to side and he saw grassy banks beside the lane, the tangled hedgerow, the leather boots, the two men standing above. One of the men – the visored one – the one with the knife – held something out to him, something in his hand, something from his own hand. A finger. His own finger, severed off.

He screamed again. He saw the other man kneel down to speak to him. But he couldn't hear what he was saying.

Zane said, 'You got off lightly, friend. Think what you do to bunny rabbits.'

North of Bristol is horse country. There are stud farms, pony clubs, event courses, stables and fields littered with jumps and rides. Horses in the fields wear smart coats and look freshly groomed. Pubs in the well-kept villages have names like Horse And Groom, The Fetlock, Rattlebones Inn. At the Old Sodbury crossroad Nick turned right and headed along deep green lanes towards the villages of Badminton and Acton Turville. Surrounding fields were lush with summer growth.

Jenny Morris lived in a rural cottage beside a copse of trees. Her narrow lane was a dusty track, and in winter it would degenerate to mud and slush. Even in summer the hawthorn and elder hedges kept the deep lane in shade. Nick hoped he had taken directions accurately. He had noted her number in the Rendox manager's office, and when he phoned her afterwards she had been cautious about seeing him, but as a friend of Babette's he had won her round. She gave detailed instructions on how to find her, but released the information grudgingly, it seemed.

He drove along the lane slowly, looking for the entrance, but still had to brake sharply when it appeared. He got out the car and breathed rural stillness, then he opened the gate, walked back to the car and drove inside. When he got out to close the gate he heard rooks cawing in the trees. Out of the shaded lane he was in the sun again and was surprised to find the day so warm. Her garden, part of a reclaimed field, was set above the lane and caught the evening sun. Flowers and vegetables grew in shared beds, but the lawn was cut, the path was tidy, and the haphazard nature of the garden was less accidental than first appeared.

The woman who emerged around the side of the stone cottage carried a canvas bag and a pair of shears. She wore a grubby smock, strong rubber boots and check trilby hat.

'Mr Chance?'

She held out a hand, then paused, pulled off the gardening glove and started again. The shears were beneath her arm.

'Glad you shut the gate.'

'Dogs?'

'The goat. Should be tethered, but he's off like a shot if he gets half a chance. Or the whole chance, in your case.' She made a wry face. 'Sorry. Nothing worse than people making jokes about your name. Never funny. Heard all them all before.'

'Can't do much with a name like Morris.'

'Don't you believe it. Morris dancing and Morris cars – you know, an old banger that never works on winter mornings. I've been called worse. Cup of tea?'

She led him round the house, through a wicket gate to a back garden given over to vigorous vegetables. Between slabs of the stone patio grew creeping herbs, and towards one side was a bank of tiny yellow flowers.

Nick grinned. 'Creeping Jenny – another pun on names?'

'I am not a creep, my man. So you know the names of flowers?'

He shrugged. 'I'm a country boy.'

She nodded, studying him. 'Baby never mentioned you.'

'Babette?'

'You didn't call her Baby?' She nodded again. 'Depends how well you knew her, I suppose. Sit out here while I boil a kettle.'

On the patio stood a sturdy wooden table and a set of chairs. As he took a seat Jenny changed her mind: 'Oh, you don't want to be stuck out here all on your own. Come in and talk while I make the tea.'

They entered through a small stone-flagged hall which led to a cluttered kitchen. A cat dozed on the kitchen windowsill and another leapt onto the wooden table and began to mew hopefully. 'No chance,' she told it as she filled the kettle. 'You'll have to change your name, my man – every second thing I say sounds like a feeble joke.'

'They get more-ish.' He pronounced it Morris.

She groaned, then replied in a heavy accent: 'We country folks have a simple sense of humour, doesn't we, m'dear?'

'Are you really a country type – it's not just your job?'

The kettle was placed on the gleaming Aga, where another cat slept between stove and wall. She said, 'I'm a country type in Wiltshire, a sophisticate in town.'

'And which is real?'

'Both, my man – and which are you?'

He shrugged. 'I'm no sophisticate.'

She leant her back against the stove. 'A friend of Babette's – in what sense?'

Nick hesitated. 'We were at school together. We lost touch. Then... we met up again about a week ago.'

She was openly studying him. 'You met up again... through animal liberation?'

'No, no, I'm not into that. I'm a musician. She was at a gig.'

Jenny seemed to absorb his words. 'And what did you want from me?'

'I'm not convinced about the way she died. I was there that day,

73

you see, I drove the car. There's been a suggestion she threw herself into the crusher – but that's crap. And an *accident* seems a bit far-fetched.'

'In what way?'

'Several ways. She had to climb up onto some kind of gantry for no apparent reason. Before she "fell" she placed her camera carefully down on the walkway. Then she got past or climbed over the safety barrier and… what was she doing up there anyway? Who was with her? They wouldn't let her wander round on her own.'

'No. What happened to the camera?'

'The cops must have it.'

'We could ask. I bet they've developed the film.'

'They're not going to tell us if they did. Look, the manager there – Reeves, d'you know him? – he told me Babette was a journalist and was working for you.'

'Well, she wasn't, my man – not in any formal way.'

'But you gave her a reference.'

'Ah, yes.' Jenny turned to the kettle. 'Just a little favour for a friend. That was some time ago, of course.'

'Why did she need it?'

'She said it was the only way she could get in. I shouldn't have done it.'

'You're the *Guardian*'s environmental correspondent – yes? Wasn't she doing a story for you?'

Jenny shrugged. 'She used to feed me titbits now and then. Take sugar and milk?'

'No sugar. This was some favour that you did – in writing, too. Why did you do that?'

Jenny filled the teapot. 'Were you her boyfriend?'

'That's beside the point.'

'Not to me it isn't.'

'After several years we met up again the day before she died. I was nothing to do with this group of hers. What kind of group was it anyway?'

'What does it matter? She left the group ages ago. Did you really only meet the day before she died?'

'Yeah—'

'You weren't seeing her earlier in the year?'

'No.'

She paused a moment. 'You're not putting me on? You really are a friend?'

He nodded. 'I want to find out why she died.'

'Hm. Because you don't believe it was an accident?'

If she was assessing him, he seemed to pass the test. She said, 'She was a lovely kid. In some ways, you know, I wish you hadn't come so soon. I heard about the accident – that was bad enough. Now you suggest... I haven't seen her for several weeks, you see? I was fond of her too.'

'Several weeks?'

She smiled sadly. 'Not since I wrote that letter for her.'

'Why did you write it, Jenny?'

She moved the teapot from the stove to the kitchen table. 'Seemed harmless enough. Pass me those cups.'

As Nick fetched them from the dresser he glanced through the door into the living room. On a desk at the side wall stood a modern PC and laser printer. He nodded towards them: 'Tools of the trade?'

'Essential, my man. Sitting at that desk I'm in contact with the world. I can file copy, write the great unfinished book, access the Internet and environmental databases, conduct research... No sugar, wasn't it?'

'That's right.'

'I'm highly techno-competent, you know. I should be, mind – since I also write for a couple of PC magazines under a different name.' She grinned. 'I shouldn't have told you that. But no one can live on a *Guardian* salary, and writing for magazines puts another string to my bow. It also gives me lots of free software: I write reviews as well, you see.'

'What's your other name?'

'Here's your cup of tea. Shall we drink it here or in the garden?'

'You don't like personal questions, do you? Isn't that what journalists thrive on?'

'We ask 'em but we don't have to answer them. Come on, I'm going outside while there's still some sun.'

I first met Babette – what? – about three years ago. She was at university then, and at first I thought she was just one of those students hooked on the latest trendy cause. If they can interest the *Guardian* they get a buzz. We're a national paper – the student's paper, you could say – and to get a story in print means they've arrived. But universities are a nursery bed, so I always give students a welcome. Some will be famous by the time they're twenty-five, and they stand out early. Successful journalism is built on a bedrock of solid contacts, people in the know. I want them on my side. When people are starting out, you see, they need publicity and I'm useful to them. By the time the tables turn and I need them, they'll have put up a defence no other journalist can get through.

That's not the only reason. I like students – *someone* has to! And for my environmental stories I deal with a good many alternative types – not that I'm exactly straightlaced myself. In my stories I don't usually get the dirt from sleek men in suits – I get the dirt *on* them, maybe, but the leads and hard stuff come from folks further down, nearer the coal face: hard-done-by workers with a grudge, dispossessed tenants, spokespersons for activist groups. That's where students shine.

Babette's first story was a smasher, though by then the BSE saga had long since run out of steam. Who cared any more? A few hundred farmers had been ruined, a million cattle had been exterminated, millions of pounds had been wasted in EC committees rumbling on – but the public was no longer interested. Yesterday's news – the day *before* yesterday. As soon as Babette mentioned BSE I groaned. But not for long. She – or whichever group she was mixed up in, because she was just the mouthpiece, I realised – claimed to have found instances where beef which should have been incinerated had been made into pet food. Hundreds of thousands of tins of the stuff were on the market, and when we broke the story (we had to be cagey; we couldn't nail it to a specific supplier) the pet food industry shot itself in the foot. You remember that, surely? Their first response was to deny that BSE was still an issue, then to claim there was no way BSE could infect household pets. It couldn't jump across the species barrier, they said. But as every reader knew, BSE had jumped the species barrier years ago – into humans. Which the food industry also denied, at the time. They trotted out some nonsense about there being no way BSE could make two jumps – from cows to pets and then from pets to humans – which we'd never suggested there was, but it helped us keep the piece alive a few more days.

It all fizzled out, of course, as stories do, but a few weeks later Babette was back with another – what was it? – yes, scrapies in sheep, and evidence that it too had crossed the species barrier. It was an alarming allegation because it suggested that, what with BSE in beef, carcinogens in chickens, lead poisoning in fish and now scrapies in our sheep, there was no meat that could be considered safe to eat, and we should all become vegetarians. Which was the whole point her group was making, of course – though their agenda was so obvious that it undermined their message. We ran the story – but well inside the paper, with no real enthusiasm. She couldn't understand that. To her, this was as big a story as the earlier one.

'But we ran your pet food story last month,' I told her. She was sitting here with me in the garden. It was colder then – we were wearing coats.

76

Babette asked, 'So what?'

'It's an old story – our readers can only take so much.'

She looked astounded. This was three years ago and she was a lot younger then. Lost inside that huge ginger coat she used to wear, she looked a kid – did you ever see it? Her legs curled beneath her in that chair... I can see her now. That little face.

Baby said, 'You have a duty to the truth.'

'You haven't worked in journalism.'

Nevertheless, we did run the story in a minor way, and I know she tried other papers without success, so it wasn't surprising that she came back to me with more tales – generally more lurid and less scientific than the scrapies one. She was a good source, though. I could rely on her, she could rely on me. We became friends.

Now, I've kicked around this wicked world far too long to think she'd picked up these tales on campus. It was obvious that she had a direct line into a specialist organisation with an impressive information base – but she'd never tell me who it was. I knew Baby for three years and she never did. The obvious guess is the Animal Liberation Front, but she'd neither deny nor confirm – and there are other large activist organisations, and God knows how many splinter groups. There's IFAW – the International Fund for Animal Welfare – which has nearly a couple of million members, though most of them do nothing more than subscribe. There's Respect For Animals, who are pretty active, and Animal Aid and Animaction and heaven knows who else. The longer I knew her, the more I suspected she was in one of the splinter groups – perhaps one so small that even I'd not heard their name. I'd ask her about them. Clearly she was the outlet for their stories, but behind that, out of sight, what else did they do? She wouldn't tell me, but once, less than a year ago, in winter – that's right, we were indoors, sitting on the carpet in front of an open fire – she began to talk of research on animals in secret units up and down the country.

'At the CJD Surveillance Unit in Edinburgh they are still doing post mortems on people who died from the disease, where the bodies are so dangerous that investigators wear rubber gloves over *chain mail* gloves over a second pair of rubber ones. Three pairs of gloves! When they've finished they incinerate the body parts. They burn the bodies of *people* who died.'

I demurred: 'We've always cremated people. The incidence of *new* CJD has fallen.'

I said this to annoy her and spur her into revealing more – an old journalistic trick.

No such luck. She said, 'So *they* say!' and changed the subject. In time, of course, Babette's interest in BSE and animal rights faded. She remembered the standard responses, but youthful passions seldom last, and she became more interested in making a living. She had left university by then, but despite a first class degree she had no settled occupation. She was selling herbal remedies and medicines door to door. Can you imagine that? It was a topic banned in this house, not because I wasn't interested but because I would not be *sold* to in my home. Baby must have been pretty good at selling the stuff because before long she was expecting to be promoted to Area Organiser. Then the firm would give her a car and she could poodle around the Cotswolds persuading people to run Party Sales among their friends. Anyone who produced half decent results, she said, would be invited to become a spare time agent, either selling the stuff direct or setting up more parties – you know the kind of thing.

Imagine how bored ordinary housewives must be to run these ghastly pseudo-parties and coerce their friends into buying Tupperware or sexy undies or, in this case, dietary supplements and skin care products? The particular "wrinkle", if you will, with Baby's company was that the products were supposed to counteract the effects of ageing – indeed, to practically stop you ageing at all. Oh, if wishing could make it so! The company used bioflavonoids and multi-vitamins and melatonin and sundry Asiatic herbs of uncertain origin (I am inundated with literature on this at the *Guardian*). The promise is that if you take their tablets regularly you'll look better, feel better, live longer – hence the name of the company, *A*genda. Like all these companies, it seemed to me, *A*genda was simply a pyramid selling operation, but whenever I suggested it she flew off the handle. It was her latest passion, of course, and she was utterly absorbed in it. Anyway, when the passion finally faded, I was heartily relieved. Baby seemed to have been cracking on about it for half a lifetime and I was delighted when she returned to dreary old animal rights. Sadly, of course, that was what killed her.

You want me to tell you the kind of group she was involved in, and what she might have been doing in the Rendox plant. But I don't know. I've heard of Rendox – disgusting company, part of QMP – but I don't recall her ever mentioning it. But she moved out of here last spring. After university, she'd lived a rootless sort of life – apart from the life-enhancing, let's-not-talk-about *A*genda, of course – and after a year of wandering she moved in with me. We were together the whole of last winter. Happy days. She'd been a salary-earning adult for over a year but her passions were young and fickle, I'm afraid. I *had* hoped she'd stay but, in truth, what can a forty year old recluse offer one so vibrant? A home, perhaps. A refuge.

'Do you know where she went – her new address?'

Jenny pursed her lips. 'I'd assumed *you'd* know it. I thought you were her lover.' She glanced across at him. 'I wouldn't want to meet her lover. Lovers. Whoever she knew.'

It was cooler now. The sun was sinking below the tops of distant trees and the fields were shaded.

'Oh God,' she said. 'This will be a miserable evening for me, my man. You've brought her back.'

Nick shook his head.

Jenny picked up her teacup but the tea was cold. 'No, I don't have her address. I don't have anything to help you.' She sniffed and gazed across the darkening garden. 'I *would* help you. But I can't.'

Nick leant back in his chair and plunged his cold hands in his pockets. He realised that he still had Babette's car keys, though her car was gone. There were other keys on the ring. If only he could find a door they might unlock.

9. (I KNOW WE'LL LOVE AGAIN) MAYBE TOMORROW

HE ARRIVED LATE for the gig – not so late they had already started but late enough to find Homer cursing the PA system and Quinnie squatting on the floor with an open toolbox and several lengths of tangled cable. Randi Page was sitting bored on a high stool smoking a cigarette, while Tiger and Cleo were huddled in a corner with a tall black girl he'd never seen before and a burly white guy he vaguely recognised. At the side of what might become a dance floor sat a sharply dressed thirty-something woman with cropped red hair, staring at her watch. She glanced at Nick without a welcome. From a side door emerged a small balding man wearing a dicky bow, who approached the smart woman with a nervous smile. Whatever he had been sent to do had clearly not been accomplished and she almost smacked him as she snapped, 'They can use newspapers.'

He scuttled away.

Tiger Guffrey called Nick across. 'Hey man, wanna cut a sax track for a commercial? Mega stuff.' He was looking jumpy, as if he'd scored.

The black girl showed her teeth in a sarcastic smile. 'Take it seriously,' she said.

Nick placed his sax case on the table beside her and said, 'I could be serious.'

She said, '*He's* taking the piss.'

Tiger said, 'Commercial break, you said.'

'Just a mention. We could up your fee.'

'Up, up, up.' Tiger was grinning inanely: early rush.

Nick turned to Cleo, who explained, 'She's from the vitamin pill company—'

'*Eh*-gender,' Tiger sneered.

'*She's* called Vanda,' said the black girl. 'From *Agenda*. You know *Agenda*, Nick – the people who pay to run stalls at your gigs? Friends of yours, supposedly.'

'What's the problem?'

'You'll like this,' Tiger said.

Vanda said, 'We could pay more.'

'If?'

'If as well as letting us run a stall you'd mention us in the show.'

Tiger repeated his earlier line, 'Commercial break,' and grinned at Cleo.

'What sort of mention?' Nick asked. 'Product endorsement?'

Cleo laughed. '*Agenda* wouldn't want to be endorsed by a clapped bunch like us. The pills are supposed to make you young and healthy.'

Vanda sniffed. 'I don't see why you're so uptight about it.'

Tiger said, 'Because the PA's up the Swannee, two of the spots have blown, and the fucking loos are out of paper. And you want a song about a vitamin pill.'

'*Agenda's* more than that. Have you read our literature?'

'He can't read music,' Cleo said lightly. 'Leave it, Tiger. Give us a break.'

Tiger gazed at Cleo like a faithful dog.

The burly man opened his mouth for the first time. He wore a para jacket. 'D'you normally kick sponsors in the teeth, Tiger? Get real.'

'You're not a sponsor, Kieran.'

The squat man stared at him. 'Maybe you should go help find the lavatory paper.'

Nick remembered him now: Kieran from the ALF.

Cleo placed a hand on Tiger's arm. 'Come on, honey. Help me tighten my skin.'

He gave a droll look and walked off with her to the drums. Nick grinned to himself: Tiger was trying too hard with her.

Vanda said, 'That man's got a gut full of acidic enzymes. You know what they do?'

'Shorten his life.'

'Since enzymes release free radicals to attack his tissues, yes, they shorten his life.'

'Aagh, science A level. Thank you, memory. I suppose you people have just the pill for it?'

'Part of a wider treatment. You've heard of bioflavonoids?'

'Actually, I have.'

Her smile grew warmer. 'Maybe you've been peeping at my leaflets.'

Kieran put his wiry head between them. 'Don't mind me. I'll talk to Quinnie.' He glanced at Vanda. 'When you've finished flirting you should join us. Steve's the only guy in this bunch talks sense.'

He grinned and left. Nick asked, 'You two together?'

Vanda leant back. 'What *do* you mean?' She smiled again and touched his arm. 'Who's been talking to you about bioflavonoids?'

It was coming back to him. 'Free radicals, I remember *that*. I thought she was talking about politics.'

'One of our representatives?'

'Forget it. Seriously, are you with Kieran – from the ALF?'

'Is that his name? No, I'm not with him. I guess I'm a free radical!' She smiled encouragingly. 'We're both here about Glastonbury but Steve was busy and I made the mistake of talking to your Scouse clown about a plug for *A*genda during your act.' She widened her eyes. 'I was just making conversation with *him*. But I'm talking now.'

Nick smiled and she touched him again. 'What I want to know, Nick, is will this little rock'n'roll band hit the big time at Glastonbury? There'll be worldwide TV.'

'MTV maybe.'

She leant closer, mouthing the words as if they were a mantra: 'Biggest rock festival in the country. Hundreds of stars. TV. Record companies. Everybody in the world who matters. This is more than a party – it's your opportunity.'

'I'm gagging for it.'

'If you're serious you must be on TV. But you'll be up against lots of competition. What can you do to stand out?'

'Be different.'

She smiled lazily. 'Mm. You really think that's enough? Tell me, that – Kieran, is that his name? – what exactly is he doing here? If he's from the Animal Liberation Front they'll be looking for coverage, won't they, at a big event like Glastonbury – something newsworthy? Are they planning something with you?'

Nick shrugged. 'We do a couple of animal rights lyrics but most of our stuff is rock'n'roll standards, jazzed up.'

'Maybe I should stay tonight and listen. If you don't finish *too* long past my bedtime.'

'Sure. Though I don't think we've got any songs about bioflavonoids.'

'I bet you've something that could be suitable.'

' "I'm Gonna Live Forever"?'

'That sort of thing.'

Nick turned away from her. 'Hey, Randi – got any songs about living forever?'

Randi was still on her high stool. She stubbed out her cigarette. 'Like "Not Fade Away"?' She coughed. 'Give me songs about a short life and an abrupt end. "I Guess It Doesn't Matter Any More". You know?' She stared at them. 'You two would be better with "Tonight's The Night" or "Why Do Fools Fall In Love".' She grinned. 'You're from *Agenda*, aren't you?'

Vanda bristled. 'You have a problem with that?'

'Hey, not me, baby. Whatever gets you through the night. Just don't step on our blue suede shoes.'

Vanda shook her head. 'I don't know what makes you people so edgy.' She turned to Nick. 'I'll see you sometime. OK?'

'You're not staying?'

'This band has lost its appeal for me. Some other time.'

Randi watched her go, then said, 'Sorry. Did I break something up?'

'We're all edgy tonight.'

'I don't think the band should let outsiders muscle in – animal liberation, health freaks, you can live forever – who needs that? It ain't rock'n'roll, baby.' She paused. 'That girlfriend of yours – wasn't she into this stuff too?'

Nick's throat closed. 'Animal rights, yeah. But not the ALF.'

'Some other group?'

He nodded.

Randi's lip curled. 'What was *her* song – "Forever Young"?'

10. AS USUAL

NICK'S FATHER WAS too young to die. Everyone agreed that, for what good it did. In his mid-fifties, in a house less than twenty miles from one he'd been born in, married to the woman he'd met thirty years before, surrounded by the ordinary possessions he and his wife had slowly gathered through the years, Nick's father, no longer earning an income, no longer able to sing along with his large record collection, no longer able to walk further than half a mile – on a good day – now spent several hours a day in bed. It would have been easy for him to spend more. No one could have blamed him for that. But he resented the hours spent there. The days left to him were dwindling, and the days on which it would be possible for him to get out of the house into the fresh salty coastal air might be few. Every time the cancer flared up again Simon wondered if he would feel the open air again. He had had his bed moved to the other side of the bedroom to catch most of the morning sun. Somehow, it didn't seem so wasteful to lie in bed in the morning while that dazzling light streamed in on him and birds sang outside and pattered at his window, but once the sun moved round he grew restless and had to struggle out of bed. He didn't mind that – the loss of sunlight was an incentive for him to move. If his bedroom had caught the afternoon sun, he reasoned, he might have stayed in bed all day, waiting for it. Sunlight was precious to him; he had to catch every drop. On the bad days when he was particularly weak Franny had to help him dress. He could manage to pull his trousers on, because bending was less difficult than stretching his arms above his head – when the pain in his chest felt as if the muscles would tear apart. To be helped into his shirt and jacket was less degrading than to have his legs folded into his trousers, and he was thankful to retain that last scrap of dignity, even with his wife. It wasn't that he minded Fran seeing him naked, but to be forced to

84

have her manipulate him into his trousers emphasised his growing feebleness and scrawny form.

Today was a good day. The sun shone fitfully through the windows and a light wind stirred the branches outside and rattled the open fanlight in its frame. There was a smell of farmyard earth and summer grass mingled with cold saltiness from the sea. Nick was here today, and his sister Helen. Simon would have liked to be able to walk that mile or so to the sea. It was too far, of course. They would go by car. The mere presence of three cars arranged outside the house – their own, which nowadays only Franny drove, joined today by Nick's and Helen's less familiar machines – showed the scattering of the family. For none of them was this the family house. Once the children were grown and off their hands (which nowadays, of course, he wished they weren't) he and Fran had moved back to the north Devon countryside they had been brought up in. Nick had stayed in Bristol, Helen had moved along the motorway to work at a large hospital in Swindon, and Alwyn had moved, as inevitably he would, to Surrey which was more convenient for him to commute to town.

'You're looking thinner, Helen.'

'*You* can talk.'

They had agreed not to skirt around the subject of his illness. His terminal disease.

'They're working you too hard.'

'I'd be all right if it wasn't for the patients.'

'It's true, though – you do look thin.

'Cancer's not hereditary, Dad.'

They stared at each other. They weren't skirting the subject, though sometimes it might be easier if they did. He shifted in his armchair. 'Medicine – long hours, low pay. God knows what made you go into it.'

'Perhaps I'm hooked on the drugs.'

They were trapped in the lines of a familiar conversation. 'Go on, say it,' she urged.

He smiled as he repeated what he always said: 'You should have stuck to music.'

'And taught ungrateful kids.'

'You were a lovely flautist.'

'Lovely to look at, painful to hear.'

'Nonsense.'

'What d'you think, Nick – a career in music? You should know.'

He had been watching clouds scud across the sky. 'One job that pays worse than medicine.'

'Help,' their father exclaimed jokily. 'Who's going to look after me in my old age?' There was the briefest silence before he added: 'For the rest of the year, anyway.'

He stared at the carpet.

Nick muttered, 'It'll be longer than that – much longer.'

Helen leant forward and placed her hand on her father's wrist. It was bony. The skin was slack. He muttered, 'Self-pitying bastard.'

Fran appeared at the door. 'And does the miserable old sod want this tray of tea?' She smiled. 'Or haven't you time for it?'

He narrowed his eyes and smiled back thinly. 'When the time comes for me to "slip away", as they call it, you'll be there with a whip to beat me back.'

'I'll claw you back with my bare hands.'

She bent to place the tray on the dark low table. 'I don't suppose you've told them the news?'

'I thought I'd save it till after tea.'

'Something good?' Nick asked.

'Oh, yes,' his father replied. 'It's date and walnut cake – your mother's speciality.'

'Ha, ha. Come on, spit it out.'

'I haven't had a mouthful yet. Come on, Fran, cut us all a slice.'

She gave him a look and picked up the knife.

They huddled together as they walked along the cliff. Although the wind had seemed gentle inland it had added freshness here, and because of Simon's growing weakness they walked so slowly they were almost standing still. They wore unseasonably heavy coats and walked in changing couples – each of them taking turns to walk with Simon; each of the couples having time alone.

'How much of an experiment will it be?' Nick asked his mother.

'They seem very confident – even optimistic. They've done any number of experiments on animals as well as some human trials. There seems no earthly reason not to go ahead.'

'And they're "optimistic"?'

'The treatment has very few side effects, they said. None serious.'

'But does it achieve anything?'

She looked up at the sky. 'Well, he's not going to see his hundredth birthday. But if it gives us a few years... As things stand at the moment he's only got a few more months. At first they said he was too far gone to start the treatment, but on the other hand... well, who better for an experiment?'

Nick put his arm round her.

She said, 'It's not preventative. It's supposed to attack existing tumours and make them regress. It uses a monoclonal antibody –

Dad and I have become frightfully technical now – and it interferes with something called an integrin receptor and blocks a signal to the blood cells that feed the tumour. Then the tumour simply starves itself to death. Sounds wonderfully simple, doesn't it?'

'It can't be.'

'No, I dare say it's really far more complicated, but that's how they explained it to us. It's a British discovery, apparently. The Americans had invented a precursor called LM609, but that wasn't tolerated very well in humans—'

'Meaning it killed them?'

'Probably. But a British lab – somewhere quite near you, actually – pushed the boundaries further, and made a product that not only worked in mice and monkeys but in humans too. I dare say all those mice and monkeys weren't given much choice about whether or not they wanted to take part in the experiment, and no doubt a lot of them laid down their lives for us, so it would seem pretty churlish to refuse to play our part.'

Nick tightened his grip on her arm. 'Christ, Mum, I don't know what to say.'

'Of course, I just want a miracle cure – something to defeat death.' She chuckled. 'That's not much to ask.'

11. NOT FADE AWAY

'A CRAP NAME for a good venue,' Vanda declared.

The Fleece And Firkin was an important date on the Bristol circuit. Featuring good up-and-coming rock bands it had developed a discerning but intolerant audience, and tonight Blue Delta had been accepted by that audience – not a foregone conclusion, given the band's strong jazz element and lack of teenage players. But the concert there – Blue Delta's first – went well and afterwards, once the band had helped Quinnie collect and stow the electrics, they waited in the darkened hall while he conducted business in the front office.

Nick had an exaggerated air of relaxation, partly because he was on a comedown after playing and partly because Vanda hovered at his side. They hadn't discussed anything – or nothing of consequence. But here she was again, despite flouncing away that previous night. Here she was when the show was done. He didn't know whether she expected him to romance her, or whether he should take it for granted she was here for the obvious reason. It was too damn late to begin a lengthy seduction.

She said, 'Finished now?'

'When Stevie's sorted out the money.'

'Then everyone goes their separate ways?'

'Uh-huh.'

'I mean, you don't go home with anybody?'

He looked in her eyes. 'No.'

'I thought maybe the blonde girl. The singer.'

'Don't worry about Randi. She's got her eye on Homer.'

'My, my. Is this band into racial harmony or what?'

He grinned. It seemed too delicate a subject for a flip riposte. 'I'll collect my sax.'

She waited while he walked across to what remained of the rostrum. Stripped of the musicians' gear the stage looked shabby and unremarkable, and yet simply by stepping up on it Nick felt the spring return to his heels. He picked up his sax case and glanced out across the hall.

'Hey, Nick, I wanted a word.'

He saw Kieran in front of the stage, looking up at him.

'Bad time,' said Nick. 'It'll have to wait.'

'I'd like to give our condolences.'

For a moment Nick didn't realise what he was talking about. Then a flash of guilt for having forgot. 'Oh, right. Yeah, thanks.' He glanced across the hall at Vanda. 'This is not the best time, Kieran.'

'She was a brave girl, Babette.'

'Brave?'

'Wouldn't you say so yourself? The way she allowed herself to get killed.'

From the corner of his eye Nick saw Vanda watching them. He said, 'Maybe we can talk tomorrow.'

'I shall be on a job. But I wouldn't mind a word about Babette.'

'Now?'

'You're not doing anything, are you?'

Well, yes, thought Nick – I was just about to screw another woman. 'OK, Kieran, five minutes. Let's talk about Babette.'

They sat alone at an unwiped table beside the bar, now closed and shuttered. Kieran seemed disappointed they couldn't get a drink. He had undone his combat jacket to reveal a dark mottled sweater in which a frayed one-inch hole showed a glimpse of white flesh on his chest. It was an odd place for a hole – as if he'd stopped a bullet, Nick thought. Or someone had.

'The thing is, Nick, we're puzzled about her death.'

Nick suppressed a frown.

'You know she worked for us – once?'

Nick nodded guardedly.

'Bit of a maverick, of course – but aren't we all?' Kieran smiled as he watched Nick, who didn't react. 'And where do you fit in?'

'I don't.' Nick ran his finger through a sticky puddle on the bar table. 'We were friends from way back. I was just in the car.'

'She never mentioned you.'

Kieran smiled again, but Nick did not elaborate.

'Did she leave anything with you – apart from the car?'

'It was stolen.'

'A *stolen* car – I thought it was hers?'

'No, next day when we went back it had been stolen.'

'We?'

Nick hesitated. 'I went back with the police to pick it up.'

Kieran sighed. 'Did she give you anything to look after?'

'No.'

'She didn't – leave anything at your flat?'

'No.'

'I have to ask you,' Kieran said. 'Are you holding something back from me?'

He was leaning forward now, staring into Nick's eyes. Nick wanted to glance around the empty clubroom but knew he shouldn't avoid Kieran's stare. 'Like what?'

Kieran smiled faintly, as if Nick ought to know.

'You wouldn't fuck with us,' Kieran said.

Nick exhaled. A sudden grief washed over him. He muttered, 'I don't know what was going on. She said the whole thing was… a jaunt, she called it. And now she's dead. Did someone kill her – is that what this is about?'

'Wouldn't we all like to know? What exactly did she say she was going to *do* in there?'

'Don't you know?'

'Not exactly. She had left the group. Hadn't she?' He held Nick's gaze again. 'When she got you to drive her to the factory, what was it exactly she said she'd do?'

'Take photographs.'

Kieran sniffed. 'Did she have anything else but the camera?'

'A handbag.'

'Might it have had a package inside?'

'What kind of package? Oh, I don't know, I didn't look inside her handbag.'

'Are you quite sure she left nothing at your flat?'

'Positive.' Nick blinked. 'Have you checked *her* flat?'

'There's nothing there.'

They know where it is, Nick realised. 'You think there should have been a package?'

Kieran didn't answer.

'Is someone else looking for it?'

'Perhaps.'

'Could Babette have been killed for it?'

Kieran paused, then said casually: 'I heard a whisper that you went back to Rendox.'

Nick narrowed his eyes. 'I couldn't believe their story about what happened. I went to see the manager.'

'Eamon Reeves? You didn't think *he* killed her?'

'I thought he might be able to shed some light.'

'He might have had a motive, yes.'

Let me tell you how we first knew her. She was at Uni and wanted to be an activist. You can always spot them. Most of the newcomers, you see, think of nothing except who they can pull into their beds. There are some studious types, of course, whose beds are strictly for reading, preferably by torchlight – but go-getters like Babette Hendry steam about the campus signing up students for petitions, madcap ideas, anti this and that societies. And I tell you, when those bright as a button, keen little activists are girls they are so sexually attractive – all that energy shining from well-scrubbed, eager little faces – it's all I can do to restrain myself from grabbing them in my arms and planting kisses on their brow.

And Babette was a *party* girl – I don't mean parties political, I mean parties that drive on through the night. She was alive. More than that: in only the second week of term she tried to close the student cafeteria because it was selling meat, and worse than that, *processed* meat. So, I thought to myself: militant vegetarian. At that time I was starting my final year – and like most men on the final lap I had cast my eye over the new girls coming in. Here they were, released from home, desperate to make their mark. Desperate to screw their parents out of their psyche. And like fresh sweet-smelling bait these delicious girls had been dropped into a pool of free-floating men – first year freshmen, hoping for several years of unending sex; plus returning students from later years looking for a chance to score anew; not to mention tutors, professors – Christ, even the groundsmen and catering staff. Fresh bait? They're like a shower of fish food dropped into a pond – you should see the thrusting goldfish spurt to the top. In the first few weeks of an academic year, I tell you the water churns.

So. Here we have Babette: she goes to parties, she's out at night – and in the mornings she has only a decorative hangover. No bags beneath the eyes. No greying skin. She is young. Strong. I want her.

So I get her out on demos. I get her fly posting at night. I get her to picket the customers of a shop that sells fur coats. Then I ask if she wants to do something serious – such as, I suggest, consumer terrorism. I say, what if we place broken glass in butcher's meat? She asks what for – to give a customer a bleeding mouth? Big deal. I say, no, my sweet Babette, first we spoil the meat, then we tip off the local food inspectorate to get down to there urgently. Close it down. But she's cheeky: she says wouldn't it be better if we told the butcher we'd found the glass, and ask what is he going to do about it? I look surprised. Does this mean, I ask, that the butcher must pay us a hundred quid or we'll tip off the inspectorate? Oh no, she says – five thousand quid or we tell the papers. And don't pick a little local butcher, but a national chain. Supermarket, maybe. Five thousand quid is no problem for them.

She was joking, of course – we never did put the blackmail plan into practice. But she continued to get involved in pranks, and from time to time I'd get back in touch. She was a livewire – but too much of an individual, too dangerous for us! She was not reliable, you know? A reliable agent would keep her head down and appear dull. She would not attract attention. But Babette was a neon light. And I was attracted to her – a moth drawn to her flame. I didn't know what to make of her – did she have potential or was she simply laughing at us? That's how it was with her. You couldn't read her.

I left university and the group kept Babette at arm's length. Her dedication to animal rights appeared rock solid and she took part in demos from time to time, and by the time she had sat her finals we'd lost close contact. That is, until we came up with a campaign idea that made me remember her – a campaign that needed a chemist. When I checked the chemists we knew it was not a long list. But, I thought, Babette had read chemistry and must surely have a good degree. I checked with the university and found that yes, she'd won a decent first – not a double first, but a decent one – but nevertheless had not walked straight into a decent post. I could guess the reason. When big firms come picking graduates, Babette would have been choosy. Big firms would not fit her high principles, and smaller firms might not have the right jobs. She could easily seem too bright: research PhDs don't like super-intelligent assistants. Men might like the way she held a test tube but don't like a girl to tell them what's inside.

They'd have had my sympathy: with Babette you never knew where you stood. I didn't know either, and we wanted a chemist we could rely on. She was a chemist with a good degree, we *ought* to be able to rely on her, and she had never let us down on smaller projects. She was still committed to animal rights. In fact, by the time I tracked her down she was hanging out with a bunch of health freaks – new age apostles preaching that the way to mega health was to eat and live meticulously. Eat well, feel well. A bunch of clean scrubbed, exfoliated individuals, pumped so full of vitamins that their eyes were about to pop. Like a religious fringe group. I tell you freely, I didn't think she'd be any use to us. Zealots I can live without. Nevertheless, I invited our little Baby for a drink.

I found myself pouring water on a plant left in the sun too long. The dried-up skin crackles and stretches. Colour returns. A husk dropped from Babette's shoulders like a winter shawl. After quarter of an hour in the country pub her chirpy smile appeared – you remember that smile? Deep inside this uptight holier-than-thou apostle lurked a good time party girl. We had a fun evening. Eventually I brought our chatter round to politics and the *specific* politics of food, then to the carnal mutilations performed every hour in a place like Rendox. I wondered aloud whether it might be possible to strike against such a company in a manner that did more than merely hurt them, but closed them down. I recalled her outrageous idea of placing ground glass in butchers' meat. Might there be some more devastating equivalent for Rendox?

The drink made her enthusiastic. Ground glass, we agreed, was a possibility but was not extreme enough. How about BSE? The original BSE scare was dead, she said, but it would only take a single high-profile episode – contamination in a food processing plant, for example – to slam the story back onto the front page of every newspaper in the land.

'Every paper across Europe,' I agreed – smiling encouragingly as I sipped my drink.

'A group did a similar thing some years back,' I continued, as if the memory had just returned. 'They targeted five major food brands – everyday stuff like yoghurt, pickles and cheese spread. It was hardly a strike for animal rights—'

'Just for money?' laughed Babette, her brown eyes gleaming.

'Absolutely. Now, this particular group – hell, who knows if it was a *group*, they were never caught—'

'They got away with it?' she whispered. I'd hooked her now.

'The group sent manufacturers contaminated jars of their product, seals apparently unbroken, just as the jars would stand on the supermarket shelf, *except* that each had been ruined with an injection of coloured dye.'

'And they threatened that next time,' Babette said, way ahead of me, 'they'd inject poison?'

'One better. A few days later, what did the manufacturers receive? A set of very well wrapped test tubes filled with bacterium – of a particularly virulent febrile disease, something like bubonic plague.'

'How on earth did they get hold of that?'

I knew she'd ask.

93

'Oh, the group must have had a chemist or a pharmacist working for them,' I answered casually. 'Perhaps they stole it from a lab. Anyway, accompanying each test tube was a short note demanding £50,000 from each company. Otherwise, the note said, the jars would be contaminated with bacterium and replaced on various supermarket shelves.'

She said, 'Fifty thousand isn't much.'

'Very affordable,' I agreed. 'Which is probably why the companies paid up.'

'Did they indeed?'

'Yes, though unfortunately that was where our friends slipped up. The money was to be paid into a foreign bank account – Austrian, I believe. The Viennese police, of course, shot round to see who would try to draw the cash. Made an arrest but only caught the messenger. But remember, this is one of many stories. The police admit to at least twenty cases a year – up to fifty some years.'

She looked disappointed. 'Then it's a well travelled path.'

'Plenty of alternatives,' I murmured. 'There was the fellow who put broken glass in jars of baby food. And don't forget the Barclays Bank letter bombs, which extorted a million pounds eventually. Supermarket chains have been targeted – pay up or we'll leave a bomb inside your store.'

'A *very* well travelled path.'

'And not necessarily a lucrative one. If you believe the publicity from brand owners and police, practically no one gets away with it. That's what they say.'

'They would, wouldn't they?' said Babette archly.

We sipped our drinks. She'd begun to realise that the conversation had not been brought round to this accidentally. 'The threat's the first part,' I said. 'Getting hold of the money is just as hard.'

She smiled at me. 'You'll have an answer for that?'

'Mhm. Forget the money.'

She looked aghast. I said, 'Those people were blackmailers pure and simple. But we don't want money, do we? We'd let the media know. One scare would cripple a factory. Two scares would kill it.'

'Three scares?'

'If we raised a scare in a different factory we'd kill the industry.'

She moved her glass on the pub table. 'Three strikes,' she murmured.

'Conceivably four. But we're not talking broken glass this time.'

'BSE,' she said.

'The golden oldie,' I agreed. 'Can we get the virus?'

'It's not a virus,' she muttered.

'Whatever. Can we get a culture of it?'

She snorted. 'Hardly. A few labs still work on it. Don't we know anyone inside?'

I held her gaze. 'No,' I said. 'It would be easy if we did.'

She wasn't stupid, as I've said. 'You want me to get a job in one. Not so easy.'

I raised my glass. 'It doesn't have to be BSE. Bubonic plague virus was used before.'

'Bacterium, not virus.'

'Whatever. Salmonella, E-coli 157. Outbreaks of those would do the trick.'

'Bubonic plague doesn't occur naturally in meat, so an infection would be easily explained away as contamination.'

'Something else,' I concurred.

'What you want me to do,' Babette said slowly, 'is give up my present well-paid job and become a lowly assistant in one of the few laboratories with stocks of lethal cultures. Then smuggle some out.'

I said, '*That* would be a good idea.'

At the time, I have to tell you, it did seem reasonably simple. We already had a "friend" working inside Rendox, so gaining access to the plant wouldn't be a problem – or alternatively we could get samples of their product. Presumably it would be easier to bring stuff out and infect it elsewhere than try to introduce the virus inside the plant. But Babette said that whatever we did we'd have to smuggle something in, and whether we were smuggling a contaminated product or just the culture, the tricky part would be getting it inside to add to bulk foods in the processor – ideally at a point where it could linger around and spread.

All of which may leave you thinking you can guess what happened on the night she died. But there's a snag. Babette couldn't get a job in the right laboratory. To even find one is surprisingly difficult, and you can't simply walk up the door and ask for a job. Now, if this was a *story* I was telling there'd be no problem – this is the kind of difficulty fiction glosses over. But in real life these humdrum little problems hold us back. Ours is not one of those mysterious all-embracing organisations beloved of crime fiction, with tentacles in centres of power throughout the land. We don't have professional agents and inside intelligence. We don't even *belong* to the ALF – you can't belong to it: you can associate your action, as long as it's in keeping with their objectives, but that's as far as it goes. There is no membership list. It's a safe structure for a world-wide organisation working at the edge.

But now we we are faced with a conundrum: Babette hadn't got the culture, so she had no reason to be inside the plant. Why was she there?

We know she was chafing at the bit. It would have been a great adventure but she couldn't get started. She had made detailed plans for getting the bacterium into Rendox via our stooge, and she'd even – here's Babette's barefaced cheek – talked herself inside as a journalist. She interviewed the management! She threatened to interview QMP – you know, QMP *owns* Rendox? I tell you, I was worried at that – I said her place was outside, not in amongst them, but she only laughed at me. She was always rash, remember? Act first, explain later. She liked the idea of getting behind enemy lines. She liked the risk. She always wanted to go as far as she could go.

On the drive back to his flat Nick was moody and uncommunicative. Vanda tried to cheer him up but by the time they arrived she was silent too. When he switched off the car there seemed every chance she would change her mind and take off for home. She stood with her coat collar around her ears while he locked the car. She was tall, her face in shadow, and he smiled at her.

'D'you want to come in?'

'I don't want to stay out here.'

He took her arm and led her to the doorway. It wasn't her fault he was down. It hadn't even been a bad evening. The set had gone well, the crowd had cheered, the club had booked another gig. It was first time for a while Nick enjoyed the music. Complete numbers went by where he never thought of Babette at all. At the end when Vanda appeared his first reaction was that he couldn't go with her, but then he thought: there was no reason he should sleep alone. Vanda was attractive and undemanding. They knew what they wanted from each other – and if Kieran hadn't interrupted, he and Vanda would have been home twenty minutes ago.

Nick glanced across the quiet street and noticed a movement in the cabin of a small truck parked opposite – a grubby white truck, parked midway between streetlights. Sitting in the front were two shadowy men. Whichever of them had moved was now sitting still.

Nick made a show of feeling in his pockets for the door key, although he already had it in his hand. No one got out of the truck. The two men simply sat and didn't look at him.

At nearly two o'clock in the morning.

Ten minutes later Nick appeared at the flat window to close the curtains, and glanced down into the street. He wasn't surprised to see the truck still there, the two men sitting in the front – though there was nothing to suggest they had been waiting for him. There was nothing to suggest they were there for any reason he could think of. The side of the truck was stencilled 'Severn Vale Vehicle Hire'.

Nick was slow getting into bed. At any minute he expected a disturbance at his door. But nothing happened. When Vanda took a moment to slip into the lavatory Nick nipped to the window and looked again. He had to squint, but the men were still sitting in the truck.

Later, when he and Vanda had gone to bed Nick found he could not perform. It was late, of course, gone two o'clock, but though the two of them filled the bed with their warm bodies, and though she stroked him with skilful hands, he felt as if he was under surveillance, as if his room was filled with hidden eyes.

12. SORRY DOESN'T ALWAYS MAKE IT RIGHT

'DON'T APOLOGISE,' she said. 'Especially now.' She widened those big brown eyes at him. 'You've made up for it.'

Her finger ran along his stomach. She was lying beside him in his bed, propped on one elbow, smiling lazily in his face. The crumpled duvet had slipped from her shoulders and her skin seemed brushed with charcoal. There were tints he hadn't noticed before, as if the surface had been coated with specks of fine rare dust. Gentle sunlight drifted through the window and where the duvet humped above the bed, a narrow sunbeam lay across Vanda's hip.

'I'm glad you stayed,' he said.

She chuckled from her throat. Snuggling lower beneath the duvet she moved her hand. 'This is cosy. Anything planned?'

'Nope.'

'Not in a hurry, are you?'

He closed his eyes. 'You know that old song,' he murmured. 'An Englishman takes his time?'

She lowered her head onto his chest. 'You mean I've got to wait another six hours?'

Her warm lips moistened Nick's nipple, and he said, 'Six minutes, at this rate.'

He slid his fingers through her straightened hair, and she moved her upper leg and lay it over his. Her breasts brushed his lower abdomen. 'Something's moving here,' she noticed. Her fingers clasped him as he stiffened. 'Definitely.'

Nick's other hand was running down her backbone. She felt firm

98

and smooth to touch, the ridges of her vertebrae hard against the surrounding skin.

Someone knocked at the door.

Nick and Vanda remained motionless in the bed. Then she lifted her head and peeped at him, one eyebrow raised. Nick frowned. They held their position for a moment and Vanda smiled conspiratorially. There came a second knock.

This time it was followed by a male voice from outside: 'Mr Chance?' Another knock. 'Anyone in?'

Nick stirred.

As he began to squirm away from her, Vanda whispered, 'They'll go away.'

But he was up now, peering at the carpet for something to wear. She reached to stop him but he was walking naked to the door. On a hook behind the door hung a dark towel dressing gown which he pulled on. Even as he shrugged himself into it there came another knock, and this time the voice called, 'Open up, Mr Chance, it's the police.'

Vanda cursed and slipped beneath the duvet. Nick opened the door.

'Sorry to wake you, sir.'

They stepped inside as if he had invited them. 'Good morning, miss.'

All that could be seen of her was a cape of straightened black hair. 'I assume it's miss.'

'Identification?' Nick demanded.

The first man smiled and reached into his pocket. 'Short memory?'

He produced his card. Nick remembered him as one of the plain clothes men at the police station on the night Babette had died. Nick had recognised the man immediately but had not placed him as a policeman because he hadn't expected to see a cop. He felt confused. When the other man held out his own card, Nick looked in its direction but didn't see it.

The first man said, 'Hope we haven't chosen an inconvenient moment.' He glanced at the bed. 'You're feeling better, I hope, sir?'

Nick went to the window and glanced at the street below. It was busier now, all the parking spaces occupied. The white truck had gone.

'Have you been keeping an eye on me?' he asked.

'Should we, sir?'

Nick turned. 'You guys never answer a direct question, do you?'

'It's not our business to.'

'How many times are we going have to go through this? Nothing better to do?'

'I don't think you could say we're pestering you, sir.'

'You keep me at the station all night. You search my flat. You come bursting in again – oh, that wasn't you, was it?'

Nick stared at him. The man stared back more patiently. Nick muttered, 'No, I'm getting you confused. I had the security guys from Rendox pay me a visit.'

'Really?'

'They denied it, of course.'

The man nodded but did not respond. For a moment, Nick thought the other cop had disappeared from sight, but then he saw him leaning against the far wall. Both men were watching him. Vanda didn't stir.

Then the man said, 'You weren't here last night.'

'Was I supposed to be?'

'We called by twice.'

'I work nights. Remember?'

The man cocked his head.

'I'm a musician.'

'Oh yes, you said.'

Nick sighed. 'Shall we get on with this? What is it you want?'

The man glanced at the mound beneath the duvet. 'It might be better if we talked alone.'

They paused. From beneath the heap Vanda said, 'I got no clothes on. I ain't coming out.'

'Then we'll wait outside, Ma'am.'

'Then what? I get dressed and walk around the block?'

'If you wouldn't mind.'

'I *do* mind.' Vanda's head appeared. 'I like it here.'

The man looked inquiringly at Nick. 'It's up to you.'

Nick shrugged.

'You told us in your statement that Babette Hendry was your girl-friend.'

'Right.'

The policeman looked meaningfully at the bed. 'And this young lady?'

Nick closed his eyes. The man said, 'I assume she has a name.'

Nick's brain had stuck and he couldn't remember the girl's name. So he said, 'She has a voice of her own.'

'Excuse me, miss, could I have your name?'

Silence.

'Miss.'

'You talking to me?'

Both policemen watched the mound of duvet. 'Miss?'

What she mumbled could not be heard.

'Would you repeat that, please, miss?'

'Vanda Craig.'

The top of her head appeared. Two eyes glared at them.

'Craig?' asked one man doubtfully.

The other nudged him. 'That isn't her,' he mumbled. 'Wrong colour.'

Leaning towards Nick the policeman asked conversationally, 'Remember Lisa Stanhope?'

'No.'

'You know – Lisa.'

'Who's she?'

'Oh, you know, sir. Miss Stanhope is an acquaintance of Miss Hendry's – works at Rendox. You mentioned her.'

'I did not.'

'Down at the station. Perhaps you don't remember. You were upset, of course.'

'I've never heard of her.'

The policemen stared at him. They let the silence hang.

Vanda said, 'They're trying it on.'

One of the men turned to her and purred, 'When did *you* last see her, Vanda?'

Vanda sunk back beneath the duvet. 'Don't be a dork.'

The men smiled and waited.

'OK,' Nick said. 'What about this Miss Stanhope?'

'Remember her now?'

'No, but *you* want to talk about her, don't you?'

'Naturally. Since she was friendly with Miss Hendry. She was part of your group, I imagine?'

'What group?'

'The one you and Miss Hendry belong to.'

Vanda called out, 'Man's in a rock group. Babette couldn't sing.'

The policeman ignored her. 'She hasn't gone back to work. She was there that day, wasn't she?'

'That night?'

The policeman nodded. 'She let Miss Hendry in.'

'You're telling me this woman was there when Babette died?'

The policeman looked at him sceptically. 'And clocked out shortly before the incident.'

'Oh.'

'So we'd like to talk to her.'

'So would I.'

'Why would that be, sir?'

Nick tightened his lips. His eyes were hard. 'There's something wrong with this.'

'Really, sir?'

Nick growled.

'You appear upset, sir.'

'Of course I'm damned upset! She was—' Nick glanced towards the bed. 'Ah, shit.'

The policeman paused. 'It would be better if you talked to us.'

'I don't *know* anything.'

'Even so. We just want to find out what happened. And I think you do too.' He caught Nick's eye. 'It would be easier if we worked together.'

Nick stared at the floor.

'You mustn't do anything rash on your own, sir.'

Nick went to the window and glanced out again. 'I was just there. I'm not involved.'

'Always better not to get involved, I think.'

Nick glared at him. 'Yeah, just leave it. Great.'

'I hear you've been asking questions.'

Nick stopped. For a moment he held the policeman's gaze, then he glanced again out through the window. Daytime traffic. Parked cars crammed along the sides of the street. No sign of the truck.

'Yes, it's better not to get involved,' the policeman said. 'Oh, by the way, we've found Miss Hendry's car. In Windmill Hill. Abandoned. Burnt out.'

Nick found it easier not to look at him. He continued staring out of his window.

'Well,' the policeman said. 'There we are. We keep telling you things. You give nothing back.'

Nick grunted.

'Don't try to be the lone hero, sir. It only causes work for the authorities.'

'Sometimes I think I'm more trouble than I'm worth.'

Malcolm handed Stan the box of slides. Malcolm's left hand was still bandaged and protected by a metal cage. This was his first day back at work since the unprovoked attack by Hell's Angels or whoever they were, when they had severed one of his fingers. He had spent the last few hours learning how few things there were he could do around the lab using only one hand.

Stan Hockendale opened the box for him, took out a slide and fitted it in the microscope. Malcolm said, 'You don't have to hand me every one.'

'Correct. You only need to look at one of them. They all show the same effect.'

Malcolm peered into the microscope, using his right hand to adjust the focus. 'My goodness. From the same animal as before?'

'Yup.'

'The cells certainly *look* normal. All of them. They've really—'

'Yup. We've taken two dozen samples now and they're all clean.'

'This is definitely the same site which had the cancerous cells?'

'Which were thriving – but not any more. The host tumours have self-destructed – and they must have killed *themselves,* because nothing else is eating them! They've gone, haven't they? By altering their adhesion receptors we've tricked the blood cells into behaving as if they had docked in the wrong place. The tumours have turned themselves off.'

Malcolm stood up from the microscope and rubbed both eyes with his good hand. 'Still no problems with the host animals?'

'None at all. The human tumours we introduced *began* attracting blood vessels normally, but when we injected our protein fragments they targeted receptors in *new* cell growth only. Normal capillaries weren't affected.'

'So you think we've cracked it?'

'What do *you* think?'

'We must have done, Stan. We've certainly stopped these particular tumours. Normally they'd trick nearby blood vessels into supplying nutrients.'

'Corrupting the adhesion receptors to create a blood supply.'

'OK, let's accept nothing's coming in – but can we be sure nothing's getting out? The tumour uses the same plumbing to disperse its wastes and flush cancer cells through the body.'

'But by stopping the tumour from creating a blood supply we've starved the thing to death.'

'Don't jump ahead, Stan. We've interfered with its molecular cue and caused the genetic program to unravel. Fine. But what about the waste matters?'

'They're just waste. Once a tumour stops getting nourishment it begins to die. Look, these are dead. They can't reproduce. We have *killed* those tumours. And there are no others forming.'

Malcolm chewed his lip. 'Nothing in the blood samples? Are all the monkeys still alive?'

'Vigorously so. The damn things are healthier in the lab than they would be in the jungle.'

'You think we're still on our own in this?'

Stan Hockendale grinned. 'Well, no one will speak up in the middle of a test programme. La Jolla's the main threat, but they're still working on a better LM609 – or I think they are! Who knows what's going on until people announce results? The damn Californians are bound to come up with something shortly – they need their grant renewed! But I think they're on the wrong track.'

Malcolm nodded happily. 'Time for human trials.'

'More specific human trials. Look.' Stan strolled through the swing doors into the animal room. Along one wall were the familiar large cages. 'To a casual observer these look like ordinary monkeys.'

Which they did. There were several to a cage – and as in a zoo, each cage was fitted with swings and makeshift climbing gear, and each was lit by a medium sized window, heavily barred. Seeing the men come in, the monkeys began their welcome dance. The noise was deafening. Monkeys began leaping about the cages like giant fleas.

'Spot the difference,' Stan continued.

Malcolm pointed out the five cages, left to right. He had to speak above the din. 'Control. LM609 on monkey tumour. LM609 on human tumour. Then we have Pro 405 on monkey tumour, and Pro 405 on human. And they're all made out of ticky-tacky, and they all look just the same.'

Stan was grinning. 'Curing monkeys of monkey tumour is pretty damn remarkable, let's face it, but here we have two sets of monkeys given fragments of pre-established *human* tumours – breast, pancreas and lung – each of which took, each of which then began to attract blood vessels which grew just as they would in man. Then we introduced the wonder treatment.'

He chuckled.

Malcolm said, 'I hate to blow a sour note, but the monkeys on LM609 look just as healthy as those on protein 405.'

The monkeys cheered as if he'd scored a debating point.

Stan raised a hand as if that might silence them. 'LM is good stuff, and it does work pretty well on human tumours in *monkeys* – almost as well as our 405 – but LM609 is *not* tolerated acceptably in human trials. Which is where Pro 405 will score.'

The monkeys showed no sign of letting up, and the rancid smell in the room was beginning to irritate Stan's nostrils. 'Two hours to feeding time,' he said as he turned away. But the monkeys were on jungle time and saw no reason the visitors should leave without paying food tribute.

'Any bananas?' Malcolm asked.

Stan was at the door. 'Of course there are – but it's still two hours to feeding.'

'They're not in training, are they? Let them have a treat.'

'You're too soft with them,' smiled Stan. As Malcolm opened the banana box the animal racket was if he'd opened Pandora's Box and released all the scourges of hell.

'They're too damn healthy,' he agreed.

Nick reached for his ringing mobile and announced his name. He didn't recognise the caller.

'Eamon Reeves. Hee, hee.'

'Who?'

'Plant Manager at Rendox. We met the other day.'

'Hm.'

'I understand the police have been talking to you about Lisa Stanhope.'

'Who? Sorry if I'm being slow.'

'She was Bab – Miss Hendry's friend. She worked here.'

'But not any longer?'

'I thought the police told you.'

'They said something about she'd been there that night. I wasn't listening.'

'Apparently she let Miss Hendry in. Then she booked herself out before anything happened.'

'So?'

'She was part of it.'

'What is this to me?'

'I'm sorry, I thought you were... Why did you come to see me?'

'Yeah, I *am* interested, but... D'you think this girl knows something?'

'Obviously. Was she part of your group?'

'Look, Mr – what was it?'

'Reeves. You really aren't very good with names, are you, Mr Chance? Hee, hee.'

'I wasn't part of this group of theirs. And as far as I know I've never met this...'

'Lisa Stanhope. Do you know her?'

'I'm finding it difficult to concentrate.'

'Well, Rendox wants to talk to Miss Stanhope. I thought you might want to too.'

'Yeah, sure. She hasn't come into work?'

'I told you. She knows she's been found out.'

'Right. Well, how are you going to track her down and talk to her?'

'We have her address and I'm going round to her flat. I wondered if you might like to come along as well.'

But why me, Nick wondered in his car. Why get me involved? I can see the company rushing after her, but why involve a stranger – especially one you think is on the other side?

When he pulled up outside the address Reeves gave him he glanced at the mobile on the seat. It was not too late to phone the police. When the plain clothes man had left his flat this morning he had seemed sympathetic, and he had left his direct phone number. Call me anytime, he'd said.

But by the sound of it, he'd then phoned Rendox.

Before Nick got out of the car he dialled the policeman's direct number. He let it ring once, then cut off the call. One touch now was all he needed to recall it. Overcautious maybe, but he slipped the mobile in his pocket and stepped out of the car.

It was a street of grey stone Victorian houses set above the road behind terraced gardens. Some of the gardens were well maintained but others were overrun with weeds – the state of the gardens indicating which houses had been turned into flats and which were still family owned. The whole street had an air of dowdy respectability. Life was peaceful here.

A car door opened and a well-dressed man got out. Eamon Reeves had been waiting in his light blue Mercedes. A comfortable car. He approached Nick and reached to shake his hand. He could have been selling Nick the house.

'Good to see you, Nick. Thought I'd wait for you. I haven't been up there yet.'

'Up where? Which floor is she on?'

'I don't know, but it's flat five. No, I meant up the garden path.'

'Is that where you're leading me?'

'Hee, hee.'

Nick tilted his head to peer inside the Mercedes. Nobody there. Reeves opened the gate. As he led the way up the stepped pathway, Nick took in his smart business suit, expensive shoes and presumably well-cut hair – greying, tightly curled and no early bald spot. About forty, maybe? Reeves rang the bell.

'I suppose flat five is empty.' He gave a slightly nervous smile. 'But it makes sense to try it first.'

There was a bank of doorbells, each with its own name card. Flat five: Stanhope. So far, so good.

'Entry phone,' Reeves declared unnecessarily. 'Should I try again?'

Nick shrugged. Whatever the game plan, he was not a party to it.

Reeves rang the bell a second time and stood on the doorstep grinning fitfully at Nick. After a while he turned to peer at the name cards. 'I wonder which one is the landlord. What d'you think – the bottom one?'

Getting no more reply from Nick than from the doorbell, he rang the one beside the lowest card. The speaker croaked into life. Reeves bent towards it: 'Excuse me, I'm looking for Miss Lisa Stanhope.'

'Not here,' the speaker crackled at him.

'Is that the landlady? I'm Miss Stanhope's employer.'

'Oh yes? Wait there.'

They waited. Reeves grinned hopefully. The front door opened to reveal a thin middle aged woman who looked as if she had been drinking vinegar. 'Come to settle her rent, I hope?'

'Not exactly.'

'She owes a month, you know.'

'Ah. She got behind?'

'And notice. She has to give notice. I mean, if she's really left.'

'Has she?'

'Another month.'

'I mean, has she left? Have her things gone?'

'Most of 'em. Except some rubbishy bits to keep up appearances. But we've had the police round, and I can tell when someone's done a bunk. You're her boss, then?'

'Yes.'

'What company?'

'Rendox. We have a plant in Avonmouth.'

'I know where it is. Just checking. You could be anyone. Rendox. Yes, she still works for you, then?'

'She hasn't been in for several days. That's why we're here.'

'She's been moonlighting on you, of course. I bet you didn't know that?'

'Working somewhere else?'

The woman nodded, grinning slyly. If she was wondering whether her information might have a price, Reeves only gave a smile. 'Would you mind if we took a look around her room?'

The woman pursed her lips. 'I don't know you, do I?'

'I'm her manager.'

'*You* say.'

Eamon Reeves paused. 'Perhaps afterwards we could talk about her rent?'

The flat was cold, sparsely decorated, and had a slightly musty smell.

A few clothes hung in the wardrobe, and a few more were in the drawers – although three of those were empty. There was nothing in the fridge. A gaping bookcase held four paperbacks, several magazines and a small vase of dead flowers. On a side table lay an out of date copy of the *TV Times*. Where the television should have been was dusty carpet and an empty space.

The landlady tried to watch the two men but they separated, opening every drawer, fingering Lisa's clothes, turning the pages of her scant reading material. To justify her presence the landlady complained.

'Never liked her much – well, not recently. Never in much, neither, just as well. Less and less, nowadays, like she's got a boyfriend – except she's never had one, not here. I keep an eye out. Goes to his place, more likely. If she's *got* a boyfriend, you never can tell. Had some women round occasionally, some of them salesgirls like her – not lesbians, I don't think so, well, at least none of them stayed overnight. Didn't look like lesbians. Too smartly dressed. They was working girls – you know, making sales calls at night? No, not at night, I mean in the evenings – they wasn't call girls, nothing like that. Selling that cosmetic stuff and herbal medicines door to door. Made good money, from the look of them.'

She squinted at Eamon Reeves.

'She was moonlighting, like I told you. Working evenings, sometimes late, I mean really late, I had to speak to her, yes, had to tell her that thumping up the stairs long past midnight's no joke, no, not when people's got to get up early in the morning to go to work. She says, "I goes to work as well, you know." "At Rendox?" I asks, because she'd told me it was Rendox when she come here, because we have to know, I mean, for security. We don't take layabouts, oh no. But that one was not a layabout – she was working hard enough for two. And I asked her, I said, "Who's this other lot? A part-time job, or what?" Because I've come across these selling jobs before. It's all marvellous to start with, oh yes. You get lots of help from the company and everything's sparkling new and you go on training courses – and that's where I thought she might have gone at first, like that time she started with the company and they took all the new ones on an induction course, lasted all weekend.'

She aimed another jibe at Reeves: 'Should've noticed that on Monday morning, shouldn't you, at Rendox? Looked exhausted, she did. "Fat lot of good that health stuff is doing you," I said. "You look worn out. Ten years older. I thought that *Agenda* muck was supposed to keep you looking young? You wait till they cop a look at you down the factory. They'll get your number, wait and see." But you never did notice, did you, down at the factory? Didn't see the way she'd drag herself in some mornings like she'd been up all night. So there you are. I'm not surprised she's scarpered. She can't work for both of you full-time. It has to stop. Besides, she told me once that she was hoping for a permanent position with them. She was only temporary, see, like most of the girls. They keeps the sales people temporary, on commission, but if you does well they take you on. And I'll tell you honestly, right to your face, that by any reckoning selling beauty products must be a lot more interesting than cutting up dead animals to make meat pies. A lot more fun, at any rate. And she was vegetarian, anyway, wasn't she? She told me she was. Not as I am one to pry.'

Her eyes gleamed self-righteously.

Nick swiftly got in a question: 'Did she mention any of her friends from work – mention them by name?'

The woman inhaled and narrowed her eyes. 'I respect my tenants' privacy,' she said.

Nick said, 'Of course you do. But you'd want to keep an eye on the girls who came here.'

'They weren't from Rendox.'

'No, but you see, perhaps one of those other girls knows where she's gone.'

'I expect they do – I *bet* they do. She's been taken on permanent at Agenda, that's my opinion, and she thinks you can stuff your Rendox job – and stuff this nice little flat as well, more's the pity. She won't come back. So if you'd like to come downstairs and settle the two month's rent the young lady owes, we can clear this whole business up.'

She was looking at Reeves, who asked, 'What about her things – won't she be wanting them?'

'She ain't coming back, believe me. This is just the rubbish that's she's left. She had lovely clothes, Miss Stanhope, and there's none of that nice stuff still here. None of her books. None of her office work. None of her pamphlets and materials.'

Reeves cleared his throat. 'What will you do with it?'

'This stuff? Keep it till the end of the month. Then take it to the tip. I might take some to Help The Aged.'

She was watching him. She knew what the businessman was working round to. But since he couldn't find the words, she suggested: 'I might sell it – for a decent offer.'

When they had loaded Lisa Stanhope's things into Eamon's car, Nick walked with him to the pub at the end of the road. Reeves was emphasising that Rendox would merely hold them in safe custody for the girl, and would hand them back on Lisa's return in exchange for an explanation of why she had walked out. Nick let him prattle on.

Eamon bought the drinks.

'What did you think?' he asked.

Nick picked up his glass of beer. 'Difficult to get any feeling of what Lisa Stanhope was like from that flat. It was anonymous.'

'But the landlady was… She had plenty to say.'

'Was any of it useful?'

Eamon wrinkled his nose. 'I don't know. We learned something, anyway. Whether it was worth the trouble I rather doubt. Hee, hee.'

'And whether her things are worth eighty quid I doubt.'

Eamon smiled. 'Depends whether one is buying or selling.'

Nick drank some beer. 'Eighty quid. Not much, is it? I guess the landlady was right – only rubbish was left behind.'

'It might tell us something.'

'Maybe. But all her paperwork had gone. What was it the woman said? Pamphlets and materials. D'you think Lisa was another animal rights activist?'

'Like Babette?' Reeves frowned, then grinned. 'These new fangled activists don't seem to wear badges or have organic jewellery threaded through their nose. Babette actually kidded me she was a journalist! Seems ridiculous now.'

'Don't blame yourself. What do journalists look like anyway?'

Eamon pulled a face. 'God knows. Hee, hee. *You're* not one, are you?'

Nick smiled back. 'Don't worry.'

Having spent over an hour with Eamon, he felt his earlier suspicions had been groundless. There appeared to be nothing sinister behind the invitation to join him in searching Lisa's flat, and equally, it seemed highly unlikely that this amiable man could have had anything to do with Babette's death.

Eamon shook his head. 'I'm not much of a judge of women.'

'Did you know Lisa well?'

'No, no. Hardly ever saw her. Quite a pretty girl – though yes, come to think of it, she often did look quite tired. Tidy, though. Hee, hee. Neat brown hair in a bun, you know? Of course, that was in the office. Different when she let it down. Yes, some of these girls are quite another cup of tea outside work. You should see them at the Christmas party! Yes. Yes…' He stared into his pint of beer. 'Quite another cup of tea.'

'But you think they *were* part of the same group?'

'Oh yes. We know that Lisa let Babette Hendry into the factory.

That was her job, I suppose, in this wretched episode. And having played her part, she nipped off sharply. The cat was out of the bag.'

Nick sniffed. 'Count yourself lucky. Babette could have got *you* to let her in.'

Eamon stared at him. When his smile appeared again it looked strained. 'She was playing us along.'

'She was the victim. We've got to remember that. Maybe it was Lisa who played you along. Maybe she played Babette along.'

'No. She signed out of the building before Babette was... before Babette died.'

Nick smiled darkly. 'So as far as you're concerned, Eamon, both girls have a clean bill of health?'

Eamon took a tiny sip of beer. 'I'm trying to remember a little more about Lisa Stanhope. She kept her head down. God, there was a lot more to her than I ever realised.' Eamon's mood was darkening. 'I never paid much attention to her, but looking back, I suppose she always was rather odd. Not a company man.'

Somebody's mobile rang. Several people looked up, and Eamon patted his jacket pocket. Then he looked at Nick. 'Yours, I think. Hee, hee.'

'Oh.'

Nick reached into his pocket and pulled out the phone. 'Nick Chance.'

'Hi Nick, had you forgotten?' A female voice he didn't recognise.

'Forgotten what?'

'I *thought* you had.'

'Who is this?'

'What d'you mean, who is this? It's Randi Page. You're supposed to be at rehearsal. Remember? Or are you still in bed with that stringy black girl?'

'With who? No. No, that was half a lifetime ago.'

'Oh.' Randi sounded hurt. 'Well. Nice life. Nice to know she came across for you. Anyway, when you're ready, Nick, perhaps you could get yourself over here.'

She didn't wait for his reply.

13. I SHOULD HAVE KNOWN BETTER

RANDI'S NEW NUMBERS fitted like fingers in a glove. Till now she had confined herself to rock and jazz standards the band knew or could ease into. Now she introduced her own material, weirder than they were used to but more up to date – songs where she turned the melody inside out. In the first verse of 'Tonight I'm Yours' the tune was almost unrecognisable. The band vamped behind with a basic accompaniment until she drifted, almost reluctantly back to the familiar melody – tasting it, stretching it, hitting it hard, giving the notes a subtly changed emphasis as if she'd sung the song a hundred times before but wouldn't sing that way again. She extended the trifling lyric to recall the memory of teenage years.

They took a break.

The band sat around the rehearsal hall tending their instruments, musing on what she'd brought. Some of this they would use at Glastonbury. Cleo went with Steve Quin to fetch cold glasses of amber liquid.

'The hell is this?' asked Tiger Guffrey.

'Free sample. Normally a pound a shot.'

'One of those isotonic slurps?'

'It's a present from your sponsor.'

Cleo smiled at Randi. 'You deserve life membership of Blue Delta. That's great material.'

Randi nodded guardedly. Homer said, 'Like the way you slowed "The Things We Do For Love", you know, we could play forever.'

Cleo gave them their glasses. 'This'll build your strength. Full of ginseng and oriental roots.'

Randi smiled. 'Meta Active One, isn't it?'

112

'You know these *Agenda* drinks?'

'Used to.' She sipped some. 'It helps, you know.'

'Man, it's free – who cares?' said Homer, swallowing a draught. 'Wow!' He coughed. 'That bites.'

Cleo handed Nick a glass. '*Agenda*'s our sponsor now?' he asked. She shrugged. 'Manner of speaking. For Glastonbury we need some push. Now that Paul Charles has dropped us from the main stages we could be a sideshow. No TV coverage. Sidelined.'

Steve heard her. 'Who told you that?'

'My brother – you know, plays with Criminal Damage? No one told *you*, Steve?'

'I'll talk to Paul. Hey, it's still a big gig.'

Tiger shook his glass to see what solution *it* contained. 'And we're a commercial for fizzy drinks?'

Steve walked away. Tiger frowned. 'This true, Cleo?'

'Yup. Criminal Damage are on the Pyramid Stage.'

Tiger cursed and put his finger in his drink.

Homer and Cleo followed Steve. Tiger trailed behind. Nick turned to Randi. 'How much will these fizzy drink people pay to sponsor us?'

She shrugged. 'They're into a lot more than fizzy drinks. Life enhancement. Life extension.' She smiled. 'Pills and potions. You've seen their stall.'

'Sounds as if you've been reading the labels.'

Her smile grew crooked. 'Didn't your black girl give you their sales spiel? She's an Event Planner.'

'You know the way they work?'

'Intimately. Listen, I want to ask a favour. You free tomorrow?'

He hesitated. 'I'd prefer the next day.'

'OK.'

'What d'you mean, "intimately"? D'you know people at *Agenda*?'

'You're the one knows them intimately.' She held his gaze. 'First Babette, now the black girl. You'll have to stop dating girls from the Network.'

He was staring at her. She said, 'Give me a lift home after rehearsal.'

What do you want to know about *Agenda*? In this neck of the woods they're strong – students for the part-time sales force and the middle classes to buy the goods. But students can be customers. Anyone can play.

They can be entry-level customers or casual agents – no, sorry,

Consultants: get the title right. Plenty of kids with alternative lifestyles are happy to push leaflets in the streets, subscribe to the magazine, sell animal-free products sanctioned by the company. The company lets low-level introductory stuff go through the field force – or Agenda house parties, you know, like Tupperware? Don't knock it – kids may be amateur, but there's a career there if they want it. Start out as Demonstrator (sales rep in your language), then Lifestyle Developer or Product Consultant, then up another step to Party Organiser (wow!) or Event Planner, like Vanda. There are higher tiers: Team Coordinators and Regional Directors. After that there's an Inner Council – for true believers: those with the skill to deliver souls.

Don't scoff. I've been there – on the fast track. Yes, little me. When I started out with Agenda I was a damn good Demonstrator because I believed. I was convinced by the product – I still think it's good. The products are much more than health foods; they transform your system, slow down the rate of ageing, help you to sleep nights and stay alert all day. They're clean, green, and don't harm animals. So. I'd been through the usual teenage manias – in fact, I was a teenager way beyond my twentieth birthday. Do we ever grow up? I'd been through the anorexia phase. I'd been vegetarian, and once I could tell the difference I was vegan. A real pain in the backside, you know? I'd done supplements and biotonics. Well, when you stop eating everything else, you *need* supplements. You've got to eat.

I joined Agenda.

In fact, you don't join them, they choose you. You can sell for the company, you can host a party, but if the company likes you, they make an approach – a "solicitation".' As a casual – an "Associate" (God, the terminology) – I was selling products to my friends and helping run a stall. Then Agenda "solicited" me and sent me on a one-day course, one of the turning points of my young life. Truly. The first thing they taught me was that I wasn't selling, I was saving people's lives. And instead of wasting time trying to *convince* people I should concentrate on those who had already convinced them-selves.

Does this make sense to you? No? You had to be there.

The one-day course was on the outskirts of Bristol at the Agenda 'Nerve Centre". (Staff joke.) We were up at dawn to meet in Colston Square. We were driven out to a low lying industrial estate in Stoke Bishop: several acres of modest buildings behind an unthreatening wire mesh fence, an ordinary security gate – nothing to arouse a second glance. Inside the compound were – still are – some offices and the warehouse. On the coach we'd been warned that when we arrived we'd be expected to join in the morning exercises – you know, like a Japanese company? Sounds foolish, but it wasn't. It wasn't even embarrassing. That day, the weather was fine and the entire staff did communal exercises on the grass – though on cold or wet days, they told us, everyone exercised indoors in a large conservatory. But they always exercised. Everybody. Every day.

The course followed the pattern of those exercises: this is how we do things at Agenda – we do it together, and we do it this way because it works. The course drummed into us that we were *not* sales people, we were helpers, bringers of light. We learnt how to recruit people, how to persuade them to host parties, how to sniff out green-thinking groups – even green companies, which do exist. Green colleges and universities.

Sounds heavy, right? But it was electrifying. Here were the people behind the concept – promoting products we already knew were cool, and these people were part of... you couldn't call it a company – it was more like a club, a fraternity. We had the same shared aim. We'd been brought in off the street for a day of training and what did we find? Their beliefs and ours were one. They kept appearing among us to evangelise (yes, that is the word) and we'd laugh about it – they'd let us laugh – because they looked so happy and convinced. They were so enthusiastic, so vibrant, it couldn't fail to rub off on us. We'd been welcomed in. We were the chosen.

You had to be there, as I say.

Later in the day the company presented us with our very own demonstration kits – smarter than those we'd had before. They showed us the Agenda Promotion Ladder – hey, what a production that was! An audio-visual spectacular in the lecture hall, evangelists running in, people leaping up on stage, trumpets blazing, and each step of the Agenda Ladder was a brighter colour. The Nerve Centre manager stood on stage, beaming and calling each of us up in turn, shaking our hands and... oh God, giving us all the Agenda hug. Oh, the Promotion Ladder glowed! He said if we made Team Coordinator, we'd get a car.

Each of us *knew* we'd make Team Coordinator.

You see, Agenda is a *modern* company. Formality is out the door. They don't pretend they're running a benevolent, something-for-nothing society: you have to work, but if you are prepared to, rewards are good. Seriously good. After that one-day course we were never on our own. We had to phone in daily for debriefing and encouragement. There were weekly get-togethers – Friday Validation Meetings, to hype us for the weekend. It was seven-day working but we didn't care, because it wasn't work; it was our life. Strenuous but fun. Out in the grey old world around us millions of dull people were stuck in a rut. We had jumped out onto the high ground, and the better we performed the better the company thought of us. They *showed* us what they thought of us, how valuable we were. They showered us with rewards – commission, prizes, Presto Points. Presto Points were what took us up the *A*genda League. Winners in the league went on the Promotion Ladder.

The next course lasted three days, residential. Not everyone from Induction had made it. But if people dropped out we kept in touch with them. No hard feelings. *A*genda doesn't like hard feelings.

This three-day course was called Awakening. Even more electric than the first. I know – you're thinking brainwashing. Sure. Brainwashing. We were *encouraged* to use the word – they knew we'd think it, so they deliberately laid it on the table. They asked us: did we think we were being brainwashed? Did we have doubts? We *must* have doubts. Get them out, put them on the table. Examine them jointly in the open air. We were taken apart and recreated. At some point in those three extraordinary days every one of us collapsed in tears. That was cool – to break down the barriers and be born again.

I can't get through to you how it felt. These are *good* people. They do believe. When I was with them, I believed. When I left them, I believed. It was just that, as time went by, I couldn't live up to their principles.

Nor could Babette – I guess you knew I'd get round to her. By the time I joined she was already a high flier – one of the chosen people, a Team Coordinator with a company car. An evangelist, smart and clean, gliding up the fast track. I didn't know her well, but I was aware of her: a bright star when I joined; but a shooting star that fell away.

She was also an animal rights extremist. No problem – *A*genda always had them in its ranks. It was unavoidable. We were all vegetarian, we all supported animal rights. Some of us were more avid, shall we say? We were the kind of people who belonged to groups. Some had links to the Animal Liberation Front. For some people, animal life is more precious than human life, perhaps more precious than their own.

I don't know how Babette felt.

Remember the Promotion Ladder? It isn't a ladder, it's a pyramid, and all the Casuals swill around the base below a smaller number of Consultants and Lifestyle Developers, who are below an even smaller number of Planners and Team Coordinators, who are themselves below a tiny uppermost pinnacle of Controllers.

Wherever you are, there are less people above you. Less weight on your shoulders, but less opportunity – less spaces for you to move into.

Me? I was a successful Team Coordinator. I met the uppermost caucus – for a while I joined their inner band. But Babette never made it. She was never called.

14. HEY – HEY –
HEY – HEY!

ZANE AND SHIEL left their motorbikes outside the Pregnancy Advice
Clinic at eleven thirty – a busy time this particular day. They were
wearing leathers but had left their helmets on their bikes. Instead they
wore goggles across their eyes and carried plastic carrier bags. They
barged into the waiting room among the handful of startled women
on hard chairs and began shouting at them:

'You've come to murder your babies! Right? To kill a living
child? This is an *abortion* factory, *isn't it*? Abortion is murder – isn't
it? Termination. Death. Face up to it, ladies – you are murderers.
Inside your stomach *now* is a living child, and it's *fully formed*.
You've come to have a baby sucked out and *thrown away*. Right?'

Women were pressed against the wall.

'Look at you. That's *right*! Look at each other, don't look at me –
look at the *murderess* beside you. Look at yourselves. Every one of
you'll let a stranger stick a spatula between your legs and scoop your
baby from your womb, covered with blood. *Your* blood. How old
will your baby be – hey? Will it cry out as it dies – hey? Will you hear
it scream? Is it a little girl or boy? Who're you gonna *murder* here
today?'

The ranting rained at them off the walls. As the terrified women
sat dumbstruck, two female staff rushed into the room and tried to
quieten the leather clad men. Zane pushed one to the floor but Shiel
grabbed the other and heaved her to his chest. He dropped the carrier
and placed a scalpel against her cheek.

'This is what they're gonna use on you! *Isn't it*? This is the knife
that slices human flesh. Look how *easily* it goes.'

Shiel flicked his hand and the woman screamed. A red line

appeared on her cheek, then flowed with blood. It was not a deep cut, but from the full flesh below her cheekbone the bright red blood streamed across her face. It looked bright. So scarlet.

'That's blood,' he cried. 'Each one of you will lose two pints when they tear your baby from your guts.' He held the struggling woman with one hand. *'Shut up!'* he shouted. 'Listen.'

Zane squatted, unwrapped his carrier bag, and drew out a shining glass specimen jar containing a foetus, six inches long, suspended in urine coloured liquid. He lifted the jar head-high.

'This is from a legitimate abortion,' he shouted. 'It's less than twenty weeks old. Look at it. Human – isn't it? Perfectly formed. *This* is what they'll wrench from your womb.'

As he waved the jar in the air the foetus bobbled in the liquid, fully recognisable as a potential child.

'How old will *your* baby be when you abort it – hey? Ten weeks? No, it will be *older* – won't it? Even at *ten* weeks you can see its little arms and legs – even its hands, its toes, its *face*. Are you gonna kill it then? No. No, you *won't* – you'll wait till it is older. How much older – hey? Four*teen* weeks? Till you can see if it's a boy or girl. The little thing will swallow and make urine. Gonna kill it then? Not you. No, because the doctors, the *abortionists* – they'll wait till it's eighteen or *twenty* weeks old – still legal to abort. Still legal to *murder* your little baby. When it's twenty weeks old, which is when you'll kill it, ladies, your baby will have been *moving* for several weeks. You'll feel the movements. The foetus will be about *seven* and a *half* inches long. Look at it – like this one here. It will have *fingerprints*. It'll have head and body hair. And at twenty weeks, you had better *kill* your baby, lady, because in another month – even if you miscarry, it might survive.'

Several of the women had begun to cry. The nurse in Shiel's arms sobbed like a woman in labour, her hand pressed against her damaged cheek, the blood running through her fingers onto her dress. Another woman came in and froze at the door. Shiel dragged the nurse towards her. 'Come in or I cut her throat.'

The woman inched inside the door.

Zane raised his jar again. 'Here's your baby. Here she goes.'

He dashed it to the floor. The jar did not break as he'd intended but the lid fell away and the amber liquid inside slurped out. As the jar rolled drunkenly across the floor the floating foetus stuck in the neck. A woman screamed. Zane stooped, picked up the jar, rammed his hand in and pulled out the foetus. 'Whoah, I'm your doctor!'

He threw the foetus at a woman petrified in her chair. She was too terrified to move. The foetus slapped against her breast and fell in her lap. She screamed. Her hands dithered above it, afraid to touch, then she scrambled to her feet and let the slippery foetus fall to the floor.

Zane said, 'Hey, they usually throw 'em in the trash can.'

The rising hysteria was like a pan coming to the boil. Shiel backed his captive to the door, but Zane hadn't finished yet. He grabbed Shiel's carrier bag and pulled out another jar – filled with scarlet fluid – and unscrewed the lid.

'Foetal blood,' he cried. '*Aborted* blood. The baby's blood and yours. Take a look.'

Holding the jar in both hands he began tossing the contents around the room. As he moved closer to the women against the wall, thick liquid slopped from its narrow neck. Pandemonium. Women shrieked. One of them tried to grab the jar and wrest it from his hands but he pushed her and she fell away, a great scarlet stain spreading down her front. Zane swung the jar so the last of the watered blood splattered across women, wallpaper and chairs. He hurled the jar against the wall but it wouldn't break – it simply bounced off and rolled away, the glass inside all streaked with blood.

As he strode to Shiel beside the door he stamped on the foetus and shouted, 'Untimely ripped, my friends!'

The two bikers backed through the corridor, Shiel clutching the wounded nurse and holding his scalpel against her face. He shouted, 'Anyone moves, I slash her face.'

They rushed from the clinic, out to the bikes at the front. No one inside had made a move. Zane leapt onto his bike, and for a moment it looked as if Shiel would heave the struggling nurse up onto his – but then he shoved her from him and she tumbled to the ground, already hurting too much to feel the gritted concrete scrape her flesh. A devil roared in her ears and the bikes were gone.

There was a cloying smell like fading *pot pourri,* and the light was gentle, as if the company kept its fluorescents on half power. The favoured colour scheme was pale apricot, the woodwork cream, and the vinyl flooring was muted green. Perhaps because of the nature of the buildings – intended for warehouses or light industrial use – the company preferred vinyl to carpet. Perhaps they found it easier to clean. Because the place *was* clean. It glowed like the inside of a fridge.

The two women across the table from him wore consciously informal clothes, their hair scraped back, with that fresh schoolgirl look which on a woman above twenty-two seems doll-like, fixed in porcelain, slightly too bright. Anxious to help him, they had said, their only contribution so far had been to fire questions – politely, pleasantly – and to note his answers on a pad. Even their pencils looked brand new.

'I doubt there is much we can say to help you, but we'll try.'

One woman smiled, and a moment later her companion smiled also – the same earnest, encouraging smile, as if she'd received the same signal along a length of wire.

'Lisa is an Associate, which means it's unlikely she'd be here on site. Stoke Bishop, you see, is Distribution and Lisa works in the field – although…' The woman glanced at her PC screen. 'She has only been a part-time worker. Losing interest, I'm afraid.'

Nick inclined his head inquiringly.

'Not much activity recently.' The woman made an amused *moue* as she tapped the flat glass screen. 'We're not one of those hard-hitting selling organisations, you know? We don't force our field workers to achieve impossible targets or work harder than they want. Lots of young people come into Agenda because they're excited by our products, and they can couple their enthusiasm with making a little money for themselves. Some last a few months, others stay with us for years.'

'And become Lifestyle Developers or Team Coordinators?'

The woman smiled. 'You know our terminology?'

'Steps on the Promotion Ladder?'

'That's right.' She smiled again. 'Not that Lisa was ever more than a Demonstrator – an Associate, not a full employee.'

'Still on computer?'

The woman stroked her keyboard. 'Of course. For tax reasons, even our casuals are recorded. We're totally above board.'

'You say Lisa is losing interest. Has she made sales recently – filed any records, that sort of thing?'

The woman glanced at her screen, which was turned away from him. 'Not in the last week or two – but for a casual Associate, that's not unusual. As I say, we have quite a high staff turnover at the entry level. It's a vetting stage, you see, where we get to know our helpers and they get to know us. Sometimes it works out, sometimes not. No hard feelings.'

The other woman spoke: 'Do you know her – personally?'

'No, just… I only knew Babette.'

She shook her head. 'Babette Hendry? That was terrible. Of course, she was no longer working for us but… It was still a shock.'

Nick was aware that both women were staring at him but for the moment he couldn't meet their gaze. He heard one say, 'We can give you Lisa Stanhope's address.'

121

'I've been there. She's gone away.'

'Really?' He heard her touch a key. 'We don't seem to have been notified. You didn't speak to her?'

'That's why I'm here.'

He could meet their gaze now. The one at the terminal clicked another key.

Nick said, 'Lisa and Babette were friends, right?'

The woman watched her screen. 'It says Babette introduced her to us. Nothing surprising in that – Lisa was a casual but Babette was Team Coordinator. Part of her job was to recruit people. They must have known each other, yes.'

'I know they did.'

Both women waited for him to continue. Nick said, 'Lisa worked at Rendox – where Babette was killed.'

'Killed?'

'Died, then.'

'Lisa worked at Rendox?'

He nodded.

'But Rendox is…'

He nodded again. 'That's right. Lisa worked in a meat processing plant. Does that sound right to you?'

'Lisa would have been violently against that sort of company.'

'Violently?'

They watched each other across the table. (At *A*genda they believed tables to be less inhibiting than desks.) One of the women licked her lips. 'We're vegetarian here.'

'I know.'

'And Lisa… both Lisa and Babette were strong believers.'

'They belonged to the ALF.'

The women demurred. 'As much as one *can* belong.'

There was a pause. A thought occurred to him. 'D'you remember another girl, called Randi Page?'

'Randi?'

'Might have called herself Miranda then. Her real name.'

'Miranda Page?' – Genuine surprise.

'You know her?'

They seemed guarded. 'Are you a detective, Mr Chance?'

He almost laughed. 'She's a friend of mine.'

The women looked beautifully polite. He added, 'We're in a rock group. Randi sings and I play the sax.'

They were assessing him. One said, 'Miranda Page would have known Babette.'

'She told me to ask *you* about her.'

122

They nodded, keeping him in their sights. 'You know several of our people, Mr Chance.'

He hesitated. Better not tell them he knew Vanda, he decided – they might think he was collecting them. He said, 'Like you said, you've a high turnover. A lot of you about.'

The one with the pencil raised it. 'Why are you pursuing Babette's link with us?'

'I'm following any link.' He paused. 'All right, I think Babette was killed. Not by you guys! She died at Rendox, the meat processors – where her friend Lisa got herself a job. And now Lisa's vanished.'

Their eyes widened. Strange how they did these things in sync. It only took a glance between them before one said, 'Babette and Lisa belonged to a group of animal rights activists. Did you know that? You might want to talk with them.'

'You have an address?'

She glanced away. 'They wouldn't want us to give it you. But if you leave us your phone number, in a little while they might call *you*.'

From Stoke Bishop it was a short drive to a spot where Nick could park the car and overlook the Avon Gorge. So close to the sea the river was estuarial, its level rising twice a day, the banks thick with mud. The other side rose sharply from the water, its rugged rocks defiant in the sun. Above the cliffs lay a wooded nature reserve. Perhaps he'd go there later, walk between the trees, maybe see a hawk hovering in the sky. It would make sense to wander through the woods while waiting for this call.

The mobile lay on the passenger seat beside him. The women had suggested that if the animal rights group rang at all they would do so soon: if Nick didn't hear within the hour they wouldn't talk to him. He wondered what link there was between the two well scrubbed women and this unnamed group of activists. Randi had said *A*genda tolerated them, but there must be more to it than that? Nick could see no reason *A*genda would tie up with a bunch of activists. Yet the women were sufficiently close to the group to set up a rendezvous.

He stared across the river at the unchanging cliffs. A few gulls soared above. Now and then one would glide down to the mud flats and choppy water. The telephone rang.

The man's voice was neutral and sounded local. He checked Nick's name, then gave a venue where they could meet.

The phone rang again when Nick was changing at his flat. 'Oh,' he said, surprised.

123

Eamon Reeves was a man who, when Nick first met him, seemed to smile too much. On the phone he kept interrupting himself with his little chuckle. He sounded nervous.

'You don't mind me phoning again?'

'No.' This was the second time Eamon had rung.

'Well, you gave me your number, hee hee. I was wondering if you'd found anything out – you know, about Lisa or Babette? You said you would try to contact… who was it? That other company she used to work for.'

'Yeah.' Nick was guarded. 'But I shouldn't think it'll get me far.'

'You haven't talked to them yet?'

'I don't know what I'm looking for.'

'There's still no sign of Lisa *here*. She hasn't been back. Though she left some personal things in her desk.'

Nick perked up. 'Anything useful?'

'Nothing obvious, hee hee. Want to have a look?'

'Are you sure that'd be all right?'

'If Lisa wants to complain, she can damn well turn up and say so.'

'Fine.'

'We could go through her things together, if you like.'

'Ah.' Nick couldn't hide his wariness.

'I feel so helpless here,' Eamon said. 'You started me thinking, Nick. I mean, the accident, well, it was terrible but I'd kind of accepted it – now Lisa's disappeared too. Not that I knew her well, of course. Babette did.'

'You're sure of that?'

'What, she knew her? Well, Lisa signed her in. I thought the police told you they knew each other?'

'It's odd she disappeared.'

'We've got to find her, Nick.'

'We?'

'Yes, if we're going to discover anything about that night. Have you found anything?'

'I'm following something up.'

'What sort of thing?'

Nick hesitated. 'I'll be speaking to some mutual friends of theirs. I can't tell you more.'

'Don't hold back on me, Nick. We won't get anywhere. What sort of friends?'

'I can't say.'

'Agenda friends or animal rights?'

'Why d'you want to know?'

'Oh Nick, for heaven's sake, hee hee. We're on the same side, aren't we? I'm willing to show you anything I've got – you know, on Lisa?'

Nick grunted, but said, 'I'm meeting these guys in Clarence Road.'

'Wow, that's rough. Whereabouts?'

'A pub.'

'Ah, they're not from *Agenda* then – they don't drink. Clarence Road… you don't mean the Nelson Arms?'

Nick hesitated, reluctant to reveal more. 'Near there.'

Eamon noticed the pause. 'That's where Babette used to meet her animal rights friends. Look, when you see these people – can I come too?'

'They wouldn't like that.'

'Please, Nick.'

'They insisted I come alone. Maybe we could meet afterwards. About six o'clock.'

'I'll come to the Nelson.'

'It'd better be somewhere else. You don't want to bump into them.'

'Won't be the first time. Will you be through with them by six?'

'I'd have thought we'd be through by then.'

'Six – hey, that's not long. What time did you say you'd meet these people?'

'Soon.'

But before Nick left he made another call.

His mother sounded unnaturally bright on the phone, but he soon prised out of her that his father was deteriorating. He was still at home but had become confined to his room – not on doctor's orders but because he was barely able to leave his bed.

'It's not so much the cancer as this treatment – this American wonder drug or whatever. There are side effects and they've laid him low.'

'He'll pull through, though, won't he?'

'I suppose so. If he doesn't ride out the side effects they'll have to stop the treatment. But then there'll be nothing left to fight the cancer.'

'Should I come down?'

'I don't know, darling. I don't think so. It's just this antibody they've been giving him – you know, this thing that targets hot spots in blood vessels around the tumour? Whatever that means. Apparently it can build up and become toxic. Or it has in Simon. Now we're waiting for the toxicity to drop.'

'Can't they do something?'

'Well, in the end, dear, they can't do much. He's got cancer. We're just buying time.'

'So he's in a bad way?'

'He can't get out of bed – well, that's not entirely true. You know your father. He won't use a bedpan, so he forces himself out of bed for that.'

'This is terrible, Ma.'

'No, not really. I know my talking about bedpans must sound sordid, but frankly, anything that gets him up is a good thing as far as I'm concerned.'

'Are they going to change the treatment?'

'I suppose so. But this seems the best there is – for the moment. They're working on something better but it's not available yet. It never is.'

'Not anywhere – not even in America?'

'I don't think so. Research is being done right now in Britain but nothing's finished yet. I suppose there's always a wonder cure around the corner, but we need it *now*. We haven't time to wait. I told them, I said if anything new does come out, we'll try it. Your father says he's quite willing to be a guinea pig. Don't waste time testing it on animals, he told the doctor, test it on *me*. I'm dying anyway. I've nothing to lose.'

'He sounds low, Ma.'

'He said all this months ago. He's quite realistic about his chances. I imagine that's why they put him on LM609 – because he was willing to take the chance. We thought at first that it might… well, not cure him, but at least buy a few more years.'

'And now?'

She paused. 'We'll just have to hope they find something else.'

The old footbridge curved above the River Avon, linking York Road and Bedminster on the south side with Clarence Road on the commercial north. Both roads were busy. Between York Road and the railway lay Bedminster Trading Estate and some undesirable housing. Behind Clarence Road on the north, another depressed oasis of flats and run-down buildings stretched to the main station and city centre. Nick stood at the centre of the iron footbridge, looking down into the muddy Avon. What was it – forty feet below? Dropped onto the banks of sticky mud rising either side were bits of city rubbish – a discarded leather bag, a boot, several pieces of wood and a supermarket trolley. Only at the higher reaches of the slimy banks did any plants achieve a foothold – scrawny sedge and willow herb, then wiry buddleia in dowdy flower. The bridge he stood on was stone flagged and its nineteenth century ironwork had been painted green. A decent piece of forgotten architecture. At the Clarence Road end stood a solitary phone box, and Nick wondered idly whether the phone inside might ring. He had been told to stand here, clearly visible, so they could check that he came alone. If they liked dramatic gestures, he thought, they might try ringing that phone. Go to the callbox for your instructions. Like in the movies.

Further along Clarence Road stood the Nelson Arms, the dingy pub where Eamon had suggested they meet. Two men had just emerged from it, and though they appeared to take no notice of Nick waiting on the bridge, he wondered whether they might be his contacts. Eamon had said that the activists used that pub and Babette used to meet them there. How did he know that? Nick watched the two men cross the road.

Alternatively they might have nothing to do with it. On the York Road side of the footbridge a car had just pulled up, and when Nick turned his head he saw three tracksuited men get out. One was leaning into the car speaking to the driver, one waited with him, and the third was coming onto the bridge. When he strolled towards Nick without really looking at him, Nick took his hands from his pockets and put his back to the rail.

As the first man reached him he had barely room to pass. But he angled his body slightly, briefly caught Nick's eye, then continued by. Nick watched him, glancing as he did so at the men from the Nelson. They were on the river side of Clarence Road, quickly approaching the bridge.

The two from the car were now following the first man. They wore the same dull navy tracksuits, and they walked side by side in the narrow stone walkway, running their fingers along the heavy green cast iron walls. The first man had slowed.

This must be them. Nick glanced at them as they approached, then back to the first who had turned to face him. Both ways cut off. The two men were closing in on him. One had his hand in the pocket of his jerkin, and two paces away he pulled out a knife. Nick saw it flash. Only because he was already tensed could he move so fast. He darted to his right, ignored the knife, and charged towards the lone man.

Who stood waiting, feet apart. Who tried to block him. Who didn't expect Nick to dive low for his knees. And bring him down.

The man crashed onto his back and softened Nick's landing. When Nick scrambled forward the man clutched at him, tangling with his limbs as Nick kicked out. The man tightened his grip and

127

Nick kicked again. The man's two companions had reached them now. One grabbed his leg.

Two other men were on the bridge, running towards them. Nick thrashed and twisted to get free, punching the face of the man on the ground and kicking out at the one with the knife. Now two of them fell on him. Nick kept his eye on the knife, grabbed the man's wrist with both his hands and forced the blade away from his body. His head was unprotected. He felt several blows. He knew the other two had joined the fray but he could only concentrate on the knife. Their tangled melee was hard against the heavy ironwork. He felt a boot thump in his ribs. He was fighting for his life. Even without the knife, the mass of bodies in the restricted space of the iron footbridge meant a heavy beating. If he faded he would be done for.

He found every reserve of strength. He kept a grip on the knifeman's wrist. Someone's hand clawed at his face but he twisted his head and got his teeth on the grasping fingers. His legs were free. As he kicked out wildly it seemed that his own desperate strength was beating them back. Their weight was lighter. Suddenly the knifeman jerked away and Nick found himself scrambling after him, his hands still grasping the man's wrist. Someone else heaved Nick away. That person held him, and for a moment Nick thought the knifeman would lunge at him, until he saw that the knifeman was being held by a new man – a heavy, redheaded man, one of those two from the pub.

But whoever held Nick had his hand round his throat. Nick thumped his head back, felt it crack against the teeth of the unseen man, then pulled away and turned to face him. As he leapt for the man he realised that the two newcomers had come to help him. But he couldn't think about it. He was one on one. He smashed through his assailant's guard and rammed heavy punches into his face. The man tried to stop him, but when he stepped back the man found himself pressed against the iron balustrade. Like a boxer on the ropes he tried to duck aside, but unlike a boxer he found no give behind him, no referee to call a break. His face broke open with blood. Nick punched him mercilessly.

He glanced to one side and saw the redheaded man struggling with the knifeman. The man had pulled his knife hand free and was trying to twist around to stab him. Leaving his opponent, Nick darted across. The knifeman saw him too late. Nick slammed one hand onto his wrist and used the other to pull back his fingers. When the man tried to kick Nick he lost his footing, and as he slithered to the stonework the other kicked him in the head.

Nick had the knife.

The knifeman struggled to his feet. But the redheaded man punched low. The knifeman stooped and fell across his shoulder. Like blundering wrestlers they crashed across the footway. They hit the iron sides and in one long, slow extended moment the force of their progress carried the knifeman further, and he soared away from the other's shoulders, his buttocks crashed on the iron rail, his torso swung, his arms flailed, his mouth opened, his legs rose above the balustrade, and he fell down, down, down into the river below.

There was the slightest pause. As Nick saw his original opponent clamber to his feet he nipped in and punched him fast. The man's head cracked against the ironwork. He sat semiconscious on the stone flagged floor.

Nick saw the third of his attackers suddenly run off along the footbridge with the second rescuer trailing in pursuit. The track-suited man reached the York Road side and scrambled into the waiting car. Almost immediately it roared away.

'Hold that one,' his pursuer yelled. But "that one" was lying crumpled by the balustrade. The red-headed man nodded at Nick, then they peered over the ironwork to the gorge below.

There was no one there.

Nick realised which way the river was flowing and crossed to look the other side. Sure enough, the knifeman had been carried under the bridge by the sluggish current and was about twenty yards downstream. He was floundering feebly to the muddy sides. The two men joined Nick and watched him struggle to the edge. He made it to the shallows. No longer swimming and no longer carried by the current, the man lay on his belly like a beached walrus. Summoning what remained of his sapped strength, he tried to crawl out of the river onto its slimy banks. But he sank to his elbows in clammy mud. He tried crawling forward but only sank deeper. Not only were his arms encased in mud but his legs were trapped as well. From the bridge they could see him straining to pull himself clear. Each movement sank him deeper. The oily mud was soft and liquid and as the man wallowed he was more encased. He was stuck now, unable to move forward or back. He looked up at the bridge, then looked away. He looked up the sides, but from where he lay the high banks were too steep for him to see anything above. They heard him call out, but his cry was as feeble as his struggles. Watching him down there, forty feet below and twenty yards downstream, was like watching a large fly in a spider's web. His movement slowed and became sporadic. His will to escape seemed to seep away.

'Tide's coming in,' Nick said nonchalantly. The man beside him laughed.

The one on the bridge who had been knocked semi-conscious scrambled to his feet – and now, realising he'd been seen, began to stumble toward the York Road exit.

'Leave him,' snapped the redheaded man. 'We're attracting attention.'

He urged them away toward Clarence Road. On each of the busy riverside roads the afternoon traffic continued to grind. Westward along Clarence Road a lone woman who might have seen what happened stared blankly at the three men on the bridge, but when she saw them heading toward her she quickly turned and scuttled away. The men quit the footbridge and walked away from her along the Clarence Road.

'Well,' said the redheaded man. 'You must be Nick Chance.'

No one in their right mind would choose to drink in the Nelson Arms, but it seemed to Nick that no one today *was* in their right mind. He bought a bottled beer because he didn't trust the barrel, and his two rescuers asked for a Mexican beer he hadn't heard of: this month's guest, they said – product of an economy slightly richer than the one outside. Two sharp-faced, shrunken men muttered in a dusty corner, while an underage kid with a shaven head sat at the bar reading a newspaper that looked as if he'd found it in the gutter. Nick joined the other two at a rickety table perched beside a fruit machine that didn't work. Like the customers.

'What was that about?' Nick asked.

'Rough area. You were standing there like a man with money in his pocket.'

They both smiled at him.

He said, 'You don't think it was personal?'

'Not unless you support Bristol Rovers.'

Comedians now. One said, 'They looked like *City* supporters to me.'

'Bit of a coincidence, wasn't it? I fix a meet with you, and while I'm waiting at the venue I get attacked. I thought it was you guys at first.'

'Thanks. You thought we'd bump you off in the middle of a public thoroughfare?'

Nick shrugged. 'No one took much notice.'

'That's the trouble. No one has a sense of duty now. Tell anyone you were coming to meet us?'

'No.'

'There you are. It was coincidence. Rising urban crime.'

They paused to let the noise of a passing fire engine subside. The wail of its siren surged through the pub and rattled its tables. Then the siren cut off.

'Ah,' said the redheaded man. 'They're going to fish our friend out of the river.'

Nick said, 'We could see if he's still alive.'

They looked at him. 'Would that be important?'

Nick shrugged. 'I don't think it was coincidence.'

The red-headed man sipped his drink. 'You were a friend of Babette's?'

'We went to school together.'

They nodded, waiting for him to continue.

'I was with her on the night she died.'

'Oh, you were the fellow outside in the car?'

'I want to know what happened.'

'Don't we all? Tell me, Nick, were you with Babette against the processors?'

'I just tagged along.'

'But were you part of it?'

'She didn't tell me what was going on.'

'But if she let you drive her there, she must have thought that she could trust you.'

'We'd known each other a long time.'

'Something more than that?'

He glared at them, dry-eyed.

'Oh, I see. Sorry, man. What made you go to Agenda today?'

'She used to work for them. I thought they might have been involved.'

'Agenda? They're a legitimate company.'

'So people say.'

'They're decent people. Sure, they don't like any company that takes dead animals and turns them into meat pies, but they wouldn't waste time on industrial espionage.'

Nick sighed. 'I don't believe Babette met with an *accident*. I thought if you could tell me what she was doing there, I might work out for myself what happened.'

A police car howled past outside, and stopped. One of the men got up to peer out of the grimy window. 'Beginning to gather a crowd. Want to watch?'

The one at the table shook his head. 'Best we stay out of it. Don't want him looking up from a stretcher and pointing a finger at us.'

The other sat down. 'Gosh, there was I hoping he'd be stuck down there till the tide came in. That's how they used to execute pirates in the old days.'

131

'Tied 'em to a post.'

The two men grinned as they imagined it.

'Well, Nick, where do you stand on animal rights?'

'I was with Babette.'

'A bit vague, old son. You vegetarian?'

He nodded falsely.

'Well, that's a start. D'you think animals *have* rights, or are humans a special case?'

'I don't like special cases.'

They narrowed their eyes, not satisfied. So Nick continued: 'Animals can't defend themselves – even the ferocious ones are hunted to extinction. Half the props of our so-called civilised society – cosmetics, foods, the clothes we wear – depend on the death or torture of helpless animals.'

Nick didn't particularly subscribe to these beliefs, but he was a professional performer and could adapt his material to what the audience wanted.

He added, 'We entertain ourselves by exploiting them or by deliberately causing misery, and we call it sport. We encourage animals to trust us, then we eat them.'

'Your band plays a number – what is it? Something about mutton—'It's never mutton on the menu, it's always lamb'. You know the one?'

Nick hadn't realised they knew Blue Delta. 'It's about live exports to the continent: "Take a rack of lamb. Simmer gently for two days"' Etcetera. We're doing stuff for the ALF this year at Glastonbury.'

'I heard Blue Delta once. You're pretty good.' The redheaded man studied him. 'Though you're not quite my scene.'

'What're you into?'

'Criminal Damage.' The man laughed. 'OK, Nick, let's work on this – not that we know much more than you do. You know Babette was let into Rendox by Lisa Stanhope – and she's vanished too?'

'I went to her flat but it was almost empty. She'd cleared it out.'

'Or someone had. You knew Lisa, then?'

Nick shook his head. 'I thought she was one of yours.'

'She is. She's been working for us in the meat processors.'

'You placed a committed vegetarian inside Rendox?'

There was a pause. 'We had plans for them.'

'Babette knew that?'

'I guess.'

'Is that why Babette was there that night, to *implement* your plan?'

'No, we don't know what she was doing there. What we do know is Babette is dead and Lisa's disappeared.'

Nick finished his beer. 'D'you know anyone else in Rendox?'

'No. Do you?'

'Kind of. Not someone I can trust.'

'They're not exactly our kind of people either. Still, if we both find what we can, we can compare notes. OK?'

'OK.' Nick stood up.

The man reached out a hand. 'Turn left outside the door, Nick. The police and fire engine are still there.'

Nick paused. 'He's not going to point me out, saying, "That's the guy I tried to stick a knife into," is he?'

'You must be careful.'

'You can count on that. How do I get in touch with you?'

The man licked his lips. 'We'll ring *you*. My name's Zane, by the way. This is Shiel.'

Nick turned left as they'd advised, pausing only to glance along the road at the hold-up in the traffic. The fire engine had been joined by a white ambulance parked across the road, its *Avon Ambulance Service* sign flickering in the flashing light of a police car. Several motorcycle cops were there as well, one of them filtering traffic into a single lane. Nick turned the corner into Temple Gate, bought an *Evening Post* – though the news would hardly have had time to make it onto local radio, let alone the newspaper – and strolled on into the bus station outside Temple Meads. The railway station was one of many pieces of Bristol's surviving Victoriana, a quaint domestic folly built by Brunel to resemble a minor West Country castle. Nick checked the bus timetables, Badger and City Line, to find one to take him out to Steve's. He'd be safer there. It was always possible, as Zane had said, that the attack had been a random walk-by robbery, but Nick didn't buy that. If the attack had been deliberate they would come again.

Nick sat on the low stone wall beside the inclined walkway. He really ought to tell the police – though where would that get him? He couldn't identify his attackers – or at least he *could* identify one of them, the one who had been hurled from the bridge and left in the mud. Who might be dead anyway. To say something would involve Zane and Shiel. He couldn't do that: he probably owed those two his life. They seemed a couple of well-meaning liberals – he couldn't betray them to the police.

He had ten minutes before the bus came, so he sat on the low wall in the sun, reached into his pocket and took out his phone. As he keyed Steve's number he watched the diverse crowd milling through the open-air bus station: mothers with toddlers in battered pushchairs, tired women with bags of shopping, idling teenage girls, young business people striding through to the train station, and some tourists to the West Country capital. A gull swooped on some pigeons and saw them off. Buses and taxis circled around the slope.

When he answered, Steve seemed to have his mouth half filled with cake. He said he was answering emails and updating the web site with a sampler from their recent 'studio' session (upstairs in a pub), but was happy for Nick to beg a bed. He was on his own, as usual. Sometimes it worried Nick that Steve lived like a hermit. Three months had passed since Paul died, yet Steve still behaved as if newly widowed.

The sun dipped to the city rooftops. Nick moved a yard along the wall to stay in the sun, then tried Vanda but she wasn't in. Having the mobile in his hand encouraged him to complete his housekeeping, so he rang Randi to let her know he wouldn't be at his flat tonight.

'We're still OK for tomorrow?' she asked.

'Yeah. Where d'you want me to pick you up?'

'I'll get a bus to Steve's. We ought to talk about tomorrow – I don't want to drop you into something you don't expect.'

'Like what?'

'I'm sorry, Nick. I should have talked you through it.'

'What is there to talk about? I thought I was just driving you someplace?'

'Well, you are, but… um… I don't want you should wear a tie or something, but can you look kind of fairly smart? I mean, like, respectable?.'

'Yeah, I can borrow something from Steve. What am I supposed to be – your chauffeur?'

'I'll tell you in the car. OK?'

'OK.'

That's all I need, Nick thought as he rang off. He glanced at his watch. But the Badger Line double decker trundled in on time. Nick stood up. The mobile rang.

'Ah, Nick? Hee, hee. It's Eamon Reeves.'

'And what do *you* want?'

'Oh, sorry, I thought we were meeting?'

Nick snorted. 'Yeah, that's right. And you chose the venue.'

'Well, no, you did actually. Am I missing something?'

Nick began walking toward the bus. 'You missed something this afternoon.'

'What do you mean?'

The last passengers had disembarked. The small queue began to climb on board.

'They were your people, right?'

'What? We're on a different wavelength, Nick.'

'I don't need a weather man to tell me which way the wind blows.'

'What are you talking about – has something happened?'

Nick stood at the end of the bus shelter. The bus showed no sign of leaving yet.

'Your security people, right? The ones who didn't come to search my flat? The ones who didn't come after me this afternoon? I hope you heard what happened to them.'

'Nick—'

'Call the dogs off, Reeves, all right?'

'For heaven's sake, Nick, I don't know what's got into you. Hee hee. But we still need to talk.'

'Yeah, very convincing.'

The trouble was, he thought, he and Eamon *did* need to talk. He had told Zane and Shiel about his contact inside Rendox, and here he was turning it off.

'Well, hee hee, gosh. I take it you don't want to meet?'

'Not tonight, Eamon.'

'Oh, not tonight. I see. Shall we meet tomorrow – same time, same place?'

'Different time and a different place.' Nick approached the bus. 'Call me tomorrow evening and I'll give you details then. Only this time, Eamon, just you and me.'

15. HAVE YOU SEEN YOUR MOTHER, BABY?

(STANDING IN THE SHADOWS)

IT REALLY WAS a different country. Apart from road signs being in two languages the Welsh motorway seemed little different to the English but once they left it to go north into hard mountains and mining valleys the rugged bleakness of the countryside and grey poverty of the villages seemed alien and unwelcoming. Trees were dark-leaved and far between. Grass struggled to root. Villages whose sole purpose was to supply human fodder for the coal mines had shrunk in on themselves since the mines had closed. Shops were little more than converted terraces with dingy produce in grimy windows. Around the scattered villages were some attempts to restart industry, and from time to time the quiet road revealed a coloured notice, falsely bright, announcing a 'Welsh Enterprise' or 'National Heritage Site'. Each sign was in two languages – always Welsh first, as if to pretend this really was a locally funded scheme and the locals really spoke Welsh. As if they didn't tune TV to English language soaps.

Nick had abandoned checking their route against the roadsigns. He had no need to distinguish Abertillery from Abercarn, or Aberbeeg from Abersychan, because Randi knew the way. He saw signs to Pontnewynydd and Pontypool, but she directed him into a dark hanging valley where muddy fields tumbled to the verge and bright modern road signs disappeared. There was stark beauty now. The high hilly countryside was left undisturbed apart from the deep-cut road and occasional remote farm. Randi became more silent as they neared her home. She had asked Nick to drive her partly because she owned no car but also, as she had warned him, because she couldn't face her parents on her own.

'Welsh dragons?'

'Unforgiving. I didn't fulfil their dreams. I should have become a teacher or married a local jerk.'

'Sounds a fun day ahead. Can I slip out to the village pub?'

'There isn't one. There's hardly a village.'

When she left school she took a year out before university, but that year out extended. She took a job in Cardiff, then moved along the coast to Barry. She worked in cafes and bars, thinking she might get work with one of the small bands playing clubs and entertainment centres.

'I was naive. And I had an accent then. They'd laugh at me – call me the girl from the Rhondda Valley. But the Rhondda's forty miles from where I live.'

Nick smiled to himself. He could hear the accent now.

'I went back to Cardiff because that's the capital, you know? A massive city. But nothing happened. I didn't get 'discovered'. My dad came on the bus to lecture me. So I went to Bristol.'

'Ran away to hide?'

'Ran away to England. I thought things would be different.'

'But they weren't?'

'Oh, they were different. Cardiff's different, but it's still Wales, you know? Bristol was like I'd emigrated. Mind, I was older then. You learn fast at that age – and when you move to a new place you can start again, you know? Be anyone you want. You can change your name.'

'Randi.'

'Well, it's not much of a change from Miranda, but it was a *statement*, you know? You're meeting everybody for the first time, so they don't know anything about you, and you tell them a name and that's what they call you. You can invent a history, if you like.'

'And did you?'

'No, not really.' He could hear the accent again. 'I'm not much good at stories. It was more the stories I left *out*. No more Rhondda valley girl, no straight-laced girl from a country village. I was a singer. I was Randi Page.'

'Page your real name?'

'Oh yes. One of my father's little jokes. He's just a page, he says – he works for a religious publisher, see? You won't have heard of them, but they're worth a fortune. They do huge runs of worthy books that stay in print for years – an essential toolkit for ministers and deacons and lay readers and Sunday School teachers and people who think it's right to have that sort of book in their sitting room. And I knew that if I became a teacher he'd expect me to have some on my own shelf and I couldn't bear it. I don't dislike my parents, Nick, but I can't live their life.'

He had expected a dark and gloomy house but it was light and airy – a mistake in Wales, because an airy house is draughty. Even in summer the rooms felt chilly. Mrs Page believed in open windows ('God's own fresh air') and God's little sunbeams bounced off the surfaces of her polished furniture. Nick sat in an enormous armchair with chintz loose covers smelling of fabric softener. The walls of the room were lined with books, mainly religious – older ones dark with robust spines, newer ones bright, garish, and selling hope.

Her parents fussed around Nick as if he were the vicar called in for tea. They had been wary at first, and when he mentioned the band they shied away as if he meant the devil's music. But when Randi's mother took her to help make a second pot of tea, Mr Page remained in the sitting room, perched on a dark wooden chair brought from the hall. He stared at Nick and asked, 'Saxophone, is it? You went to music school?'

'I learnt the clarinet – you know, school orchestra? – then moved up.'

'Ah, formal training, then?'

'Grade eight clarinet, grade six flute. I preferred the clarinet.'

'It's a boy's instrument. So you played in an orchestra? – Nick.' He tried the name.

'You could call it that. Lots of woodwind, too little brass, too many violins.'

Her father smiled. 'Oh, those "vile dins" make a terrible noise. I've had to sit through some painful performances. Miranda played the flute. Given it up now, though.'

'The flute?'

'Oh yes. Not much call for it in your jazz band, I don't suppose?'

'No. My sister played flute.'

'Ah yes, the flute's a lovely instrument for a girl.' Her father licked his lips. 'D'you think Miranda's a good singer?'

'Sure. You've heard her?'

'No, not really. She sang in the choir, mind, but that's not the same. She sang a solo once in a school concert.'

'And you've not heard her since?'

'She did invite us once to come down to Barry. Apparently she was going to sing in a smart hotel? But we didn't go. Mother doesn't care for Barry. It's too crowded.'

'It might not have been your kind of music.'

'No. We went to a hotel in Tenby once, years ago. There was a woman there who sang Ivor Novello – that was nice.' He smiled, remembering. 'That isn't Miranda's cup of tea.' He glanced at the door. 'How long have you known her – Nick?'

'A couple of weeks.'

'Oh, not long, then? You weren't around when she first went down to Bristol?'

'I was there but we didn't know each other.'

Her father seemed relieved. 'Well, what else do you do, Nick, apart from play the saxophone? You don't make a living from it, surely?'

'I try.'

Randi and her mother came in. Though her mother – a wisp of a woman, dark haired – had a fine underlying bone structure, her lack of make-up left her unnecessarily plain. Her face had hardened. She carried a tray of crockery and scones. Randi held the pot. Her mother looked at her husband: 'Had a good chat, then, have you?'

'Oh yes. We talked about his saxophone.'

Her mother frowned and Mr Page continued: 'Nick hasn't known Miranda long.'

'Oh.' She studied him. 'You just gave her a lift? I see.'

Randi laughed. 'Mum thinks I've brought you to be looked over – you know, boyfriend, serious? Dad hasn't been asking your *intentions*, has he?'

Mr Page said, a little too loudly, 'Nick has only known Miranda for two weeks.'

Her mother brightened. 'Well, don't embarrass the boy! We'll have another cup of tea. You like scones?'

'Love 'em.'

'Miranda needs a friend in Bristol.' She smiled. 'Someone to look after her.'

'Mum!'

'Someone you can rely on, love – not like those you were mixed up with before.'

Randi sighed as she poured the tea. Her mother said, 'It's a big city, Bristol, isn't it?'

'Yes.'

'That's what I always say. There's your tea and a nice little scone, Nick, and don't you hold back asking for another. There's plenty to eat.' She glanced at Randi. 'I like a man with an appetite.' Nick dutifully bit the scone. 'Aren't you eating, Miranda?'

'I've had enough, Mum.'

'Not dieting again, are you? You're as thin as a rake.'

'It wasn't a diet—'

'A man likes a girl who likes her food,' her mother declared. 'Doesn't he, Nick?'

'Some people don't need as much food as the rest of us.'

'A few months ago, you know, Miranda was under seven stone.' She wanted to say more but wasn't sure if she should. 'Used to be a beauty consultant, see? And they're all anorexic, isn't it? But that's in the past. None of that silly nonsense now.'

She didn't seem able to drop the subject.

Mr Page asked, 'Do you like that scone, Nick? Mother's very good at them.'

She agreed. 'They were Miranda's favourite but now she doesn't eat a thing.'

'They never were my favourite. And I do eat, Mum – but not all the time.'

'Not unless it's *made* of multi-vitamins. Oh, I'm sorry, Nick, what will you think of us? She's lovely, really. Just doesn't like her mother's food.'

'Oh, give me a biscuit,' Randi conceded.

Her mother hesitated. 'They're chocolate ones. I didn't think.'

Randi reached out her hand. 'Chocolate's all right.'

'From a packet.'

'Fine, Mum.'

Randi took one and bit off a piece. Her mother gaped as if she had nibbled a raw fish.

Mr Page stirred on his chair. 'Well, Nick, I hope you're on good terms with *your* parents?'

As they drove back, the sun disappeared behind the steep sides of the valleys and the black copses of trees could have hidden wolves. Nick and Randi hardly spoke.

'I'd expected demons,' he said eventually. 'But they seemed... ordinary.'

'They're ashamed of me.'

'I think they love you.'

'Because they nag at me like scolding birds? That's just habit. Parents and kids, you know, in the same small house – the kid growing up, the parents growing old?'

'It isn't a small house.'

'For teenagers and adults it's always small.'

She was feeling raw, he thought, so he stared ahead through the window. The valley bottom lay deep in shadow. He switched on half lights.

'First I didn't go to university. Then I worked in bars and hung around with punks and rock groups. I failed twice, you see.'

'I didn't go to university.'

She ignored his words. 'Cardiff and Barry were Sinks Of Iniquity, that's what they thought. Bristol was in England – they knew nothing about it. When I went across the Severn I was… like a pilgrim sailing for the New World.'

'Your parents aren't that isolated.'

'Not unless you live with them.'

'The way you warned me they were religious I thought they'd rant at us or start a prayer meeting. They didn't ram their faith down my throat. I quite liked them.'

'They were on their best behaviour.'

'Thinking I was a potential husband?'

'Why else would a girl bring a young man home?'

They emerged onto a wide trunk road but he left the lights on. Though skies were darkening he needed less concentration to drive from here. It was a normal road down to the motorway. Welshness disappeared.

She shivered. 'It's claustrophobic in that house. No life, no contact with the living world.'

'They'd say *they* were in touch with the living world.'

She touched his thigh. 'Thanks for taking me, Nick. I – I ought to be able to face them on my own but… it's not fair, I know. I mean, I do love them, I suppose, but whenever I see them, I always get this great sense of reproach. I want them to take me as I am, but no, they're hurt and they can't hide it. They can't understand where they went wrong. They look in my eyes and can't find the answer. But *they* didn't go wrong – I did.'

'Bullshit.'

'You don't know the half of it. Dropped out, went wrong, blew a decent job.' She chuckled. 'Maybe they'll feel better about it, now they've seen you.'

'They've seen the devil?'

'The devil's acceptable face.'

He asked carefully, 'What was this decent job you blew?'

'Oh, you know about that. I told you.'

'*Agenda*, right? You were promoted and then dropped out. Well, even their personnel people admit a high staff turnover.'

'Not at the top, they don't.'

141

'You got to the top?'

They passed a sign to Cwmcarn and Pontywaun – and those were the *English* spellings; they hadn't left Wales yet.

She said, 'I was a fallen angel.' He grunted. 'They're decent people. I just couldn't hack it.'

She moved away from him in the car. But he wouldn't let it go: 'What, you just walked out on them?'

'I fell from grace.'

He waited.

'I had a nervous breakdown. OK? I was under too much strain. They tried to sort me out but... OK, when I tried to kill myself they had to send for help.' She glanced defiantly but he didn't react. 'The last thing they needed was a suicide on the premises. I was *living* at Masterfield, part of the inner caucus. If I died on site the police would have been brought in.'

'There was something to hide?'

'Nothing the police would find.'

'What's Masterfield?'

'The inner sanctum. You could call it the corporate HQ – except that *A*genda doesn't go in for business labels. No, it's just Masterfield, and it's where the inner caucus lives.'

'You were living there? It's private, I guess?'

'Secluded. Don't get the wrong idea, Nick, nothing happens there. We lived in harmony.' She chuckled. 'There I go again. Harmony – Cornelius liked the word.'

'Cornelius?'

She paused. 'Cornelius Clayton. He owns *A*genda – though he'd say every member owns it. He's the inspiration.'

'Did Babette go there – to Masterfield?'

Randi turned to him. 'Still thinking of her? I shouldn't think so. She was only a Team Coordinator, that's as far as she got.' She shook her head. 'I was a different person, you know? I was, like, possessed.' She chuckled. 'I certainly was.'

'And Lisa Stanhope?'

'Who's she?'

'Oh, another girl who worked for *A*genda.'

'What is this, an interrogation?'

'Well.' He chose his words carefully. 'I keep meeting people who worked for the company.'

'Oh, yeah. What did you do with – what's her name? – Vanda the other night? Drill her and grill her, was that the scene?'

'No—'

'Don't blame *A*genda for your girlfriend's death. She sneaked

142

into a meat factory, for God's sake. She worked as an activist for animal rights.'

'She wasn't an activist—'

'What was she, a hygiene inspector? If you want to quiz someone, quiz the folks at Rendox.'

'I did. And I'll quiz them again.'

'Ho hum. Well. This Babette creature got under your skin.'

'I've known Babette since she was twelve. I mean, I *knew* her since… oh, shit.'

'Yeah, shit.' She paused. 'I'm sorry, Nick, I'm being a bitch. I'm sorry, right?'

'So you're sorry. We're both sorry.'

He drove in silence, then said, 'I want to take a look at *A*genda as well.'

'I thought you'd done that?'

'Bishops Stoke is hardly where it's at. Where exactly is this Masterfield place?'

'Don't go down there, Nick.' She touched his arm. 'They wouldn't let you in.'

'Would they let *you* in?'

'No way, Nick. I can't go there again.'

'No way you can't – or no way they'd let you in?'

She hesitated. 'They'd let me in. But I couldn't go there. That's where I had my breakdown.'

'You're over that.'

'Really?'

'Could you get *me* in?'

'There's nothing there. They're decent people.'

'Everybody *tells* me that. Everyone says "they're decent people". What do they do – brainwash you and drum it into your heads?'

'Watch the road, Nick. They don't brainwash anybody. They…'

'You said they did. Except they're decent people. At least we've got *that* clear.'

She hesitated. 'Nick, you're externalising your grief.'

'Oh, thanks! If ever I need a psychiatrist—'

'Don't push me away!' She glared at him. 'You're like a wounded animal that won't let anyone near.'

She touched his arm. 'Let me help you. I could try to soothe your pain.'

When he swallowed, his throat was dry. 'Well, I'm going anyway. D'you want to help?'

'I can't.'

'I thought you might help a wounded animal.'

She shut her eyes. 'That isn't fair.'

'No. I'm sorry, Randi, but I'm a wilful bastard. Tell me I can't do something and I go right ahead and do it. Listen. Maybe we both should go down there. Maybe we both have a demon to confront."

16. (WHEN YOU FIND YOUR SWEETHEART IN THE ARMS OF A FRIEND) THAT'S WHEN YOUR HEARTACHES BEGIN

IN DAYLIGHT, ROCKY'S Bar looked like any other small city pub, tucked down at the end of a short cobbled alley between high waterside buildings near the floating harbour. Inside was a notice claiming there had been an inn on this site for over two hundred years, a meeting place for traders, a sailor's hideaway – though the bar had only recently been called Rocky's. In the evening the gloomy alley was brightened by the pub's welcome lights and glowing windows, but in daytime its awkward placing made the bar a quiet venue – a good place to meet people and conduct private business.

In this part of Bristol were few places to park a car, so Nick left his in a multi-storey and walked through the back streets. It was a warm, dusty afternoon – warm in the shadows of the streets. Few people were about. Walking in this reclaimed area near the docks made Nick realise how much water there was, how many bridges – both the large, traffic-bearing carriageways and the small pedestrian ones refurbished. Although the docks still functioned, their main revenue now came from tourists.

Or from business people, sipping wine in waterside eateries. That would be how Eamon discovered Rocky's – for an occasional lunch with grey-suited buyers among carefully converted warehouses and dockside cottages. He was waiting when Nick arrived. He sat in a rickety chair at a table formed from an old wine barrel, and in his hand was an enormous wine glass that would take half a bottle to fill. Rocky's was the kind of bar that sold the bottle with a couple of glasses, sat you at a table and left you to it. So you drank more.

Nick felt edgy. He walked straight through the bar and through the far door to check outside. Coming back he glanced round the interior, but only two tables were occupied and they did not look threatening. He paused at Eamon's wine barrel.

'No one waiting for a second hit?'

Eamon chuckled. 'You've got a thing about this, Nick. What happened?'

'Their report must have been pretty vague.'

Eamon offered a placatory wine glass. 'Chardonnay OK, or would you like red?'

'Chardonnay's fine.'

Nick sat down. They looked at each other. Eamon said, 'Still no sign of Lisa, I'm afraid. Been back to her flat?'

Nick shook his head. 'She won't be back. Once she got Babette inside the plant her job was finished. Game over. Maybe she showed her up to your crushing machine. Oh, I don't know. Think she worked alone?'

'Unlikely – especially since she clocked out before the... incident. That would have left Miss Hendry alone with whoever it was she'd come to meet. As you say, Lisa's task was to get her inside. After that, who knows?'

'But you agree it wasn't an accident?'

Eamon sighed. 'It never did seem very likely, Nick. She was after something, wasn't she?'

'You tell me.'

Eamon smiled – his automatic smile. 'I wish I knew. I get these horrific pictures in my head. You know, poor Bab – Miss Hendry led up onto the gantry and thrown into... Could Lisa have knowingly led her into a trap?'

'I don't know what to think.'

Eamon shuddered. 'I mean, she couldn't have been dragged her up there – she must have gone willingly. Perhaps they said they'd show her something. That could have been it.'

Nick watched him silently.

'Or perhaps she climbed the stairs alone but when she reached the top she found two men waiting for her. Oh God, I don't know. I don't know why I'm talking like this. The images won't leave my head.' Eamon looked up angrily. 'It drives me mad.'

Nick stayed impassive. 'Two men, you reckon?'

'I don't know.'

'There were three at the Nelson.' Nick stared at him. 'Weren't there?'

'Three?' Eamon swirled his glass of wine. 'You keep on about this attack but I don't know anything about it. Honestly. We've got to trust each other, Nick.'

'Why?'

Eamon giggled sadly. 'To stand any chance of understanding what's going on. Some men attacked you. You think I sent them, don't you?'

'Welcome to the real world, Mr Reeves.'

'Eamon.'

'It's Mr Reeves till you explain this. I had to meet some people at the Nelson Arms. The only person who knew was you. So, I'm waiting outside the Nelson when three men appear from nowhere and try to knife me. They have come for me specifically. Right? Specifically. Now, you tell me, *Mr* Reeves, how'd they know I'd be there?'

'They came for you *specifically* – did they use your name?'

Nick tapped the table. 'I don't know – I don't remember. They wanted me, and the only person who knew I'd be there was you. They didn't need my name.'

Eamon ran a finger round the rim of his large wine glass. 'It could've been coincidence. Perhaps they were muggers. Have you thought of that?'

'A guy walks up to me, says nothing, and tries to stick a knife into my guts. He was not a mugger.'

Eamon continued toying with his glass. 'I can't explain it. I didn't tell anyone – not unless someone bugged my phone,' he giggled.

'What about the security guys you sent round to my flat?'

'I didn't—'

'Forget it,' Nick snapped. 'I'll grant you that the security guys in my flat were not the same as those on the bridge. Even so.' He leant across the table. 'Too many coincidences.'

Eamon breathed into his goblet and clouded the glass. 'This attack at the Nelson – you claim I'm the only one who knew you were there… but what about those animal rights people you went to meet?'

'They're the guys who saved me.'

'Oh.' Eamon gulped some wine. 'You don't think they set it up?'

'They pushed one of the bastards off the bridge. He could be dead.'

Eamon looked aghast and muttered, 'You don't think they could have told anyone?'

'The animal rights guys? No.'

Eamon poured himself another glass of wine. 'At Rendox, we don't have a security department, Nick – just a man on the gate.'

'They were security men who came to my flat.'

'But we don't have security.'

'No? Perhaps they were from another department – corporate hospitality? Customer care? And who's the guy with the Northern Ireland accent, the blond prissy hair?'

Eamon froze and put down his glass. Nick watched him. Eamon repeated, 'Northern Ireland accent?'

'Blond hair.'

'Tall man, slight limp?'

Nick paused. 'I didn't notice a limp. What about the hair?'

Eamon nodded. 'White blond. Very tight curls?'

'We are making contact. Who is this man?'

'I know who he could be. But no, it's too unlikely.'

'Spit it out.'

'I mean, they'd have no reason—'

'His name?'

Eamon reached to pick up his glass but withdrew his hand. 'Derek Cranham – no, it can't be him.'

'Go on.'

'Well, he is in security, that's true – but for a client, our biggest client actually, not for us. He works for Tradefair, you know?' Eamon giggled. 'But they wouldn't be into this – I mean, attacking people, etcetera. Heavens, no.'

'But he might have searched my flat?'

Eamon smiled again. 'Well, they did give our factory the once-over, and… and he was down recently – spot check, that sort of thing. He's very meticulous – obsessive, you might say. Hee, hee. It's Cranham's job to check out any company Tradefair works with – even us, though we're both owned by QMP. Tradefair is a highly ethical company, you know?'

'Not another one.'

'They can't be too careful – with their reputation.' Eamon smiled.

'What reputation?'

'Blue chip, Triple A rated. They're trade facilitators – but you'll know who they are, Nick, obviously.'

'No.'

Eamon shook his head condescendingly. 'They're a global company. They arrange major international trade deals, but these are good people, Nick—'

Nick sighed.

'Tradefair works for charities and NGOs, which is why they have

148

to be scrupulous about their business partners – even us. Everything has to be above board. Hence Derek Cranham – though I can't imagine he'd be interested in you, Nick. No offence intended.'

'NGOs?'

'Non-Governmental Organisations – Tradefair works with Unicef, Unesco, that sort of thing.'

'Are they local?'

'International. Their head office is in Docklands – that's their UK HQ – and they have an admin centre in Staines.'

'Any "Staines" on their character?'

'Hee, hee. No. Oh, for goodness sake, Nick, don't start building conspiracy theories about Tradefair. It's like attacking Oxfam.' Eamon stopped chuckling as a thought occurred to him. 'Babette didn't mention them to you, did she?'

'No.' Nick watched him.

'She had a bee in her bonnet about Tradefair. God knows why.'

'Did Cranham investigate her?'

'He'd never heard of her.'

'Why should she have a bee in her bonnet about Tradefair?'

Eamon puffed out his cheeks and blew. 'I think we're buzzing down the wrong track, hee, hee. No. But she never mentioned them to you?' Nick shook his head. 'How well did you know Babette?'

'We were at school together.'

Eamon nodded, watching him. 'That's it then – nothing more? Until you joined this animal rights group?'

'I'm not a member.'

'You don't have to deny it, Nick. Why else are you here?' Eamon chuckled sadly. 'Everyone wants to talk about Babette, but I'm the only one who cares.' His eyes were damp. 'You even suspect me of being involved in her death, which is ridiculous. Yet, you – you all think…'

He was no longer smiling. His mood suddenly changed, like the sky in spring. He stared into his empty wine glass and said, 'I loved her, Nick. I still do.'

It should be therapeutic to talk about it – but is there a remedy for grief? Of course not, that's asking too much. I want therapy, not a remedy – therapy: a palliative, something to help me through the pain. Remedy suggests a cure. There is no cure. Every hour of every day, I think of her. I wake from dreaming of her in the night. Beneath my sadness is guilt – not conventional guilt, the guilt I'm supposed to feel for having betrayed my marriage. I should feel that, but I can't get round to it, somehow. Some day, perhaps, but for the moment my marriage doesn't seem important. I could sacrifice it – I would willingly sacrifice it – to bring Babette back. We live in Keynsham, four up, two down: wife, two children, a dog. An orderly but terminal existence. Nothing wrong with it – my wife doesn't suspect. Why should she? She no longer notices me; she is simply content to find me there. I haven't stopped loving my wife – in the calm, undemanding way you love someone with whom you have lived for eleven years. Nothing wrong with that kind of marriage, I dare say, but not much right with it either. A kind of living, nothing more. If it ended tomorrow I would not feel sad. People would expect me to feel sad, and perhaps that would encourage me, if not to act sad, at least to imagine I was sad. After all, if you are told you should feel in a particular way, it's easier to go along with it, not to question it, not even to let the thought that you could question it come into your head. So, yes, I probably would feel sad, a little sad – a sweet melancholy, as it were. But provided nothing unpleasant happened to my wife, I could lose her tomorrow with no more sadness than at the loss of last year's coat.

I do feel guilt about Babette's death. I could have saved her, surely? I truly think I could, though not on the actual night she died – I knew nothing about her plans. There's the tragedy. A few weeks earlier and I might have known: she would have told me, she would have involved me in her plans – because I could have helped her. It was in my power. She wanted access to the Rendox plant, just as she had the first time we met. Although she told me she was a journalist, I soon realised it wasn't the whole story. No one could be as committed as Babette and keep their beliefs concealed. She was vegetarian, for goodness sake! Now, all right, being vegetarian didn't automatically mean she was an animal rights fanatic, but it was a little odd that she should start an affair with the manager of a meat processing plant, wouldn't you say? Yet it didn't seem odd, at the time. Not to me. She came to see me at the factory twice, was it, three times? She could have asked again, I'd have let her in. I'd have given her anything, as she well knew.

Why didn't she ask me, that fateful night? You know what I think? I believe that because her purpose was not innocent she wouldn't involve me in her scheme. She was thinking of me, you see? A more selfish girl would have asked – and the tragedy is that if she had asked me, if I could have been with her that night, she would be alive today.

I feel so guilty.

We had few secrets. Does that surprise you? For example, I knew she was vegetarian right from the beginning – on our first date. Oh, yes. She invited me out to supper. Nothing wrong with that, of course: she was a journalist, or was supposed to be at the time. She was buying information with a meal. Nothing wrong with it – except that I didn't tell my wife I was spending the evening with an attractive young female journalist. What man would? We went to the Greenleaf: vegetarian, no meat on the menu – Babette didn't ask if I approved. She simply took me there. Said they were bound to have something I could eat.

'Think what it's like to be vegetarian,' she said. 'At most conventional eating houses my only choice is salad or omelette.'

I assured her the place was fine.

'The Greenleaf may not serve steak,' she said. 'But at least you can eat anything on the menu. When I'm in a conventional place I can't.'

I wasn't sure I could eat everything on that menu – there were some pretty formidable dishes – but she had said it with a smile, and didn't follow up by subjecting me to an evening of improving lectures. In fact, we spent our first date role playing – Babette asking journalistic questions, me phrasing careful replies. She looked cool and efficient. Before the main course was over I knew I fancied her, and by the end of the meal, as we lingered over coffee (frightful stuff, but ethically sound) I was trying to think of some way to see her again. I plumped for the direct approach:

'May I see you again?'

Any hesitation was covered by Babette's sweet, open – I have to tell you, devastating – smile. She was a decade younger than me. 'I'll phone you,' she replied.

I wanted to get her number but since she'd said she would phone me I had no reason to ask outright. As we paid up and left the restaurant I tried to be light and witty. I wanted to leave her with the best possible impression. We had come in separate cars – nowadays a girl can't be too careful on her first date – and as we paused in the darkened street beside the cars there came a moment from my youth, a moment I had not experienced for twenty years, that drawn out moment where you prolong your farewell, where there's something you desperately want to say – yet daren't say it – where you cover your embarrassment with jokes.

Then she was gone. Her car pulled away and left me alone on the pavement, waving after her in the dark. There was another moment – not a gauche and tender moment this time, not from one's youth, but a moment full of the sour languor of adult marriage: I got into my dull and empty car, slumped in the seat and stared sightlessly through the window, putting off the moment for going home.

Two days later Babette phoned. The intervening time had been bad. My wife had started by complaining – uncharacteristically – about the meal. Perhaps I showed traces of leftover excitement – I don't know – but she grumbled that I never took her out. It was all right for me, she said, to be blasé about restaurants and to assure her she had missed nothing, but she would like the opportunity occasionally to be blasé herself. Let's go out then, dear, I said. When, she asked? What should she wear? I remember standing before her in our dull, boring bedroom, numb from nagging, having to switch my thoughts from Babette to my wife's wardrobe and what it lacked. Having to remember the shops that my wife shopped in. Having to agree that she could buy a particular frock she'd seen – she went out and bought it the very next day. Perhaps that was why she nagged – she needed an excuse to buy the dress. That's marriage, you see – reality. I had returned from a fairy tale to the horror story of normality.

Perhaps I exaggerate. But which is worse, I ask you – a marriage between warring souls, or a joyless union lacking the spur to break apart? The first can be ended; the second won't. I'm dribbling on – you don't want to hear about my marriage. I only mention it to excuse myself – if excuse is needed – for spending the next two days waiting for Babette to call. Would she ring? Why should she? What could she possibly see in me?

That first day I couldn't concentrate on my work. I was nervous, light-headed, I kept staring at the phone. I was like a stagnant murky pond when fresh water is introduced – water which has not yet mingled and become lost, but which lies clear, cool and sparkling at its edge. But she didn't phone. That evening I went home. I remember thinking that I must look as guilty as if I'd spent the whole day in bed with her. I was obsessed. Nothing like it had touched my life for fifteen years. Parts of me that I thought had withered and died creaked into wakefulness. It wasn't just the meal we had shared, there had been her visit to the plant, when I guided her round and instructed her, while she seemed to hang on my every word. Does this sound distasteful to you – a middle-aged married man besotted with a young girl? Well, she was not a young girl, she was in her mid-twenties. And I am not middle-aged yet, I'm not forty – no, not forty, my gosh, not quite. In some ways I'm at my peak, though in recent years the romantic side of my life has… been suppressed.

But Babette phoned me. Yes! Late on the second day. We made a date. One advantage in being older is that I can seize an opportunity. You may say I had no need to seize it – she phoned me to make the date – but no: she phoned only to confirm points in her story. I made the date.

Another advantage in being older – or in having a position that comes with being older – is that I could take the next day off. I didn't wait till the weekend – not that I could have seen her then; the weekend is when a married man is most restricted – but I took her out the very next day and we drove to the Forest of Dean. The memories come flooding back. There's a pub I know deep in the Forest with a decent restaurant, where we had a light but delicious lunch – hark at me, the old roué again, impressing the maiden with my credit card – and we walked among tall green trees, admired scenery and picked wild flowers. She wanted to see Tintern Abbey, which – I don't know whether you know the place? – is a charming, rather impressive ruin lost in the forest. You may even have been there yourself. Babette told me she had been once before, on a school trip, as a child. It brought back memories, she said.

That day there were no school trips in the Forest – just the inevitable few tourists strolling round. They were middle aged. D'you know, I was reading something recently from the National Trust – an odd statistic: at any of their sites, apparently, less than five per cent of visitors stray more than two hundred yards from the car park. Makes you wonder why they go: why not stay at home and read the guide book? Anyway, when Babette and I strolled away from Tintern – she wanted to see the river, she said, those childhood memories again – we were very soon alone. It was high summer, a glorious day, dappled sunlight, that sort of thing. I'm not one for descriptions. There was no one around. We walked part of the time beside the river and part up the wooded banks where she picked scrubby little weeds that she insisted were wild flowers – which I suppose they were, if you want to call them so, but neither of us knew their names. She crushed one between thumb and finger and got me to smell it – a straggly weed that she said used to be stuffed inside a lady's mattress to make it sweet. Did I think it smelled sweet? A weed! Well, maybe it did smell and maybe it didn't, but it gave me the chance to hold her hand.

There we were, two soppy children, picking wild flowers – not the kind of afternoon I had in mind. Babette was looking for a particular spot down by the river, a place she remembered from a school trip years before – but I don't know that we ever found it. What we did find was the absolute peace and loneliness of the forest. Birds, I suppose, though I don't remember them. Water certainly, brilliantly clear and cold, rushing over stones and mossy branches. Steep sides to the little valley – tricky to walk because there were no paths. Tangled trees and little clearings in the sun. It was in one of these… well, I'll spare you the details, or spare myself the embarrassment, but in one of those pretty woodland clearings beside the trickling river – where both the sun and time seem trapped, where the grass had not been trodden – Babette and I at last made love.

The grass, yes, I remember its thick and spongy texture, the sour-sweet smell, and the plants that grew among it. We lay afterwards, cool green blades against our skin, our faces so close to the ground that among the leaves of grass we could see each tiny cress and clover. I watched a ladybird run to the top of a shining blade and balance on the tip. Though the glade was bright with sunshine the grass was cold and still felt damp.

Her hair was extraordinarily soft. You may remember that Babette's hair was long and auburn but you won't know how achingly soft it was to touch. You won't know how it felt to run your fingers through and press it your face – oh, its scent! Her hair smelled of grass and flowers. It glinted in the sun. It held her essence. It was so… young.

She made me feel young as well. I must tell you this: making love in the open air brings a wonderful sense of freedom. The world slips away. I forgot my work, my wife, my children. I was reborn. After a while Babette got up and walked to the river bank, where she sat, feet in the stream. I sat beside her and the water sparkled, clear and cool. She sat easy in her skirt, but I felt foolish in rolled up trousers so I took them off. She said, 'Take everything off. There's no one here.' I hesitated – the outside world returning – then I removed my shirt. 'Go on,' she said, until I took everything off. I know this sounds ridiculous, and at the time I was afraid I'd look ridiculous, I was worried she might be tricking me somehow. I'm ashamed to think that now. Because even then, even there, even when alone with Babette at a perfect time, I admit I doubted her – only for a moment perhaps, but I doubted her. It was only a moment because – I confess to you – when I moved out into the rushing water and stood naked in the middle of the stream I experienced a massive surge of joy. And a massive erection too. I looked like a satyr in the woodland stream. Then Babette, my fairy queen, came in to join me. She was almost fully clothed, only tights and shoes removed, skirt gathered in her hand, and she waded through cool surging water to where I waited like a god to welcome her. We made love again, standing in the centre of the running stream – me with my feet apart and Babette with her long slender legs wrapped around my waist, the ends of her skirt trailing in the water. The growing force of our passion and the precariousness of our position eventually brought us crashing down – a slow motion, stumbling fall into cold water. And I stayed inside her! I was half sitting, half on my back, and she was spread astride me as if riding a dolphin in the spume. My body tingled with delight – but I couldn't stay in that pinioned position and I playfully tangled with her, wrestling midstream, until I turned her over and rammed myself into her, again and again, forcefully now, while she fought back, laughing in my face, sometimes rolling me onto my side, sometimes collapsing into the stream – and all the while the tinkling cold water surged past our thrusting bodies, down into the shadows beneath the trees. We threshed in the chilly water. Suddenly Babette cried out – and came. Almost painfully I came too. A great bolt of ice shot into her womb and left us exhausted in the water. We lay like cross-channel swimmers who have reached the shallows. Then, awkwardly, because for the first time we could feel the stones in the river floor, we staggered upright and waded ashore.

It was cool, of course – and quiet. Coming out of the water was as if a loud motor had been switched off. We heard only our breathing and a few faint background sounds – the water itself a delicate tinkle, the birds silent as I recall. The power of our lovemaking left us strangely shy with each other. We hardly spoke. Whereas normally, satiated lovers put on their clothes, Babette's were so soaked she had to take them off. It was the first time I had seen her naked. But she was utterly unaffected – she wrung out her saturated clothes and lay them on the sunniest spots of grass. This was England, of course, the Forest of Dean, and the sun would never be enough to dry them. It was a little chilly, to tell the truth, but obviously I could not put my clothes on while she was naked, so we sat close together in the forest glade like nude models in an Arcadian painting.

I don't suppose we sat there long. There was no possibility that her clothes would dry, and though I tried to make her wear my Ralph Lauren shirt she eventually pulled her own sodden clothes on and we returned quickly to my parked car. Babette wore damp clothes the whole way home, and we kept the heater blowing and, to be honest, our conversation was a little forced: she must have been uncomfortable, and I was worried that she'd catch a chill.

She didn't. We saw each other several times again. Yes, twice she came to the factory – which was a little awkward: one, because the staff knew I was married and two, because I knew she was a journalist. But she was interested in me, not the wretched factory. I believed that until the day she died.

Or did I – really? Our relationship created doubt. I was married, she was not. I was old enough to be her father. She was a journalist writing a story on my plant. And, what with my being married and Babette leading her own life, we were unable to see each other as often as I wanted. I began to wonder if it was as often as she wanted.

155

I wondered where she might be and what she might do when we were apart. Whether there were someone else. I was the older man with doubts. You must forgive me. You were not in love with her. You won't understand.

Eamon seemed unaware of Nick's stunned silence. Slightly flushed, Eamon gazed imploringly across the table, seeking a reaction. He had exposed himself in a way that for him was wholly uncharacteristic. Opposite him, Nick gazed at the smears of wine in his balloon glass and seemed lost in contemplation. He didn't know what to say. He didn't care what he said; he didn't care what anybody said; he didn't care about anything in the world.

Someone had selected a ballad on the jukebox – an Elvis Presley song from the '50s. Because the bar was almost empty the volume was turned down low, and the mournful, throbbing lyric rolled softly among the tables, treble cut and bass saturated. It echoed like a funeral bell. Nick began to hum along with it, hardly aware of Eamon rising to his feet.

'We'll keep in touch then, Nick.'

He nodded.

'Take care of yourself. Hee, hee. Don't let the blighters... you know.'

He took a couple of steps backwards but realising Nick wasn't watching him he turned awkwardly and walked away. When he reached the door Nick did look up, but only to stare grimly at Eamon's back. Eamon slipped outside. Nick continued to stare at the door, trying to make the Presley song drown his thoughts. But the record finished, too soon.

Babette had been with Eamon Reeves. She had had an affair with him. She had set her cap at him, inviting him specifically for a meal, then phoning again for a second date. Whose idea was it to go to the Forest? Why had she taken him to Tintern Abbey? Why had she gone any damn place with the man at all? Eamon Reeves, who had sat here at the table, pathetically insisting he was under forty, as if being thirty-nine would have made it any better. Eamon Reeves, a meat factory manager.

From the alley outside Nick heard a car shoot by at speed, its screaming engine making people in the bar look up. There was thump, somebody shouted. The note of the engine flickered and passed by.

It broke the peace of the afternoon. Someone shouted again. Over by the door were two women at a small table. One got up, went to the door and peered through the crack.

156

Nick felt his stomach clench. The woman said something, disappeared outside, then the other woman rose too. Nick heard a chair scrape. Somebody moved. He too moved, scrambling from his chair and running to the doorway. He jostled the woman and barged outside. For one moment in bright daylight he thought nothing had happened. Then he saw three people in a tableau: the woman from the bar, a kneeling man, and a third person crumpled in the road. Nick went towards them. From the bar behind, others emerged. Another door opened. More people appeared. Nick stared at the still form in the road. He knew it was Eamon Reeves.

He asked the kneeling man, 'Is he dead?'

'I think so. Oh, my God.'

The woman gasped. Then gasped again. Eamon's body had buckled. It was a bloodied heap, thrown to the side of the road. One look at his skull showed he was dead. His eyes were open. He had blood on his chest and lay like an empty suit of clothes.

'Did you see what happened?'

'Yeah.' The man gulped. There were voices all around, but Nick concentrated on what the kneeling man would say. 'He was kind of crossing the road. No, he was just...'

'He was just what?'

Someone bumped into Nick. People wanted a look.

The man said, 'Better phone for an ambulance.'

Nick asked, 'Did it look deliberate?'

The man stared up at him. 'What d'you mean?'

But he knew what Nick meant.

'Did you get the number of the car that hit him?'

In the growing clamour his words might have been lost but the man stared back at him as if he and Nick were in a private conference. 'No, it was... It all happened so fast. Some kind of van.'

Another man squatted beside them, and he prodded the body as if he might wake the dead man up. He didn't behave like a doctor. Nick asked, 'What sort of van?'

'It was too fast, you know? A white van.'

Nick was bumped again. He didn't turn round. Among all the people in the alley he and the kneeling man were on their own. 'A white van – anything written on its side?'

'Yeah, something... I don't know. Severn something. I don't know.'

'Severn Vale Hire?'

'Yes.' The man nodded slowly, gazing at Nick with approaching horror. 'Vale Hire, Van Hire – something. You know who did it?'

'No.'

157

Nick stepped away.

'But you were with him, weren't you? I mean, in Rocky's Bar?'

Nick pushed his way backwards against the tide. The man continued to stare up at him, as if he and Nick really were in a separate film. Everyone else strained to see the body, and as Nick pushed back against their mass they muscled past for a better view. The kneeling man didn't want to stand up. Nick was soon behind the small crowd, at a point where the man could no longer see him. He turned on his heel and walked away.

17. (FOR GOODNESS SAKE,)
DO THE HIPPY, HIPPY SHAKE!

He was driving like an automaton. Randi, at his side, had given up trying to talk with him. If anyone was entitled to brood, she thought, she was: she had only agreed to come because he had begged her, saying that without her he wouldn't be able to get in. He had asked her coming back from Wales, when he had taken her to see her family, when she was under an obligation to him in return. She hadn't agreed then. She'd explained that when she'd had the break-down she had promised herself she'd never go back, but Nick had come back with some guff about the dragons one had to face, the kind of crap they came out with at the Sanctuary: he could have read the book. Dragons, Christ, as if her parents were not enough. How many memories had a girl to face?

Nick seemed to think *Agenda* might hold the key to his sweet-heart's death – just because she'd once worked for them! He didn't want to face the obvious: that she was an animal rights activist who'd got in over her head. Literally, as it turned out. OK, it was sad for him, but wasn't he milking it? He had only been going with the girl two days – how much a part of him could she have been? Perhaps that was the point: he had known her for a few golden hours of romance, before reality showed through. Plenty of people seem OK for the first few hours.

She glanced at his profile in the car. Set like concrete. Staring ahead. You'd think he'd been on the motorway twelve hours. In a minute she'd have to nudge him to take the exit – otherwise he'd plough on till he reached the sea. They passed the one-mile sign. She'd better say something.

'Next exit.'

'Yeah, Glastonbury,' he said.

So he was awake. At the half-mile sign he raised his foot and eased the speed. As they approached the exit, Randi chewed her lip. She recognised landmarks: the Sedgemoor service station at Brent Knoll, the flat banked rivers, the Huntspill canal. When they finally did turn off, the road seemed astonishingly familiar – a spine road, built above the flat green moorland as if on ramparts lined with trees. Each side of the road revealed long views. To her, this countryside had always seemed muddy and monotonous. Now, on a journey she had never meant to take again, it seemed to carry a lurking threat. She had driven on this raised road once in a thunderstorm, the sudden flares of lightning exposing the empty landscape so starkly that it looked primeval, the leafless trees etched against the sky. But in today's warm summer stillness the trees were asleep. The houses they passed showed no sign of life. Randi opened the window to let in some air.

She said, 'Next right.'

They were dropping down across King's Sedge Moor, where the reclaimed peat bogs stretched away from Glastonbury, though once or twice, out to the left, they caught a glimpse of the lone monument on the Tor. From the low deep green countryside, that seemingly artificial hill was visible five miles away, and the tower on top was like a finger pointing to the sky. That was the idea, presumably. Down through the centuries, religious orders had been particular where they built monuments. They built their churches with tall spires to help passing travellers spy them across the fields. Down here in remote Somerset the spires were flat-topped, castellated, solidly square, but in the peat flatness around them they could be seen for miles. Even the monasteries, which were plentiful, were unmissable – as if the medieval monks, far from retreating from the world, sought their penitents from afar.

'Take a right,' she said. 'Through Moorlinch and Sutton Mallet.'

Three hundred years ago in the low meadows near Westonzoyland a fierce battle had been fought: ill-armed peasantry hacking into each other's bodies with heavy swords, the smell of gunpowder in the air. Now bare fields mouldered in the sun.

Nick spoke. 'Remote place for a head office.'

'This is the Sanctuary. It's not what you'd think of as an HQ.'

She felt a fluttering in her stomach. When she glanced at Nick he was staring ahead again, concentrating on the narrowing road.

Nick felt as if he himself were trying to hide. As he drove beside the empty fields he felt detached from the outside world, as if nothing were real. He was about to enter what Agenda called the Sanctuary, their inner sanctum. He was, quite possibly, about to present himself to the very people who wanted to kill him. Somehow, in this remote fastness, he hoped to find the truth about this oh-so-ethical organisation Babette had worked for, which lurked at the fringe of everywhere she'd been. There was no justifiable reason to suspect Agenda – everyone told him they were decent people – yet their omnipresence nagged at him, and in the absence of any other clue he had to follow his instinct. There was no obvious explanation for what was going on. It wasn't even certain something was going on. Babette's death might have been an accident – the only thing that interested the police was how she had tricked her way inside the plant. Eamon Reeves could have died in another accident, a hit and run. The security men at Nick's flat might have been following everyday company procedure – Eamon had said Cranham took his job very seriously. Obsessive, he'd said. And the men on the bridge might have been muggers – it was just coincidence that Nick had been there. Everything could be coincidence.

Yeah, maybe.

Maybe Agenda products could help you live forever.

No, Eamon had been killed. Someone had known he'd be at Rocky's Bar and had waited at the end of the alley. That someone must have also known who Eamon had gone to see. If Nick had left first, would they have run him down? Did they want Eamon or both of them? There were two ways Nick could find out: come and face the potential killers or wait until they felt like trying again. To hell with the second way.

Perhaps Agenda were the good guys. Eamon said the security men came from a client company, Tradefair, another oh-so-ethical concern. And the guy kneeling by Eamon's body said the van had been labelled Severn Vale Hire. Like the van driven by the security men.

That made Agenda a less likely suspect. Maybe Nick could strike them off the list.

The black cast-iron gate was wide and hung between stone gateposts in a high wall. In a discreet niche at the right hand side was a dull metal entry phone, and as Randi approached it she glanced between the slender black uprights to the empty drive. It was too familiar. She pressed the button which had been there so long it appeared part of the wall, waited, and gave her name.

She didn't recognise the voice that answered, but everything changes over time. The gate creaked open as she returned to the car.

'We're expected,' she said. 'Just follow the drive.'

Perhaps fifty years ago, these tree-lined verges would have been well maintained, but now the encroaching woodland had crept forward and the long grass, brambles and cow parsley had spilled over and softened the roadside edges. The drive curved between the trees, then opened onto a wild flower meadow and meandered on to the large main house. In front of the grey stone building the once formal gardens had degenerated into vegetable plots and an unkempt lawn. The old retaining wall had been extended to block the drive.

'Does it matter where I park the car?'

'There on the right.'

In a hard-court area between road and field stood a van and two cars.

She said, 'We'll have to walk up to the house.'

'And creep round to the tradesman's entrance?'

'Vehicles aren't allowed inside the garden. It keeps it special.'

He parked the car and they climbed out into peaceful silence. Nick leant towards her. 'I assume it's safe to talk – the wall isn't bugged?'

'Don't build it up. These people are not that abnormal. Look.'

Across the low wall they could see two women walking across the lawn. The women glanced towards them, then continued on their way, chatting as they approached the house. Randi said, 'You'll find it very ordinary.'

'As long as I behave myself?'

They were heading to a narrow turnstile in the wall.

She said. 'Play clever if you like, but they'll just clam up.'

They eased through the gap in the wall and came out on a gravel path.

He said, 'They'll be watching us.'

'Paranoid, and you've only just arrived.'

As they approached the house he persisted: 'Could be someone in there with a pair of binoculars.'

'They know who we are, Nick.'

She sensed him stiffen as they crossed the lawn. He was unsettled because no one had come out to greet them, and once inside he could wander as freely as in a public park. He was looking for phantoms that were not there.

Various outbuildings remained in use, and towards one side of the lawn stood the timber statue she recalled so well: a weathered Saint Andrew's cross on a round wooden dais two feet above the grass.

Nick had seen it. 'That's the platform for the Exultations?'

'Yes.' She had explained this. 'Powerful, isn't it?'

He shrugged. 'You come out in every weather?'

'The worse the weather the stronger the effect.'

A picture flashed into her mind of Cornelius standing arms and legs akimbo in pouring rain before the cross, his face towards the sky as if defying lightning to strike him down. She touched Nick as they reached the steps. 'Stay cool.'

The iron knocker looked as if it had been there since the house was built, but she knew that Cornelius had found it a couple of years ago. It was a laurel wreath, symbol of victory and longevity. She rapped three times.

She had barely lowered her hand when the door swung open. The young girl who greeted them must have been waiting just inside. She was dressed in yellow, so was pre-enlightenment.

Randi said their names.

'We've been expecting you.'

Nick made to go inside but didn't know the rules: the girl stepped out to them, closing the door. 'I'll take you to the Consultation Block.'

Her fair hair had been cropped to an inch all over, but it was soft and rippled in the breeze. As she glided past, Randi caught a faint aroma of rosemary and lavender. She remembered the ceremony of natural oils. Walking along the front of the house she saw Nick glance towards the Exultation platform and she wondered what pictures lurked in his mind. She hadn't told him everything.

The fair girl led the way, but Randi knew where they were going. The Consultation Block was the Sanctuary's only office suite and was where conventional visitors were welcomed. The business was no longer managed from the Sanctuary, but from the 'Nerve Centre' at Stoke Bishop. The girl led them round the side of the house, past the herb gardens, to the converted barn that formed the office suite. It had a washed-down rustic look, but before she could take them through the door she entered a key number and swiped her card.

They went inside.

'Please wait here,' she said softly, pointing to a pair of low settees. Though the office held half a dozen desks only two were occupied. Each housed a terminal at which sat a young woman with short cropped hair. One was in yellow, one wore green. When the girl spoke to her, the woman in green glanced across at Randi and smiled. Randi nodded back. 'Hi, Maggie.'

Maggie left her desk. 'You're early. I must say it's wonderful to have you back.'

'Flying visit.'

Maggie touched her arm. 'This time, perhaps. But we've missed you, you know?'

'This is Nicholas Chance.'

Maggie gave him the benefit of her tender stare. 'Yes,' she said, and nodded. 'I can feel your pain.'

Nick flinched.

Randi nudged him. 'He finds it hard to talk about it.'

Maggie touched his arm as she had touched Randi's a moment before. 'You're among friends here. You both are. Try not to hold back.'

He grunted.

She smiled. 'I know it's harder for men, but you've taken the first step, haven't you?'

He shrugged. Suddenly he asked, 'Did you know Babette?'

She looked puzzled. Randi said, 'That's the girl who died – she used to work for us.'

'Did she ever come to the Sanctuary?'

'No,' Randi answered. 'Product Consultant.'

'Then, sorry.' Maggie shook her head. 'I didn't know her.' She turned to Randi. 'You're about an hour early.'

'Nick's a fast driver.'

'I'm not sure what's best to fill the time. Perhaps you'd like to—'

'I know where Cornelius will be just now.' Randi paused. 'Don't I?'

Maggie glanced at Nick doubtfully. 'Better not.'

Randi said, 'We haven't got all day.'

Once they had left the office Randi led him across the rear lawns away from the main house onto a path through a copse of trees. Maggie had stayed behind. Nick asked where they were going.

'To meet Cornelius.'

He saw the secretive grin on her face. The nervousness from when they first arrived seemed to be melting. To Nick there seemed nothing threatening here and he assumed that Randi had realised her fears were groundless. To tramp about in familiar territory must be a relief. Her head was up now and she was glancing fondly at the trees. She had faced her demon. She'd want to convince Nick there was nothing evil in this place.

Maybe so. But these might be the people who had killed Babette and Eamon Reeves.

They stepped out of the trees into a sunny field.

Randi said, 'Hello, Cornelius. Meet Nicholas Chance.'

The sun was directly in front of them – still high, but bright enough to snag and dazzle their eyes, making Nick briefly squint. Dug into the green grass was a small round pool, the size of a king size bed. It could only have been two feet deep, for Cornelius Clayton lounged in it as if in a bath, water lapping his chest. Beside him in the pool sat a girl about half his age, her long black hair wet from when her head had been beneath the water. Cornelius's own hair was the colour of stripped pine, and he wore it scraped back into a moist pony tail. It must have been the last male pony tail in Britain.

Cornelius reached out a hand. 'Welcome to the Sanctuary.'

'Thanks. Don't stand up.'

Nick stayed a yard or so from the pool. The water was cloudy – unnaturally blue – and the sun glinted off its surface. He thought there might be steam rising from it too.

Cornelius smiled. He looked about fifty, and from the build of his shoulders he still worked out. 'A proper midday break keeps you alert all afternoon.'

'Shops and Offices Act?'

'Common sense. Look after your body and inner soul.'

'Like regular maintenance on your car.'

'Our bodies last longer. I'm sorry, are you tired after your journey?'

'We'll pass on the bath, if you don't mind.'

Cornelius moved in the water. 'You'd find it invigorating.' He stood up, stark naked as Nick had feared. 'Be kind to your body. Never abuse it.'

He reached for a towel on the grass at his side. He was demonstrably unselfconscious. The girl with damp mermaid tresses grinned up at Nick. 'It isn't cold in here,' she said.

Maybe not, but now that Cornelius had stepped out of the bath he dried vigorously. His pubic hair was the same stripped pine colour as that on his head, but Nick wasn't convinced either set was authentic. Did the guy dye his pubes to match?

He averted his gaze to the newly-built brick barn nearby. A faint line in the grass connected the barn to the pool, where they would have laid the conduit.

'Is this a thermal spring?' he asked innocently.

Cornelius was stepping into his linen chinos. He did not wear underpants. 'No. It's spring water, which we strain though natural peat.'

'Heated, though?'

Cornelius buttoned his fly. 'We give nature a little help.' He stood legs apart, sun warming his muscular shoulders, and nodded at the new brick barn. 'The refrigeration plant gives off spare heat. We let nothing waste.'

The black-haired girl slid beneath the heated water. Her hair floated like seaweed.

Cornelius said, 'We re-use the heat in the main house.'

The mermaid surfaced. 'We have solar heating too.'

Water dripped tantalisingly from her breasts, but Nick felt impatient and moved away. He wondered whether this had been laid on for him. Cornelius buttoned his shirt.

'Shall we go?' Nick asked, glancing curiously at the barn.

'It's a lovely day. Let's not hurry indoors. Let me give you a sense of how we live here.'

Randi had seen Cornelius on show before, and now, after months away, she noted how deftly he steered them on his path. When he led them from the Field of Elysium he made no reference to the barn or the Sacred Grove, and as they strolled through the cool copse of trees he walked with Nick, talking earnestly about the scientific theories behind *Agenda*'s creed – but didn't let them wander off through the trees. He ignored the side path to the Dionysian temple and took them to the Consultation Block.

He showed the small spotless lab – a relic now – where years before *Agenda* had conducted research into bioflavonoids, and he mentioned the larger one in La Jolla where they had tested how effective each was as a free radical scavenger. Proanthocyanidins, he said, were the most powerful weapon to prevent oxidative damage to human cells and tissues. He mentioned DHEA, the 'goddess of hormones' as he called it, manufactured in human adrenal glands to control vital metabolic functions – sex hormone balance, stress and energy levels, creation of lean body mass rather than fat, and the rate of ageing. Body levels of DHEA decline in humans from their twentieth birthday and it is the loss of DHEA, he said, that constitutes the ageing process. Stop the decline and you slow the rate of ageing. Increase the production of proanthocyanidins and you increase the life of your cells and tissues. Essential proanthocyanidins are drastically reduced and even eliminated from daily foods by modern processing. 'We owe it to our bodies to put these essentials back.'

Nick's eyes had glazed, but he came back with his earlier analogy: 'Like replacing the oil in your car?'

Cornelius smiled indulgently. 'You seem fond of cars, Nick.'

'I guess you're against them? We had to leave ours outside.'

'To let you walk the last fifty yards. Our house already had a protective garden wall and we felt it should continue to emphasise our separation from pollution outside. It is only a gesture, Nick. We don't want to return to horses and carts – far from it, *Agenda* is a forward-looking institution. We are based in science. We use science to prolong human life.'

He rested his long fingers on a computer terminal. Randi watched him in profile as he concentrated his personality on Nick Chance. Cornelius had the relaxed grace of a big cat stalking wild savannah. He had a lean body, country-boy looks, a Richard Branson smile. But his pale blue eyes occasionally became unreadable, especially when he was concentrating. He seemed to switch his attention on and off, as if conserving the drain from an internal battery. Randy felt his power, and was relieved it wasn't aimed at her.

Nick was wilting – not from any spell woven by Cornelius, she thought, but from the weight of biochemical information. She said, 'The sun's still shining. Let's go back outside.'

She had interrupted Cornelius's flow. When they came out to wander round to the front of the house his speech became more hesitant. He hadn't finished his scientific sell and, as she remembered well, he was so fascinated by its intricacies that he was easily tempted to dwell longer than lay listeners could stand.

Longer than some managers could stand. Before living at the Sanctuary, Randi had worked both at Bishops Stoke and in the real world selling to customers. She had thought of the Sanctuary as the command centre, the centre of knowledge – the place where the founder lived and did his great work. Once she had been invited in as a member of the Inner Caucus, she had slowly realised that the company's power no longer rested in the Sanctuary, but was distributed. The very network Cornelius had created worked against the centralisation of power. *Agenda* had no need for a nucleus. It was self perpetuating. It was in everyone's interest for the company to grow: the more successful *Agenda* was the more successful they themselves became. Cornelius was not supplanted – he was necessary, an inspirational figure, but he no longer had the same power. Perhaps no one had.

He was murmuring to Nick as they turned at the end to rewalk the front lawn.

Facing them across the grass was the Exultation platform, and in front of the cross stood a girl – the dark-haired mermaid from the pool – clad now in a simple dress of red. Afternoon shadows fell behind her at the foot of the cross, and the girl was illuminated by bright sunlight from the side. For a moment Randi thought the girl might begin her own mantra of exultation – but she was standing on the grass, not on the raised platform of Exultation.

Cornelius was expounding on the quest for everlasting life. 'There is no reason why human beings should not live two hundred years. Seriously. It is already possible for us to reach a hundred and twenty or even forty, isn't it? We can do that today. We can go further with the correct diet, correct exercises, correct way of life.'

'That rules me out,' muttered Nick.

'We must avoid toxins, carcinogenics and mutagenic substances.'

'Right out.'

'Don't joke, Nick – it's not too late. By taking in more bioflavanoids, vitamins, minerals, proanthocyanidins, antioxidants—'

'Your products, in other words.'

Cornelius chuckled. 'Not necessarily. To improve metabolic efficiency just supplement your diet with any products that restore collagen and scourge free radicals—'

'Such as your products.'

'Money, Nick. What's it for? I'm not motivated by money – I'm an evangelist, my message can save mankind. Literally – I can give you half your life again. I see you don't smoke?'

Nick shook his head.

'I meet those who do. I smell it on them. Anyone can smell it on them, especially here in our clean country air. But they have only to give up and invest the same amount on products to improve their diet, and they'll transform their lives. Stop smoking – add ten or twenty years. Take proper supplements – add thirty years. These are modest estimates, easily achieved. If you add an exercise regime and revitalise your body with tissue nutrients and active enzyme formulations, then someone of your age, Nick, might ultimately stretch their life a hundred years. Hasn't that got to be worth thinking about? I know I preach – but it is surely right for me to preach; I should preach, because this message is the most important you'll ever hear.'

They had reached the platform now. The dark-haired girl smiled. But she was stoned.

'We concentrate on your age group, Nick, because at your age we can have most effect. We'll be at Glastonbury, yes, we'll run a stall and distribute literature – but we need bands like yours to proselytise through music. You are our conduit, Nick.'

They stood before the dark-haired girl and Cornelius wrapped an arm around Nick's shoulder. He was standing taller now in the sunlight, self-assurance fully restored. This was the Cornelius Randi remembered, and seeing him now it was easy to believe that nothing had troubled him for a decade, he had no doubts. At tomorrow morning's Exultation he would be in rare form. He would stand on the wooden platform, arms raised to align with the cross behind, and he'd sing hosannas across the lawn. As his proud profile caught the rising sun, the girls in the Inner Caucus (they would all be girls) would gaze in admiration at the chosen man.

Today the girl in red leant forward and kissed Nick on the lips. 'Welcome to the new millennium,' she breathed.

On the drive back Nick seemed more cheerful. As she guided him through tangled lanes up to the spine road he said the day had yielded a great deal. Randi waited for him to elaborate, but he didn't. 'One less option,' was all he said.

For her, a weight had shifted. Before they'd come, Nick had insisted that having faced her parents she should face the greater demon in her mind. Pop psychology, she thought, especially since Nick had his own reasons for wanting to get inside the Sanctuary. But it wasn't the ordeal she had feared. She thought of the dark-haired girl in red – one of the handmaidens, as she had been. Seeing that girl in front of the Saint Andrew's cross had been like seeing herself. Except that the girl was dark-haired and wore it long. She looked nothing like Randi at all.

But she had shared the pool with Cornelius – his private pool, his font. She was stoned on locally grown marijuana, which she would have eaten in chocolate cakes – hash brownies – since Cornelius disapproved of smoking. And she'd been dressed in red.

Nick seemed tuned in to her thoughts: 'The little mermaid was stoned out of her mind. They grow their own?'

'Yeah.'

'Are they all stoned?'

'Maggie wasn't.'

'No.'

'But the stuff's around if someone needs it.'

'She needed it – to go skinny dipping with the old man.'

Randi glanced across at him. 'Jealous?'

'No way.'

'She was pretty.'

'Pretty stoned.'

'Enjoy the kiss?'

Nick snorted. 'That was nothing. She didn't open her mouth.'

Randi laughed. 'She wasn't asking you to bed. It was a goodbye kiss.'

'The place was like a free love commune – you know, like from the Sixties?'

'Maybe that's what Cornelius wanted you to think.'

It was his turn to glance at her. 'He was giving me the run-around?'

She sighed. 'So… the old man, as you called him – how old d'you think he was?'

Nick pulled a face. 'Is this a trick question? I mean, all those life enhancing pills – you're going to tell me he's a hundred and two?'

'Close.'

'You're joking!'

'Not far short.'

Nick was momentarily dumbfounded. 'I don't believe it. Come on – what, ninety-two, eighty-two? No way.'

'Those pills really slow things. I mean, the mermaid, as you call her – I don't know how old she is exactly, but she's been with Cornelius nigh on twenty years.'

'Twenty… She hardly looked twenty years old herself! Oh, come on, are you telling me those pills really work?'

Randi shrugged. Nick shook his head. Randi said, 'Maybe it's the pool – you know, the font of life?'

'No way, Randi. A hot water pipe came from the barn.'

'I didn't say it was a natural spring. But has it got to be natural water – is using science a cheat?'

Nick exhaled. For a moment he concentrated on driving. 'Screwy.'

'How old d'you think I am?' Randi asked.

The car briefly swerved.

'Careful,' she said. 'I'm not immortal.'

'Well, I don't know, Randi – how old?'

She paused. 'If I brought you some of these pills, would you take them?'

'I'd have to think.'

She nodded. 'Ever cautious. Maybe I should let you into the secret.'

'Maybe you should.'

'I don't know.'

'Come on, Randi.'

She paused. 'Ever hear of Phineas Barnum?' She paused again. 'His golden rule: there's a sucker born every minute.'

He hesitated. 'You're kidding?'

She smiled. 'See how easy it is?'

Cornelius had not been kidding. As she and Nick drove up the motorway Randi explained his New Age beliefs – sanctity of life, veneration of the body, Science holds the key. She told how his evangelistic zeal made the company so widely known. She also admitted that seeing the place afresh suggested that Cornelius no longer had control.

'Who has?'

'No one. It's like a kid on a push bike. You run alongside for a while, hand on the saddle, then you let go and your kid rides on his own. That's parenthood. Little birdies fly. Cornelius is sitting on an empty nest.'

And a nest-egg of money, she thought. Purely as a piece of property the Sanctuary could be worth two million pounds, and to the company that was an excellent investment. Had Cornelius really lost control? Would he know if he had? Was there a board somewhere that paid him lip service or did the company simply continue without a head? It was possible. As long as everyone thought someone was in command and there was some kind of accepted order, the machine would run and run. And if Cornelius was the Wizard of Oz he didn't have to hide behind a curtain and growl through a hidden microphone. He ruled in the Sanctuary and delivered empty edicts.

Randi sat in the car thinking of the dark-haired girl in red. Assuming nothing had changed, there would be four of them – handmaidens in the literal sense of the word. To Cornelius, the greatest of life's great mysteries was that of seed. It was the greatest marvel, the essence of life. To produce seed was man's one godlike act, and to sow seed randomly was to waste his most precious gift. When farmers sow they aim for continual improvement, collecting seed from the finest specimens and discarding the rest. From the finest specimens every seed is precious. Such specimens are hand reared in sheltered conditions, and when they reach fruition every seed is carefully gathered and stored. This applies to both plants and animals. It should apply to man.

Every day at dawn Cornelius celebrates Exultation with a handmaiden. Though all four disciples go to the platform, though all four partake in the disrobing ceremony, they take it turns working with Cornelius in gathering seed. The four girls sing the paean, then stroke and worship their master. But at his command three retire – remaining close nearby, singing softly while that day's handmaiden gathers seed. The girl kisses his stamen, caresses his anther, nuzzles Cornelius like a bee. Like humming insects each girl has her own technique for gathering pollen: one is fast and angry; one soft and drowsy. Randi used to use her tongue like a butterfly.

More variations are wrung by the British weather. On cold rain-

171

lashed days the pace quickens, and the chosen girl rubs her wet body close to her master to keep him warm. Sometimes in winter all four handmaidens have to press around him, writhing together till the knot of bodies becomes so tangled that Cornelius can no longer tell who owns which limb. But as the weather warms – as their bodies grow used to the open air – the three votive maidens station themselves further away, leaving the chosen one to perform the beautiful act alone. For Cornelius these must be the most sensual times. Already aroused by communal disrobing and play, he lies on his back on the wooden platform beneath the cross while the girl works him slowly, tantalising every drop of life-creating fluid from his stalk. It is her duty, he says, to extract every drop.

Randi realised that on this journey she was leaving the Sanctuary – finally getting away. Today she looked back on what had happened with the dazed disbelief of one who returns to school and finds the classrooms have grown smaller. The master was just a man. Cornelius had looked about fifty and, despite her joke with Nick, probably was about fifty. Powerful – mesmeric even – but just a man.

She leant towards Nick and whispered, 'He was just a man.'

'Who?'

She leaned closer and kissed him on the cheek. 'Thanks.'

'Oh. You're the second pretty girl who's kissed me today.'

'Don't you like it?'

'I could learn to.'

The gig that night was one of those corporate functions where the music had to be toned down to suit office workers having a night out. They wanted the Conga and stupid chicken songs and their idea of a rock classic was Waterloo. Nick modelled his sax playing on Lester Young, and Homer's guitar was so subdued it could have been a lute. Steve Quin set his keyboard to be as syrupy as a Wurlitzer in the dark.

Afterwards, they packed their instruments in subdued mood. Nick sensed that Randi had distanced herself from him, in case he thought that having spent the day together they might share the night. Maybe seeing Cornelius with fresh eyes had depressed her. She had withdrawn again, hunched inside her duffel coat, and only Cleo could bring a smile. That was fine with Nick. At Agenda he'd been on edge and this dreary evening session left him drained. He wanted sleep. In a few minutes he'd drive across Bristol to his flat. But would he sleep? He'd eliminated Agenda as a threat – hadn't he? – but Babette and Eamon had been killed, and he himself had narrowly escaped death on the footbridge. Why? He had driven Babette that night. Was that enough he should be killed? It was too incredible. Babette had gone there to take photographs. She would have been a nuisance, nothing more.

Was he a nuisance?

Cleo and Tiger were with Steve Quin. Tiger seemed upset. 'We're appearing there on Saturday.'

'I'll talk to them.'

Tiger threw an imaginary cornet to the floor. 'Talk to the bastards? Stevie, I am not spending the rest of my life playing twelfth rate gigs, and at Glastonbury if we're stuck out on the rim with the ice cream stalls we are twelfth rate.'

Cleo touched his elbow. 'Come on, Tiger.'

Tiger threw his arms out. He didn't want to argue with her. 'Cleo, even your brother's on the Pyramid. Criminal Damage, Cleo – they're just a pop group.'

'That's where the money is.'

Tiger shook his head.

Nick joined them. Steve said, 'There are several stages. It's an enormous gig.'

'But where are the cameras?' Tiger asked.

Steve said, 'I'll phone Paul Charles in the morning. I've got a hundred emails in from fans—'

'What good will they do? Internet!'

'And we can apply pressure through our sponsors—'

'Oh, a lot of use! Steve, it's serious. If we're just also-rans, then… well frankly, son, I'm off.'

Steve looked at him damply, but Cleo said, 'Thanks, Tiger. Leave us in the shit.'

He avoided her eye. 'I mean afterwards. I'll do Glastonbury.'

Cleo spoke to Steve: 'Why are we on the sidelines?'

'Who knows?'

'You asked?'

'Come on, Cleo. Don't start.'

'I'll speak to my brother. Not that he can do anything – but Tiger's right, Steve: Criminal Damage is even less of a name than we are. I'll ask him what they did.'

'Thanks.'

They looked at each other. It was late. Cleo led Tiger off.

Nick punched Steve playfully on the chest. 'You wanted to be manager.'

'I'd have preferred to be Stevie Winwood.'

Nick smiled. 'I don't want to pile on the agony, but this could split the band apart.'

'Blue Delta – weren't they a band once?' Steve bit his lip.

Nick said, 'Nobody blames you, Steve. It's not an easy game.'

'Yeah, but… Criminal Damage…'

'They appeal to a different audience.'

'Yeah, like Barry Manilow.'

Nick grinned. 'I thought you fancied him?'

'Not my type.' Steve tried to rouse a smile. 'I like 'em butch, you know?'

Nick reddened. 'I was going to ask if you could put me up again tonight – you know, spare bed… But—'

'Does it have to be the spare bed?' Steve arched his eyebrows. 'I've got an enormous one. Just teasing, honey. Why d'you need the bed again?'

'It's complicated.'

'It must be.'

Steve held his gaze. 'You're always welcome at my place, Nick.'

'Just a bed, please.'

'Strictly platonic?'

'Less of the Platonic. I've heard about the ancient Greeks!'

Stevie smiled. 'Well, sir, I think I can accommodate you.' He studied Nick more seriously. 'Are you in trouble, Nick?'

'You could say that.'

18. GREAT BALLS
OF FIRE

THE SUMMER EVENING had turned to twilight but from inside the neon-lit lab they looked onto night. The windows had become mirrors, reflecting back. Almost everyone had gone home. Stan Hockendale, white coat open over shirt and slacks, enjoyed a celebratory cup of coffee. Malcolm, in buttoned-up white coat and his hand still bandaged, stood with his backside against a table and shook his head.

'You're like a father who won't give up his child.'

'I've got two of them – they're yours for free.'

'No, thanks! For teenagers I'd want rent. But seriously—'

'Soon, I promise you.'

Malcolm clucked his tongue. Stan said, 'We mustn't announce results too soon. All our effort and painstaking work could be thrown away.'

'I know, Stan. But while we hang around here polishing results someone else will pip us to the post. We're not alone on this – only ahead.'

'When we go public we'll be under intense scrutiny. Jealousy, professional cynicism – all our weak spots will be exposed.'

With his good hand Malcolm reached for his own cup of coffee and raised it awkwardly to his lips. 'Don't worry, Stan, we're bomb-proof. We've been through hundreds of guinea pigs in there.' He gestured towards the door. 'The side effects are negligible.'

Stan scoffed. 'I've heard that before.'

'What d'you want – another year of observation?'

'That would be nice, but—'

'Every week we sit on this, another hundred people die. I mean, forget the fame and flattery, Stan, think of the people out there dying. Think what their families would say if asked.'

'Think what they'd say if we rushed the research.'

'Rushed! Stan, in two hundred cases of starving tumours to death and eradicating them with Pro 405 – there've been no side effects. What's the risk? Say we do a *thousand* cases – will you be happy then?'

'Happier.'

'You want to know my opinion? If we do a thousand cases and one of those thousand fails – yes, one of the monkeys dies – I tell you, those people out there, those desperate families with someone dying of cancer, they're going to say, "Give me that protein". Christ, one in a thousand chance – as they see it, they've a *thousand* in a thousand chance of dying – unless we get to them.'

Stan put down his empty cup. 'Let's not over-dramatise. Cancer's not the killer it was. Hundreds of thousands of sufferers are curable already, and hundreds of thousands won't be – with or without Pro 405. We'll dent the figures, certainly—'

'A big dent.'

Stan raised a hand. 'Yes, a big dent. A big step forward. But let's make sure we're stepping out on secure ground.'

Malcolm pursed his lips. 'How long are you going to wait?'

Stan moved away.

'How long, Stan?'

'Well, we've completed our trials on lung, skin and larynx. Pancreas and bowel are nearly done. And I think the brain trials will prove—'

'How long?'

Stan looked at him and blinked several times. 'Well, I suppose to tidy everything up—'

'We can't wait for every last dot and comma. We don't need to, we've got enough, Stan. But you've got to get those notes in order, that's priority now. We've made the breakthrough, we've done the work – but no one would know it from your notes.'

Stan nodded glumly. 'They are a mess.'

'How long to bring them up to scratch?'

'Well, first I've got to—'

'No, nothing else comes first. The rest of us can sort the routine work, but only you can do the notes.'

Stan puffed out his cheeks and grinned. 'I thought I was running this project?'

Malcolm grinned. 'Not any more. Those days are over. You're about to become a part of something bigger.'

As Stan came out into darkening fresh air he sniffed the scents on the evening breeze. Curry, he thought – that's odd. Then he remembered the nearby bush of philadelphus was in flower. Mock orange blossom, they called it, though it smelt of pepper. A lovely smell.

He felt a tingle of anticipation because he knew Malcolm was right. The project was finished now, all bar the shouting. He'd sort the data, write it up, and publish! Then the shouting would really start. He understood why Malcolm was impatient: the work was done, they'd made a clear leap forward in applied anti-angiogenesis and the next step was the exciting one – the climactic one – of making those findings known. In his paper, Stan would be generous to his assistants, acknowledging the constructive help and long hours Malcolm and the team had contributed. They'd be properly credited. Stan knew he'd been reluctant to let go, but it was finished now. He crossed the tarmac to his car and remembered Becky with her homework on Madame Curie. She had sniffed disparagingly at the story of Curie spending years in a garden shed working her way through two tons of pitchblende, boiling huge pots of it to isolate a single decigram of radium. Becky had not grasped that in science miraculous discoveries did not burst out effortlessly as they do in films, but took years of dedication and hard research. Towards the end of his wife's work, Pierre Curie had grown impatient too, pressing her to drop the laborious project that had filled her life. But she did not stop. Finally one evening she led her husband by the hand into that darkened shed and revealed the phosphorescent particles they had sought, glowing in glass receptacles in the dark. A magical story. Why hadn't it touched the child?

Stan opened the door to his car, sighed softly, and eased wearily into the driving seat. He turned the key to the ignition.

They watched the car explode from a hundred yards away, in the deep shadow of a lime tree – the flash of light followed immediately by a crack like metal slapped against a wall. The car seemed to sag, hesitate, and burst into flame.

Zane said, 'That'll teach the bastard to torture animals.'

The flames looked clean, the first blaze of a freshly kindled bonfire, though a pall of oily smoke shot into the air and hovered on rising heat a few yards above. But they had bungled it. As they watched, they saw the car door swing open to let a man tumble out and fall to the ground. His clothes had blackened and he was wrapped in a cloak of small, dancing yellow flames. He writhed on the tarmac. Shiel made a move – either to help the man or finish him off – but Zane restrained him:

177

'We've made our point.'

Now a door opened from the laboratory and a man dashed out. It was Malcolm, though Zane and Shiel had forgotten they'd ever met him – he was just a lab worker from inside. They saw him pull off his white coat and try to smother the flames licking his companion on the ground. He tried to wrap him in his thin white coat as if it were a fire blanket. But it was ineffective. The white coat discoloured and began to smoulder. Just as Malcolm turned to the building and screamed for help, another man appeared, a pile of white coats heaped in his arms. He dashed across and flung them over the blazing man at Malcolm's feet.

The two men knelt beside the body, uncertain whether to touch or leave alone. There were so many coats heaped upon him that they couldn't tell whether the flames were doused or still alight. But he wasn't moving.

Shiel sniffed. 'That's the smell of burning flesh.'

'Just the cloth.'

'No, I know what cloth smells like – it makes a cloying smell.'

'Petrol, then.'

'You may be right.'

'I am right. Don't get fanciful. We can't even feel the heat from here.'

They watched the tableau in the car park. The two kneeling men looked at each other, then one stood up and stumbled away into the building. With his bandaged hand Malcolm gently prodded Stan's body on the tarmac. There was no response.

19. (IF LOVING YOU IS WRONG) I DON'T WANT TO BE RIGHT

LONDON'S ROYAL DOCKS look like old Hollywood. Around the brown water docks the flattened land is littered with futuristic buildings dropped indifferently among dirty tenements and abandoned warehouses. The buildings have no relationship to each other. They look like sets for different films.

Nick found it a difficult place to get to. The tube line didn't run there and although an old overground railway was marked on the map he didn't trust it. Taxis didn't want to know. He had to take one to London City Airport and walk from there.

Close to the river, between the docks, he expected something similar to Bristol, but in the denser traffic of the capital he couldn't smell the river at all. He smelt dust. He walked along a narrow pavement, stepping off from time to time where cables were being laid. A high wire mesh fence rattled beside him. The ground trembled from workmen's drills.

The wire mesh was interrupted by a red barrier at the entrance. Across the small crowded car park stood a gleaming office block, glass and steel. Nick was wearing a tie and the nearest he had for a suit, and he hoped these would ease him inside the headquarters of Tradefair UK. He thought he looked the part, but the man in the gatehouse frowned at him as if he should have come by taxi or his own car. Standing on the pavement in dusty shoes was not the best of starts.

'Derek Cranham, please.'

'Which company?'

'Oh, I'm from – the Delta group.'

'Which company are you visiting?'

'Tradefair. Don't they own the building?'

'One of the tenants.'

The man ran his finger down a grubby computer screen, then jabbed a key. 'Cranham. That's with an aitch? Right. Mr Cranham expecting you?'

'Of course,' Nick lied.

'Straight across the compound, through the main entrance, take the lift to the third floor to reception. You picked a busy day.'

Indoors was cocooned from outside. Decor: dark blue. A sign in the lift said Tradefair occupied the third, fourth and fifth floors. There was Information Services, Information Technology and Information Processing. There was Overseas Development and International Aid. Reception shared a floor with Human Resources and Secretariat. Nick thought about skipping reception and barging straight onto another floor but it wouldn't gain him anything. They'd be waiting in reception.

He gave his name to a glossy girl in cream, sitting at a fancier terminal than the one at the gate. She keyed his details in, and they watched together as a tiny printer regurgitated the details onto a tally roll. Briskly, she ripped off the ticket and folded it into a perspex lapel badge holder. She offered coffee but he declined.

He stood by some low blue chairs arranged in an L shape around a dark wood table on which the day's newspapers and some magazines had been immaculately arranged. Part of her job, he guessed, was to tidy them after every visitor. He left them alone.

She looked up from her switchboard. 'Mr Cranham is expecting you?'

'Yeah.' Nick glanced at his watch. 'Twelve thirty,' he added nonchalantly.

She repeated this into her mouthpiece, then looked up. 'It isn't in his diary.'

Nick shrugged. 'I'll have a word with him.'

'He isn't available, I'm afraid.' She smiled discouragingly. 'Can any one else help?'

'Doubt it. This is a confidential matter. Security.'

'It would be.'

'Mr Cranham knows me. Nick Chance. Tell him it's about Babette Hendry.'

He watched her face as he said it, but the name seemed to mean nothing to her. She repeated it into the phone. As she flicked off the switch she said, 'That was Mr Cranham's PA. Would you like to wait?'

She had become more formal, as if she suspected it didn't matter whether he waited or not. She did not offer coffee again. Nick looked at the low blue chairs, and then sat down.

Though there were no other visitors the receptionist was busy. The phone kept ringing, and people flittering past her desk would pause to snatch a word. Whether they phoned or came in person they expected her to know the precise whereabouts of anyone in the building. And she did seem informed – answering most enquiries with a 'Yes, they're in Special Projects' or 'No, they've left Resources. They're in QMP.' Nick glanced at her desk to see if she had a CCTV terminal, but there was only her PC. Maybe she was telepathic.

No one asked about him. People scurrying by acted as if he wasn't there. He glanced at the line of magazines but it seemed a shame to disturb their precise arrangement. He folded his arms. After five minutes he eased himself upright to stretch his legs. The girl looked up sharply, and kept her eye on him when he wandered to the staff notice board. He'd recognised a logo from across the room: beside such exciting reads as 'QMP Policy For Health And Safety' and 'Operation Tidy-up' was a staff sales sheet from *Agenda*. They had a rep here – Phoebe on the fourth floor. Call her any time to see her catalogue. Didn't it seem odd, he wondered, that an aseptic company like Tradefair allowed an 'alternative' catalogue to be posted openly? Presumably not: it sat easily enough with other corporate sops to a greener lifestyle. A drawing of a photocopier: 'Be Environmentally Minded – Do It Double Sided'. An appeal for Action Aid. A diagram showing How To Find The Fire Exit.

Nick left the notice board feeling none the wiser. Safe and innocuous. Nothing that Granny shouldn't read. He was aware that the receptionist was still watching him, so he returned to the low blue seating and sat down. He could be in for a long sit. Slowly, the girl stopped glancing at him and as he became less and less distinguishable from the furniture – invisible almost – he began to wonder what would happen if next time he stood up he were to slowly wander away. He was part of the scenery now. He belonged.

He moved his feet closer to the chair, ready to stand up, and was surprised to hear a new voice murmur his name.

'Mr Chance?'

A large man, uncomfortable in his suit: 'Sorry to keep you waiting. Would you come with me?'

Nick had been expecting Derek Cranham and it took a moment before he remembered the man as one of those who had been with him that first morning, searching his flat. From his manner, anyone would think they had never met before.

He led Nick to the lift, pressed the button and waited silently. They stepped inside. Here, the blue was darker, as if the lighter blue outside had started dark but had faded. The dark blue embraced them. The air felt dense.

Nick said, 'We meet again.'

The man did not reply.

The door opened at the fifth floor and the man stepped out. Blue again: deep blue carpet, mid-blue walls. As Nick started into the corridor the man placed his hand against Nick's chest and muttered 'Wait.'

He was staring along the corridor. At the far end Nick saw a gaggle of suits shambling into an office. They looked like a tour party – and not one that travelled economy. Only when the last had left the corridor did the big man let Nick leave the lift. He led him in the same direction, except that half way along he stopped to tap at a pale wooden door. Nick had time to read the name plate as they walked in. Instead of 'Security' or 'Derek Cranham' the gold letters read 'Michael McDonnell – UK CEO'.

'This is Mr Chance, sir.'

Beneath Nick's feet lay soft blue carpet. Restful paintings hung on pale blue walls. The man at the desk did not stand up. He sported a dark striped suit that shouted money, and had thick brown hair. His silk tie cost twice as much as *any* shirt Nick owned. His eyes flicked to the security man and back to Nick. 'You're sure?'

'Yes, sir, this is him.'

McDonnell studied Nick, who stared back levelly. He was trying to work out what CEO stood for – Central Eradication Officer? Remembering Eamon Reeves, that didn't seem so funny.

'You searched him?'

'No sir, I – not yet.'

McDonnell scowled. 'You let him in without a proper search? You know what these bastards are.'

The big man scuttled forward. 'Feet apart,' he said roughly. 'Arms out.'

His frisk was far from cursory. As he prodded, McDonnell snapped, 'Where's his briefcase? He leave it downstairs?'

A wild look flickered in the big man's eyes. Nick said, 'I didn't bring one.'

McDonnell ignored his words. 'Did he leave anything in reception?'

'No, sir, I don't – I'll go and look.'

'Don't bother.' McDonnell snatched a phone. 'Cynthia? Gentleman who called just now – came up to me. Did he leave a briefcase – a parcel? Can you see where he was sitting – anything there?' McDonnell waited. 'You're sure? No, just a precaution. Oh, while he was waiting, did he go to the loo? Anywhere? Right. Thank you, Cynthia.'

He put down the phone.

The big man said, 'He's clean.'

'Matter of opinion, I'd say.'

McDonnell eyed Nick bleakly. 'Well, Mr Chance, I won't pretend your visit's a surprise.'

Nick looked noncommittal.

McDonnell continued: 'You picked today deliberately?'

Nick thought a nod seemed best.

'That's just too bad, because you'll be staying here.'

'Meaning?'

'You don't leave this room.'

Nick glanced at the big man by his side. He would have turned to see how far the door was but that might have made him look weak. 'How long d'you intend to keep me here?'

'Until they've gone. How did you get through the gate up to reception?'

'I walked.'

'No one accompanied you?'

McDonnell turned to the security man. 'Check with the gate. Use Nancy's phone – she's with our European friends. Then wait outside the door. Wait!' McDonnell reached inside a drawer. 'Lock the door behind you.'

He tossed a key across, then let the big man leave. They heard the key turn.

'Now, Mr Chance, if that is your name – what have you come to say?'

'I want to know what's happening.'

McDonnell paused. 'About what?'

'Two deaths. Two I know about.'

'Two deaths,' McDonnell repeated.

'You know which two – you're not losing count?'

McDonnell studied him. 'Are you wired?'

'No.'

'Then why this curious start? I'm supposed to say something incriminating? We do know who you are, Mr Chance. We know why you're here.'

'Tell me.'

'Money. The root of most things, isn't it? Please take your jacket off.'

'My jacket?'

'I need to know you're clean. Take it off, please.'

Nick hesitated, then removed his jacket and handed it across the desk. McDonnell felt the lapels, then slid his hand into each of its pockets. 'Still can't be certain,' he said, and he threw the jacket across the office. Nick looked in amazement as it landed in a heap against the wall.

McDonnell rose and came round the desk. He was older than Nick, carrying a little weight, but he approached Nick with the confidence of a man used to getting his way.

'Unbutton your shirt.'

Nick stared at him. Like a doting father, McDonnell reached forward and began to undo the knot in his tie. Nick smacked his hand away. McDonnell glared. 'Do as you're told.' He reached for the knot again and tugged impatiently.

'I'll do it,' Nick said. He was puzzled: why was he going along with this? He pulled off the tie, handed it to McDonnell and backed a step away from him. They had been so close that anyone walking in would have thought it a scene from Modern Satyricon. Nick unbuttoned his collar and stopped.

'Go on.'

'I'm not taking this off.'

McDonnell reached for the buttons on Nick's chest.

'Get away!'

'Do it.'

They stared at each other. Nick undid the buttons. He hesitated, then opened the shirt, revealing his chest as if on some kind of beauty parade. He felt ridiculous, a male centrefold, but he pulled the shirt off and stood like a topless mannequin while the dark-suited man inspected him. McDonnell walked slowly round him. Nick began to wonder if the man really was looking for a mike or had some other reason to see his skin.

'Nothing there.'

'Right.'

Nick slipped an arm back into his shirt as McDonnell said, 'Drop your trousers.'

'Get stuffed.'

'Don't be tiresome.' McDonnell jabbed a finger at him, prodding his flesh. 'So far, all I've seen is that you're not wired above the belt.'

'You've seen enough.'

Nick pushed his other arm into his shirt. McDonnell reached for his belt buckle. Nick stepped back as if he'd been scalded.

'Keep your hands off!'

McDonnell stared at him. 'You really do fancy yourself, don't you? If you'd prefer a strip search I'll call my man in. But you wouldn't prefer that, believe me.'

They stared at each other.

'Drop your trousers,' said McDonnell softly. 'You can keep your underpants on, if you're wearing any.'

'Of course I'm...'

Nick glowered at him. McDonnell showed the faintest smile. He said, 'As the Chinese Grandma said – don't get cocky now!'

He remained a yard in front of Nick and waited. Nick exhaled. Then he undid the belt to his trousers and let them drop.

'Kick 'em off.'

Nick coloured. Before he could pull the trousers off, he had to stoop to remove his shoes. He did so, then removed his trousers. In shirt, underpants and socks he felt more naked than if he'd been nude. McDonnell put his hand out for the pants. 'Might as well be sure.'

He looked inside the trousers, slipped his hand into each pocket, then marched across the room. He dropped the trousers onto Nick's jacket and started back. 'Now we can talk.'

'No.'

Nick marched toward his clothes but McDonnell blocked his path. 'You can put your trousers on. But the jacket stays.'

Nick shouldered past and picked up his pants.

McDonnell said, 'I didn't think you'd wear a mike in your pants, but you never know with a jacket.'

Nick pulled the trousers on. 'You watch too many movies.'

'Do I?' asked McDonnell thoughtfully. He picked up the jacket, took it across the room and rapped at the door. The key rattled and the door swung open. McDonnell handed Nick's jacket to the big security man. 'Look after this.'

The big man frowned. McDonnell closed the door.

Nick had returned to the desk to collect his shoes.

'No,' said McDonnell. 'Trousers, yes but shoes, no.'

Nick leant against his desk and pulled on a shoe. McDonnell opened his mouth, but it wasn't worth the fight. Nick put on the other shoe.

McDonnell said, 'You were saying?'

Nick didn't reply.

McDonnell strode past Nick and looked out the window. The

sun glinted on his expensive hair. He said, 'Purely out of interest, Mr Chance, how did you find out about today's visit?'

Since Nick didn't know what McDonnell was talking about, he shrugged.

McDonnell asked, 'D'you have a mole in here?'

Nick shrugged again.

McDonnell sighed. 'Do you intend to say anything?'

'I came for a talk.'

McDonnell squinted at him from the window. He nodded through the glass as Nick strolled across. 'Well, there they are – though they can't hear you through this window.'

Nick looked down into the rear car park, where a visiting party was being escorted to three large grey cars. At each one stood a uniformed driver holding open a door. 'You came too late,' McDonnell whispered.

'Couldn't get a taxi.'

'Oh yes, taxis still hate coming here. For this visit we hired three cars a full day each – just to ferry those elegant backsides to and from the airport. Ten minutes walk.'

'Fifteen. I walked it.'

'Oh, you came by plane?' McDonnell looked impressed. Nick didn't correct him.

McDonnell said, 'You could have met our friends at the airport.' He snorted. 'But you wouldn't really want to talk to them, would you?' He watched the visitors climbing into the cars. 'You just want to threaten you might.'

'My idea of fun,' Nick muttered enigmatically.

The first car moved off. 'There go your EC Grant Coordinators,' said McDonnell with a satisfied smile. 'So sorry you won't get to meet them. That next car, the one with the face you recognised, is of course from the Ministry of Agriculture – including Mrs OTM herself.' He caught Nick's frown. 'The Over Thirty Months Scheme, as you ought to know.' He paused as the third car crept forward. 'And now the NGOs. Where would we be without them? Sweet. You noticed the gratitude on their honest black faces? Thank you, massa, for dat lovely food aid. Thank you, bass, from my starving people. Thank you for de fat brown envelope.' McDonnell's smile had soured. 'You really think you have something to tell those people? You think they'd be shocked?'

Nick hazarded a guess. 'Babette Hendry thought so. And you thought she might be right.'

McDonnell shrugged. 'She spoke for all of you, didn't she – your messenger?'

Nick shrugged. 'In a way.'

'A messenger shouldn't bring bad news.' McDonnell turned from the window. 'There goes the last car. You've missed them.'

'It was you I came to see.' Nick let the words hang.

McDonnell stared back. 'Come for a second bite? You have a nerve.'

Nick didn't know what was best to say.

'You think you'll get another half million pounds? You'll be lucky if you leave at all.' He pointed. 'You owe us.'

Nick tried not to react to the sum of money. He said, 'If it was worth half a million then...'

'Oh, in the scale of the overall contract – at that particular moment, yes. But now? No. Sorry. What's your position in this group?'

Nick shrugged again.

'What are you – anarchists? No one in a specified position? No one in authority, joint decisions all the way? Wouldn't surprise me. How many are there of you again?'

Nick countered: 'Why did you kill Babette?'

McDonnell stared at him thoughtfully. 'Any reason we shouldn't kill you?'

He returned to his desk and placed his hand on the telephone. 'Let's say I pick this up and call Security. That's who you asked for when you arrived – Derek Cranham. Why him?'

Nick moistened his lips. 'You did ask if you had a mole in here.'

McDonnell laughed. 'Don't give me that. He catches moles. You took a gamble asking for Cranham – he hates your people. He's... otherwise engaged today, but his colleague outside that door – remember him? I'm sure he'd be delighted to see to you. Shall I ask him in?'

Nick's throat was dry. 'I came to see you.'

'No, you didn't. You asked for Cranham.' McDonnell's eyes narrowed. 'That was the only name you knew, wasn't it? You used his name to get in. Let me tell you something, Mr Chance – you took a chance too many. You got half a million out of us. But you gave the papers back, we got the contracts signed, and now everything's tidy. Those people you've just seen leave – you think they want it blown apart? No. They want a peaceful life. If you've come with another piece of paper – a copy, is it? – I'll tell you what they'll say. They'll say 'It's too late for this. Sort it. Tidy up.' You know what that means? It means remove the evidence. Which as you know, we have done once. You returned the papers and we burned them. Now you appear. We should burn you.'

'Like you killed Babette?'

McDonnell pursed his lips. 'You want to hear me say that, don't you? Let me tell you something more interesting. You're in my office, the door's locked, you're on private property. If we kill you here – right here where you're standing, who outside will ever know? Yes, yes, some friend will say you came here – but we'll insist you never arrived. We'll show them the signing-in book.'

'I signed at the gate.'

McDonnell snorted. 'Oh, really? We can't alter it? Do grow up. You're on Tradefair territory – subject to Tradefair rules. Do you think anyone outside has any idea what happens here? D'you think they care? We pay our taxes. We have our books audited. End of story. What we do is our affair. We are the law here.'

'Not quite.' Nick's mind was racing. 'We could blow this scam of yours wide open.'

'No longer. Your price was high but, as you know, we did expect to get the money back. We'd still like it back, Mr Chance.' McDonnell smiled at him. 'Suppose we keep you here. Hold you to ransom, as it were?'

'I'm worth about two quid.'

McDonnell nodded. 'What should we do, then – kill you? That's the way you people think. For you, robbery, extortion – even blowing up an abattoir – is fair game. You take the moral ground, of course – you're the green activists, the holier-than-thou brigade – you can do anything. But we – the hardworking businessmen, the people who supply you with your goods, who finance your cushy lifestyle, who put clothes on your backs and food in your overfed spoilt mouths – the people who make it possible for you to scrounge off the state and lie around dreaming up daft ideas – we must do what you say. We can't farm animals and feed the world. We can't run profitable businesses. And Christ, if you ever get a sniff that once in a while we might cream off a little extra profit for ourselves – oh what a pious hullabaloo! I told your precious Miss Hendry this: do you think it matters if we're paid twice? D'you think the Grant Commissioners and Min of Ag would care if they found they were both paying the same subsidy? D'you think they'd want the administrative inconvenience of sorting it out? No, we dump food in starving African mouths, so they're happy. Would you sanctimonious evangelists rather we destroyed the EC food mountain than give it to starving peasants? You think we should destroy it, rather than let a few of us make a nice profit off the back? So what if we get paid twice? The food is still cheaper for Africans than you can buy in the shops.'

'Everyone a winner,' Nick said sarcastically.

McDonnell nodded. 'Everybody's a winner. Remember this also: those pathetic starving natives in Wogga-Wogga Land – they don't pay twice. They don't pay for the food at all. So don't go bleeding heart on me. No one pays twice.'

'Two people pay once.'

'The European Community and the Overseas Aid Department. It isn't real money.'

Nick shook his head. 'That's what a car thief says: it isn't real money – it comes from insurance companies.'

'You think your taxes would be one jot lower if we didn't work this little scam? You think Tradefair is the only one? Everyone's at it – charities, NGOs—'

'What the hell is an NGO?'

'Oh, for goodness sake! You've heard of a quango? That's a quasi autonomous NGO, right? NGO means Non-Governmental Organisation – a body that isn't elected, isn't political, supposedly, and doesn't have to justify itself by making anything so sordid as a commercial profit. A high-minded, self-perpetuating, self-monitoring user of other people's cash. Untouchable. Unimpeachable. Isn't that a beautiful conceit? You know something? Tradefair is damn nearly an NGO itself. We're practically a charity!'

Nick snorted. 'Who do you help, apart from yourselves?'

'We put food in millions of starving mouths.'

'And cream off a huge profit.'

'Profit is not a dirty word – it's what makes business tick. Yes, we "cream" some off – so what? If your baby was dying and I gave you a bottle of free milk, would you come back and demand the cream? No, you'd be grateful for what you'd got. That's how the world works – and it's what your kind don't realise. Profit is the lifeblood. Profit is the oil that makes things happen. All over Europe. All over the world. Half the world economy relies on people creaming a little off the top. If we can't get our share of cream, you don't get milk.'

Through the bright window behind him a light aircraft rose above the nearby buildings. It must have been taking off from the airport.

Nick said, 'That's your justification for cheating ordinary people out of millions of pounds? That's what made you kill Babette?'

The aircraft disappeared. McDonnell sighed. 'We didn't kill your messenger – though I don't pretend the thought did not occur to us. But we didn't kill her. We thought you did.'

'Me?'

'Your organisation. The girl was carrying half a million pounds,

189

wasn't she? I know you people pretend to have high principles, but – excuse me – that's because most of you are too damn useless to earn a living. High principles! Ever notice how most of the fellows who invent high principles for the rest of us dream up those principles sitting on their backsides doing nothing all day? Don't talk to me about principles.'

Nick had been staring at the floor. 'You think… my organisation killed her for the cash?'

'Why not?' McDonnell looked at him blandly. 'Isn't that why you are here? Look, Mr Chance – Nick – let's set our cards out on the table. A dollop of plain speaking. You came here to see Cranham because he was one of the few names you knew. Right? So point one: why here? How did you know he worked for Tradefair? He didn't tell you. Point two: why have you really come? Don't give me that "because people died" shit. There are two reasons I can see – though I'm an open minded man: if you've another, I'll listen. Why are you here?'

'What are your two guesses?'

McDonnell looked exasperated. 'For goodness sake! You've come to say something, so say it. Do you realise – no, you don't: you people know nothing about business – do you realise how lucky you are – how privileged – to have this time with me? I'm chief executive, I'm out of the country two days a week, my time is valuable. But Cranham's away and you've picked a day when the whole site is overrun with important visitors. My fellow board members have gone with them now, for lunch. Feed the starving! But my colleagues don't want me there because the negotiations are "too delicate". I like plain speaking – I'm an import-export man. I know the ins and outs of HM Customs, bills of lading, how to make a percentage at every turn, but today's meeting concerns "ethics" – your kind of shit – moral principles. So I'm left out. I'm no good at it. Well, spare me the waffle, Nick. Show me the bottom line.'

Nick tried to sound sympathetic. 'People forget you're the guy who runs the place.'

McDonnell wandered back to the window and stared out bitterly. 'God knows who runs it now.'

'The workers have taken over the factory.'

'The lunatics have taken over the asylum.' He turned from the window and stared at Nick glumly, as if he at least was not his enemy. 'No one controls anything any more. It's all too big.' He snorted. 'Someone like me, head of Tradefair UK – I can't keep tabs on everything. I have to delegate. So I lose control. Don't misunderstand me—' He pointed his finger. 'I don't lose it to a rival. I just lose it. We all lose it. In a huge organisation like this, whatever anyone says gets watered down. We can only hope that some of it gets through. Authority – control – is spread so thin, God knows what happens. The organisation runs itself. It's autonomous.' He snorted again. 'We call it collective responsibility and pretend that we meant it to be like this.' He stared at Nick. 'Why are you here? To get more money out of us?'

He waited. Nick shook his head.

McDonnell shrugged. 'We have the documents now. No one can touch us. I'll tell you why I think you're here – one of two reasons. One: to expose us – you blackmailed us once and got away with half a million pounds, but you copied the documents and want to make them public. High principles, not money. Is that what it's about?'

'No.'

'I didn't think so. Then the second possibility gives me the first laugh I've had all day. You want the original half million pounds. Am I right? You never got it in the first place, did you, Nick?'

'No.'

McDonnell smirked. 'I guessed as much. What happened that day – did Miss Hendry disappear, or just pretend we never paid?'

Nick gave a half smile back. 'Pretend? You really paid her?'

McDonnell chortled to himself. 'I knew it. The bitch screwed all of us.'

The room seemed close and stuffy. Nick took a breath. 'Or someone else did.'

'I doubt it.' His eyes glinted as he studied Nick. 'All right. You're not wired, so you're not dangerous. Who knows? Perhaps you can fill in the odd gap.'

'It's worth a try.'

The first we knew of it was a little packet arrived in the post, addressed to Derek Cranham, Head of Security. And just in case Derek was tempted to try to hide the thing away, several members of the board received letters also – a short letter, each identical, each in an identical envelope, each telling the recipient to check with Cranham what he had received. There was an email too – again, one to each of those board members. Our email addresses aren't secret, but they're not openly available, shall we say? To have access to them meant the sender had more than a passing knowledge of our internal procedures.

So we could hardly ignore the little packet.

It contained a few photocopies but an accompanying letter made it clear the copies were extracted from larger documents held by the person who had signed the letter – a childish touch here: it was signed Nemesis. The papers were all internal Tradefair documents, and together they clearly mapped the progress of several large consignments of Food Aid – mainly frozen meat and meat products – sponsored, or paid for, by different NGOs, grant-making organisations and our own government. It was embarrassingly clear that each consignment had been sponsored by more than one body, and that Tradefair had been paid twice – indeed, in one case, thrice.

Let me make it clear: these were exceptional transactions. We don't get all our exports paid twice! But occasionally, with a little artful obfuscation, we can slip a sly one through the system. Bear in mind, please, that the various inspectorates are a bureaucratic nightmare – not only to honest traders but to the inspectorates themselves. The bodies are international, for a start, so not only do all documents have to be translated into several languages, the procedures have to accord with those in force in different countries. They also have to accord with the supranational rules of the EC and with whatever bizarre rules apply at the final destination. The paperwork is stultifyingly dull. One can hardly expect clerks to give undivided attention. As long as the documents match up in sets, and as long as the numbers within them balance, the weary clerks will let them through – especially when the documents come from a recognised institution like Tradefair, an institution which has been thoroughly audited in the past and found to be as honest as the day is long. Remember that with these food aid cargoes we are doing good works, so there is a presumption in our favour before we begin. Remember also that the EC has a permanent backlog of around a million tonnes of community beef in cold storage – they need to dump it somewhere, and they do not need some jumped-up clerk to get picky with the paperwork.

Any more than Tradefair needed this packet on Cranham's desk.

We received a telephone call at lunchtime – I received it actually. Naturally, I suppose, being Chief Executive, although Cranham expected it to come to him. He was all set up to trace the thing. But it came through on my mobile, from a mobile, and simply said that we had two days to pay half a million pounds. Half a million! I tried to call her bluff – yes, it was Miss Hendry, though at the time we didn't know her name – but she just rang off.

When was it? Around teatime, I think, she rang again. This time she subjected me to a short harangue on the iniquities of our trade – a rather garbled tirade about forcing meat down the throats of naturally vegetarian natives, with the dubious claim that money we earned slaughtering animals was no better than that earned from slaughtering people in war. I didn't really follow her, to be frank, but

I raised an argument to keep her on the line long enough for Derek to trace the call. She said if we didn't come up with the money she would be perfectly happy – indeed, she would prefer – to expose us to the press. She'd prefer to close us down. Harangue, harangue, put down the phone.

Derek had her number now, but it was no help. When he rang Vodaphone they confirmed that the call had come from a stolen mobile.

What to do? The initiative was with her. The following morning when she called (one day left!) it was to explain how affordable half a million was, set against the huge profits we had made on the deal. Which was true, but hardly the point.

On her next call – that afternoon – she dropped a bombshell: she no longer wanted the money; the group had decided there was more mileage in exposing our wickedness and closing us down. The campaign wouldn't stop with us, she said, but would continue until the whole crooked structure of rigged food aid had collapsed. Not true – she was over-dramatising – but if her group had gone to the press there would have been a huge international brouhaha, and Tradefair would have been a casualty. We couldn't let her do that. Suddenly I had to switch from negotiating down her demand for half a million pounds to virtually pleading with her to take it. She, of course, became reluctant: the group might have taken the half million pounds originally, she said – indeed, they might conceivably still be persuadable – but they'd changed their mind. Besides, she said, from what I had been saying, she'd assumed we'd been unable to raise half a million in cash. We'd done it, I said. We were ready to give it her.

Was there nothing she could do?

She'd think about it, she said tersely, putting down the phone.

I had to point out to my colleagues that she hadn't closed the door. I said, I've been a trader all my life – I can read the signs. She'll call us back tonight for a higher price. We either shift the deadline or start raising some more cash. Do you know – that was the only time this year I've been in a position of true leadership. Just for once they needed me. Just for once the problem would not solve itself. Just for once those cautious PC literate accountants needed someone who could actually take a decision.

She rang. As I'd predicted. And she rang to deal.

'£100,000 more,' she said. 'Separately for me alone.'

'How d'you want it paid?'

No, I didn't argue. To tell the truth, a hundred thousand was a lot less than I'd thought she'd want. Half a million was a lot of money, but set against the trading value of the company was just a dent in our bottom line. A hundred thousand was petty cash. And it made her personally involved. 'Separately for me alone' – music to my ears. Get this absolutely clear: she had persuaded them to take the half million so she could skim off an extra hundred thou off the top. For herself. Excellent. Until that reassuring flash of greed there had always been the risk that these high-minded activists really would prefer to forsake the money and bring us down. But now we had someone in their camp with a personal stake in ensuring the financial deal went through. She'd want her money. We'd get our documents back.

We arranged to meet on neutral ground – three people either side – confirm the packages, go our separate ways. She'd choose the venue – but: she'd only tell us it the following morning. She was only being professional. She wanted the deal to go through.

As you can imagine, the following morning saw us here in the office bright and early, practically on a war footing – several board members, your friend Cranham and his team. The money was placed in a soft black carry-all. You'd be surprised how little room it took: half a million – six hundred pounds actually – quite literally a small fortune. For many people a sum like that would allow them to never work again. A lifetime in a single black leatherette bag. Right here, sitting on my desk, shapeless, a sleeping dog. You could almost see it breathe.

We glanced at it, we wandered round the desk, but no one wanted to take ownership, as it were. No one wanted to be responsible – except me. No, that's not fair – Derek Cranham did: he'd have been prepared to run the project. Like me, he'd have made sure the exchange was done properly. He'd have handled half a million pounds as lightly as if it had been soiled laundry. But the others? No. Given the choice, they'd have preferred not to have been in the room, not to have been involved. We were about to give away half a million pounds. We were hoping to get the documents. In – what? – a half minute ceremony, one of us would go alone to an as yet unnamed place to meet whoever was appointed by the other side, and in those few seconds the two representatives would each glance inside a packet and take a decision upon which Tradefair's whole future hung. A big moment. And in this room that morning I smelt my colleague's fear.

Well, I may not have much of a role left in this company but, like the figurehead on a sailing ship, I can lead.

The call came agonisingly late – about ten o'clock: Miss Hendry again, though at that time we still didn't know her name. We never did until she died.

'Nemesis,' she said, as if it were a codeword. 'You have the money?'

'Two packets, as we agreed.'

'Come to your other place at Staines.'

'Knowle Green?'

'Use your company car – the Jaguar.' She even knew the car I drove. 'Be there by eleven o'clock.'

'That's pushing it. The traffic—'

'Leave your mobile on.'

That was the clue, and Cranham spotted it. 'It's a run-around,' he said. 'They want us on the road before telling us where we're going. Once we're out, she'll switch directions.'

He was right, of course – though he hadn't spotted the significance of west London, Knowle Green. Staines is convenient for the M4 – the fastest route to Bristol.

It took us an hour to get across town, and she phoned twice to check our progress. She had insisted there be only three of us – three from our side, three from hers – and I went with Cranham and his man Haydon. I let Haydon drive. Sure enough, once we were on the M4 but before Exit Three, she said we could forget about Knowle Green and head instead for the Heston service station.

'Going west,' she said. 'Stay in the car park.'

'How will we recognise you?'

'We'll come to you.'

I was keeping my mobile free of calls, but Derek was on his immediately with the change of venue. He had two more men in a following car, you see. He had them overtake.

Heston is a rather dull, untidy service station, not unduly large. When we rolled in with the Jaguar we were an easy mark. I had Haydon park it to one side, and I deliberately ignored our other security car, which Derek had told to take up a position near the exit. We sat and waited.

Have you ever sat in a crowded place waiting for someone you have never met? It's a curious feeling. All these people milling about – any one of whom could be the one. Not those harassed couples with young kids. Not those old people. Nor those teenagers, surely – sloppily dressed, aimless, too loud. Not those – yes, oh my God, yes – this person rapping at the side window – this menacing Hell's Angel in black leather. This hulk who asks, 'Which one of you is McDonnell?'

'I am.'

'Out. Only you. The other two stay in the car.'

Derek Cranham speaks: 'No, we all come. Three of you, three of us. That's the deal.'

'Sorry, you two sit and watch. Like we do.'

The hulk indicates another one, standing by two bikes. I ask, 'Where's the woman?'

'Over there.'

He points away from us, to our left, across the ranks of warm parked cars, to where someone – yes, we see her: that's her, surely? – that unexpectedly glamorous creature leaning against a little hatch-back, a head scarf hiding her hair. Dark sunglasses, smart suit. She stands with a black briefcase across her thighs.

No one is in her car.

The hulk says, 'You've got the money.' He says it flatly. It is not a question. I wonder whether he knows the price went up a hundred thousand, and that she asked for the extra to be in a separate packet. No way he did.

'Take it across to her.'

'Are the papers in her briefcase?'

'Don't worry – she'll show you. We all stay here. It's like, she shows you hers, you show her yours.'

Cranham shifted in his seat. I believe I've already told you that Cranham doesn't forgive easily. Between the seat and the door he had a hand-gun, and I tried to forget that it was there. Cranham leant out the window: 'Tell your biker friend to come here.'

'Why?'

'We're stuck in the car. He's free. If Mr McDonnell comes out, it's two of you to our one.'

I said, 'It's my call. I'm going across to her. Stay here.'

The hulk said, 'You two stay in the car. We'll stay with the bikes.'

I didn't want Cranham to get riled. By now I had opened the door. I said, 'It's between her and me.' I got out the car.

'Don't get smart because she's a woman.'

I felt good in the open. 'If she has the documents, she gets paid. Otherwise she doesn't.'

'Enjoy.'

I heaved the hold-all out of the car and started across the busy car park. The bag was bulky and surprisingly heavy, as if it had been filled with cans of beans. Six hundred thousand is several reams of paper. They're heavy. I felt sunshine on my head. And I felt an unex-pected sense of freedom – a kind of power. All these people on their little journeys, scurrying between cars and the service station, think-ing about ice creams and lavatories and cups of tea. No one gave me a second glance. Behind my back as I picked between them I was watched by Cranham, Haydon and the two bikers. Directly in front, leaning against that little hatchback, the girl smiled briefly and

196

shifted her feet. She was worth a second glance. Among the harassed travellers she was as cool as a model on a shoot. She had a model's stance. What she really looked like was hard to tell, but the head scarf, sunglasses and smart suit – not to mention that tantalising briefcase – gave her a timeless look. She had class.

'Mr McDonnell, I presume?'

I smiled. 'Sorry, I can't remember your name.'

She ignored that and said, 'Nice to put a face to the voice. Let's get inside.'

I paused a moment to make sure Cranham's second car could see us. They needed to know exactly which car was hers. She asked, 'Frightened? Such a big boy, too. Why don't you sit behind the wheel? I'll keep the key.'

'Fair enough.'

She opened the door. I peered inside and got in. She walked round the car. I – well, I'll admit to you – I had a frisson of excitement: she and I alone in the car with half a million pounds. A glamorous girl. I could smell her perfume in the car. I still couldn't tell exactly what she looked like, but it was a safe bet that she was the best looker in the car park.

She slid in beside me and closed the door.

'Swops?'

We exchanged bags. Being behind the wheel I was cramped, but she had room to open the hold-all and peep inside. 'I'll have to count it.'

'While I check these documents.'

'The brown paper parcel,' she said. 'I assume that's for me?'

'A hundred thousand. I assume you'll give it all to the Green Party?'

She put the hold-all on the floor, rested the parcel on her lap and slit the top. 'I love brown paper packages.'

The notes had been banded by the bank, two thousand in a band. She rifled through a couple of packs, then counted the rest in bulk. It didn't take long. She had only to count to fifty, and we hadn't cheated. Her money was there.

I began to leaf through the documents. She had itemised what they had when she phoned, and just as we hadn't held back on the money, I didn't expect her to hold back any documents – not those she had told me about: our worry was there might be more. Certainly if I had been in their shoes I'd have sold the bulk for the initial ransom but held a couple of plums back for a second call. We didn't think she'd done that, but we couldn't be sure. There was no way to know. I could hardly ask her as we sat cosily in the car. We'd have to wait. We didn't like it, but had no choice.

I checked the documents. She counted her money. She slid the brown packet into a plastic carrier and hid it under her seat. It took her longer to count the half million.

'Can I keep the hold-all?' she asked sweetly.

'Cheapskate.'

I'm sure that if I could have seen through her mirror shades I'd have seen her eyes twinkle. I would have liked to have seen that. It was ridiculous: here was a girl calmly stinging me for six hundred thou, and I had the hots for her. I looked down at the hold-all and saw her knees below her skirt. I glanced at her jacket buttons. She shook her head.

'You're not concentrating.'

'Yes, I am.' I inhaled her perfume.

'You're happy with the documents?'

'I don't think "happy" is the word I'd use.'

She leant towards me. 'We aim to give satisfaction. It's all there.'

'What happens next?'

'Good question. We can't stay in this car all day – people will talk. Do your men know about my own hundred thousand pounds?'

'They do.'

'Are they going to tell my colleagues?'

'They wouldn't tell them the time of day. No, don't worry, I told them not to.'

'Good. Well. Time we all went home.' She smiled at me. 'Goodbye.'

As I say, it sounds ridiculous but I almost kissed her. Instead, I climbed out of her car and returned to mine. Cranham and Haydon were still in it and the Hell's Angel stood outside. He nodded. 'All done?'

'You can go now.'

I wanted him to go. Cranham probably had that highly illegal pistol in his hand. Now I'd returned with the documents he'd want to get the money. I didn't want a fracas in the car park.

'OK, Haydon, ' I said. 'Let's be moving.' I opened the rear door.

But as Haydon switched on the engine the biker slammed my door shut. 'Wait,' he snapped. 'We want a couple of minutes start.'

A faint sweat broke on my brow. Cranham was losing patience. He had the gun.

He growled, 'What's going on?'

He wasn't even looking at the biker.

The other man was heading for the hatchback. He crossed with Miss Hendry striding towards him, hauling the heavy black hold-all, almost dragging it along the ground. He grabbed it from her and turned back to his bike.

Cranham shouted, 'Mr McDonnell, get in the car!'

He pushed his door open.

The biker started running and I shouted, 'Derek, not in the car park!'

But he had jumped out and as he rushed after the biker I squinted over the car roof to make sure he didn't have the pistol in his hand. Thank God! He caught the biker. As I dithered by the car, Haydon was also out across the tarmac. I saw the biker slam two low blows to Cranham's body, then turn and run. Haydon lumbered after. But the biker easily outran him. To tell the truth, I think my mother would have outrun him. Haydon is big – perhaps he's too big, he carries excess weight – or perhaps his bravery didn't match his size, but the bikers jumped on their bikes.

Cranham ran for the car.

'In the back,' he panted. 'We're going after them.'

As we clambered in I heard the motorbikes roar. We jolted forward. Cranham swore. He tried to hurtle in pursuit but was impeded by ordinary, slower cars manoeuvring in and out of parking spaces. I saw Haydon step in front of us to be picked up. I saw his startled face as we shot past.

Cranham threw me something hard and compact in the back. I recoiled. I couldn't fire a pistol in a public car park. Nor on the motorway.

'Get through to Dirkin on the phone.'

It was his mobile he'd thrown me.

'Tell Dirkin to forget the hatchback and chase the bikers.'

I keyed the 'recall' button.

As the number zipped through, Cranham yelled, 'What about the girl?'

'Later. Get the money. Ah, Dirkin?'

But Dirkin had seen what had happened and was already on the trail. Except he was only a hundred yards in front of us, and the two bikers were barely in sight.

'We'll lose them,' Cranham snarled.

'Go faster,' I commanded. As if he could.

I checked with Dirkin. He remained in front of us as we dashed down the motorway, but the chance of his catching them was infinitesimal. His was a faster car than ours, but against a couple of 750 cc machines our only hope was that they crashed.

'Or the police stop 'em for speeding,' I quipped.

'They'd never catch the motorbikes. They'll take us instead.'

'Get your foot down.'

I imagined thirty thousand twenty-pound notes fluttering

through the air.

'We've got the documents, ' I muttered.

'That's definite?'

'Oh, yes. They must have known that we'd chase them. They're not stupid. We can't expect them to make it easy for us.'

'You going soft on them?'

I snorted – though in a curious way I was. I admired the audacity – *her* audacity – I admired the way she had chatted so coolly in the hatchback. I admired the way an attractive woman took command.

We ground on, top speed, foot to the floor and engine roaring – but we had no hope of catching motorbikes. Then Dirkin spluttered through the mobile. I jolted forward in my seat as Cranham braked. We slewed across the motorway, screeched into the slowest lane, and the car crunched to a halt on the hard shoulder.

'What's up?' I hadn't been looking.

'Dirkin's car.'

Cranham was already scrambling out. Dirkin's car had stopped behind us. When I got out Cranham was shouting at his two men. We had passed beneath a footbridge and Dirkin was pointing up. On the far side, still above the motorway, the bikers were running across with the bag.

But the bridge was a hundred yards back and by the time we reached the first step up they were coming down the other side. Cranham charged up our steps like a madman. We followed. I was last onto the bridge, but even as the other three rushed across I could see it was pointless. At the foot of the steps the other side was a car. The bikers jumped in and it pulled away. By the time I was on the bridge the escaping car had started back to London. We stood on the gantry and watched it go. Then, slowly, we returned to the out-of-town side of the motorway.

We had the papers – each of which had been original. If they had been copies we could have refuted them, called them irritating forgeries. But as you know, your people had our original papers with the actual ink – and probably our fingerprints. We had to get them back. The rules of the game were that to get them back we had to pay five hundred thousand pounds. Six hundred, in the end. We'd get the papers, you'd get the money – game over, as you might say. We played the game, stuck to the rules. But once we had the documents, there was nothing to stop us trying to get our money back. We were not bound by the rules of good sportsmanship. You had cheated in order to start the game, so we could cheat to end it. Half a million was worth a chase, wasn't it? Two hours wasted in a fast car.

Wasted: yes, it was wasted – in that we lost the money. You got away. We were sad about that – annoyed – but in the end, you know, half a million is not an awful lot. And, as I have freely admitted, I did find something admirable in the way your delectable Miss Hendry managed the scam. She'd have known that we wouldn't stand by and watch her team drive away. She must have known that we would chase – indeed, she did know, which is why she had another car waiting beside the footbridge on the other side of the motorway. Yes, she knew we'd chase, but… only for so long, only so far. Not to the ends of the earth.

20. I WONDER IF I CARE AS MUCH

(As I Did Before)

WHEN HOMER HEAVED the PA speaker onto his shoulder he looked like Desperate Dan shifting the stove. His knees buckled less from the weight than from the sheer awkwardness of keeping the thing balanced. He tottered across the yard, stooped, then slid the box into the back of the van. Tiger applauded. He and the others were watching because Homer always insisted he move the speakers alone. He liked the chalenge of it. He knew that they knew that each huge box was almost empty – just a speaker and a lot of air – but the trick looked awesome.

'Staggering,' Tiger commented.

Homer grinned, flexed his shoulders and strolled to the other case. Tiger jumped up on the trailer to guide it in. The two speaker cases were always lain along the floor, filling it almost, with the amp wedged in alongside and the rest of the gear on top.

'Won't even need this stuff,' Steve said.

They were behaving nonchalantly, as if gigs like Glastonbury came every week, as if playing to an audience of a hundred thousand – and millions more on TV and radio – was a regular part of their performing life. The fact that the organiser's instructions had itemised the far superior PA which would be made available at the festival – the fact that they were given instructions at all – didn't dissuade them from loading their usual gear, just in case. To turn up at a gig carrying nothing more than their instruments would be like arriving naked. They had to have their own power amp and speakers. Steve took his toolkit, Randi her spare mike, and Tiger suggested they bring lights. He was joking, of course – or he hoped he was, given the feebleness of their lamps – and once he had finished on the trailer he jumped down to loiter by Cleo's drum kit like a Russian sentry.

Cleo was on the phone.

Outwardly, Nick was as light-hearted as the others but although he tried to josh with them his thoughts kept returning to his trip to Tradefair the previous day, and to what Michael McDonnell had revealed. The picture he had painted of Babette contrasted sharply with Nick's own – in fact, each of the sketches people drew showed Babette's face in a different light. Every picture told a different story.

'Hey, Stevie,' called Tiger. 'Do we get a private dressing room or do I just have to muck in with Mick Jagger again?'

'Dream on!'

'Because listen, if it helps, I could squeeze in with the New Spice Girls.'

'Showing your age, Tiger.'

'I'd show 'em more than that.'

'Nothing they haven't seen before.' Steve pointed at the truck. 'There's your dressing room.'

McDonnell had seemed convinced Babette set the scam up. According to his version, she wasn't a pawn in some wider game plan; she had planned it, led it and seen the jaunt through. McDonnell didn't see her as a high-minded activist. He saw her – or he painted her – as being prepared to skim a hundred thousand off the top. Nick couldn't buy that: he knew Babette too well. McDonnell had spoken to her on the phone and had met her only once – in highly charged circumstances – so his view would be coloured. He hadn't known the girl Nick had known.

'Here comes Cleo. Thought she was snacking that phone.'

OK: Nick hadn't known Babette in recent years. Three years at college, two more since then – but their last two days together proved that she was the same girl she had always been. Nothing had changed.

Cleo grinned at them. 'They've given in.'

'What?'

'Yes!'

Blue Delta had won the lottery.

Cleo opened her arms. 'We're on a main stage.'

'Which one?'

'Jazz and World Music.'

'Fantastic!'

'You're a genius, girl.'

Homer grinned broadly. He stretched out a hand and she moved to it. As the group closed in on her, Randi said, 'Someone has to give that girl a kiss.'

Cleo glanced hopefully at Homer as he squeezed her hand, but it was Stevie Quin who kissed her cheek. Randi joined the threesome. Nick hung off with Tiger.

Jenny Morris had described Babette as a student radical who jettisoned her causes to earn a living with *Agenda*. Kieran suggested she might have been active in the ALF. Eamon Reeves had had an affair with her.

Cleo said, 'I was just the one they broke the news to.'

Homer laughed. 'Come on, girl – you badgered those people.'

Tiger said, 'Brilliant, Cleo, you are so brilliant.'

Steve was smiling warmly. 'I don't know how you do it.'

Cleo looked close to weeping. 'I didn't do anything – someone must have put in a word for us.'

'Your brother?'

She laughed. 'No way! I mean, he loves me dearly but he's not going to push his sister's group, is he? He's been loving this. I don't know, guys, I just don't know.'

Steve wanted to be absolutely sure: 'No buts, no maybes? We're not in the Dance Tent—'

Tiger interrupted, laughing: 'We're not on the Avalon, with freaks and weirdoes?'

'No way,' Cleo laughed back.

Steve shook his head. 'We're on a main stage.'

'You said it.'

'And not at three in the morning?'

'No one plays at three in the morning. Though...' She grinned. 'They did ask if we might be playing Agenda For Love – I mean, we don't have to, they said...'

'You think *Agenda* did this?'

'Well, they are our sponsor.'

Steve chuckled incredulously. 'But they can't push Paul Charles – he's immovable.'

Homer was rambling: 'It's the *Agenda* bender! Man, there's pushing and pushing. Wheels within wheels. Wheels on fire, right? A quiet word to Mr Charles from a friend who's been there for him. That's what makes the wheels turn, baby. Turn, turn, turn.'

'Wow,' Steve said with a whistle. 'We're in *Agenda*'s pocket now?'

Homer hooted. 'No way, no pockets, man! It's Cleo. She showed that Mr Charles some class.'

Cleo shrugged. 'Maybe it was down to *Agenda*.'

'No,' said Steve firmly. 'They may have influenced it, but you did the work, Cleo. You moved us from an also-ran to a main contender. That's... fantastic – really. I think you should be our manager.' He continued over her laugh. 'I'm serious. I'm no good at this job – I'm not a manager. I play keyboard.'

'And the Internet,' said Tiger. 'Multi-talented.'

Steve smiled. 'Yeah, social secretary. Seriously – listen now, guys. I have a proposition.' He waited for the inevitable hoot from Tiger before continuing: 'I think Cleo should be our boss.'

'Boss!' she laughed.

Homer knelt at her feet. 'Man, I second that!'

Cleo touched his head. 'Come on, guys, let's just do the show.'

Homer leapt up. 'Yes, ma'am! That's right. Anything you say, ma'am. You hear that, people? She says, let's do this show!'

Something about going to London makes provincial men wear ties. They don't feel they can slob about the city as if at home. Yet the fact that they are not comfortable makes their clothes sit uneasily, as if bought specially for the occasion, ready made. Londoners can spot them – folks from the sticks, wearing their best. Londoners are more casual: businessmen move easily in suits. People say that in London you can wear anything, there are no rules. But there are. Those provincials in last year's fashions – no-time fashions, fashions that never were – wrong colours, wrong smelling perfume, wrong shoes. Women in blue suits or floral dresses, hair sprayed rigidly into place. Men in tweed jackets with curious pockets stuck on as an after-thought. Children who gawp. People who consult the price guide to the tube. People who unfold a map in the streets and stand frowning at it, embarrassed, thinking that to consult a map in public proves they don't belong, while Londoners swear by their own map book, the *A to Z*, without which any journey beyond their own neighbour-hood is unthinkable.

Zane and Shiel have on dark suits. In their white shirts and poly-ester ties they look like Mormons – visiting missionaries to the town. Their shoes sparkle and each inevitable blemish they pick up in the crowded streets stands out as a reproach, a slur on the fine leather worked hard for that shine. The two men have designed their wardrobe on the Gerry Adams style of public dressing – sombre suits and erect stance, as deliberately deceptive as the black garb of Hell'n'Damnation itinerant preachers who once stalked the old Wild West. Zane is even wearing spectacles. Horn rimmed.

But sitting in easy chairs beside the office window they still look out of place. Jenny Morris fetches coffee, and as a sign of respect for their new-found status she transfers the coffee, out of sight, from plastic cups dispensed from the machine to the china ones reserved for guests. Shiel eyes his as if it might be drugged.

She says, 'It's from Africa,' as if that might make machine-made coffee taste good.

Since Shiel still doesn't pick his up, Zane takes his lead and the two men sit piously, as if vended coffee is a grave insult to their religion. They are in a small private room away from the eyes and ears of other journalists, but in the additional company of a pale man in an ancient cardigan who Jenny has introduced as Peter Lafferty from Editorial. They are suspicious of him. They know Jenny, in that she is a columnist and they know her name, but at this delicate stage they view any newcomer with caution.

Zane stares at Lafferty. 'This must be off the record.'

'Oh, yes,' he says. 'Totally confidential. Nothing to fear.'

Shiel grunts. 'Can you really talk confidentially with a journalist?'

'Happens all the time,' says Lafferty. 'Which one's the sugar, Jenny?'

She moves a cup. 'Peter's here because this is such an important story.' She smiles encouragingly. 'With any luck, we can put you on the front page.'

Lafferty stirs. 'But we have to know your story's genuine. Now, I understand that you have documents?'

Zane nods.

'Brought them with you?'

Zane bought a briefcase especially. It lies beside his feet, shiny as his shoes. He says, 'Once we show the documents, you've got the story.'

'And you've lost your bargaining counter? Don't worry, that's how the game has to be played. The only way a punter proves a story is to show it.' He shrugs. 'We don't cheat.'

'This is the *Guardian*,' Jenny says.

Zane shifts in his chair. 'Well, we brought the documents,' he says. It seems wrong to simply hand them over, as if acquiring the papers has taken no more effort than taking them out of a drawer. But he puts the briefcase on the table. Lafferty looks at him. Zane opens it.

Lafferty takes the sheaf of papers and sits back with a sniff. 'Photocopies.'

'They're the genuine article,' Shiel tells him.

There is a short silence as Lafferty flicks through the documents. Jenny breaks it. 'These are the documents they killed Babette for?'

Zane says, 'She challenged corporate Britain. To even question Big Business makes you its enemy.'

'Not just in Britain,' Shiel adds. 'World-wide capitalism ignores the law. These huge corporations are all-powerful. No one controls them or polices them – they set the rules.'

Lafferty buries his face over the papers.

Zane intones, 'From the slaughter of animals it's an easy step to slaughtering people. You know, of course, that the QMP group owns farms and abattoirs. They have clinics, vets and research labs. They run the whole show, cradle to grave – their vets help breed the animals, their farmers fatten them, their abattoirs slaughter them, their trading companies sell the meat. They sponsor MPs, journalists—'

'Not us!' Jenny says.

'Don't be so sure. Who funds your pro-Choice journalists?' Zane adjusts his spectacles. 'Remember, QMP invests in abortion clinics and private health as well. We're talking about an international corporation with a higher turnover than Britain's annual GDP.'

'Scotland's, maybe,' says Lafferty. 'Let's not exaggerate. There isn't much in these papers about QMP.'

'But they own Tradefair,' Zane responds. 'I tell you, QMP has the whole business covered, every step along the line.'

'They don't own Tradefair, they're affiliated.'

'It's all the same. They've got a stake in more businesses than – than the government.'

'Abortion clinics?' Lafferty thumbs the papers. 'Can't see that here.'

'They have some, though.'

Lafferty looks at him. 'That'd be interesting. Are your activists Pro-Life as well?'

Zane shrugs. 'We're talking animals today.'

'There've been several American-style attacks on British abortion clinics – similar to your attacks on abattoirs and the medical research lab. Haven't there?'

Zane turns on Jenny Morris: 'What've you told this man?'

She shows her hands. 'Peter has to be sure you're the real thing. You see, these documents are all very well, but we want a story. Like your attack on the Gilman Thompson lab – that's a story, one that puts you personally in the frame. It establishes you as environmental crusaders.'

Lafferty says, 'A stolen file is a leak story. Killing a research chemist is a scoop.'

Zane sniffs. Shiel asks, 'Is he dead then?'

'Hockendale? Yes. Died in hospital. Now, we have to be careful which way we present this. You know, any terrorist story can have two very different slants – depending on whether we write about the poor man who died or about your high moral purpose.'

'Poor man? He was experimenting on animals, murdering them, seeing how much pain they could stand before they died.'

Lafferty shrugs. 'One version. Of course, we could talk to his wife and family. He had children—'

Zane taps the table. 'There's more at stake here than one man's family. Our campaign concerns the whole of society – how we live.'

Shiel says, 'It's our mission to give the world a clean start to the new millennium.'

Lafferty nods. Jenny notes the phrase.

Zane says, 'We've exposed a multi-million pound fraud, international conspiracy.'

'Are you running a vendetta against QMP?'

'No way!' says Shiel.

Zane explains: 'We don't indulge in the politics of revenge. But it is true that QMP murdered one of our volunteers – you know, Babette Hendry?'

'You can prove that?'

Zane dismisses him irritably. 'That's not the point. We've come to you, the *Guardian*, because although you're still a part of the capitalist system you're the most sympathetic paper to our cause. Of course, if you think we should have gone to the *Independent*...'

He pauses expectantly, but Lafferty will not be drawn.

Jenny says, 'No, we're interested in these stories and in the material you've brought along – though as Peter says, it's the action that our readers will latch onto. The fraud stuff is all very well, but it's just big business, isn't it? It's what people expect. Our readers want a story. And you two are a story – you're actively engaged in the fight against animal exploitation. You've put your own lives on the line – after Babette Hendry, the first martyr. That's the kind of thing we want.' She smiles at Zane and holds his gaze. 'You could both become media stars.'

Zane shakes his head. 'We're not here for personal advancement.'

'Just as well,' remarks Peter Lafferty. 'We may run the story, but we can't afford large fees.'

'We are the *Guardian*,' Jenny apologises.

Shiel folds his arms. Zane takes a breath. 'We didn't take the risk of revealing ourselves to the media for monetary gain. What we want is sympathetic coverage – we want you to understand our point of view and give these stories the prominence they deserve.'

Shiel says, 'Otherwise we could try the *Independent*.'

Lafferty sighs. 'Forget the bloody *Independent*! Let's say we run the stories – can we use your names?'

'Of course not,' Zane snorts.

'Anonymous,' mutters Lafferty. 'Pictures then?'

'Afraid not.'

Lafferty turns to Jenny. 'Have we a shot of this Hendry girl?'

He looks enquiringly at the two men. Zane shakes his head and Jenny flushes. 'Well, actually, of course, I knew her. I mean, I have a photo – well, several, though whether they'd be suitable...'

'Personal shots?' asks Lafferty. 'Informal? Intimate?'

Her head shoots back. 'Babette was a friend. A dear friend.'

Lafferty says, 'OK, good, so we've got photographs. We can keep these documents?'

Zane glances at Shiel. Lafferty exhales. 'Well, they are only photocopies – so we'll keep them, right? You won't change your mind about being anonymous?'

'We can't.'

'Pity.' Lafferty smiles. 'Good looking pair of fellows. You'd have the right image for this story. A picture would really crown it – make you king.'

'Lead the police straight to our door.'

'We could make sure the story didn't say that you personally broke the law. I mean, it wasn't you personally who killed Doctor Hockendale. Was it?' he prompts meaningfully.

Zane pauses. 'It's not our policy to encourage the cult of person-alities—'

'We don't name names,' Shiel agrees.

Jenny sits forward. 'We could photograph you back-lit – you know, faces darkened?'

'Then the police ask you to show them the originals?' asks Shiel.

'We can always use actors,' says Lafferty. 'But give it some thought. If you want to make world headlines, then at some point you have to let us take pictures. You do want to be the stars of this story?'

They hesitate.

Jenny says, 'Babette Hendry is the star.'

'Well yes, she's dead – that does make it easier. Was she a good-looking girl?'

'Yes,' says Jenny stoutly.

'Good. For you two, then, we'll use code names. Any prefer-ences?'

Zane pauses. 'Zane,' he says. 'That can be my name.'

'Oh, right,' says Shiel. 'Um… I'll be Shiel.'

'Fine,' responds Lafferty. 'As unlikely a pair of names as anyone could dream up. We'll get to work then. Keep us posted with any progress. And no more of this 'try the *Independent*' nonsense! What d'you think, Jenny? We could bill Zane and Shiel as our Environmental Task Force.'

'I prefer eco-terrorists,' she says. 'We have to excite the readers – even frighten them – before we persuade them to take these two to their hearts.'

Zane smiles at Shiel. They are about to become part of the establishment.

21. C'MON EVERYBODY!

THE LAST TIME Nick came to Glastonbury it cost him £75 for a weekend ticket. Like thousands of others, he and some friends shared a tent and an inordinate quantity of beer. For two weeks before the festival and the whole of the weekend the summer rain dropped remorselessly, turning the Somerset meadows into acres of clinging mud. Their tent had been near the Dance Tent, and in the worst of the foul weather Nick and his mates had to choose between crouching under their own leaking canvas swilling beer, the Dance Tent disco thumping beside them, or braving the rain to hear live bands elsewhere. After squatting in the tent listening to the muffled sounds of Primal Scream and Death In Vegas, Nick opted for rain.

He'd been young enough to enjoy it.

This time he found it quietly exhilarating to drive down with Randi the second day, to park (relatively) easily in the performers' car park, meet up with the rest of Blue Delta and concentrate on the set-up – rather than mill around with a hundred thousand fans, wondering which unmissable band he had already missed. This year the sun was in summer mood and the 600 acre site wallowed in light. Music shimmered above the fields like a heat haze, and the smell of bonfires obliterated both the sweet smell of marijuana and the foul smell of chemical lavatories. Beyond the trucks and trailers in the performers' car park was a shifting mass of teeming people. The band playing nearest sounded like Radiohead. Wasn't it too early for them? Good music, though. And loud.

The Blue Delta Band strolled about the car park, trying not to strut. Steve and Cleo were talking with a Glastonbury technician – he looked like a technician but at Glastonbury, who knows? He could be anyone – the Festival's chief accountant or an old hippy from Status Quo. Homer was in a deeply technical discussion with a slender brown Rasta from a retro Trip Hop band, comparing sunglasses. Tiger was introducing Randi to a group that looked like and probably was Red Snapper, and from the way he was jigging up and down he'd had a sniff of something good. Nick hoped Randi didn't meet too many competitive bands, because the festival was a tempting place for musicians to make new alliances. Few other bands would have heard her sing – but by the end of the night she'd have sung to perhaps twenty thousand visitors and she might even have featured on worldwide TV.

Between the parked trucks Nick could see the edge of the huge crowd, the fans peering through to the enclosure, hoping to see someone famous. But at the moment there were only roadies, Glastonbury workers, contractors or members of smaller bands like his, new to the experience, unknown, free to walk in the light. Set apart from the crowd they felt like stars. But like the crowd, they too were starstruck: while wandering in this hallowed enclosure they might have a casual word – one professional to another – to a legendary name.

'Nick Chance. A word with you.'

Nick turned. He knew the face, but...

'I'll be introducing you tonight.'

Animal rights. Kieran, from the ALF.

'You'll not mind if I say we're sponsoring you?'

'You're giving us money?'

'Not directly.'

'Surprise. Then how come you'll introduce us? What will you say?'

Kieran grinned. 'Hardly a word. You know these audiences – impatient. They've got all weekend, but... I'll just say 'Let's have a big hand for Blue Delta', and I'll say 'We're all here for animal rights, aren't we?' – then I'll go. Blink your eyes and you'll not see me.'

'You're sponsoring?'

'I won't even mention the word. You are doing an animal rights number?'

'Speak to Steve – no, Cleo: she's managing us now.'

Kieran pulled a face. 'Ah. We fixed this earlier with Steve.'

'It's Cleo now. And she talked sponsorship with *A*genda.'

Kieran frowned and left.

Sponsorship was something Nick didn't have to think about. He wondered if Tiger and Randi were talking to Red Snapper or just their look-alikes. Maybe he could meet someone really famous.

They stood powered up in the draughty wings of the Jazz and World Stage, throats dry, stomachs hollow, listening – or not listening, since they couldn't concentrate – to Vanda telling the audience how proud Agenda was to introduce Blue Delta. She'd out-bidded Kieran. Around them, the long summer evening had faded and the night air felt cool. Beside them on the platform vast canvas side-sheets rippled like pond water. The wooden planking and open air gave the stage a nautical atmosphere and the muffled sound of the expectant audience was like an impending storm. Vanda's words were lost in the wind: something about Agenda's fabulous scientific discoveries, amino acids, extended life, enhanced sex drive, how to use a health drink as an oral cosmetic – far too many words, to the wrong people at the wrong time. Shortly before, as they waited backstage, she had given each of the band a small cup of the isotonic drink, Nliven, saying it was full of ginseng and minerals to help sustain them as they played. For their first worldwide event, she said, they needed energy and life.

Tiger slipped a tab in his.

The first number blasted out across the huge audience like a long-needed wake-up call. After the group before them – hypnotic but soporific – the screaming brass and reed of Blue Delta knocked the audience on their heels. The enhanced PA of the festival stage amplified the opening clarion louder than the band had ever been heard before. Tiger's strident horn melted around Nick's raucous sax, Homer's guitar sung like a startled bird above Quinnie's chords, and Cleo's drums sounded as drums can only sound when live – the motor driving the band. For these first few frantic minutes Randi stayed out of sight off stage. The huge standing throng, lulled by the worthy act before, began to sway – arms raised, feet trampling on the grass. Passers-by at the edges of the crowd moved closer, drawn to this immediate sound rather than to the vaguer promise of a farther stage. As the crowd swelled, the band segued effortlessly from their opening into the jerkier rhythms of 'Rip It Up' – Cleo, Tiger and Nick pounding the triplets of the underbeat, Quinnie on the tune and Homer decorating the melody. Blue Delta's was such a heavily syncopated version that half the audience would have struggled to name the tune. But to that rhythm they could not stand still. The band had placed these two blinding numbers at the start so they'd grip the audience and not let go – and standing above them on the stage, looking out across that undulating mass, each musician knew that their programming had worked.

In the less packed areas of the crowd people were dancing. The whole mass was moving. Down at one side, near the stage, there were some idiots who had presumably had too much to drink (hadn't everybody?) starting a fight. They were trying to force their way forward towards the stage, but at the front the crowd was at its most dense, and in any case the final, tiny corridor between fans and stage was guarded by Glastonbury security and volunteers from the ALF, granted this minor role to compensate them for not introducing the band. Their boys would enjoy a strop.

As the band hit the climax the crowd erupted in applause. The huge cheer – from a larger audience than Blue Delta had ever played – seemed to echo from the darkened sky. The group staggered across stage, gasping for breath, acknowledging cheers. Tiger and Nick grabbed plastic cups of tangy Nliven and eased their throats. They drank quickly. They mustn't sag. Steve Quin had already begun the slow measured intro to 'What's Love Got To Do With It?' and the two wind players were needed for the low sobbing sustained notes that gave the number its haunting feel. They played the whole riff twice – once to establish the change of tempo, once for Randi to make her entrance. She was dressed in shredded black, her short blonde hair sprayed to an eerie near-white sheen. Fragile, slender, she stood over the shortened mike and sheltered the mesh cage like a dying spliff on a windy night. For six slow bars at front stage she stood unmoving before the backbeat. Then she begun to sing. As she sighed the words she made them convey a new, anguished message and her huddled body projected pain. While she sang, the band moaned restlessly beneath her. Homer's guitar echoed her words. When the instruments finally took over they wailed like bloodhounds at their mothers' grave. But Cleo's drumbeat drove them forward. The audience knew that this mournful melody was about to burst from its chains and soar above them into the night. Some of the older hands expected the old jazzband ruse of a sudden break into double time, but this was not a night for cliché. When Randi came back in they found the mood had changed – but not to the easy freedom of double time: instead she slammed into the lyric with awesome defiance, twisting words that never before had much significance and ramming them into the face of every man she'd known.

What had love got to do with it?

The crowd roared their support. During the instrumental section, Nick noticed further disturbance in the crowd, but even drunks must realise that this was not the time. He watched the audience as Randi took a curiously modest bow: there did seem to be a small phalanx of trouble makers down there but they were a spit in the ocean of riotous approval. Cleo hit a flashy roll and the band went straight into their jauntier version of 'Three O'clock Thrill'. Randi sung this with unexpected humour, ludicrously emphasised, tongue in cheek – fairly true to the original words, except that a girl called Jill became a boy called Bill. This was light relief before her next raunchier number. But it was also a better opportunity for the aggressive group in the crowd to stir up trouble. Nick peered into the darkness – what was their problem?

By now, most of the security men had made their way to that side of the crowd and seemed not so much fighting them as trying to hold them back. Nick didn't want to watch – he'd lose concentration – though for a moment he saw, or thought he saw, a face he recognised. It couldn't be, surely? He made himself look away, staring out above the bobbing crowd to let the tiny disturbance regain proportion. He glanced back, but this time he couldn't see the unexpected big man. For a moment he could have sworn he'd seen Haydon, the Tradefair geek.

Tiger nudged him – sharply – to bring him back on time. 'Three O'clock Thrill' was a deceptively simple number but it depended not only on Randi's over-the-top mugging of the lyric but on intricate clowning from Tiger and Nick. He had to follow the trumpet. Tiger rolled his eyes at him – it was seldom Nick who had to be brought back in line. Nick realised that those few seconds of lost concentration had taken him off the boil, and he had to work now to bring back the heat. But he mustn't force it. He had to float and sail around Tiger's trumpet like an angry bee. He blew too hard and squeaked.

Nick was beginning to sweat. For one panicky moment he realised that he was on the biggest stage of his life – and his technique was faltering. He stared at Tiger's trumpet as Tiger leant close to increase their bond. Tiger would know the feeling – he'd been there himself. But tonight it was as if Nick had taken a trip too far. But he hadn't. Tiger had taken a tab, but Nick had swallowed nothing more than that glass of Nliven. Could that be it? He was feeling high – but Nliven was only melon juice with an apricot flavour.

He was back on song now. Let that be a lesson, he thought: music is not easy – it only sounds that way. In a brief two-bar break Nick shook his head. Perhaps he'd picked up Tiger's adapted drink by mistake. But his head had cleared. Performer's panic, that's all.

Just as you can't help picking at an uneven fingernail, Nick couldn't help another glance into the crowd. Strange. There was no sign of him. The guy was as big as a PA speaker – about the same shape as well – and yet had melted into the crowd. There must be ten thousand out there but few the size of that great hulk. He should stand out. There was just a sea of undulating faces. People say that

215

when a passenger is swept overboard he disappears instantly – his little white face in the water indistinguishable among flecks of foam.

Tiger nudged him again.

Nick leant into him, following his riff, underpinning the staccato brass. Tiger had introduced a new cross rhythm and Nick joined to parody a show band treatment. Randi was distorting the lyric with a punk inflection and the two-man wind section punctuated her words with a fast series of little quintuplets – the wait-a-little-bits as Tiger called them. If Tiger had bolstered their drinks he showed no sign of it. His horn had crystal clarity. Both Steve and Cleo slid in behind. Now only Homer and Randi kept with the tune. Randi pulled the hand-mike out from the stand and began prancing along the edge of the stage, leaning out across her audience, stooping low, mocking the swaying fans with exaggerated homage to the boy called Bill, her three o'clock thrill.

The crowd were loving it, joining in the chorus, shouting back at her, lapping the stage when suddenly, like storm water breaching a sea wall, a section to one side burst through Security and rushed the stage. They crashed into the waiting line of stewards and ALF men. Suddenly, Glastonbury, home of peace and universal brotherhood, showed another face. The stewards, backs to the stage, faced the interruption to their humdrum evening with transparent glee. The ALF men, opposed to man's cruelty to animals, outdid the professional controllers in smothering the outburst. The breakaway rioters found the few yards separating them from the stage harder going than they supposed. They had expected sheer force of will to carry them through and had come unarmed, whereas the stewards and ALF men upheld peace with batons and soft coshes. They beat the invaders to the ground. And the band played on.

Nick and Tiger dropped the wait-a-little-bits and brought back the melody, keeping the noise level high in case Randi wavered on the words. But she was fine. She stepped back from the edge and directed her delivery to the middle of the crowd. Steve called from the keyboard, 'Keep going. Don't end yet.' But no one in the band needed telling. They'd repeat and improvise till the fuss died down.

A man had broken through the guards. He started clambering onto the stage but Homer took two easy steps and kicked him in the chest. The man fell back into the dark. For all the band knew he could have drowned. They never saw the man again.

The crowd noise had changed. The huge mass of newly converted fans were furious with the troublemakers and though normally the crowd would have disapproved of the techniques used to quell them, this no time for being reasonable. This was Blue Delta. This was one of those bands you hadn't heard of which blasted through to become a crucial memory of the festival. This was why you paid a hundred pounds a ticket. This was the point of the weekend.

Trample the troublemakers into the mud.

Steve had his hand up, finger pointing, for one last refrain as the first bomb came. No noise. Nothing you could hear above the din. Just a sudden flash of flame, a sheet of light, and the centre stage was a pool of fire. Steve leapt from his keyboard amid yellow flames. Cleo stopped the drums. Nick paused horrified on his sax but Tiger rippled on. As Steve dithered at his keyboard Randi shouldered past and ran off stage – coming back immediately with a bucket of sand. Only Tiger was playing now. Nick and Steve ran into the wings, Cleo extricated herself from her drums, and Homer stood, guitar hanging loose, staring incredulously at the fire. Nick and Steve reappeared on stage with buckets of sand. They had hardly got there when two more petrol bombs arrived. One missed the stage, landing in front among the battle wounded, but the other fell at Homer's feet. Impulsively he kicked it away. The ball of flame rolled across the stage and Homer clutched at his foot to stifle flames around his leg. Tiger turned his back to the fire and made one last attempt to keep the show alive. Closing on his mike, he abandoned 'Three O'clock Thrill' for his solo set piece, 'Tiger Rag'. As flames rose higher on stage around him, Tiger huddled over his gleaming horn and ripped into the unmistakable

> Whoa! Catch that tiger!
> Wup! Catch that tiger!
> Wup! Catch that tiger!
> Catch that cat.

In the stark light of the floods the glow from the flames was lost, enfeebled, a toy fire, a stage effect, an illusion created by the band. The man huddled over his trumpet was a tramp on a cold street corner, hustling for pennies in the rain. The two men scuttling across to him seemed emblematic figures of authority to move him on. Whatever happened was melodrama. The audience, outraged to see the show collapse, sympathetic to the last Chaplinesque character with his horn, howled like groundlings in the pit. Bring back the band. Put out the fire. But they had to watch the trumpet man led away. Every musician left the stage. Orange flames reached the wood and fabric wings and then, eerily, the lurid light swelled to win its battle with the floods.

The audience quietened. They heard the distant sound of a concert elsewhere – a tamer, more routine rock song floating on the wind. It was like the sound of a neighbour's radio. They were left staring at the burning stage, unsure what would happen next and whether to go or stay. It was like the end of a bonfire party, when the guests stand around wondering whether the fireworks have finished or whether there may still be one more display.

In the trampled field behind the looming stage the musicians were spectators, nothing more. Around them in the dark moved purposeful men with buckets and extinguishers. Behind the giant stage the sound of the audience was muffled and lost in the shouts of firemen going about their work. No one spoke to the band. Cleo tended Homer's leg. Randi and Nick looked after Steve's superficial burns. He seemed badly stunned. Tiger stood by himself, horn at his feet, hands thrust deep in his pockets, glaring at the people scurrying past as if they were to blame.

Nick said, 'Let's get away.'

Randi stared at him. 'The guys who did this,' she said. 'You need help.'

'Nothing to do with me,' he muttered.

She continued staring. 'You're OK then?'

'I'm fine. You?'

'Oh, I'm fine. We're all fine.' She gave a tired smile. 'It's our party, and we can cry if we want to.'

She led Steve away from the fire. Nick and Cleo supported Homer as he hobbled across the field. Tiger stayed. The flames died and turned to smoke. The musicians picked their way between the vehicles, then paused in the semi darkness and watched the firemen at the stage. They could see Tiger, still standing there, a dark shape against the glow. Most of the light came from one side, from the smouldering embers of one wing. High in the wing the embers brightened and the top section shifted from the backdrop and as it slowly parted from the upright its orange light became a V. There was a shower of sparks. The side piece fell.

They saw Tiger silhouetted against the sudden flame, motionless against the light. The flat fell and flared behind him. He didn't notice. He picked up his horn and drifted away.

Homer grimaced. 'My guitar, man. It's on the ground there.'

'And my sax. I'll bring them over.'

Nick glanced at Cleo. 'How about your drums?'

'Insured.'

'Yeah, but…'

'Yeah.'

She tightened her lips as if she had tasted something unpleasant. 'They'll be a write-off. Sums up the evening.'

Nick grunted. Walking toward the smouldering stage he heard the PA kick into life. Someone said, 'OK folks,' then something unintelligible, then coughed and started again. Nick wasn't listening. Some kind of apology – an announcement stating the obvious, that the show would not restart. At least he and Homer had their instruments. Cleo's drums were gone, Steve would certainly have lost his keyboards – and the electrics: amplifiers, mixer unit, speakers. Nick cursed. Then he remembered that most of the electrics had been supplied by the organisers. They could take the hit.

He found the instruments and paused for a moment to watch the work. Everyone seemed to know what they were doing. Maybe they rehearsed. Standing with a guitar in one hand and sax in the other, Nick was just an extra. That burned-out stage should have given the band their greatest opportunity – it almost had – but instead it would be remembered only for the fire. In days to come, people might ask, 'Which band was playing when the fire started?' and those they asked would shake their heads. Trivial Pursuit. The new-found stars were just nobodies in the way.

Was that right? Had the band been in the way, or were they the object of the attack? Was he the object? Since that night at Rendox the band had been confronted by angry workers, their posters had been defaced and they had been bombarded on the Internet. Now they had been bombarded in real life. No, not they – he had been. The whole band had been attacked, though they were not to blame. Any more than he was.

As he turned and walked away the sound of the PA came seeping through. A male voice, not an organiser's – someone angry. Nick hesitated. One of his attackers? No, Kieran: one of his defenders, you could say.

'—what we're up against. Anyone fights for defenceless animals finds that they are defenceless too. The voice of protest is being stamped out. Is that what you want?'

There was a desultory 'No' – but even a desultory *No* from ten thousand people can sound loud. Nick went through the vehicles to Cleo and Homer.

'—and destroyed any chance for a band with the courage to speak out. Don't be fooled, friends – these weren't hooligans you saw tonight. They were the paid mercenaries of big business.'

Nick found Cleo and Homer by an empty trailer. She had her arm around his waist, though he no longer needed her support.

Homer nodded at his guitar. 'Thanks, man.'

'No problem,' Nick said, putting the sax and guitar down. 'Where's Steve and Randi?'

219

'Gone to the van, I think.'

'Seen Tiger?'

Cleo snorted. 'He's out of it tonight.'

She stayed close to Homer – who asked, 'That mother sayin' about us? I thought we'd swopped animal rights shit for these Agenda mothers?'

Nick shrugged. 'Everyone takes a ride with us. I want to find Tiger.'

'Not in this crowd, man.'

Cleo said, 'He's happier on his own.'

'He isn't happy. Look after my sax. I'll find him.'

Nick picked his way through the trailers to the other side of the burnt-out stage. The crowd noise was louder here, and the PA had normalised: '- other stages right now. Make your way over to the Pyramid, a new show in ten minutes, or to the Acoustic where you can hear Kathryn Tickell at this very moment. Meanwhile, on the Avalon Stage—'

Forget Blue Delta. The show goes on.

Nick struck out from the side towards the west enclosure. If Tiger had joined the main crowd Nick would never find him. Only in these more secluded areas was it possible to move at reasonable speed. In most of the 800-acre site the crowd density and general lethargy prevented anything more than a mindless trudge through large camp sites and surrounding car parks. Main walkways between stages were near impassable.

Close to the stage was prohibited to non-performers and by crossing the restricted area Nick could cut towards what used to be the NME Stage but was now simply the Other Stage, where Red Snapper would be appearing. On the broken Jazz and World stage a lighting tower had tilted and one of the spotlights hung askew, blazing its light across this empty patch of ground. As Nick passed through it he wondered if Tiger might see him picked out by the beam and come across to join him. He paused a few moments, peering out into the crowd, but the spotlight blinded him. He carried on. He was looking for Tiger; Tiger wasn't looking for him.

He came out of the spotlight and moved into near darkness between empty trailers. Beyond lay a muddy patch of ground where contractors had unloaded and assembled the day before. Crowd noise reduced here, and even the tannoy sounded faint. The chattering crowd was like a million starlings. There were smells of frying and a thousand bonfires. He went between two trucks to emerge the other side.

Someone grabbed him.

A large hand clamped across his mouth and heaved him backwards. Nick kicked behind but whoever was there had his feet apart. Nick struggled but a rod of metal came along his cheek and he heard: 'Don't move! I'll fucking shoot you.'

The rod moved. The end of the barrel prodded against his face. But he tilted back to see who held him. Not that he had to. Dark as it was he knew it would be Haydon.

The big man leant down to him. 'Not a fucking sound,' he whispered.

Haydon's hand remained across Nick's mouth. His other rested on Nick's shoulder and the gun jabbed against Nick's cheek.

When he squirmed, Haydon pulled him tighter and slid the gun to beside Nick's eye. He held him so tight Nick could hardly breathe. He tried to bite but couldn't move his jaw.

Haydon seemed in no hurry. Nick stared across at a second line of trucks waiting in the darkness. He could hear the distant strains of music and apparent closeness of a vast mass of people. He couldn't make out a particular conversation but could have sworn there were people trudging past the other end of the truck.

So Haydon wouldn't try anything. Would he?

He already had. When a hundred thousand rock fans laughed and romped in darkened fields, if some rocker fired a gun they wouldn't blink an eye.

Haydon tensed.

He was listening. Waiting for something.

Somebody.

Movement between the trucks. Someone emerged. Nick stared in disbelief. He stared at her. She stared back. Three yards away. Her huge eyes seemed wider in the dark. She held a hand up to her throat.

Haydon said, 'No one moves.'

They were frozen statues. Something had to give. Nick felt the gun move, as it repositioned to cover Babette. He couldn't move now. If he jogged Haydon's arm the gun would fire.

She licked her lips. Her eyes flicked from Nick to the levelled gun. Haydon said, 'I knew you'd be here. I knew you'd want to meet your boyfriend.'

Nick couldn't speak. There were a thousand questions he had to ask. But even if Haydon took his hand away he would be dumb. He hadn't a breath left in his body.

Haydon twitched. He was about to speak or shoot. But Babette disappeared – vanished back between the trucks. Haydon stumbled forward, releasing Nick as unimportant. Nick's foot shot out. Haydon tripped. But he was too big a man to fall and wasn't going fast enough. Nick crashed against him and Haydon, off balance, fell on one knee. Nick went for the gun, leaping at Haydon's wrist with both his hands and forcing the man's arm down to the ground. Haydon thumped his ribs. Nick wouldn't let go. Haydon thumped again. Nick rammed his head into Haydon's face. At the same time he whipped his hand from Haydon's wrist and wrapped it round the gun. But Haydon wouldn't let go. Nick tried to force the gun up, bending the man's hand against his forearm. He used his other hand, but Haydon still would not let go. Wriggling on the ground Haydon aimed his left fist at Nick's head. Nick ducked and butted Haydon in the face. Haydon shifted to wrestle better – and as he moved his legs, Nick kneed him in the groin. It wasn't powerful but it slowed Haydon enough for Nick to knee him again. Haydon roared – more in anger than pain – and as he reared back Nick threw his weight against the gun. It went off. The blast caused no ripple in the passing crowd but it shocked the two men enough for them to loosen their grip. Nick twisted the gun and Haydon lost it. Even as Nick got his hand there he knew he wouldn't use it. Nick had never fired a weapon in his life. He couldn't shoot a man at close range. As the pistol loosened he obeyed an instinctive reaction and hurled the weapon across the grass. His hands were free now and in another instinctive reaction he tightened them round Haydon's throat. Haydon bucked on the ground. He grabbed at Nick's fingers but before he could pry them loose Nick butted him again across the face. Haydon's fury broke him free. He tossed Nick aside and tried to stand. But Nick was smaller, nimbler. Haydon was still rising when Nick kicked him in the face.

Haydon's face was streaked and flecked with blood. He knelt erect like a wounded walrus and Nick came again for a second kick. Twice is once too much. Haydon grabbed his foot and though he didn't catch it cleanly he twisted Nick down to the mud.

Now Haydon could use his weight. Clutching Nick's ankle he slithered across his legs. Nick tried to use his fists but Haydon pinned him to the ground. He held onto Nick's arms. He heaved himself along Nick's body till he could use his knees to hold him down. Now Haydon's hands were free. Nick was defenceless. He could only watch as Haydon pulled back his heavy fist and smashed it into his cheek. But Nick had turned his head and part of the blow thumped in the mud. That was the first blow. Haydon raised his fist again, watching carefully where he should aim. His battered face dripped spots of blood. He grinned triumphantly. As he swung his fist his red embittered face burst apart with a sudden bang. He toppled forward. Nick wrestled, struggling with his weight. The huge hulk became inert. Nick pushed it away and as he clambered into a sitting position he found himself at Babette's feet. She held a gun, the pistol, aimed at Haydon's corpse.

'I wouldn't leave you,' Babette said.

As they hurried through the darkness Nick's feet seemed stuck in treacle. To get to the performers' car park he and Babette had to thread their way through a sprawl of bedraggled tents. They tangled in guy ropes and stumbled over unseen objects in the grass. Most tents seemed empty, though one or two suspicious faces peered from flaps into the darkness in case they were tent thieves or vandals, raiding the pitch while the occupants were at the sound stages. There were occasional camp fires, the sweet smell of dope.

They must find his car, she said. The man she'd killed wouldn't be the only one on her trail. He'd been watching Nick, waiting for her to get in touch. Nick was a link to her – perhaps the only one. Whether the man she'd killed had started the fracas at the concert she couldn't say. It seemed unlikely he'd throw petrol bombs to flush Nick out. That must have been some other guy, not this one, the man she'd killed.

She kept calling Haydon 'the man she'd killed'. Nothing personal. She hurried Nick to find his car but the more she hassled the more slowly they seemed to proceed. Even where tents were thinly pitched, the open ground seemed littered with trash and trenches – even a stray dog yelped and followed for several yards. When they reached the compound Nick couldn't remember how to get in, and once inside he couldn't find his car in a sea of vehicles. His head was spinning. Was it the fight? Had Tiger slipped a tab in his drink? Was it a dream?

No. He walked beside a dead girl. She had saved his life. They had killed a man. Other men were here to kill her – because she was dead. They'd kill him too. Because he knew she wasn't.

It wasn't till they were on the empty road that he found reality. After locating the car they had stumbled through another shambles getting out. The car parking procedure was designed to help late arrivals come in. There was no easy way to drive out.

Then, in the dark lane as he squinted down the tunnel of trees, the way the shaft of light from his headlamps picked out branches and overgrown verges made them seem unreal. He wanted to understand what had happened. But she hushed him and said there'd be plenty of time on the long drive home.

'Home?'

'Your place. Your flat.'

223

He felt an idiot. He didn't know the plot. Over the years a dream had visited him in which he was an actor waiting in the wings, and only when he went on stage did he realise that he'd never rehearsed this play, had only the faintest idea how it ran, and didn't know the answer to any line. Each one might be a cue. Whoever spoke waited for him to say or do some specific thing. He had to improvise the part, trying to guess the required response, but play the part so the audience would never know he was in the dark.

'It's so good to see you again, Nico.'

'I could say the same. I mean...' He petered out.

The view through the windscreen was a moving film. When they moved onto the main road to the motorway they began to pass other vehicles coming towards them. Their lights filled his car. It was as if no one bothered to use their dip. But nothing seemed real to Nick. There were no people inside those cars – they were just part of tonight's dream. What he saw through glass could not be real.

He glanced at Babette, sitting by his side. She seemed relaxed and had a half smile on her lips. Sometimes she stared through the windscreen, sometimes she closed her eyes.

'I'm tired, Nico. On the run you don't get much sleep.'

'Who are you running from?'

When she turned to face him in the car, her smile was the only thing that was real. 'I'll tell you everything. But concentrate on the road.'

He wanted to stop. He wanted to hold her. He wanted to tell her he thought she'd died.

But she knew that. She knew everything.

It was fun, you know? When I used to demonstrate for animal rights it was a giggle. I was at Uni. Like students everywhere we'd sign petitions, hold meetings, go fly posting at night – but loitering on the fringes of our groups were professionals, come to recruit. Like the days when spies were recruited at universities, though whether that really happened I don't know. These people had nothing to do with MI5. They were head-hunters from the anarchists, libertarian socialists, Irish Republicans, animal rights. It didn't matter what they stood for, their techniques were much the same: they joined your group, watched you, then gently led you astray. They made an offer you couldn't refuse: their excitement for your self-righteousness. At first, they'd use you as cannon fodder on some risky jape but if you showed flair you'd be invited in. But each time I was put to the test (they never told you you were being tested) I'd think I'd done well but I wouldn't be accepted. It hurt my ego.

Why didn't they want me? It wasn't because I was a woman (traditional excuse) because although activism seems a male preserve, there are female activists, and they're not all lesbians. It wasn't that. Was I not brave enough, not foolhardy enough or (perish the thought) not bright enough? Hardly. In my student days I was considered a shining beacon. Was that my problem – was I too brave, too bright, too foolhardy?

I've never been one for introspection. I thought: animal rights is fun and I believe in it, but if I can only be a foot soldier I'll give up. Officer class or nothing, me. I made the kind of transformation you often see at university – the student radical goes for a good degree. Some students become radicals; some radicals go back to books.

As a result, perhaps, I got the degree – chemistry – but nothing more: a degree, some job interviews, but no job. Once again, I performed well – I always thought I was the sort of person I would want to employ – but I couldn't get a job. At each interview my smile became more fixed. A few months after university I became seriously depressed. In my blacker moments I'd ask myself what I had ever really achieved – whether I was half as good as I thought myself. I couldn't get a job; I hadn't been accepted as an activist; perhaps I wasn't as good as I imagined.

I had to find something I could do.

As you know, I've always been vegetarian, and I was intrigued at the time by the latest theories about healthy eating and a cleaner life. I'd studied the chemistry of it. And I'd heard of a company which offered a way to combine my own beliefs with a realistic route to make my fortune.

I may not eat meat but I do like money.

So I joined Agenda and became a demonstrator on the road. Once again, I looked the part, spoke the part – I even ate and exercised the part. I went on courses, read the literature – I was a model sales person (sorry, Demonstrator, Agenda speak).

But I didn't sell a lot.

There I was again. Familiar situation. I tried to do right, but it didn't work. Maybe there's something wrong with me, I thought. And believe me, in your early twenties you're as lacking in confidence as any teenager. I was, anyway. Meanwhile, people who had been at university with me – I mean at my very own university, not just any university anywhere – people I knew were in the real world, making money.

While I did everything right, and got nowhere.

Till I bumped into someone I had known at university – a guy (no, I didn't have an affair with him) – a guy called Kieran. He suggested that maybe I had been doing everything too right. What did that mean? He was like Mephistopheles, that guy – he plied me with drink, he listened, he smiled. Question the rules, he said. Expand your boundaries. Accept an ordinary job – as a lab assistant, say, below your capabilities – but set your own objectives. To hell with their objectives, he said: if they don't give you a proper job, you don't owe them anything – you can use them, instead of letting them use you. As a chemist, he said, you could make a strike for animal rights. Wouldn't that be more fun? What kind of outrageous strike could you make?

We came up with a mad idea (it must have been the drink talking) of my working in a CJD research lab and stealing bacterium to infect meat in an abattoir or meat processor – it didn't matter which. Crazy? He had thought it out beforehand. Kieran had a mole in a local processing plant – Rendox – and if I stole the bacterium, she'd do the rest and... well, I hadn't had that much to drink: I could tell a set-up when I saw one. Kieran clearly had the whole scheme mapped out. But I didn't mind – I wanted to do something. He stressed that I didn't have to get a job that fitted my abilities – I could accept any lowly job as long as it helped me achieve my objective.

There was one little flaw: I couldn't get that lowly job.

I applied to labs around the country – to tell the truth, there weren't many that actually had the bacterium – but none of them would employ me. The old slap-down again. I had a good degree, I wrote a good application – and they wouldn't even see me for the job. I'd failed again. I'd have to crawl back to Kieran and tell him they wouldn't even let me sweep the floor.

Then I thought back on what he'd told me.

This local firm, Rendox, is part of a group called QMP – who the ALF have been investigating for a long time. Investigating! They've been subjecting QMP to guerrilla warfare – raids on subsidiary companies, exposures in the press, bombs in abattoirs, attacks on staff, that sort of thing. They even have a mole in QMP itself – yes, I know, another lowly worker who can walk into any job she wants while I, a supposedly bright graduate, can't get inside the front gate. Great. I was working overtime on my ego, just to stop it smothering. OK, Kieran, I said, tell me again about QMP.

'Not QMP itself,' he said impatiently. 'Their main UK presence, Tradefair – who are running a multi-million scam.'

We were sitting at the waterside outside the Arnolfini – eating one of their slightly too earnest salads. Too many beans. Too little dressing. And you know those heavy wooden tables they have outside? A seagull had crapped on ours. You can get too close to nature.

'And you'll threaten Tradefair you'll expose them?'

But Kieran could be po-faced when it suited him. 'The ALF is not into blackmail.'

He meant it. The ALF weren't interested in a multi-million scam because no animal suffering was involved – I mean, no more than Tradefair owes their entire existence to. I was stunned. If one of Tradefair's associate companies packed a few too many lambs into a truck, the ALF would be out with cameras and press packs and demos. But if the company systematically ripped off governments and institutions to the tune of millions and millions of pounds, that was OK. All right, it wasn't 'OK', but it wasn't the ALF's affair!

Can you credit it?

I'm as strong for animal rights as the next girl, but I am a product of my generation.

'How many million is "multi" million?' I wanted to know.

He shrugged. 'I've no idea, but quite a few million every year. We don't know the exact sum – it's very difficult to pin down. The actual amount is unimportant. What matters is the immorality of the meat trade.'

Oh yes, of course. I took a long draught of my wine. Several million pounds a year. That's not important.

'What is their scam, exactly?'

He didn't want to tell me. I don't think it interested him. He sat at the wooden table – a sunny day, water running by, families at other tables, people popping in and out of the gallery – trailing his finger through some spilt beer, and in a bored voice he told me a story which he said was 'typical of big business everywhere'. Well, I'm sorry, Kieran, I thought, let's get real a moment, shall we? This is not typical, no way.

Shall I tell you what was going on?

Tradefair was subcontracted by the EC – not as a business, he said, but as an NGO – to organise the distribution of surplus meat from the beef mountain to the third world. Feeding the poor is a nice little earner. You can make a career of it. But Tradefair wasn't satisfied to take a percentage, they wanted more. Commercial companies like Tradefair have to be sharp and efficient to survive, while the fat cat lazy institutions of government and the EC are neither sharp nor efficient. Their survival is not in doubt. When the big corruption scandal broke and the EC sacked all its commissioners, what happened the very next day? They all turned up for work as if nothing had happened. They couldn't stay at home – they had a lunch to go to.

'Government institutions are self-perpetuating,' Kieran said. 'They love complexity, but they can't unravel their own red tape.'

227

Big business can. And it can introduce additional knots of its own. In this case, Kieran said, Tradefair were shipping consignments they invoiced twice. The EC 'chose' to pay those invoices – regardless of the fact that most of the shipments were paid again by national governments, charities, or receiving nations. One paid in advance, one in arrears. One paid on shipment, one on receipt.

'You can prove this?' I exclaimed.

You should have seen his face – he looked offended. 'Proving is not the point. We *know* they're doing it. We have documents.'

'Which do prove it?'

He gave another frown. 'I wish you'd keep to the matter in hand.'

He wouldn't be forthcoming. Like a hasty lover, he'd built me up then let me down. It was just the beer talking.

I've always been a trier – you'll grant me that. While Kieran doodled in his beer I chatted girlishly, flattered him, joked – and got the name of the ALF's mole at QMP. I already knew who it was in Rendox.

I followed them up. I talked to the girl at QMP – and learned that what Kieran had told me about Tradefair's scam was true, but we couldn't prove it. We had some documents, but they were incomplete. She showed me some invoices for consignments already paid. 'Where's the duplicate?' I asked. 'Can we show they're both for the same consignment?' No, not exactly.

Thanks a bunch.

I tried Rendox. Lisa, the girl we'd planted in the factory, said the manager there – Eamon somebody – fancied himself a ladies' man, and was as silly as a baby when he'd had a drink. He became talkative, she said. Music to my ears.

He was at that age – maybe men are always at that age when if an attractive girl smiles at him he can't refuse. He'd already had a fling with Lisa – he thought it was his idea – and had lain in bed confessing in the afterglow, and though he hadn't told her everything I could see his story didn't quite tally with Kieran's. Eamon's was more interesting.

I followed up in the most blatant way I could – by pretending to be a journalist. It's a good ruse – it polarises: people either clam up and won't speak to you or they spill the contents of every secret lumber box and lay their hoard out, looking for praise. That was Eamon. He showed me round the factory. He should have delegated this but I flashed my great big eyes at him and before you know it, there we were, parading around the factory in white coats. He wanted to date me, but didn't have the balls – being married, of course. I let him stew a couple of days, then I phoned him. You don't want to hear the details – pretty sordid stuff – but I delved into what he'd told Lisa and boy, she hadn't heard the half of it. He didn't spill the whole tale in one night – he wasn't that pathetic – but it dribbled out fast enough. The pathetic wretch wanted to talk about it – though he tried to hold some back, hoping it might keep me coming back for more. He didn't realise that once I'd got the gist I could have Lisa ferret out the rest.

So, you ask – what was Eamon's secret?

Rendox and Tradefair are both part of QMP. Tradefair was moving the beef mountain to the third world – at a profit – and Rendox was processing British beef. Note the euphemism: *processing* – that's processing as in destroying. Back in the distant past when British beef was supposedly best in the world, Rendox processed it into pies and sausages and did all the other disgusting things people do to turn dead animals into food. But after BSE, British beef was good for nothing – literally – it was often worse than nothing and couldn't be sold. Factories and abattoirs which had previously turned flesh into food suddenly switched to 'rendering' it – cooking it at far above the boiling point of water to produce the kind of slurry that was safe enough for disposal. It's not too dissimilar a practice to cooking meat for sausages and meat pies, when you come to think of it. And Rendox thought about it. They realised that when they cooked meat for consumption they 'rendered' it at a lower temperature. Cooking is cheaper and makes more profit. Though there's still a profit in rendering, provided you're in the rendering business, and you're not some poor schmuck of a farmer who's had to breed the animals, feed and care for them and pay for their transport to the knacker's yard. Tradefair saw an opportunity: why not process infected meat as if it were any other meat? Why not turn it into human food?

Eamon defended this – to me, a committed vegetarian. The BSE thing, he said, had faded into almost total insignificance. The guy had a point, if you looked only at the death statistics. I know he was only trotting out what QMP's PR machine had drummed into him, but the reality is that despite all the hysterical media hype, the so-called 'new' CJD only killed around forty people ever. That's less than are killed on Britain's roads every week. One of those who died was a lifelong vegetarian! If you follow the reasonable argument of guys like Eamon and his cohorts from the meat processing industry, there's less risk from eating beef than from crossing the road. It's a criminal shame to waste it. And if some British beef was a bit strong for Western stomachs, there were plenty of other people out in the world with no such qualms. The infinitesimal risk would be laughable to a starving black man. Ask *him* what he meant by risk.

See how easily an animal killer satisfies his conscience! In the early days, Eamon told himself he was just the manager at Rendox – his plant was rendering meat as before. It was Tradefair that sold it, so neither Eamon nor Rendox were breaking the law. Rendox rendered meat supplied by QMP farmers, then passed it on to another QMP company for disposal. His hands were clean.

QMP were already being paid twice to feed the starving with left-overs from the beef mountain. Now, Rendox could accept further EC grants to kill, render and destroy British beef – but could pass the supposedly destroyed meat to Tradefair for distribution to the third world. Rendox then, like Tradefair, could be paid twice – first for destroying the meat, then for selling it to Tradefair. A tasty profit, you might say.

Eamon, incidentally, didn't know the other half of this scam – he knew Tradefair were adding his infected slurry to the meat they sold the starving, but he didn't realise they were being paid twice for each consignment! Meat which was supposedly so tainted it had to be destroyed was in reality being sold at full price several times over. It had become the most profitable beef in the country.

When I pieced all this together, imagine how I felt. I wasn't shocked by Rendox, Tradefair or QMP. Nothing a meat processing company does will ever shock me. But I now knew what was happening at both Rendox and at Tradefair. Eamon knew about the Rendox scam – and he was beginning to realise that Lisa knew, which worried him. He didn't know about Tradefair double-selling the onward cargo. And at Tradefair, our Phoebe knew the Tradefair part but didn't realise that Rendox had also found a way of being paid twice. If she didn't know, it was a fair bet that neither did many in Tradefair's management. I knew, and someone in QMP must know. But QMP has only a tiny presence in the UK. They are represented here by Tradefair. So did anyone know? Was I the only one?

When you want to know if a nest is empty you poke it with a stick. I contacted the Tradefair board – or to be accurate, *we* contacted the Tradefair board. Tradefair was well aware of the ALF, having had several run-ins with them in the past, so I decided that what I had to say would sound better if it came from the ALF. I'm a canny girl, though – I didn't give my ALF team the full story: I stuck to the double-dealing Tradefair scam which they already knew. I soon found that some ALF members were more worldly-wise than Kieran, and could see the virtue of a little blackmail – or they did when I suggested we ask for half a million pounds.

I say this casually, because I know you've heard how much we got from Tradefair. But how much do you know? You've heard Michael

McDonnell's story from Tradefair but I haven't spoken to him since the sting. Understandably!

We asked for half a million pounds in used bank notes – a foolish move, showing us to be amateurs. Banks can't easily produce that large a sum in old notes. And if you ask a bank to be paid in old notes it sets some obvious alarm bells ringing. These little gems I learned over the telephone on Day One from Mr McDonnell – a guy who seemed to thoroughly enjoy the whole malarkey. First bit of excitement he'd had in years.

Did he tell you about the additional hundred thousand? Yes, I thought he might. That was to be my own little earner on the top – a secret between himself and me, in exchange for my keeping secret the initial scam at Rendox. I thought there'd be hardly anyone who knew both sides of the scam, and I was right: he knew, but most of his board didn't. And Eamon's board only knew how to make meat pies. Yet for McDonnell it was the Rendox scam that frightened him – feeding the starving with tainted meat: can you imagine! He went along with me to pretend that the whole sting was about Tradefair's double dealing but in reality, he knew that (a) we didn't have sufficient proof and (b) it was the tainted meat story that could bring them down. So it suited both of us to talk up the double dealing – and by slipping me another hundred K he thought he could keep me on side.

We fixed a meeting place at a service station on the M4. I'd asked him to bring a bag containing the five hundred thousand, plus another hundred K for me in a separate pack. We sat in my car and I checked the money while he checked the documents. That was quite a moment, you know? The two of us snuggled up in my car, conducting a mutually satisfactory deal. And remember, only he and I knew what the deal was really about. He had his henchmen with him, I had mine – but we made them wait outside. They skulked around the car park, keeping an eye on each other, each worried that the other would try to pull a stroke – but in fact, McDonnell and I sat in the car as peacefully as if I were an antiquarian bookseller supplying him with a rare first edition for his private collection of erotica.

But I'm not entirely gullible.

Nice as he behaved sitting beside me in the car, I didn't expect him to let me drive away unchallenged with half a million pounds. Once I'd seen him flick through Lisa's packet I was on my guard. I had a plan.

My guess was that I'd be followed down the motorway, either by someone from Tradefair or the police. I knew no one had staked out the service station because I'd kept them in the dark about where the

231

exchange would take place. There hadn't been time for a stake-out. But there were a lot of cars in that car park – which was why I'd chosen it – and any one of them could be waiting to get on my tail. So I had my two henchmen turn up on motorbikes – and at the last moment I gave them the money bag and they roared away. Sure enough, McDonnell's car shot after them – and so did their nippy back-up number hovering by the exit. I was left in the car park on my own. I was like the warm-up in a rock concert, you might say – a forgotten player, unimportant now.

So I followed them down the motorway. It was the one snag with that venue – only one exit, onto the same stretch of motorway. But I had told my two men to hammer down the motorway a few miles, past a couple of exits, on to where a pedestrian bridge crossed to the other side. I knew that on their motorbikes they'd be well ahead of any car – but I couldn't guarantee Tradefair hadn't contacted the police and that the police hadn't sealed the next few exits. And it was just possible that a car – or who knows, another motorbike – could have caught up with them. But of course, when my two men abandoned their bikes and ran across the bridge – to where Lisa was waiting in another car – any pursuit was stymied. It doesn't matter how fast your car is when you're on the wrong side of the crash barrier facing the wrong way.

I'd like to have seen that, but I was dawdling two miles behind them on the motorway. By the time I arrived, there was no one at the footbridge, so I stopped the car – a hatchback – heaved the motorbikes into the rear and carried on.

Meanwhile my confederates were making haste to London with McDonnell's bag in Lisa's car. We had a safe house in Shepherd's Bush and a couple of hours later I wandered in. They did not look happy.

'The bastards cheated us.'

I looked puzzled. 'Counterfeit money?'

They pointed to the cash lying on the table. (Yes, very unprofessional of them to leave it scattered about, but with the ALF you take what you get.) I picked through the wads of banknotes. (And I wasn't unprofessional: at no time in that house did I not wear gloves.) Looking at the money on the table I could see we had two types of bundle – a minority of banknotes as they should have been, but the rest comprising neatly cut sheets of plain white paper.

I looked dumbly while they angrily explained: 'All the crap was at the bottom, with the genuine stuff on top.'

'But I checked,' I spluttered. 'I rootled through the bag, sitting in the car.'

232

'How far down did you go? The real stuff went quite deep. Did you push your hand right down inside?'

'I thought so. I checked several bundles – including some from the middle of the bag.'

'There were three or four layers of money, then it changed to crap.'

I felt a tear run from my eye. OK, that was not professional of me. 'I can't believe it. I sat beside McDonnell and looked at any number of bundles while he read the documents. The guy must have been a card sharp.'

'Did he keep you talking?'

'Yes, but…'

You can imagine the atmosphere. Lisa tried to comfort me by saying that to make up the bag Tradefair had had to use a lot of real money for the top layers, so we hadn't come out empty-handed.

'How much did we make?' I asked helplessly.

'About a hundred thousand.'

I won't drag this out. You can guess what happened. I had turned up at the meet with a couple of carriers filled with bundles of plain paper 'banknotes' I'd prepared earlier and I swapped them for the real half million McDonnell gave me. Once he left the car I only needed twenty seconds to make the switch. I used the 'personal' hundred thousand to top up the hold-all and I gave that to my biker friend in the car park. While everybody else kept their eyes on the hold-all, I drove off with my half million carriers under the seat. Naturally, I unloaded them before Shepherd's Bush. During an uncomfortable evening with the lads in the house I appeared contrite and angry for being such a dork, but gradually everyone came round to Lisa's point of view (which I surreptitiously encouraged) that the hundred thousand pounds was a qualified triumph in the battle against the food fascists.

But the story of my life is that although I perform exceptionally well, I always trip at the last fence. Whatever I try never seems to work. To keep the half million I thought I need only hang around with the gang a few days – long enough to convince them of my innocence and contrition – then I could slip away without a stain on my character.

But next day, one of my two bikers came round to see me, looking excited. I feared the worst. What he intended to do, he said, was phone McDonnell and say that since Tradefair had reneged on the money, the ALF felt morally free to spill the beans on their financial scam.

'We'll get the bastards,' he said. 'They cheated us of our money.'

'Is that wise?' I asked, playing for time. 'Now they've got the documents they've nothing to fear. They could set up a meeting and hand us to the police.'

'They won't want the police involved. Bad publicity.'

'Not in a blackmail case,' I extemporised. 'The police never reveal the dirty details – it's part of the deal. They'd rather catch the blackmailer.'

He bit his lip. 'They won't use the cops.'

'They'd be silly not to. And why should they meet us – unless it's to hand us over to the police? We've still got their hundred thousand pounds. They'd like it back.'

It was a convincing argument, you must admit. He muttered something and looked around my room for a motorbike to kick.

I added sweetly, 'A hundred thousand's better than nothing. I'd hate to lose it.'

He got on his high white charger: 'It's not our hundred thousand. It's for the cause.'

'All the more reason,' I insisted, 'not to be trapped into handing it back.'

He continued to grumble but saw my point. Eventually he left, muttering about 'putting it down to experience', and I hoped that the hundred thousand I'd let them keep was just enough: a hundred thousand in the hand against a rather doubtful five hundred thousand in the bush. I know which I'd choose.

But he had me worried. It was one thing to convince him while he was in my sight, but what about later? I'd convinced him, but what about the others when he reported back? Once the bunch of them sat around drinking herbal tea and decaffeinated coffee, wouldn't they bluster and curse the class enemy and evil businessmen? I couldn't guarantee the outcome. One of those headstrong veggies could call Tradefair any time. How McDonnell would laugh. How he'd love to tell them they'd been two-timed by their own lieutenant.

Then I would have everyone after me. McDonnell's men would want their money back – half a million is half a million, after all, and they'd know I was on my own. I might joke about veggie bikers, but these are the guys who blow up abattoirs and vivisection labs: they've wounded people – I think they killed a man last week.

I had to disappear.

Nick kept his eyes focused on the motorway. It was dark now, and the beam of his headlamps lay bleakly on the road surface. The engine noise was a drone.

Eventually he muttered, 'You set the whole thing up.'

Babette touched his wrist. 'I couldn't tell you.'

'Why not?'

'Darling, you'd have...' She leant forward to look into his face. 'I'm really sorry, Nico, but I... needed you to grieve. I know it was awful, but when the police came I needed you to look devastated. You know? If you'd been acting the part, they'd have known. My death had to hurt you, Nico. They had to see that.'

Nick's throat felt as dry as the concrete road outside.

She said, 'I'll make it up to you.'

He shook his head.

She said, 'And I'm back now. I'm back for good. We can't stay in Bristol, of course, but with half a million we can make a fresh start anywhere.'

'You put me through this for half a million?' He tried to swallow but found nothing there. 'That's why you sought me out at the Art College concert – you needed some sucker to shed a tear for you? Good old Nick – he was always soft.'

She squeezed his wrist. 'Don't, Nico. Don't torture yourself. Punish me – I deserve it. But I didn't use you, Nico. I'm... awfully fond of you. And I didn't seek you out: I just happened to come to the concert and saw you there. Even then, I didn't think—'

'*Happened to come?* You were on the run – and you strolled in to a concert?'

'Oh, Nico. Things just turned out that way.'

He had slowed, and they turned off the motorway. There was more traffic now. He swung beneath the carriageway onto the long Portway that snaked into Bristol beside the river. The uninhabited southern bank was dark. He remained silent till they stopped at a traffic light.

'Those two days together were just a sham, weren't they? You just wanted me for Rendox.'

Her voice was low. 'They were wonderful days. I hadn't seen you for years and... I was at my lowest and... suddenly you were there – the same guy that I... fell in love with at school.'

'Don't wind me up.'

'I'm not.'

The lights had changed and he eased forward, one other car behind.

She said, 'Those two days, Nico, you tore me apart. I began to realise... what I could do, but I could see what that might do to you. I didn't think I could go through with it. I hated myself. Some of the time, Nico – you must have noticed? – I clung to you so desperately: you were the one good thing in my life, and I fouled you up.'

235

'You did that, all right.'

'I don't ask much. Why don't things ever work?'

'You set me up.'

'We're going to be good together.'

'You set us all up: me, Rendox, Lisa, your stupid group – what happened to Lisa?'

'Nico.'

'What?'

'Let's go to your flat.'

He turned off Portway.

He asked again, 'What happened to Lisa?' But he knew now. She knew he knew.

She said, 'Remember that film, *Sleeping With The Enemy*? That's what Lisa did.'

'Slept with Eamon Reeves?'

'Yes.'

'You did too.'

'No!'

'You told me—'

'I didn't—'

'*He* told me. You made love to him in the forest near Tintern Abbey. Remember the forest?'

'I didn't make love to him. I... didn't. I don't know what he told you. But it was Lisa – she made love to him. She had an affair with him. She had gone over...'

'To the enemy? That makes it right?'

He had to concentrate on his driving as the street narrowed on the hill.

Babette said, 'She went over to the meat processors. She let him paw her. She should have been our mole – now she's a martyr. She'll like that.'

'You pushed her into the pulveriser?'

'No, she... No. Nico, they were going to kill me. I had to find some way to disappear – not just to vanish but to really... I had to die. Seem to. Then everyone would... stop looking for me.'

'You pushed Lisa into the pulveriser.'

'Well—'

'So they'd think she was you.'

'Everyone had to wear the same white overalls.'

'They found your red blouson as well.'

'Bits of it, I guess.'

'Yeah, bits of your sweet little red jacket. Lots of sweet red flesh.'

She leant across. 'Oh, Nico, I'm sorry—'

236

'You killed the girl, for Christ's sake.'

'For my sake, not his.' She laughed slightly, then stared in his face. 'I've been trying so hard, Nico. Always. I try so hard.'

'I want to drive.'

'You think I murdered her. It wasn't like that. She was sleeping with—'

'Don't give me that!'

'She wanted to be a martyr. Honestly, Nico, the ALF is full of idiots like that.'

'Did you swap clothes with her? Before or afterwards?'

'It wasn't like that. I just… threw my jacket in.'

They were in his street. He slowed the car, looking for a spot.

He said, 'They said she'd gone home.'

'I'd clocked her out – after she let me in.'

'After she'd served her purpose?'

He braked savagely and engaged reverse. It wasn't a large spot. But it would do.

Babette said, 'I was desperate. I wasn't thinking straight.'

Nick switched off the engine. He shifted in his seat but couldn't turn and face her. He said, 'I don't want you in my flat.'

'I came to find you, Nico. Despite the risk.'

'I'll drive you home.'

'You mustn't leave me, Nico. I killed a man for you tonight.'

He paused.

She said, 'I've been in some very dark places. I need you, Nick.'

'You don't need me. You've got the money. Everyone else still thinks you're dead.'

'Tradefair never believed it.' She was trembling now. 'They sent that man.'

'On the off chance. They just weren't sure.'

'I haven't got the money.'

Now he looked at her. 'That's why they're after you.'

'I haven't got it. You have, Nick.'

'It's in my flat? Christ, they searched it.'

'Do you still have my car keys?'

'Yeah, somewhere. But they're no use to you. The car was stolen and burned out. Oh, don't tell me – the money was in the car, wasn't it? What a joke.'

'I need the key ring.'

She smiled. He didn't. She said, 'I tell you everything but you don't listen. One of the keys is to a left luggage locker. That's where the money is. You've still got my keys?'

He nodded.

'Let's get them.'

Nick took a breath. 'I'll get them. You wait here.'

'But—'

'I told you, I don't want you in my flat.'

'Nick! What do you think I'm going to do?'

'I don't care. I just want out.'

He opened the door. When he was outside he pointed his finger at her. 'Stay there.'

She looked so young – her face pinched and frightened. 'Don't leave me on my own, Nico – please.'

He walked along the street and crossed to his flat. At the door he glanced back along the line of sleeping cars to make sure she was still inside. He could see her face peering out from behind the windscreen.

As he climbed the stairs he wouldn't let himself ask questions. He'd fetch her keys and let her drive away. No, she couldn't drive away: she didn't have a car. She'd ask him to drive her. Nick shook his head. Her problem. Don't even think about it. She could find a taxi.

He opened the door.

The flat was airless. He paused in the doorway and would have left it open to let some air in, but he felt a twinge and pulled it shut. He stood listening. It was a tiny flat. He should hear the slightest breath.

There were no sounds. No unfamiliar perfume.

He walked to the dresser and opened his oddments drawer. It hadn't been disturbed. He saw his spare wallet, an old comb, a shoe lace, various slips of paper. He saw her keys.

Nick slipped them in his pocket and wandered to the window to look down at the street. His own keys were in the ignition and he half hoped she would drive the car away. But she didn't want his car. She wanted the keys. He glanced at them in his hand: half a million pounds. Somewhere. He squinted down at the street again to check she was still in his car. Being in the passenger seat away from the centre of the road he could barely see her. From Nick's side of the street a man crossed to the car. Nick glanced – then looked again. He recognised him. Derek Cranham.

From Nick's bedroom the sounds of the street were hardly audible. Cranham may have worn soft shoes. From high above Nick saw Cranham reach inside his jacket. It seemed to be happening in a silent film. Cranham produced a long pistol. Babette moved across the car. She tried to open the driver's door. But Nick saw the pistol jerk in Cranham's hand – and that was the first sound he heard, a faint sigh of breaking glass. He saw the pistol jerk again. He heard another sound – his own voice: 'No!'

He forced the window open. He shouted something. The man did not look up.

Cranham walked quickly across the street. From further along the kerb a white van pulled out and glided closer. It barely paused as he jumped in. The van didn't speed up, but drifted to the end of the street, then turned and disappeared.

Why was Nick still staring from the window?

He ran from the room, down the stairs into the street. As he ran along the centre of the road he felt like a character from that silent film. The road was lined with silent cars. Walled with silent houses. He came to a halt beside his car.

The girl was dead this time. She had slumped across the driving seat, her head crooked against the door, blood dripping from her smashed skull into the footwell. Nick gazed in through the empty passenger window. Shards of shattered glass hung in the frame.

He looked up at the surrounding houses. Surely somebody…

Each curtained window was a blank. When he looked along the street it lay empty in the night. It was two o'clock in the morning and Nick realised that what he'd thought was the curiously long belly of Cranham's pistol had been its silencer. Part of the silent film. A puff of dust in the small hours, a thud of glass, an outraged sigh. End titles.

Nick had no desire to touch her. She lay so limply. Yet from the neck down she did not look lifeless. The position she was propped up in looked so uncomfortable that she surely must move soon. No. She wouldn't move again.

He mustn't look.

Nick turned – and if anyone had been watching from their window they might have thought he had turned to gag. But he was wondering what to do. According to the records she was already dead, but that didn't mean he could ignore her. Stupid thoughts flickered through his brain. A man couldn't be tried twice for the same murder – but how about a girl who was murdered twice? Nick would be the one they tried for it. She was his girlfriend; they had been together both nights she died. Cranham could not be linked to her – he worked for Tradefair, not Rendox, and would produce a dozen witnesses to say he was a hundred miles from here tonight.

Nick couldn't leave her near his flat.

He reached through the shattered window, leant across and hauled her body off the driver's seat so he could prop it upright against the door. But when he stepped away her body slumped sideways and drooped towards him through the window. He pushed her back.

Nick stood by the car wondering whether to move her to the back seat. She could loll around there and do no harm. He could dump her on the floor. The only way he could cope was by depersonalising her, treating the carcass as a shipping problem he had to solve. A piece of meat. This was how they worked in abattoirs. It was how she worked.

Somewhere in the dreary darkness would be a lonely place to dump her body. He need make no particular effort to hide it – he'd heard too many stories of ingeniously hidden corpses coming to light. He would leave the body somewhere where it wouldn't be found for several hours – easy enough in the dark. He could try the river – being tidal, the corpse might float out to sea. Depending which way the tide was. But with his luck – and hers – the tide would float her body back into town. Where to do it? On this side of Portway were too many houses, and on the other were too few: a creeping car at night would be noticed.

There must be a field somewhere. Some piece of land forever England. Why not Wales? It was only an hour's drive. Put her body over there and the police might look for a Welsh connection. Why go to Wales? Why not the forest – a lonely copse near Tintern Abbey?

He knew just the one.

He walked round the car and got in the driver's side. When his shoe slipped on the mat he knew it had slithered on her blood. Don't think about it.

He reached in his pocket and pulled out her key ring. He stared at it for a moment, wondering why it looked unfamiliar. Then he realised that his own key was in the ignition where he'd left it. He weighed Babette's keys in his hand. One of those – it must be that one – fitted the door to half a million pounds. That key. A plain key. That key might fit any locker, anywhere. But which, and where? He'd never find it. The key was valueless. Its value had been erased. He tossed it in her lap.

He switched on the car and eased out into the street. At the end he signalled before turning right, then he drove at a legal speed into the darkness.

MYSTERY

JAMES   James, Russell
         Oh no, not my baby